THE INVICTUS

Volume 2 in the Relentless Enemy series

KEITH GOAD

North Carolina

Published in the United States by BQB Publishing
(an imprint of Boutique of Quality Book Publishing Company, Inc.)
www.bqbpublishing.com

ISBN 978-1-952782-91-6 (p)
ISBN 978-1-952782-92-3 (e)

Library of Congress Control Number 2022950594

Book design by Robin Krauss, www.bookformatters.com
Cover design by Rebecca Lown, www.rebeccalowndesign.com

First editor: Caleb Guard
Second editor: Allison Itterly

*Dedicated to the beloved memory of my father,
Norman Robert Goad Sr. (1936–2019), whose family
and heritage are the inspiration for this epic tale.*

INVICTUS

Out of the night that covers me,
Black as the pit from pole to pole,
I thank whatever gods may be
For my unconquerable soul.

In the fell clutch of circumstance
I have not winced nor cried aloud.
Under the bludgeonings of chance
My head is bloody, but unbowed.

Beyond this place of wrath and tears
Looms but the Horror of the shade,
And yet the menace of the years
Finds and shall find me unafraid.

It matters not how strait the gate,
How charged with punishments the scroll,
I am the master of my fate,
I am the captain of my soul.

—William Ernest Henley

CONTENTS

PROLOGUE
THE LATIN GATE

AD 92
Rome

A single ray of light shone through a crack in the blocks of a dark, dank hold where John was held. It touched upon his forehead, and the old man, nearing his eightieth year, felt bathed in warmth. As he meditated in the dark and squalid stone room, his mind and spirit anchored to the frail beam of light.

The source of light was the sun that was now beginning to set, coloring the entire city in a bright orange glow. The hold was in a Tullianum prison near a southern portion of Rome's Servian wall. Within the room, all that remained of the light as it washed across the city was the thin beam that split the darkness. Still, it was enough to sustain John against exhaustion and the strain under which he found himself.

John's arms were bound together above his head and held taut by a chain that extended from the ceiling where it was affixed. His legs were shackled together and rooted to an iron loop on the stone floor. A thin, earth-colored tunic clung to his frail body, one that wouldn't have kept an ordinary man from shivering in the cold of the room. But despite the damp chill and discomfort, John focused intently on the beam of light that reached his head and felt pain free and warm inside.

He had led the spread of the gospel across Ephesus and

helped to govern an array of churches throughout Asia. The growing fervor of Christianity had drawn the attention of the Roman Emperor Domitian. Following his victory in the wars of Britannia and the Dacian conflicts, the emperor felt emboldened to turn his attention to what he saw as the growing threat of the Christian beliefs, and he launched a widespread campaign of persecution against them. Upon learning of John's influence in the region, Domitian commanded Roman forces to seek him out and bring him to Rome. He would make an example of John.

Now, strung up in chains, John awaited the return of the Roman guards to learn his fate. He was alone in this cell, which offered no hope or comfort other than the thin ray of light on which he focused to sustain himself. Or at least he had thought he was alone.

"*Annuit coeptis*," Archangel Michael whispered from the ether within the cell. "The Father assures that you will endure the pain and trial that await."

Remaining connected to the light and to comfort, John opened his eyes to mere slits and said, "So, the last remaining follower has now lived to be the oldest, only to be brought here and destined to meet the same fate as his brethren?"

"No," whispered the angel. "He requires your help in documenting and revealing to all followers their final journey—how they will ultimately return home."

"Am I to suffer the same fate as Paul and Peter before me at the hands of this great persecutor?" John asked. "I've traveled far and endured much. Do not placate me and minimize what lies ahead."

"Your resilience will be as He has commanded it, and you will be the portal through which the final revelation will be shared with others," Michael answered.

John challenged him. "What profit is there in my blood if I am to submit to this again? Will my dust praise Him and declare my faithfulness?" John tilted his head up to the ceiling. "Hear me, oh Lord, and have mercy upon me."

Michael ignored his pleas. "It is impossible to retire from your service to Him. Is this not what you agreed to in the garden all those years ago?"

"Aye," John responded, his eyes moistened with the memory of the promise he had made in a garden of olive trees. "And I would agree to it again now, if He were present to ask it of me." He lowered his head. "Will Azrael be with me if this is to be the end?"

Michael's voice became purposeful. "Your time here is not yet done, John. These men cannot end your life—you know this. The Father has unfinished work for you."

John, exhausted by the years that weighed heavily on his thin frame, grew irritated.

Michael encouraged him to persevere. "This is part of His plan. The vision of all things and how they are to conclude will be revealed to you in Patmos."

"What is this Patmos?" John asked. "Is it a place?"

John had not noticed the two guards who had reentered the chamber to retrieve him. They removed their helmets and, in the absence of any perceived threat from the old man, they lacked the customary daggers slung around their waists, just below the armor of their chest plates.

"Quit muttering to yourself, old man," one of them said. "Your time has come." They quickly and roughly released the chain from the ceiling and unshackled his legs from the floor mount. John crumpled to the stone floor, his limbs distended. He groaned in pain.

"Shut up, old fool!" one guard bellowed as he slammed a

thick fist into John's face. The blow sent John sprawling to the ground, and a gash opened across his cheek.

"Let's get him out there," the other guard urged. "The emperor is ready now. Come on, get to your feet." They dragged him up and each placed one of his arms across their shoulders. Then they ushered him through the door of the stone chamber and down a long a hallway toward the entrance to the prison.

The sun was quickly sinking into dusk, and the elderly man struggled to keep pace with the soldiers who guided him to a gate in the city's large stone wall.

They turned the corner just outside the gate to find a large assembly of noblemen and senators waiting for them, arranged in a half circle. A large wooden platform atop a stone parapet near the wall supported a huge steaming pot with a cantilever apparatus above it. It was a large metal vat—large enough to hold a full-grown man—with a wooden arm that extended from a tripod beam. A rope and leather harness dangled near the wooden arm and hung down near the base of the pot.

Beyond the encircled group was another stone parapet, this one serving as a platform for the Roman Emperor Domitian, who sat ready to take in the festivities he had arranged. Domitian was flanked on one side by a large praetorian guard whose armor and clothing bore more colorful ornamentation than that of a typical Roman soldier.

In a shrill, whiny voice, Domitian made an announcement to herald the arrival of the prisoner as he was brought before the group. "And here comes our guest of honor!"

As John approached, half-carried by the guards, still wrapped in his tattered tunic, he looked disheveled and exhausted. While he had been freed from his leg irons, his hands remained fastened together by a leather strap. It was quite a sight for a gathering of senators and noblemen to take in: an old man, worn and weathered but with a venerable and virginally pure face, contemplative eyes, and stark white hair and beard. He appeared simultaneously human and angelic, bent by the weight of his years.

As John was brought before the emperor, Domitian looked down upon him and spoke, his voice directed to the crowd. "This prophet speaks of a long-deceased deity who will come back to judge us all and grant everlasting life to those who believe in him. Let us demonstrate tonight what great folly this is and give him the chance to renounce the troubles he has caused this republic."

John stood up to face the emperor as the crowd of Rome's elite gathered behind him. As the soldiers stepped back from the prisoner so he could face his audience with Domitian alone, the guard who had punched John's face was puzzled. Where was the gash he had inflicted on the old man's face just moments ago?

A hush fell over the crowd as Domitian said, "Old man, you've been brought here to be granted a privilege that is so unique, others may only dream of it: the opportunity to renounce the discord you've sown in exchange for your life to be spared."

John straightened up even more and stared unflinchingly at the Emperor of Rome. "The venators you sent to Ephesus did not intimidate me there, just as they do not here," he responded, looking back at the two guards who had dragged him out to the gathering.

"The impudence and gall with which you speak!" Domitian seemed to have anticipated John's challenge to him. "Do you not understand? I am truly *Dominus et Deus*—master of all."

John countered, "I've seen many mere men like you,

determined to deliver pain and keep God's children in bondage."

Visibly agitated, Domitian leaned forward on his makeshift throne. "You will understand: look at all who kneel before me . . . and those who do not." He waved his hand. The buzz of conversation that had circulated through the crowd quieted, and slowly they all kneeled, including the large soldier next to Domitian. Yet there was a group John had not noticed when he was first brought outside. Domitian nodded as John realized who they were. "Indeed. They are followers of your word, but not of mine. You might have the chance to save their lives tonight, to keep them from suffering death for the treason they have committed against the republic. You need only to admit to them and these noblemen of Rome that what you preach and believe is nothing more than the prattling of a huckster."

Shaking his head wearily, as if he had had this discussion with other oppressors throughout his long life, John said, "I believe in God the Father Almighty, creator of heaven and earth—"

"Heaven and earth?" Domitian interrupted. "You speak of my domain, old man."

"I believe in Jesus Christ, God's only Son and our Lord—"

Domitian's rage flashed. "Christ? Do not say his name! *Damnatio memoriae*—that is what will become of that name and its history this evening!" With these words, Domitian declared his intent to purge the Christians and their beliefs from all memory and mention.

The group of noblemen had arisen, and anticipation stirred among them, as if they knew what would soon befall John. They seemed enthralled by the staging of what would be a grotesque spectacle on such a pleasant, cool October evening.

John, too, sensed that the exchange was approaching a climax. He turned his gaze toward the group of a dozen or more Christians the emperor had brought to meet their death. Some looked to be at peace, while others were nervous and afraid. Others looked down to avoid the confrontation between the supreme leader of Rome and the frail, aged prophet who served as the standard-bearer of the beliefs they held so fervently.

As if speaking to himself more than to the emperor, John closed his eyes and said, "There is no greater love than to lay down one's life for others." He turned his gaze back to Domitian. "Great Caesar, allow me to offer my own sacrifice so that those poor souls, regardless of how they came to their beliefs, will be spared death."

Domitian seemed genuinely surprised that John would offer such a bargain. "You willingly embrace the punishment I've constructed for you? The price for your loose tongue in my empire?"

John nodded. "My life can be the price so that they may live, albeit in the choice and manner of their banishment that you see fit."

Domitian's lips curled into a smile. "I will allow it to be so. Then it is time to proceed, old man."

John became terrified as he suddenly understood the earthly consequence of what he had just agreed to. "No, wait! It doesn't need to be this way. There is a manner in which we can all coexist."

Domitian quickly responded, "Your tongue has once again spoken of bargains and agreements that you know are folly. It's time to end the charade that you've fomented, which has only served to misguide your followers and insult these great nobles of Rome."

Then the emperor sneered, "Throw him in!"

The guards were quickly on him. They began to drag him up the ramp of wooden steps toward the vat. John protested and struggled frantically, trying to break free, but he was no match for the younger and stronger soldiers. In his blind fear, he could not make out the diatribe Domitian started delivering to the others who gathered, hearing only that it was about the false beliefs that would end with John's life.

Atop the wooden parapet, one guard strapped the leather band that held John's wrists to the end of the rope that was tied to the wooden cantilever, which was positioned to swing his body out and over the boiling oil. Terrified, John pleaded and begged them not to carry out the commandment.

While one guard held the wooden cantilever structure, the other pulled with all his force, lifting John off the ground. As John dangled by the rope in the air, the other guard swung the wooden arm that held him precariously over the boiling pot.

"No! Please!" John screamed as he felt the overwhelming heat rising up over his thinly clad body.

Eyes wide in anticipation, Domitian yelled, "Now!"

The guard who was holding the rope released his grip, and John fell feet first into the roiling oil. As he landed in the pot, a cloud of hot steam shot into the air. Bellows of pain and the gurgling sound of John's voice rose out of the vessel along with the sounds of sizzling oil. The nobles cringed at the desperate screams of a man being boiled alive. The Christians shrank as well; several of them made the sign of the cross, believing that John was descending into a hell on earth.

Then something strange happened. The stability of the huge pot of oil began to give way. It rolled back and forth, as if within the pot was no longer a dying man, but rather some caged animal attempting to escape.

Domitian looked puzzled and alarmed. "What is happening?" he yelled.

With a great thrust from inside, the pot tipped over, spilling its steaming contents from atop the parapet and onto the cobblestones lining the entranceway to the gate. John rolled out of the pot and landed with a thud as the oil splashed onto the stone. The guards nearest the wooden structure jumped back in alarm. The crowd gasped in disbelief. John was naked. The tunic, the leather that had bound his hands—even his hair—had been burned from his body. His flesh was melting, dripping off his body in smoldering clumps. John screamed and writhed in agony.

"What manner of sorcery is this?" Domitian demanded.

Then, as if his survival wasn't extraordinary enough, the burning and melting of John's skin abruptly stopped. And as moments passed, time itself seemed to have turned backward. John's flesh appeared to be repairing itself, restoring his body to the state it had been in when he stood before the emperor, all but hair and clothing to cover his nudity.

"Amazing! It's a miracle!" people exclaimed. "It is a sign from the gods that he is to be spared!" noblemen and senators shouted. Even the Christians, who had been brought there to be put to death, found themselves restored in faith and prayed and wept in happiness.

Domitian was astonished. He had sought to put to death John and the other Christians this evening before Roman citizens, both to rid himself of the nuisance they had brought to the empire and to convey his absolute power over his subjects. Instead, he was faced with a miracle. The prophet had survived, and the manner in which he had done so now stoked fervor among Christians and Romans alike.

It was in this moment of confusion that the countenance of the praetorian soldier standing beside Domitian changed. His expression shifted from the disbelief and alarm, which was mirrored in the faces of everyone who had witnessed this miracle, to the look of someone at ease, satisfied with what had transpired.

The Archangel Michael possessed the soldier, and he leaned down to Domitian and whispered, "He must be banished quickly. To Patmos. Have him sent to Patmos. We can stamp out the knowledge among those who've witnessed this tonight and ensure that he can never cause the empire further trouble."

Domitian, still gape-mouthed in disbelief, agreed. "Yes, yes, of course. See to it." Domitian then arose quickly and was escorted by several other guards to an awaiting chariot so he could be removed from the spectacle.

As Domitian's chariot receded, John gradually emerged from the intense pain he had endured. His flesh continued its metamorphosis, restoring itself. The amazement that had gripped the crowd continued, and they shouted to one another, wondering how such a miracle was possible.

The mind and body of Domitian's guard remained under Michael's influence. The praetorian marched forward, shouting orders to the other guards, demanding that John be returned to the prison, clothed, and prepared for a journey by boat to the island of Patmos. He ordered the release of the Christians who were being held captive. Then he watched as John's naked body was escorted back into the prison.

Several hours had passed since the event outside the gate. John sat silent and alone in a stone cell, a fresh tunic covering his body. All of the burns and injuries had completely vanished, and he felt as if the excruciating, terrifying event had never happened. Suddenly, a vision of Michael floating a few feet off the floor appeared. Translucent white, he looked strong and powerful, covered in a white robe, the hem of which trailed off in a slow-moving mist.

"Bless you, child. You were strong and have endured, as I said would happen." John closed his eyes and nodded in agreement. "Your work is close to completion, but the Great Rabbi needs you to attend to two matters."

"What would those be?" John asked.

"When you arrive on Patmos, your mind will become open to receiving revelations from the Father that must be documented. This is so that all believers henceforth will know how the end times will come to pass."

John assured him, "I can keep my mind open, pure, and prepared for when the Father wishes to speak through me."

Michael appeared most pleased. "You have come so far and done so much. Your work on Patmos to document what you learn is extremely important. Yet it is only one of the two tasks you must complete.

"Oh?" John questioned. "What is the other?"

"Remember what the rabbi gifted to you in your hands in the garden? That ability to draw out the truth and protect others? It is the same energy that has sustained you and protected you from the harm that the dark hearts of mankind have tried to levy against you throughout your life. Within your palm is a single point of light to resist the darkness. Do not let it end in its solitude. Pass it on as you were instructed to do."

"I do understand the power His touch has bestowed upon me," John responded.

"Then you must remember what He said to you in the garden. He asked that if you accepted this gift within the flesh of your hands, you would commit to passing it on to others who are worthy to wield the same power. Doing so will maintain a resistance against the four horsemen you witnessed spring forth from the Dark One in that garden so long ago. Do you not remember how important his instructions were on this point?"

"Of course, I remember."

"You must endeavor to pass on the gift you received from our savior to several others—the divinity within you makes this possible. There cannot be just one line that extends from you because it will be too vulnerable, too easily snuffed out. But if there are several, then your power could potentially live in a number of others throughout the ages. A light to repel the agents of darkness who seek to thwart the good works of those who believe."

Michael's voice took on a more somber tone. "You will create the *Invictus*, a lineage of those who cannot be harmed by men, just as you could not this evening. Those descended from you will live to serve and protect others from the horsemen that the Dark One has unleashed upon this world.

"Remember: those to whom you choose to pass on this power must know that the aggression of ordinary men cannot harm those who accept it. The four Dark Descendants are the only beings who can do such harm. Pass on the gift! But choose wisely because you'll only have enough strength to pass the gift on to a few. Then, in time, the gift can be passed on to another, or more, depending on how pure of heart they are."

"I understand," John replied. "My delay in doing so should

not be interpreted as a failing in my heart, only the failing of an increasingly weary body."

"All the more reason to choose others soon, either on your journey to Patmos or once on the island. You mustn't delay. While the actions of ordinary men cannot prevail against you, the slow artillery of time and its impact on your body ultimately will."

John nodded his head in respectful reverence. "Of course. Glory be to Christ and the Father."

"Glory indeed," Michael said. "Fare-thee-well, John."

And with that, the shadowy white mist of the Archangel Michael form faded. John felt renewed in strength, understanding the purpose that lay ahead, and the peace for him that would follow.

Soon after, the cell door opened. A young Roman soldier strode in. His face held an expression that John had not seen among the other guards: a look of concern. This centurion seemed to lack aggression.

"Old man, are you well? Are you healed?" he asked.

"Aye," John replied. He cast his gaze downward as he spoke.

"I want you to know that I believe," the soldier said. "I understand the goodness you seek to bring into the hearts of others. I wish to be a part of it. I must do so in secret, but I can at least offer you comfortable passage to Patmos. I will protect you, ensure that no further harm may come to you. I ask only that you teach me, open my eyes to the glory and the goodness of what you've preached." The soldier lowered his head, clearly humbled. "I feel called to it."

He quickly regained his composure and looked into John's eyes. "But we must move swiftly. When the other guards come, they will know that I am in charge. You should trust that I will keep you safe even when I pretend otherwise in front of them. Do you understand?"

"Of course, my son. Bless you," John answered. "What is your name?"

"I've privately forsaken my given name, choosing instead to be known as . . . Daniel."

1

THE SECOND DAY

2003
Chicago, Illinois

"Let's recap from our last session and then see if we can go further. Your cousin Danny, who was a detective with the Chicago Police Department at the time, was there with you when the images appeared."

"That's right," Craig said. "I met him at the church. I wanted to make sure he would be okay. I knew he was going to confront the serial killer he'd been tracking."

"And it was there that you and Danny did exactly that: confronted the man who attacked you. And sometime during the attack, you saw a vision of how your father had died."

"Exactly," Craig replied.

Craig Henriksen was sitting in a comfortable armchair in Dr. Janet Burris's office in suburban Chicago, next to a large picture window that faced the street. Craig wore tennis shoes, jeans, and a dark polo. Two days' worth of stubble framed his jawline. Dr. Burris sat in a similar chair, rigidly upright, writing in a notepad as they talked.

He hadn't seen her in several months, and it had been nearly a year and a half since he and his cousin had endured the terrifying experience she was recapping. They had both almost died in the encounter with the serial killer. But from what exactly, and why? This was still a mystery, despite Craig's having tried ever since to solve it.

The vision had revealed details of his father's mysterious murder. And before he passed into unconsciousness, Craig was sure he had heard his father speaking to him. Craig was a small child when his father was killed. Finally learning the reason his father was killed and the manner in which it happened was a penultimate moment for him. Many unanswered questions he had always struggled with had started to come into view. But not everything was revealed during the ordeal, and these sessions with Dr. Burris were part of his quest to understand. "But wait," she said. "How did you know where Danny was going to confront the killer? Did he tell you? That would seem strange to me, revealing details of a pending police investigation to a family member."

"No, he didn't," Craig responded truthfully. He was finding it easier to be honest with the doctor now than he had in their last session. "And I'm really not sure how I knew. I just had this powerful intuition that made me feel like I was supposed to go to my father's old church in Iowa. That things would somehow play out there. Not sure why. To this day, I still don't know."

It had been an incredible turn of events that led to the confrontation in the church Craig referenced. While he helped decipher clues for Danny at the murder scenes, one had involved a serial killer who later toyed and taunted Danny. The killer finally took the brazen step to kill Danny's girlfriend, which threw his cousin into a fit of rage. It was then that Craig's gut led him to follow his cousin back to Iowa —where Craig had grown up—in an effort to aid Danny.

He found Danny gravely injured when he arrived. It was then he learned from the serial killer, who referred to himself as the Tourist, that Craig had been his target all along. All the killer's actions and efforts up to that point were intended to draw Craig out in the open and into a place where he would destroy Craig.

When he confronted the killer in that church, Craig realized he had greater abilities beyond those he'd already known. He had known he could re-create images of past violent events by touching spilled blood, seeing those episodes play out as shadows and silhouettes. He also had the power to sense the thoughts and emotions of others. His dreams sometimes foreshadowed events he would encounter in the future. But the ability he discovered while protecting Danny was different—it went beyond the intuitive and the visual and into the physical. He'd discovered that he could project powerful waves of force from the palms of his hands; so potent, in fact, that they had kept the inhuman attacker at bay. He was certain that this unexpected, uninvited power was the only reason he and Danny had survived the ordeal. Their assailant had died, though Craig still could not explain how.

Several moments of silence passed. Dr. Burris looked steadily at him and then returned to scribbling on her notepad. Craig noticed that her appearance hadn't changed much at all over the years. Short and slightly boxy, she sat primly in a modest, conservative business dress, her salt-and-pepper hair closely cropped, holding her notepad, with metal-framed glasses perched low on her nose. She often looked over them at her patient.

It was an overcast morning, with clouds just starting to break apart in the sky. Craig looked out the window and caught his reflection. He'd changed a lot in the last two years. He was nearing his thirtieth birthday and no longer looked so young. Instead, he felt more seasoned. His light brown hair had a few

18 The Invictus

gray ones at the margin. And his smooth, clean complexion now had several deep wrinkles around his eyes and on his brow, born from a new fortitude, internal and external, forged during these recent struggles.

Dr. Burris looked up from her notepad. "And the other thing that happened, beyond the vision . . . what you did with your hands. You see that as a greater manifestation of what you could do before using 'tactile transference,' as you called it, this ability to re-create images of violent events. Am I summarizing that correctly?"

"Yes," Craig answered. "But when we were in the church, and I learned the murderer was the same man who had killed my father years ago, I felt this . . . this deep *rage*. It felt like something erupted inside of me, and that's when I discovered I could project blasts of force from my hands."

"To protect you and your cousin?" Dr. Burris sought to clarify.

"Right, because Danny had been stabbed by this thing, and he was bleeding out."

"You just referred to the attacker as a 'thing,'" Dr. Burris pushed.

Craig knew he was taking a chance in explaining further, mainly because he still wasn't exactly sure himself what the attacker was, and his attempts to learn more had come up empty. And anyway, his newfound ability, as well as all the strange, old ones he'd gotten used to—had been dormant since the battle with the Tourist, the name the killer had given himself.

At first, he was grateful for the respite. Trying to manage powers he couldn't explain was a burden. During this quiet period of normalcy, many aspects of Craig's life had lightened up. He was in a relationship. He was continuing his martial arts training. He felt stronger and healthier than ever before. He had unexpectedly come into a sum of money, which convinced him he could return to grad school. But he had been feeling a persistent void for well over a year. He suspected the powers he possessed likely came with a heavy burden, and he now realized that sense of purpose had been important to him. Part of the reason he was consulting the psychologist—though he hadn't yet expressed it to her—was in the hope that she could help him tap into them again.

So, Craig decided to wade into more honesty with his therapist. "You know how I've told you I could re-create the image of a crime scene from the blood of a victim? Well, this time was the first where I could channel the images from a cross I found in the church. And not just any cross, it was one my dad used to wear. When I touched it, I was able to re-create the scene when he was murdered. It was right after that, Danny and I were attacked by the thing that killed my father."

"There it is again," Dr. Burris said. "Why 'thing'? What was it about the assailant that made you describe him as inhuman? It almost sounds like a mythical thing to me."

"Because it didn't behave as if it were human. Danny and I injured it in ways that no human could've survived, but it still came after us. Like it couldn't be stopped. Like it wasn't human. It was relentless."

Craig paused. He wasn't ready to theorize on what the attacker was or why it was so determined in its effort to kill both him and Danny. He still didn't understand it. Craig began to feel vulnerable. He had already revealed a lot to her. But he wasn't ready to tell Dr. Burris how the spirit of his father arrived just in time to save them as Danny's life was slipping away. Nor would he tell her about the ensuing conversation he'd had with his deceased father. This seemed a bridge too far. In his mind, Craig remained convinced it had happened. But he did not want to appear crazy.

Feeling the uncomfortable silence between them, Craig broke it. "But maybe I'm sharing a little too much. Too far? You're not buying this, are you?"

Dr. Burris remained calm, dispassionate, as she removed her glasses and looked at him. "You need to trust that I'm trying to meet you where you are in your memories of this experience," she said. "When we met months ago, I got the sense that you may not have felt I was taking this as seriously as you do."

Craig remembered that session well. It was shortly after the ordeal, and he hadn't been as open.

"At the time, details about your ordeal in the church were sparse," she continued, "and there were no conclusions about the killer's intense interest in your detective cousin."

Craig remembered being grateful that not much had gotten out in the press. As far as he was concerned, the less details known, the better.

"Well, since then, I've done more research," Dr. Burris continued. "Your cousin was quite prominent in the news-papers with his cases, and quite successful. The reports of his pursuit of this serial killer highlighted that this was the case that almost killed him. And," she paused for a moment, "as I look back through our notes and how you've described helping him, let's just say I resolved to have a more open mind."

Craig was surprised that she had made the effort, and a touch impressed. He thought it could be a good time to explain his previous apprehension about telling her the truth.

"When I've explained to you the strange things I can do, you seemed to think it was all in my head. So, I guess

I wouldn't be surprised if you question the new ability I've described to you today. The fact that it's evolved from visions and insights into something physical."

"I was skeptical when you first described the re-creations you said you could 'conjure." And now you're telling me you can project a force from your hands? Well, if I'm also being honest, I have to say that is equally bizarre."

Craig felt his guard coming up and his expectations sinking.

Dr. Burris must have sensed his emotions. "But, Craig, as I said before, I have done a little research of my own. Something truly extraordinary must have happened to you in the church, even if it isn't all that clear or easily explained."

She took a breath, then said, "I've looked into some extraordinary human phenomena in the literature, paranormal abilities that don't fit a clinical view of what people are supposed to be capable of. As far-fetched as it may sound, I've studied, for example"—she flipped through a stack of papers in a folder—"aura reading."

Craig's puzzlement showed as Dr. Burris continued to explain. "Aura reading is the perception of energy fields surrounding places, people, and things. I've also looked into out-of-body experiences. Bilocation is the process of being in multiple places at the same time. Divination is gaining unexplained insight into a situation. Mediumship, also known as channeling. Precognition, which involves the perception of events before they happen. And lastly, psychokinesis, which is the ability to manipulate objects through thought. Oh, and there's also retrocognition."

"What's that?" Craig asked.

"The perception of past events."

"Wow, I am impressed. So, which one of those do you think I have?"

"It sounds like a little of all of them," she said. "There's no doubt, Craig, that you experienced *something* in that church." She paused. "Let's just say it was outside the range of the normal human experience."

Finally, Craig thought. *Maybe she's willing to explore this with me.*

"As for why none of these things have happened lately, which might give you a chance to understand them better, it could be because your condition has been displaced by happier circumstances."

"My 'condition'? That's an interesting term for it."

Dr. Burris seemed intent on underscoring a point. "You've told me about everything that has been going well for you lately. Think about it: have any of these phenomena manifested since your life has gotten easier?"

"No," Craig conceded. He did feel good; there was no denying that. Things had been going well. He was optimistic about his relationship with Lauren. He had also recently learned that his father had set up a fund that he could access. This provided financial security. All of this should make him feel good, but he still couldn't shake a vague sense of emptiness. After years of unanswered questions, he had received some answers when they confronted the Tourist. His powers had evolved, and the words he heard from his father in the church spoke to a purpose and legacy to his abilities. Not pursuing this further felt like a waste.

Craig had recently started to remember more details of that early winter evening. The Tourist mentioned there were others who sought to destroy people like Craig and Danny. If that were the case, Craig felt he should at least be able to access his powers for self-defense. Were all of the positive turns in his life keeping him from exploring this? What did his powers mean and what sort of obligations were attached to them? All these questions had been troubling him, but he hadn't realized how much so until this moment. *This must be why I'm giving Dr. Burris another try*, he thought. *But have I grown too content to where I can't connect the dots?*

"Maybe the negative feelings you felt when you were younger have been replaced by positive feelings and life circumstances," Dr. Burris said. "So you could look to the positive side. Hidden secrets were revealed and explained to you, and you were able to save your cousin and yourself and escape from the church before the killer was himself killed by, the paper said, an explosive harness he was wearing."

Craig remained grateful that the public understood that the Tourist died from suicide.

"Now that things are good for you, and everything related to that encounter has been resolved for the better, you could put it behind you and see what a happier future has in store for you."

"Or?" Craig anticipated.

"Well, the fact that you're back here tells me you're still searching for something."

Craig felt suddenly vulnerable. She seemed to be zeroing in on the feelings that had just passed through him. He tried to calm himself by pushing his bubbling anxiety to the side. *Don't let it get to you. This is her job, and this is what she does.*

"Yes, maybe life's finally looking up for me, and I shouldn't look that gift horse in the mouth."

"Maybe. But why did you come back?" she countered. For the first time, Craig sensed the dynamics between them shifting. He'd always tried to convince her that the things he could do were real, but now she seemed to be challenging him about them, even urging him to examine them more closely.

Dr. Burris pushed ahead. "It would seem that something incredibly powerful and enlightening was revealed to you in Iowa. Maybe you should ask why. For what purpose?"

"Yeah, I guess there are still some things to think about." This was uncomfortable, and Craig felt like retreating.

She pointed to his chest. "You will want to find out what's in there and why." Then she paused and looked at him. "Craig, have you heard the Mark Twain quote about the two most important days of your life? The first is when you were born—"

"And the second is the day you understand why," Craig finished. "Yeah. I'm pretty sure Lauren has teased me with that one."

"Lauren . . . your girlfriend?"

"Yeah, she's one of the things in my life that is going well right now."

Anchoring back to that, Craig wondered why he would want to risk his current good fortune. There hadn't been any need for his powers recently, so why should he seek to explore them more with the doctor? He felt satisfied with their session today; he had been heard—a big step. She was finally coming around to believing him. That was enough for now.

"For once, I think it's my turn to say that our time is up. There's a bunch of stuff I've got to get done today to support those positive turns we talked about. Registering for classes, for starters, and a bunch of other stuff. Thank you. Really. This has been helpful. And we will do it again," Craig said.

But the doctor wasn't quite ready to end their session. "Maybe something in your thoughts, or at your core, has manifested in the form of your special abilities," she suggested.

"There definitely seems to be an extraordinary type of energy to them. Being trained as a clinician, it's not easy for me to conclude that. But as I said, I've been reading up."

But Craig had already checked out. He wasn't upset by her continued probing, just resolved to finish the session and get on with his day.

"Yeah, maybe. Listen, I truly appreciate your trying to meet me halfway on all this craziness."

"It's not crazy if it's had such a foundational impact on you," she replied.

As he got up to leave, she stood up and extended her hand to shake. He clasped it warmly in both of his. "Thank you. I appreciate your listening and trying to understand and help me make sense of everything."

She smiled slightly, seeming embarrassed. Craig felt a current of electricity pass between his palms just as he let go of her hand. Dr. Burris's eyes widened, but she said nothing as she returned her hand to her side.

"You will see me again soon. I promise," Craig said. He turned to leave.

"Wait," Dr. Burris said. Craig turned to face her. "You have a chance," she said, "a window during which you might be able to understand what happened that evening. I know it's been difficult to talk about, but I believe you've been given a chance to more deeply understand what lies at the heart of your experiences. Don't waste it."

Craig wasn't sure what she meant and was about to ask when the phone in his pocket buzzed. "And I will explore it with you. Next time. For sure," he said. He mouthed a silent "thank you" to Dr. Burris and slipped out into the hallway. He picked up the phone.

"Hey, Mr. Unemployed," the voice on the phone said. It

was Danny. "I called your apartment and Lauren said you were giving the shrink another try."

"I gave it a shot," Craig said. "Just finished up with her."

"Any new insights?" Danny asked.

"Nah, same old stuff."

Then Craig remembered Danny had a big day coming up very soon. "Hey, are you going to talk to that new lieutenant tomorrow?"

Danny had made strides since rejoining the force, but the injuries he sustained during the attack had left their mark. His leg had been broken so severely that he still needed a cane to walk, and his forearm had been amputated and was replaced with an advanced prosthetic. As a result, he hadn't been cleared to return full-time as a detective. That was a hurdle in his career he sought to clear soon.

"Maybe," Danny downplayed. "I'm gonna try and corner him and see where it goes from there. He's been a tough read. Not at all like Hammond."

As Craig descended the stairwell and exited the building, he thought about Danny's old boss. Hammond had been extremely helpful in smoothing over the unexplained aspects of their encounter with the serial killer. He also seemed to have some tacit awareness of the strange powers Craig had used to help Danny, although he had made it clear he didn't want to get involved in trying to understand them.

"Well, you've got to let me know how it goes," he told Danny. "This is your time, man, I can feel it. The city is about to get the full Detective Walsh experience again!"

"Slow down, pal," Danny said. "Someone seems to be in a good mood."

"Call me tomorrow if that's when it goes down," Craig said. Then he had an idea. "Or, better yet, let's get together.

Dinner. You and me and Lauren. This time we'll be dining with *my* lady friend—"

Craig wanted to swallow the words as they were leaving his lips. Emma had been killed by the Tourist. She and Danny had been romantically involved. Craig felt like an ass for bringing it up.

"Hey, listen, man. I'm sorry . . ."

Danny jumped in. "Dude, let it go. No worries. For sure we can do dinner. It'll be good to see Lauren again. Let me just see how the next couple of days go and I'll reach out."

"Of course," Craig said, relieved.

"Let me know how the grad school thing starts. Gotta go. Talk to you soon, Craig."

Craig's heart was heavy as he hung up the phone; he knew he had chilled the moment. He'd wanted more time to talk with his cousin, but Danny was always in a hurry. And now Craig realized that Danny didn't get a chance to say what he had called about. Craig stuck the phone back into his jeans and proceeded down the street toward the bus stop.

2

SPECIAL DUTY

"All this 9/11 shit keeps us jumping through hoops, you know?" Detective Ramirez complained about an all too familiar situation as they made their way toward an auditorium in Chicago's Seventh Precinct.

"Maybe they're changing the color of the threat level again," Danny piled on, faking trepidation. "Hopefully, it hasn't reached hot pink!"

It was midmorning, and Detective Danny Walsh and his colleague were being called in to yet another impromptu briefing. Ramirez, a detective in narcotics, was wearing a T-shirt and jeans—his usual daily attire—with his shield and identification on a lanyard around his neck. Danny wore a sport coat and slacks and used a plain fiberglass cane to assist with walking.

As they neared the auditorium, Danny continued to vent. "With all our resources getting pulled in every potential threat related to 9/11, you'd think the city would be ready to take any help they could get with the normal bullshit: the trafficking rings, homicides, the mob, and everything else in the stew."

"For real," Ramirez agreed. "You itching to get back at it, my man?"

"You know it. Homicide was always good for me, but now I'd even settle for something in Organized Crime."

"Walsh, you know that none of those wise guys wants a piece of you." Ramirez spoke of Danny's reputation.

"Sure. Something like that." Danny knew Ramirez didn't mean it. He would have meant it in the past, but things were different now, and they both knew it. Danny's injuries had left him less than intimating compared to his old self. He still talked a good game, but the nagging doubts echoed in his mind.

As the officers gathered for the meeting, Danny couldn't help but feel invisible. Before the attack, his commanding presence and gregarious nature would have generated buzz and banter in the room. He'd always been the center of attention. But consciously or subconsciously, his colleagues were treating him differently. The novelty of his return to the force after a dramatic, life-threatening experience had worn off. Now, with each passing day, he felt less like a cop and more like a walking publicity stunt. Devalued, marginalized.

In the year that had passed since the ceremony that reintroduced him to the force, he had become resigned to covering cursory duties that left him feeling frustrated: desk work, research, and an occasional investigation. The attack occurred at the end of 2000, and he hadn't made enough progress to rejoin the force in limited capacity until the spring of 2002. While he had gone through a lot of changes to get to that point, there had also been changes in the law enforcement landscape during that time. The Chicago Police Department's attention and resources were being pulled into preparing for, assessing, and investigating real or suspected threats from Al Qaeda and other potential terrorist cells in the city.

The seats in the auditorium were small and cramped, and Danny had some difficulty settling in with his cane. At the front of the auditorium, Jack Mason, his new lieutenant, stood beside a woman who was preparing to get the meeting started. Danny saw that the lieutenant had noticed how he'd settled into his seat. Danny caught his eye and gave a nod and a half smile in a gesture of respect.

Mason reminded Danny much of the way he used to be; if he were being honest, he'd admit that Mason was probably a more impressive version. Mason had been a Green Beret and had left the military unexpectedly several years ago. The departure was rumored to have been about a family issue, and Danny had been wary about asking about it.

Danny's main focus was on his own continuing convale-scence, sharpening his physical fitness, and his policing skills. He'd been working up to a conversation with the new lieutenant in the hopes of gaining his confidence enough to the point where he could once again be assigned the more demanding types of investigative action where he felt most useful. A parade of lieutenants had passed through the precinct since Danny's old boss, Eric Hammond, opted for an administrative role at headquarters several months ago. But, despite the turnover, it appeared that Jack Mason was there to stay. And because of that, Danny had taken time to ready himself for the conversation.

The briefing started with an overview of a new Office of Emergency Management and Communications, as well as "Alert Chicago," a website designed to keep citizens aware and connected to the actions of the Department of Homeland Security.

After reviewing and sharing more perfunctory information, Mason zeroed in on a discussion of terrorist threats. "We know the Willis Tower was on the original list of the 9/11 hijackers.

So, we know the city was and probably remains a target. I'm gonna ask for your coordination with Homeland. But at the same time, be as vigilant as you can behind the scenes. Learn more, connect the dots, but do it quietly. We can't let the public feel like they're trapped between an increasing police state and fear of imminent attack," he said. His face flushed red, and his voice rose. "We can't let these bastards disrupt our way of life and how we operate as a country!"

Danny wasn't the only one taken aback by Mason's passion. And warning a bunch of cops about a police state? That struck Danny as especially odd, and he believed it probably did a number on the other officers too.

Mason's posture and tone seemed to ease as he wrapped up his comments, touching on several investigative efforts underway related to suspected terrorist activities. Then he shifted emotional gears, becoming more guarded as he prepared to hand the discussion over to the woman who had joined him.

"And as we come across potential suspects in these cells, the force has decided to draw on some additional psychological resources to help us in these efforts." He turned to the woman, clearly unenthusiastic about her presence. "Deborah Wood is from Homeland. She's going to walk us through the resources they're making available to us."

Wood told the assembled officers that Homeland would be sending military experts to various large city police departments, including Chicago, for use in tactics for dealing with potential enemy combatants, including interrogations. Given Mason's military background, Danny wondered if he was skeptical of the military assistance.

As Wood continued her briefing, Danny's mind wandered,

mulling over how to approach Mason. He was tied to the administrative work he had been relegated to since returning to work, wanting instead to return to the detective work where he excelled. Today would be the day. Danny was eager to get back into action, both for himself and to show those close to him that despite his obvious physical limitations, he was otherwise fully recovered.

As Wood droned on, Danny's colleague, who was seated behind him, leaned forward and said, "Hey, Walsh. Munitions has something waiting for you. A special duty weapon that Hammond arranged."

This was news to Danny. "Really? Are you sure?"

"Yeah. The quartermaster wanted me to make sure you swing by and get it soon. 'Cause he doesn't want to keep hiding it on the down-low." Danny was opened his mouth to ask for clarification when Mason's stern voice boomed from the front of the room.

"Hey, guys, we're trying to have a meeting here," the lieutenant admonished.

Shit. thought Danny. This was not the impression he wanted to make today.

Danny made an effort to refocus his attention on the woman from Homeland. What she was saying now was thought provoking. "The gentleman we have identified to assist the CPD is someone who served time as a POW in Vietnam. Specifically, he has skills and experience in dealing with the guerrilla tactics of enemy combatants. To be honest, Colonel Bishop tends to be reclusive, but we've convinced him to spend some time with your investigators."

Reclusive? Now Danny was intrigued.

Wood wrapped up the discussion by laying out a general

timetable for when the colonel might visit the precinct. Then Mason closed the meeting with several reminders and general updates.

As the group filed out, Danny held back. He wanted to let the room clear so he could talk to Mason in private. He caught the lieutenant as he started to head for the door. "Chief, can I get a minute?"

Mason appeared unwilling to engage, responding over his shoulder, "Walsh, I got a lot lined up for today. Is this something that can wait?"

"No, not really."

Mason turned to face him, eyebrows raised.

"I wanted to let you know . . . I know it's been a long road back. It's taken time and a lot of work. But I'm ready now."

"Ready for what exactly?" Mason said, his tone dismissive.

Danny was caught off balance by a curt response right out of the gate. Mason appeared to sense this and adjusted his tone.

"Listen, let's rewind a second, all right? There's nothing personal here. The city's got things jumping off in all directions: coordinating with DHS on this terrorist stuff, homicides left and right, racketeering, the mob."

"I know. And I want to pull my weight," Danny pressed. "I'm good at what I do. I can deliver for this department."

"I've read up on your file, and I know what you *used* to do."

Danny tilted his head and squinted, irritated by Mason's insinuation that those days might be over. Standing at six foot three with closely cropped blond hair, Mason was as imposing as Danny had been when he was at full strength. Typically in such a tense encounter, others were intimidated by Danny. Mason was unfazed.

"Walsh, I just have a lot of questions, is all. I've read up on you about how all this happened," he said, gesturing to Danny's prosthetic and cane. "But I need to know more. And I need to be sure of where your head is at and whether you really are capable of performing up to my standards for this department."

"Fine, sure," Danny agreed. "Let's talk it through."

Mason looked Danny up and down again. "As far as getting back in the field . . . I mean, can you even qualify with the stuff you gotta deal with?"

"I assure you that I can take care of myself and whatever I'm up against," Danny said, his initial apprehension about the conversation giving way to impatience. "And I'm a damn good detective. If you've read up on me, you know that's an understatement. I just need a chance to prove it again."

Mason stood silently, as if processing what Danny had said. Then a uniformed officer entered the auditorium. "Lieutenant, we got a situation. We've still got that informant in holding— the mob guy we need to either catch or release. Well, now we got more rolling in on gang charges. We need that holding space. What do you want to do with the informant?"

Mason kneaded his forehead before coming to a decision. "Okay, Walsh. Let's start with you helping *me* out. You know how much of our resources have been pulled from mob cases and all these other rabbit holes we're running down with the feds. I know you did Organized Crime before Homicide. How about you handle this guy in holding?"

Danny let out his breath. "Yeah. Absolutely."

"Okay. We'll talk more later about what you want. For now, focus on lightening the load we have right now. That'll be a big step in the right direction."

It wasn't exactly a return to the work he was best at, but Danny was eager to take it. It was a crack in the wall, and he was intent on making it wider. "You got it," he responded before turning to the uniformed officer. "Which hold is the guy in?"

"Twelve, the one along the back hallway."

Mason appeared satisfied with the compromise and nodded to Danny as he left the room with the uniformed officer.

Encouraged by the conversation, Danny set off toward the hold, determined to see whether the man cooling his heels there had anything of value to offer.

When he arrived at an administrative area outside the holding rooms, he spent some time reviewing the informant's background and history. His name was James Walters. As Danny read the arresting officer's report, he learned that Walters had always been a reliable source in helping the department understand the organized crime groups that moved in and out of the area. But he'd gone dark in recent weeks. Then he'd been picked up overnight by an arresting patrol officer on a breaking-and-entering charge.

The attending guard buzzed Danny through, and he entered the interrogation room.

"So, it says James here, but you look more like a Jimmy to me. What's your story, pal?" Danny said.

His sudden entrance had briefly startled Jimmy, who was sitting behind a metal desk in the center of the room. The young man was dressed in faded blue jeans and a black concert T-shirt. His greasy, disheveled hair reached below his ears. Recovering from his surprise, he settled back and displayed a dismissive, uncooperative attitude. He looked like he practiced that a lot.

"Whatever, bro. I'm just looking to bounce pretty soon and hit some breakfast somewhere is all."

Danny leaned casually against the concrete block wall,

staring at a file folder. "You've got three outstanding warrants on you, Jimmy, so you and I are gonna chat for a little bit before you go anywhere. Why the cold shoulder lately? What's new around the Stockyards or New City?" Danny was referring to areas within Chicago's industrial corridor. With the ongoing revitalization in those parts of town, it was known as a hub of various gang and mob activities related to the work and resources changing hands there. "You don't call, you don't write. What gives?"

"Who says I oughta know shit about the new crews around there?"

"So there have been some new arrivals," Danny said sarcastically. "Do tell."

"Listen, Officer Whatever—"

"It's detective." Danny spun a chair around to straddle it as he stared down the informant.

"Oh boy. Wow. Okay. *Detective*, how about you just throw me back in over there and we'll see what I can really learn. I won't do you much good if I gotta leave my ass pinched up here in the joint."

He was cocky, acting as if he held all the cards, but Danny was used to the attitude and knew just how to handle these characters.

"Let me give you a little news flash, Jimmy—" he started, then stopped abruptly. He had noticed something curious about Jimmy's body language after Danny took a seat closer to him. The informant shifted defensively and crossed his arms. On his outer bicep, there appeared to be a new branding: ornate letters that spelled out C–O–I.

Danny sat as still as stone as his mind flashed back to the strange things he and Craig had been through together. It finally landed on an old letter he remembered Craig had found. The letter spoke to the death of someone on Craig's father's side. It was cryptic and referenced a group to which the ancestor belonged. The letters that referenced this group were the same as those on the informant's arm: *C, O, I*.

Immediately intrigued, he pressed for answers. "What's the mark for, Jimmy?" The stupid boy didn't seem to understand the question at first, but when Danny asked a second time, gesturing explicitly at the bicep, the informant's demeanor changed instantly.

"What? What of it? Whaddya mean?" A slick of sweat suddenly shone on his forehead.

"That mark." Danny pointed. "Right there. I'm looking at it. It sure looks fresh."

"What do you know about it?" The punk's anxiety was clearly growing. "They gotten to you?"

"Hold up there, Jimmy. You seem a little rattled. Let's get back to the information we're looking for. The arresting officer's notes say you've been helpful in recent months but not so much lately."

"That cop didn't say there'd be any questions about no mark."

"Somebody do this to you, Jimmy?" Danny asked, half concerned, and half intrigued.

"All's I know is that arresting cop said I could be in and out after a quick chat. You know, that really tall Black cop."

Danny wasn't sure where this discussion was going, but his mind was now preoccupied with the letters. He had clearly hit a nerve with his line of questioning; something or someone associated with that brand was making Jimmy scared. And another thing: Danny didn't recall any particularly tall Black patrol officers on duty in the precinct at this time of day. Being tall himself, he thought he would have noticed that.

"Why don't you just wait here for a minute—"

"No, man," Jimmy interrupted. "Listen, just lemme outta here and I'll get some real good info about what's been going down in the warehouses."

"Okay, so we're talking about the warehousing district, huh?" But Danny's emphasis on the location only seemed to alarm Jimmy more. It was as if each new exchange between them put Jimmy in greater personal jeopardy. Danny could tell by his body language that the guy's apprehension was genuine.

"Just hold up for a minute. Let me see if we can close the loop with the officer who brought you in. Then we can get to some kind of agreement on whether you'll be able to help us out today."

Jimmy started to protest again, but Danny filled his chest with air and barked, "Just shut the hell up for a minute!" Asserting himself that way—the way he used to—felt terrific. He got up to leave. "I'll be back," he said over his shoulder as the secure door clicked shut.

Danny started down the hall to the precinct's common area in search of the officer Jimmy had described, but before he could get very far, he was stopped by the same detective who had leaned over his shoulder during the briefing.

"Walsh! For real, you gotta get your ass down to the Q and get that package Hammond sent you," he said, referencing the quartermaster, the police official in charge of weapons and ammunition for the precinct. For whatever reason, taking possession of that package from Eric Hammond was clearly a priority.

The punk would keep, Danny decided. He decided to take the time as he descended a stairwell—relying on his cane to get down quickly, albeit gingerly—and headed toward the munitions area of the Bureau of Support Services.

Quartermaster Crowe greeted him with a gruff "'Bout damn time, Walsh." But he was smiling. "Come on back here. You gotta see this shit."

He led Danny through the caged area and into a more secluded part of the room. "Your boy Hammond is really looking out for your ass. It's a weapon, but it's certainly not regulation, aside from the fact that there's a Remington eight-seventy twelve-gauge shotgun involved."

"What the hell are you talking about?" Danny asked.

Crowe placed a wooden cane covered in heavy stain and varnish on the table. It was elegant, a classic. "She's a beauty, all right," he said. "Quite the special-duty weapon."

It looked exactly like a cane, but as Danny lifted it to inspect it, he saw that it held within it a single-barrel shotgun. The arched end of the cane, which fit perfectly in his hand, had an almost imperceptible latch that could be pulled down to form a trigger. The end that met the floor was lined with rubber for traction.

"So, now you've got this to lean on, in addition to your Smith & Wesson semiauto if the shit jumps off. 'Lean on' . . . get it?"

Danny ignored Crowe's half-hearted attempt at banter as he hefted the cane. He had to admit it was an impressive weapon, and its real purpose was well concealed. As Danny admired it, he momentarily forgot about the informant and his mission to locate the arresting officer.

"All right, that joke was lame," Crowe admitted. "But Hammond reached out to me and let me know he had this made for you. So you can have, you know, a little more personal backup when you get back on the streets."

While the cane highlighted Danny's need for an additional

weapon for him to be effective, he was genuinely touched that Hammond had it made for him.

I've got to get together with Hammond, Danny thought. He wanted to thank him. He also wanted to hear his thoughts on Mason, to better understand why this ex-Beret had opted for a desk job. But most importantly, he wanted to get Hammond's take on the fresh letters that were branded on the informant.

"Wow, I need to thank Eric for this," he said hastily. "And thanks to you, too, Crowe," he added, grinning his appreciation. He snatched up the cane. "I can take this now, right? It's mine?"

"You betcha. You just need to keep it under wraps. Let's just say it didn't go through regular channels."

"For sure. Here, let's trade."

Danny snatched the new cane and left the one he had been using with Crowe. "I've gotta run, but this is awesome. Thanks!"

"One thing, though—it's important," Crowe added as Danny turned to leave, lowering his voice to a harsh whisper. "That shit ain't loaded yet."

As Danny made his way out of the area, the cane felt good in his hand, sturdy and balanced. It might have been a weapon, but it was also a good cane, helping him climb the stairs and walk quickly back to the interrogation rooms. As he passed the intake area, he saw the commotion caused by the influx of arrests. Now was not a good time to ask about the Black uniformed officer, so he decided to go back into the hold and get a better description from Jimmy to use when things settled down. Or perhaps he'd lead Jimmy out and they'd go looking for the officer together, to get an on-the-spot ID.

But when he returned to the hold, the door to the interrogation room was open. The room was empty.

"What the fuck!" Danny exclaimed. He went over to the guard who had access control to that room.

"That kid who was in here. A guy named James Walters—Jimmy. Where the hell is he?"

The guard shrugged. "Beats me. Word came from out front that we needed space, and he was a dead end anyway, figured he could go—"

"Word from who?" Danny interrupted. He was irritated. He understood that wires sometimes got crossed with informants and what the precinct was looking to do with them, but this seemed out of character.

"Listen, Walsh. Take it up with the folks out front. We got a shitload of douchebags making their way back here, and we're going to need the space for that mess."

Danny knew he would have to drop it, but the guard's dismissive tone made him seethe on the inside. No respect. *This wouldn't have happened before*, he thought.

Danny was grateful for the weapon Hammond had made for him. And he appreciated the opportunity Mason was giving him to get more mainstreamed. But the informant being set free was gnawing at him—as were those letters. He couldn't understand why, but his gut told him those letters were somehow connected to ones he and Craig had attempted to decipher more than two years ago.

3

SPRING SEMESTER

Craig pushed his way through the lobby doors and out of the Loyola administration building on the Water Tower Campus. He squinted as the midmorning sun washed over him.

He had spent the majority of the preceding hour finalizing his registration for graduate school. He felt apprehensive, but also excited about taking the next step to further his education. He would pursue an MBA, but as for a specialization, he did not yet know. But he was encouraged, and the warm early spring weather that greeted him matched his optimistic mood.

The Water Tower was one of a few buildings to have survived the Great Chicago Fire of 1871. Craig always liked to look at the building whenever he visited the city's Near North Side. Standing just over 180 feet tall, the castle-like structure currently served as Chicago's Office of Tourism and was the hub of a near constant buzz of activity in the area.

He crossed a side street to Byrne Plaza, a green space that surrounded the ornate building. Craig drew in a deep breath and smiled.

In recent years, it had seemed like he was just plodding along, puzzled and bewildered by the strange things he had discovered about himself: the "paranormal abilities," as Dr. Burris had termed them during his last session, that his cousin Danny had exploited to help solve crimes. But then came their climactic battle with what Craig could only describe as a supernatural being, and with it some clarity about the mysteries of his past, particularly about his father. Since then, he had felt empowered by an inner strength and resolve he had never known before.

All of those events had forced him out of his comfort zone, and now he was making the conscious decision to leave that zone again, this time by quitting his job with the accounting firm of Gray Parker & Harris to start grad school full time. Given how hard he'd been working to physically prepare for whatever lay ahead, he reasoned it would be good to expand his mind as well. That way, both body and mind would be strengthened.

Craig was grateful for the opportunity to take this new path in life—to stop plodding and instead start mapping a deliberate course—and that the First Bank of Chicago had come through and paid his tuition. He thought it odd that he hadn't learned earlier about the college fund his father had set up for him, strange that the bank hadn't reached out to him at some point. But his name had never been in the papers before, and it wasn't until shortly after the sensational reports of the encounter in the church were published that someone there had finally made contact. Regardless of how the connection was made, the important thing was that he now had the benefit of that money, and at what seemed like exactly the right time.

He hadn't carried a backpack since his undergraduate days, and it felt unfamiliar. He strolled over to one of the curved stone benches that lined the plaza, let the bag slide off his shoulder, and sat down. Lauren had been challenging him to take more "strategic pauses," as she called them: brief bits of time when he could step back to get a sense of where he was and where he was heading. Knowing that he had about an hour before his martial arts session a few blocks away, he decided to do just that.

He watched the many passersby headed here and there. What were they moving toward or away from? Did they plan to assess where they were as well?

And then his thoughts inevitably turned to Danny. Craig wondered if his cousin was having any luck getting over his hurdle at work since they had last spoken. It was a long shot, Craig thought, though he would never admit it to Danny. But walking with a cane and a titanium and plastic prosthesis in place of where his good, strong arm had once been . . . how could someone so physically compromised be considered fit enough to pull his weight in the field? Craig still felt enormous responsibility for the whole situation. After all, Danny had been so severely injured because he was hunting a serial killer who was ultimately after Craig. And his surging career had been derailed because of it.

Craig took a deep breath and exhaled, wishing at least some measure of what Danny wanted for himself would come true. As he relaxed, he felt grateful for his own life, and particularly for Lauren's influence in it. His heart lifted as he thought about how fortunate he was to have her in his world. The confidence she had in him was obvious. The optimism she exuded was contagious.

Craig felt the buzz of his cell phone in his pocket, which pulled him from his thoughts. He looked at the number on the display and smiled.

"Hey there," he answered.

"Hey. How's it going?" Lauren said. "I know you had a lot lined up for today."

"So far, so good," Craig responded. "Got registered. Did a

little research on what fields I might be interested in. Really glad the bank money got transferred into my student account in time. I'll be hopping over to aikido in a few."

"How was Madison?" Lauren interjected. "Were you able to make it by to see her?" Madison was Lauren's friend whose job it was to coordinate volunteer efforts to help refugees new to the Chicago area settle in. Lauren had been pushing for Craig to help out while he was preparing for school now that he no longer had the daily obligations of a full-time job.

"No, not yet. I was just stealing a few minutes for a pause before I head to my session," Craig said, a playful hint about what she had been encouraging him to do.

There were a few moments of silence. Craig could sense she wasn't happy.

"What's up?" he asked. "Remind me why you think it's important that I connect with her."

"We talked about this. About how you might have a unique perspective to help these people cope with having to leave their families behind. Because you had to go for such a long time disconnected from your own family history." Lauren knew Craig had lost his mother to cancer when he was a child, and then his father was killed. He had been raised by Danny's parents since he was ten and had known little about his father for most of his life.

"Oh yeah, right. Yeah, that makes sense. Still, didn't you say that I should take time to find my own way?"

"Well . . . yes," she responded, her tone sounding like a parent whose child had predictably made the wrong choice.

"Don't worry, though, I'll work it in today. Promise."

"You'd better." She softened. "Okay, well, I hope the rest of your day goes great. I'll see you tonight." Craig was glad when their call ended with her typical optimism.

After they hung up, he tried to recenter his mind to take in the beautiful morning. He looked across Michigan Avenue, past the Water Tower, to the community playhouse. His phone buzzed again, and he heaved a sigh. Was there some hidden force conspiring against having some quiet time for reflection?

It was Danny. He answered quickly, eager for news of how things were going at the police station.

"So? What's the word?" Craig asked.

"The word is, well, getting there."

"Wait, that's two words," Craig joked. "What happened with the new guy? Murphy, right?"

"Mason. And it went kinda okay," Danny answered. "He agreed to let me take on a little bit more of the investigative load. Look into a few gang things."

"Well, isn't that a step in the right direction?"

"Sure, sure . . . " Danny seemed preoccupied. "Listen, I got a question for you. Remember those initials you found on that letter addressed to your dad?"

Whoa, that was out of left field. "It was addressed to my grandfather," Craig corrected, "but yeah, I remember. Where's this coming from?"

"Nowhere. I was just going back through some things in my mind, stuff we learned during . . . I guess knowing that I'm getting back into investigating has gotten these juices flowing again."

"I think I get it. It was *C, O, I,* remember?"

"Right, exactly. That's what I thought. Going to need to think more about that." Danny paused. "I also called to ask whether you've had anything come back—you know, your old . . . talents. Any of those come to light recently?"

"Dude, you know I would've told you if they did." Craig

knew Danny was checking yet again whether Craig's supernatural abilities had returned. It seemed odd that Danny was
bringing it up out of the blue, on a phone call. "No, nothing
other than conjuring the images at the crime scenes you
worked, but you haven't done that kind of work in quite a
while."

"True," Danny acknowledged. "Hopefully, there will be
other opportunities if I'm able to get back to Homicide. What
about that thing you did with your palms at the church?"

"Nope, not that either."

"Any seeing into people's heads?"

"Nada."

"Dreams? Those dreams where you could kinda see what
might happen?"

"Zilch."

Danny sighed.

Craig adjusted how he was sitting and cradled the phone
to his ear. "Hey, why are you asking about this stuff?" It
was strange that he was being pushed to think about his
extraordinary powers twice in less than a week, starting with
Dr. Burris, and especially about the fact that they'd gone
dormant.

"It just seems strange that it's all gone cold for . . . how
long? Over a year now?" Danny asked.

"I don't know what to tell you, man."

"And I've been thinking about what happened at the
police ceremony when you cut your hand," Danny continued.
The incident was an extraordinary development. Moments
before the event in which Danny was to be reintroduced to
the force with great fanfare, Craig had hastily tried to help his
cousin in cutting the tag off his new dress jacket. Danny had
accidentally sliced into Craig's hand, causing a deep cut. But

then, miraculously and in an instance, the injury healed itself as if it had never happened.

"I remember," Craig said.

"Well, I think that's really the wildest thing of all," Danny said. "It's almost like maybe you couldn't really be hurt."

That was pretty wild conjecture, especially coming out of nowhere like it did. Challenging the hypothesis, Craig countered, "You remember when I fell out of that tree when I was twelve? I broke my arm in two places. I think we've seen I can definitely be injured."

"Yeah, true," Danny admitted.

"Where are you going with this, cousin?"

"Well, since I'm on the verge of getting back into action, I'm thinking maybe now's the time to see whether you might be able to help me again."

"Yeah, maybe." But Craig was suddenly tired of talking about it. "Look, I'm focused on other things. I'll be starting this school gig pretty soon."

"Oh, right," Danny recalled. "How's that going?"

"Good! I knocked out some of the legwork today. Now I'm headed to aikido." He glanced down at his watch, noticing that class was about to start. He got up, shouldered his backpack, and headed in the direction of the gym. "Clearly we need to catch up on stuff. We were going to try and do dinner, remember?"

"Yeah, but Lauren will be there, and I'm never sure how much she knows," Danny reminded him.

"She knows most. Well, some." Craig relented. "If we do dinner, let's just you and me meet a little ahead of time and then she can join us."

Danny jumped on the idea. "When were you thinking?"

"I'll touch base in a week or so after I get a better idea of

my schedule." For once, it was Craig who felt like he needed
to wrap up their call.

"Okay, but let's make it soon. Hopefully, work will be
spiking for me, and I wanna do dinner before that happens. I
also need to make time to connect with Hammond."

"You're meeting with Eric?" Craig asked. "Let him know
I said hi."

Danny chuckled, as if he found it funny that Craig might
be on a first-name basis with Hammond. "Sure thing."

Craig wrapped up the call about a block away from his
martial arts class. He slowed as he approached the old building;
he had noticed something odd. A young woman was leaning
against the building next to the studio. She wore gray sweats
and a long-sleeved gym shirt. She was tall and lean, with pale
skin and dark brown hair, and looked very fit. Craig thought
she looked striking—strong, intense, determined. Her eyes
darted back and forth among the pedestrians on the street, as
if she were searching for someone or something.

A man in his mid-fifties and dressed in slacks and a jacket
walked past the woman. She stepped away from the wall,
appearing to confront him. From his vantage point, Craig
could see that the woman's body language was aggressive,
intimidating. Their voices were rising now, though Craig
couldn't make out any words.

Their back-and-forth continued. Then the woman's arm
darted out and she pushed the man in the chest. He pointed
at her, a gesture that seemed to say, "Don't try that again."
She grabbed his outstretched wrist, twisted upward with both
hands, and forced him to the sidewalk on his knees. The man
bellowed in pain.

Seeing the older man being decked by a martial arts move
he knew well, Craig instinctively launched himself across

the street to help—and into the path of an oncoming car. A blaring horn and screeching tires got his attention, and he turned to face the car. But it was too late to evade it. As he turned toward the car, he braced for impact. The car skidded into him, and he slapped the hood squarely with his hands, attempting something like a handstand. The move kept him from being flattened, but Craig was tossed through the air. As he was about to land, he twisted his body to keep his arms in front of him to absorb the impact. His palms burned as he slid along the pavement.

He lay face down, stunned for a moment. Then he lifted his head to find that traffic had stopped in both directions. Craig turned his attention back to the scene he'd been tracking, quickly spotting the tall woman in the sweats who still held the man under her control. Their eyes met, and she squinted in puzzlement, seeming to wonder why she was the object of his attention. Then she released the man's wrist, turned on her heel, and walked briskly up the street.

Craig cautiously stood up.

"Hey, pal! You all right? Hey! Hey, I'm talking to you!" a motorist yelled.

The woman he had been so determined to confront had escaped, and Craig was flooded with embarrassment and anger at himself.

Another motorist called out, "Hey, are you okay? You need help?"

"Yeah, I'm all right. Goddammit!" he hollered, swiveling his head to take in all the drivers surrounding him. "I'm fine already. Sorry!"

Craig retreated to the sidewalk as the cars resumed their trips prior to his barging into the middle of them.

What was I thinking? Craig thought. He stood for a

moment, staring across the street to where the confrontation had occurred, and saw the man get up, glance around furtively, and move quickly out of sight in the opposite direction from where the woman had gone. His behavior didn't seem to be that of someone who had just been wrongly assaulted, but rather that of a man who desperately wanted to retreat from view, hoping that the confrontation had gone unnoticed amid the commotion Craig had caused.

Craig struggled to understand what he had seen and what prompted his action. Why had he felt compelled to launch himself through traffic to intervene without any concern for his own safety?

His hands that had burned from their impact with the asphalt showed no signs of injury. Once again his body had instantly repaired itself. None of it made any sense.

Having gathered himself, he crossed the street—safely in the crosswalk and with the light this time—and made his way to his gym.

Craig was now late. He hurriedly dressed for his martial arts session.

He emerged from the locker room knowing that he didn't have time to dwell on the altercation he saw or nearly getting hit.

The studio was located on the third floor of an older building that was being renovated. Construction was clearly still ongoing in this room. Exposed brick flanked the large leaded glass windows that looked out onto the city. Old, worn wooden floor planks still covered a large area where training mats were laid out.

Craig apologized to his sensei, Master Jason. He stretched while Jason waited for him on the mat. He was feeling lethargic after coming off the surge of excitement he felt when he arrived.

"Craig? Are you ready? A little groundwork perhaps?" The sensei's voice broke through, and Craig realized he'd been just staring into space.

"Sure," he responded.

"What's up with you, Craig?" his instructor asked. Jason was a fit Asian American man in his late thirties and stood at five foot five, six inches shorter than Craig. His dark hair was tousled and slightly damp with sweat from two previous sessions with other students.

"Nothing. I'm good," Craig responded.

Jason nodded at the cross that hung outside Craig's martial arts uniform. "You're still going to roll with that thing around your neck?"

"You know it." Craig smiled wryly as he patted the cross, then tucked it under his top. "Remember? It never comes off."

The cross had a history, and he had grown superstitious about wearing it. It had belonged to his father. Craig had found it in the church where he and Danny were attacked, and it had served as the portal through which Craig saw how his father had been killed. Even before that, Craig had dreamt of his father wearing it. So now it held special meaning for Craig, symbolizing his father's life and the sacrifices he had made to ensure that Craig would survive.

"As you wish. Let's get started then," Jason said, motioning him onto the mat.

After they did a few leg sweeps, they were on the mat grappling with one another. Craig always thought of the workout as a physical chess match, where each opponent probed for a weakness or flaw. He was noticeably slow today, compared with other sessions. Usually, his movements were much sharper.

"You dragging a bit today, Mr. Henriksen?" Jason asked.

Craig had gotten quite good in the couple of years since the incident. He had learned aikido and become adept at it during his late teens and throughout his twenties. But since the attack, he was no longer satisfied with that level of skill, and he had thrown himself into improving. It didn't seem to be working today.

"Maybe—not sure why." Craig could feel his fatigue, and mentally he wasn't entirely present. For one thing, he was still preoccupied with the events that had occurred on the street. And then there was his conversation with Dr. Burris and Danny quizzing him on why his powers had gone dormant.

"You'll find it hard to channel physical energy when you have a lot on your mind," Jason said. "Certainly, the head, the heart, and the body . . . are all connected and reliant upon one another . . . to perform at their peak," Jason said between breaths. He was also tiring, but not as much as Craig was. "Things on your head or your heart today, Craig?"

"Not sure." Craig was struggling to keep up now.

"I sense that there is. Your movements and technique are lacking today." Jason was simply stating the facts, honestly noting what he observed in his student, as was his way.

But Craig felt like his effort was being called out. He shook his head and refocused his thoughts on the matter at hand, ramping up his intensity.

Jason noted it. "Ah, there we are. Better." He parried the attacks Craig now levied as they spun and launched themselves about on the mat.

Jason then dialed up his own intensity and the degree of difficulty Craig had to face. Recently, Craig had been able to rise to the occasion when his instructor did this, but not today.

Jason twisted his way behind his student, pinning one of Craig's arms awkwardly behind his back. "If you're feeling pressure, Craig, just tap out," he said.

"No way," Craig grunted. Resolving not to submit, he tried a range of techniques to free his arm from the lock.

"Careful," Jason cautioned as he felt the reverse pressure Craig was trying to apply. In a bold effort to escape, Craig planted his feet on the mat and launched off them, looking to spin in midair to free his arm. As he landed on the mat, he instead felt the unmistakable snap of his humerus. Jason immediately released his arm. Craig coiled into a ball on the mat, cradling his injured arm.

"Craig!" Jason shouted. "Are you all right? Oh my god, it's broken, isn't it?"

"Just . . . just give me a minute," he gasped, grimacing. Jason crouched over him, waiting to learn how bad the break was.

Initially, the pain was searing, agonizing. But as the seconds rolled by, it started to ebb, and the area around his bicep felt cold and hard. After a few moments, Craig slowly released the injured arm, and to his amazement, he was able to fully bend it. It was completely healed.

He looked at Jason. "I think it's gonna be okay," he said.

"Craig, it's broken. I felt it pop."

"No, really, see?" Craig brazenly flexed his biceps.

Jason sank onto the mat, shaking his head in disbelief. "But how? I don't understand . . ."

"C'mon, sensei. This has to have happened before. Probably just popped my shoulder out for a minute." Craig hoped that sounded like a plausible enough explanation because he wouldn't be able to explain himself.

Still confused, his instructor let it go. "Okay, so long as you are sure you're all right." He switched out of concerned mode and back into teaching. "That was a countermove you should've known wouldn't work. It was a lazy shortcut. Work out of it next time."

Craig nodded, but the words hadn't really registered; he was processing the gravity of what had just happened. He had emerged unscathed from significant injury. He knew Danny would be most interested in this, especially following the phone call where Danny had been quizzing him about his abilities reemerging.

After sparring, they went to a bench to towel off sweat and grab some water.

"You really decided to put me in my place there, didn't you?" Craig joked, deflecting. "Always looking to crank it up a notch just when I start getting confident."

"That's part of the improvement process; you know this, Craig."

"Yeah, I get it. No stress, no growth, you always say," Craig teased. "But, seriously, as good as you are, does it ever scare you to think just how medieval you could go on someone?"

Jason took a philosophical turn. "It is true that it is our potential power, not our shortcomings, that scares one the most."

"Well, it's gonna be some time before I'm anywhere near your level," Craig said. "You'll have to share some of your closest secrets if I'm ever going to be that good."

Jason became intent. "Ah, remember that it was Bruce Lee who once said, 'A teacher is never a giver of truth, but instead a guide who points to a truth that the student must discover for themselves.'"

Craig was still too preoccupied for metaphysical ideas. "I'll have to give that some thought." Then he remembered the woman in the street. "Let me ask you something, sensei. I saw a woman down the street, a block or so away. She was really giving a guy the business. She had some obvious aikido skills."

"Did she have dark brown hair? Thin?"

"That's her."

"Yes, she usually comes in here on Mondays and Fridays to spar in my open sessions."

"The encounter was odd," Craig said. "What do you know about her?"

"Honestly, not much. She started coming in a few months ago. Already very skilled in the art when she arrived. She seems to keep to herself," Jason sounded lamented, as if he enjoyed getting to know his students, as he had with Craig. "But very, very skilled. You think she caused trouble out there?"

"It definitely was a confrontation, and it kinda seemed like she started it," Craig said.

Jason looked concerned. "She does not strike me at all as inappropriately aggressive. She has always shown great respect for the martial arts with me."

That wasn't much info to go on, but it seemed to be all Jason had. Craig remained intrigued by her and what he had seen her do. He wasn't sure why, but he decided he would try to cross paths with her soon during one of the open classes. Maybe then he would understand why she had so captured his attention.

4

AN ANCIENT ALLIANCE

New York City

It was getting late in the evening and the night air felt chilly. Two men stood outside a large brick building in Manhattan near a dead-end alley. No one else was in the vicinity.

"Remind me again why the boss wants us to hang out here freezing our asses off?" Tommy asked.

"Hell if I know," Frank said. "He just said we needed to be on the lookout for a stray."

Frank grimaced his skepticism. "I know the boss has got a way of seeing things coming. But this seems a bit of a reach, even for him."

The two men were key enforcers in the mysterious Venator crime syndicate. Given the nature of their work, they had little reason to feel apprehensive, despite standing in such a foreboding location and waiting to see if anyone might wander so close to an area they controlled. Both men wore black bomber jackets, dark pants, and boots. They were clean shaven with short-cropped hair.

Frank reached into his coat and pulled out a pack of cigarettes. He withdrew one and held it to his lips as he raised the lighter. But instead of lighting it, he paused. His eyes

had caught the unmistakable outline of a man in a long coat
making his way down the alley toward them.

The cigarette bounced up and down in his lips as he awaited
the arrival of the stranger their boss had predicted. "Well, will
you look at this?" Frank said. He snatched the cigarette out of
his mouth. "Guess the boss nailed it after all. Again."

Tommy nodded. "Yup, the dude knows what he's talking
about."

Frank tossed aside the unlit cigarette as Tommy motioned
to the middle of the alleyway where they could intercept their
visitor. They stood shoulder to shoulder in a show of strength,
blocking the stranger's path.

As the dark outline of the stranger gave way, they saw that
he was slim, and older, his gray hair peeking out from beneath
a dark driving hat. His clothing appeared nondescript beneath
an open trench coat.

"What are you doing out here so late, old-timer?" Frank
asked.

Without hesitation, the stranger responded, "I have
important information for the man you take orders from.
Things that I am sure he would like to know."

"Oh, really?" Tommy jumped in. "Lucky for you that we
just happen to be out here tonight. You sure you wanna come
in here and talk to our guy though? By yourself?"

"But of course. I've traveled far in order to speak with
him. May I please come in? The night air is cold." The older
man was polite but not deferential, his tone matter of fact. If
the two enforcers sought to make him feel uneasy, that hadn't
succeeded.

"Sure, pal," said Tommy as he pointed to the doorway at
the back of the building. "Let's get you on in there then." He
led the way to the door and the older man followed. Frank

closed the space behind him as the three of them headed into the building.

Once inside, Frank slid a deadbolt in place that secured a large steel door. They stood in a small, windowless room. A few dusty hanging light bulbs inadequately illuminated a spartan industrial setting. There was a wooden table surrounded by four wooden chairs, and there was a large candle placed in the center. On the opposite wall was another door that was opened and appeared to lead into a larger area.

Frank withdrew his lighter and lit the candle. The flame shone brightly but did little to further illuminate the room. The older man shuffled up to the table and paused, looking at the flickering flame, but stopped short of taking a seat. Mistaking this hesitation for apprehension, Frank sought to take advantage. "What are you waiting for? Have a seat, old man. And show a little respect, will ya?" With a flip of his wrist, he popped the old man's hat off his head and it fell to the floor.

His eyes now unshielded, the old man squinted, as if even the dim light in the room was somehow still too bright. He glanced down at the hat, then looked up and locked eyes with Frank, his gaze menacing.

Tommy, observing the scene, feigned defense of the old man. "Aw, leave the old bastard alone. Besides, he's got a set of stones on him for coming out here by himself to talk to the boss."

The old man's flashing stare seemed to soften. "Indeed," he said. "As for my hat, I'm sure you mean to retrieve it for me. Don't you?" His lip curled very slightly into a snarl.

What happened next caught Frank completely by surprise. His insides flooded with fear. He felt hot and nauseous. Sweat beaded across his brow. He hastily reached down to retrieve the hat, despite not understanding why he felt the impulse to do it, thinking it was the only way to alleviate the sense of dread that had been stirred up within him. Cautiously, he placed the hat on the table in front of the old man. And sure enough, his internal distress eased.

Tommy stood silently, his head cocked to one side, clearly confused by his colleague's deferential behavior.

"Ah, that's better. Thank you, my boy," the old man said as he snatched it up. Then he complied with the request to take a seat.

Before either gangster could explore the old man's intentions or the reason for his seemingly relaxed attitude, the door behind them opened. The pair immediately straightened in unison.

"What do we have?" a deep voice asked.

A hulking man walked into the room, barely fitting through the door. He stood well over six feet. A dark gray suit and white shirt were stretched across his impressive frame. He wore a red tie. He had a dark complexion and a cleanly shaven bald head. Salt-and-pepper stubble lined a powerful jawline. His countenance was solemn, yet he appeared slightly bored.

Frank addressed his boss nervously. "Oh, hey. We were just getting this old guy settled in for you. Found him back in the alley just like you said we would. He says he wants to talk with you. That he's got info you wanted."

The boss and the old man eyed each other up and down.

"Yeah, it was just like you said, Boss," said Tommy. "He walked right up to us like he had an appointment or somethin—"

"Leave us," the boss said, raising a massive hand.

"What?" Frank said. "Boss, you sure? We don't know

anything 'bout this guy. I mean, you said someone might show up tonight, but don't you think—"

Hand still raised, the boss kept his gaze trained on the old man. "Get out. Now," he whispered.

All too familiar with that tone, the pair quickly exited the room, moving into the building's interior and out of earshot.

"What the hell was that all about?" Frank asked.

"I dunno. You think the boss knows that guy? That why he knew he'd show up?" Tommy said.

"I'm not sure. But something about that old-timer ain't right," Frank offered.

"What do you mean? Is that why you gave him back his hat?"

"I just don't think he's right. He's bad news of some kind," Frank replied without acknowledging the sense of dread he'd felt.

"He may be. But he's about to find out the boss is way worse news."

The room was silent. The boss pulled out the wooden chair and sat down across from the old man. Motionless, they looked at each other for a long moment.

The old man spoke first. "You felt it, didn't you?"

The boss ignored the question. "It's been a very long time since I've seen you. Why do you deem it practical to seek me out now?"

The old man persisted. "But you felt it, did you not? It may have taken some time for the awareness to ripple here, and it was longer still before I joined you here tonight. But undoubtedly, you have felt it."

"Yes, brother, I have," the boss finally admitted. A mix of disgust and resignation clouded his face. "The second of the four of us has now fallen. And perhaps we must discuss it. But it is not wise for the two of us to be in proximity."

The old man nodded. "Agreed. But an event such as this has happened only once before. And that was nearly a hundred years ago. The fact that it has happened again necessitates that we meet to confer, that we may better understand the nature of this new player and the challenges he presents."

The boss looked off into the shadows of the room beyond the candlelight. "You and I attend to our work in our own way. Our brother operated differently."

"Yes," the old man agreed. "I have found it quite easy to appeal to the darkness in others, to instill within them the proper motivation to assist me. You seem to have done the same."

"Exactly. I've created a very powerful organization here in the city. And you might imagine that among the millions here, there are many who seek to follow the light. I have been most effective in bringing some to the darkness." He returned his gaze to the old man. "Though our brother worked in solitude, it should not have been possible for any human to destroy him. At least when the first among us fell so long ago, it took more than a mortal to end his work."

Pushing what he believed to be the most pressing matter, the boss continued. "We need to stay focused on our task. We have had a lot of success in eradicating others in this line."

"This is true," the old man mused. "But we do not yet know enough about this newest one. It is curious. It appears that the only way he could have destroyed our brother was if he was being aided by our enemy."

"Yes, but how?"

"He must have offered a most precious sacrifice during their encounter in order for our enemy to bring him such assistance."

"Ah, so this is how you interpret what happened?" the boss asked.

"It is the only way we know of that he could destroy one of us," the old man answered. "Which makes him a threat that is both serious and different from what we have known before." The old man leaned forward, his voice calm but his eyes narrowed, intent on conveying his concern. "I'll say it again: we don't yet know enough about this newest one. But we do know that another of our brothers has fallen. We are now half of the numbers we once were, and both losses have occurred in the last century."

Speaking in his deep baritone, the boss sought to assuage the old man's concern. "Relax. Perhaps it was mere carelessness on our brother's part. Or the bastard just got lucky somehow." His large frame fidgeted in his seat, betraying his own unease about this turn of events, and the wooden chair creaked in protest. He clasped his hands on the table in front of him. A flash of light glinted off a gold signet ring that adorned one of his fingers.

"This development doesn't give you pause?" the older man questioned.

"Not at all," the boss maintained. "You and I took a decidedly different path than our brother. He was most effective in the shadows and working alone. We've found ourselves equally effective working somewhat more openly, but with the benefit of insulation against the curious. Look at our progress. Their numbers dwindle, do they not?"

"Nonetheless," the old man responded sternly, "we should not understate the loss we have sustained. The gravity of it has drawn us together—much like when our other brother perished so long ago."

"Agreed." The boss cracked his knuckles. "But you and I have an advantage that our two deceased brothers did not. We remain well protected by others. Our approach is more surgical, more selective. Until the end, when they meet their fate."

The boss's eyes narrowed, and he leaned forward. "This new follower likely doesn't understand that you and I look different than the others. This will be an advantage for us. And we shouldn't fear that his ability is any more advanced than that of the others in the line."

A fiendish smile creased the wrinkled skin of the older man's face. He leaned back in his chair. "Of course, you are right. You and I have built elements of both protection and subterfuge. This has increased our success compared to our brothers. We will prevail, so long as we are able to work together."

"As we always have when it has been necessary," replied the boss.

The smile on the older man's face faded. "But we should also remember that whoever this new actor is, he is different from any of the others we have faced."

The boss straightened, and his enormous chest seemed to grow further. "When the time comes, we will deliver our blows . . . until he falls."

"Agreed. We should coordinate how and where we will confront him, and how he is to be eliminated. But first, we must find him."

"Has this been difficult?" asked the boss. "What have you learned?"

"Not much yet. Just his name, and that he's somehow aligned with the police. All else has eluded us."

"How can that be?" asked the boss. "Even with police protection, it should be relatively easy to identify and reacquire him."

"It is curious," the old man mused. "The trail has gone cold. We've sensed no more use of his 'gifts,' and his alignment with law enforcement is murky. Perhaps this lack of understanding has contributed to our inability to detect him."

"If that is the case, he could be manipulated if his role hasn't been revealed to him." The boss squeezed his hands into fists. "If he is a blank slate, he may not yet have learned to channel his abilities." The seriousness of this theory seemed to sink in. "He must be dealt with. Soon."

"Then we agree that he poses a greater threat than the others," the old man replied. "Remember what we learned when our first brother fell so long ago—that the only way to receive divine aid is by offering one's own soul *and* being oblivious to the meaning of the act. If he can be tempted, we might be able to convince him that he would be better served by becoming an ally."

The boss's eyes widened, and he nodded vigorously as understanding dawned. "Then not only would his line cease to exist, but he could also become a powerful instrument for us."

"Indeed!"

The boss smiled. "His talents alone would provide strong temptation. And if he has the hubris to match"—he raised one eyebrow—"he could be tempted to stray from his intended path."

"That would accelerate our work!" the old man eagerly added.

With that, the two men lapsed into silence.

"When we find him," the boss finally said, "we must appeal to his attraction to power. Or if that fails, we must be close enough to strike him down."

"Yes," the old man agreed. He reached a hand toward the flickering candle flame and let his fingertips carelessly dance through it. Yellow tongues of fire surrounded his fingers as the candle continued to burn. "If he is able to embrace our perspective, he will understand the appeal of the fire, how lovely it is to watch it lay waste. We'll either find out that he can be used, or we will destroy him. In any case, this line of foolish guardians will be snuffed out forever."

The old man extinguished the flame between his thumb and finger, holding on to the end of the wick as dark smoke curled up from below.

"Let us make it so," the boss said in a husky voice.

5

RESISTANCE

Chicago

Craig had been restless for most of the night, his mind racing from the events at the martial arts studio. His subconscious flashed with a myriad of hazy images that finally coalesced into a dream.

He was standing in the middle of the living area of what seemed to be the apartment where he had lived before moving in with Lauren. He could hear sobbing.

"Hello? Who's here?" he called out. There was no response, but the sobbing continued. He looked around the apartment but couldn't see anyone. He called out again, "Where are you? What's wrong?" He felt a great sense of apprehension, and for some reason, he was drawn to his old bedroom. He walked to the doorway and looked inside.

Emma was sitting on the edge of his bed. She was Danny's girlfriend and one of the serial killer's victims. Her head was turned away from him. The sobbing stopped. Next to her on the bed lay an old box of memorabilia within which Craig had found a letter addressed to his grandfather with the cryptic initials: *C, O, I.*

Emma turned to look at him, her eyes dry as if she had not been crying at all. "How can you have moved on?" she asked

Craig. "Why have you left us already?" Her hand gestured toward the box. "You were supposed to protect us."

"What do you mean?" Craig asked, baffled. "Protect who?"

"I don't mean me, of course. It's too late for me—what's done is done. But everyone else like me. All the others. Are you just going to turn your back on us?"

"Turn my back on who? I still don't understand. Please explain—what are you talking about?" Craig pleaded.

Ignoring the question, she responded, "This is what it feels like to us." She stood, turned, and walked toward the wall. Her outline blurred as she approached the wall, then seemed to blend into it, and then disappeared.

"Wait! Don't go!" Craig begged. "I need to understand. What're you talking about?"

Craig bolted upright in bed, panting. His arm was outstretched toward the wall.

"Craig? What's going on?" Now Lauren was awake, groggy but concerned.

Unsure of what the dream meant and unwilling to try to describe it to her in the middle of the night, Craig encouraged her to go back to sleep.

"Nothing. It was nothing. Just a bad dream. Get some sleep."

Lauren nodded as if she understood and rolled over. Craig glanced at the digital clock on the nightstand and saw it was 2:30 a.m. He lay on his back and stared at the dark ceiling, puzzling over the dream until, after some time, a blanket of tiredness descended upon him and he fell soundly back to sleep.

Craig had overslept. While his classes hadn't started yet and he didn't have any other commitments that day, he liked to get up when Lauren did so he could spend some time with her as she got ready for work. The whirr of the blender in the kitchenette of the Wicker Park apartment they shared announced that she had already showered and was preparing to leave.

"Lauren, you're leaving already?" Craig called out. Though he had slept in, it was still earlier than she usually left for work.

"In a bit," she responded. "I'm going to Minneapolis for a few days. I need to head toward the airport soon."

Craig's bare feet hit the floor as he arose in a T-shirt and gym shorts. He quickly freshened up in the bathroom, then headed to the kitchenette. He stood in the doorway as Lauren finished prepping her breakfast drink and said, "Remind me why you're going up to Minneapolis and how long you'll be gone."

"Recruiting. Going to find the best and brightest." She squinted one eye skeptically. "Hey, I found you, didn't I?"

"I was already working there, I'll remind you," he quipped.

"Not anymore, baby," Lauren played along as she poured a smoothie into a container. Wearing a knit sweater and wool slacks, she looked as radiant and chipper as she always did in the morning. Craig loved the way her thick auburn hair swept across her shoulders as she moved.

"Seriously, why do you still have to travel for recruiting so much? It's not like GPH needs to hire a ton of new people all the time." Craig referred by acronym to *Gray, Parker & Harris*, the accounting firm at which Lauren worked in HR.

Lauren turned and smiled at him. "Now, Craig. Am I

sensing a touch of worry or jealousy? For pity's sake, I let you move in, didn't I?"

She liked to joke and keep things light, and Craig was grateful for that. It was one of the qualities that helped pull him out of the frequent spells of depression he had suffered before they met and when they first got together—spells that fortunately weren't so common anymore.

"It's just . . . I don't know. I was looking to run some stuff by you."

"Then call me," she countered.

"It's not the same," he said.

Looking concerned, she asked, "What's up, sweetie? You're talking like you did when we first dated. All shrouded in mystery and whatnot. Something has you conflicted again?"

"I've been thinking, is all. I mean, things are really good right now."

"Right now?" She raised an eyebrow.

"No, they have been. Don't get me wrong. I've just been feeling, I don't know, a little more anxious."

"How come?" Lauren gently challenged him. "You've been talking about this new phase for a while. No work obligations. Getting to go back to school, focusing on martial arts again. Haven't you been looking forward to getting to *exactly* where you are now?"

"I know. But I've also gotten sidetracked from something I think matters too: figuring out how and why I used to be able to do the strange stuff I could do. And for what purpose, I guess."

Lauren shrugged her shoulders. "But you have the freedom of not needing to work now, and you can focus on other things. And that certainly seems to have agreed with you and your mood."

"You're right. But there's also times, especially when I talk with Danny, that I'm reminded of all that unusual stuff, and also the trauma he went through." The emphasis on Danny was actually a dodge. His frame of mind really had more to do with the sudden return of his capacity to heal himself. And now his dream of Emma.

"But Danny's been able to have his own break too," Lauren replied. "Hasn't he been on desk duty? You shouldn't feel like you're letting him down. He hasn't needed you to try to help re-create images—or whatever you did at the crime scenes."

Craig hadn't told her how much Danny wanted to get back to the work he was so good at. Or that he had just brought up again that old letter Craig had found.

"Isn't it all good how things are going now for both you and him?"

Craig sighed. Each high point she had mentioned about this new phase of his life had given him pause recently, and he felt nagging unresolved aspects of each. He remained quiet.

"Is there something I'm missing here?" Lauren asked. "You haven't told me about any new episodes, like getting glimpses of people's thoughts or feelings the way you did with . . . it was Danny's girlfriend, right?"

Emma, Craig thought. He remembered telling Lauren how he could see into Emma's mind. Her mentioning Emma so soon after the odd dream seemed too much of a coincidence, so he decided to open up a little more.

"No. Not glimpses. But a bunch of other strange things seem to be popping up all at once. Like the other day, I was heading to aikido after I registered for classes, and I saw a young woman working this older guy over with some aikido moves. It was weird. Didn't make sense. But I found myself charging across the street to see what was going on. Damn near got run over."

"So, wait. You're telling me you got some weird feelings about a girl you saw on your way to karate—"

"Aikido."

"Whatever. And that made you run into traffic?" She was clearly growing annoyed. "Wasn't this the same day you said you were going to talk with Madison about volunteering?"

"Yeah."

"And didn't?"

Craig lowered his eyes and nodded.

"Now maybe it's me who should be a little jealous." She went back to gathering her work bag and other items together.

"No, it's not like that," Craig reassured her.

"Why is it not like that?" She furrowed her brow.

"Well, because nearly getting hit by a car threw me off a little, and then I felt like I needed to catch up with Danny on some things."

"Why would you need to do that?"

"Because . . ." He felt like he was back on his heels now. "Because it's been a couple years, and I've gotten used to being, well, normal. Maybe I've ignored too many things that I should have figured out by now. Things I really need to resolve."

"I'm not trying to be rude, but the things you've struggled with are visions, dreams, glimpses into other people's heads. The progress you're making right now is real. It involves tangible things."

Craig had never told her about his ability to heal his own wounds and project force from the palms of his hands. The latter had undoubtedly saved his and Danny's lives that night in Iowa—it didn't get more tangible than that. But he still didn't feel ready to share those experiences with her.

Instead, he said, "But remember when this all started to happen? There was an arc to this, Lauren. Like how it all linked back to my dad, and that the killer in Chicago was the same person who killed my dad and the same one we fought in the church. And I really want to know: Are my abilities similar to my dad's? And if so, what does that mean for me, and what I'm doing with my life? How am I supposed to use them?"

Lauren shrugged. It was the first time she seemed dismissive about Craig's past.

He pressed ahead. "It just seems like there's a bunch a stuff lately that's pushing me to get clarity about my past."

"Why do you choose to exist *there?*"

Craig thought that was an odd question. "What are you saying?"

"You seem so preoccupied with those things, with where your special abilities may have come from and why. What about looking inside yourself and trying to understand what you're supposed to do today? And the day after that? Move forward, Craig. Use your experience to help people, now and in the future, like volunteering. Go back to school like you're planning. Stop dwelling on the past."

Now it was Craig's turn to bristle. "That's not really the advice I thought you'd give. The point is that my abilities have gone cold. Maybe I need to try to figure out why that is before I move on."

"I've been making a bunch of suggestions about figuring yourself out. But so far, you've blown me off. Is there something you're not telling me? Something else that's been going through that head of yours?"

"Yes, I'm questioning my purpose. And I'm wondering whether I'm being a little too selfish. Maybe I just need to warm these things up in my mind again and examine what I find. What's the harm in doing that and thinking them through?"

Craig wouldn't admit it to her—he had really only started to sense it himself—but he had begun to feel like the enlightenment he had achieved during the encounter in the church was beginning to wane. And for some reason he couldn't explain, he found that distressing, and he felt like he needed to do something about it.

Lauren let out a dramatic sigh. "To be sure, if you've grown colder after being so close to a roaring fire, make no mistake: it isn't the fire that has moved."

"Okay. Weird," Craig said. He was used to indulging in her eccentric comments, but he felt like this conversation was going nowhere.

"I think I follow," he said. "I've been getting fragments of info, and I need to move a little closer to them to see how they might fit together?"

"A person always encounters more resistance when they start to get closer to learning the truth."

It felt like a throwaway line to Craig, and he treated it as such. "It certainly feels that way this morning."

She looked at him, her disappointment plain. "Whatever you think you need to explore, just go there. Figure it out. I need to jump on the L and get up to O'Hare."

"When will you be back? I told Danny the three of us could grab dinner later this week."

"Just call me and tell me the reservation time. I'll see if I can wrap things up in Minneapolis before then." She smiled. "I just really need to get moving. I'm already late."

As she headed for the front door, Craig was confused. She had been so supportive over the many months they'd been together. Why was she being so judgmental now about where Craig should focus his energy and attention?

Craig's phone buzzed on the counter where he had left it the night before. When he picked it up, he saw that it was Danny. He didn't want to let it go to voicemail, so he hurried to address Lauren. "I need to take this, but I'll call you and let you know about dinner."

She rolled her eyes.

"Are we okay?" Craig asked.

"Sure." And with that she was out the door.

He turned back to the phone in his hand and answered it just in time.

"Hey, Danny."

"Listen, Craig, I'm gonna need you to . . ."

There was a moment of silence, and then Craig heard another voice in the background say, "Hang up the phone, Walsh."

"Just hold on a sec," Craig heard Danny say.

The voice in the background came through again, more sternly: "Hang up the damn phone."

With a click, the call disconnected.

Craig stared at the phone, puzzled. It didn't sound like Danny was in any kind of trouble—the dangerous kind of trouble. Rather, it sounded like he had been admonished for something.

6

TRAUMA

Danny stood alone in a conference room, looking out a window that allowed him to see the buzz of activity in Chicago's Seventh Precinct.

He was thinking through his next move. Since getting a partial green light from his new lieutenant to assist with investigations, he had been making slow but steady progress in reinserting himself into the daily flow of police activity. But he wasn't satisfied that the course he was on would yield what he sought. There was also the curious case of the informant he had interrogated the week before, and those cryptic letters that were branded on his arm. He was trying to balance his own self-interest and curiosity. It was important that his colleagues started to see him as a legitimate detective again, despite his physical challenges.

What to do next? he thought. He decided to treat his personal situation the way he would when solving any case: take a patient approach and wait for an opportunity to emerge that pointed in a direction toward further progress.

He watched as a group of men entered through the common area of the precinct. They weren't law enforcement personnel. Most looked to be in their late twenties or early thirties, but in their midst was an older man with graying hair. He wore a conservative suit and walked with a limp. Behind them was

Deborah Wood from Homeland Security. Lieutenant Mason, who seemed annoyed, trailed behind.

Danny decided to join the group in the hopes that there would be an opportunity to integrate with his new boss. He placed his nearly empty coffee cup on the conference table, snatched up the new cane that Hammond had made for him, and walked out the door. He was still getting used to walking quickly with the cane, but he found it surprisingly easy to work with, a nice complement to his size and gait.

By the time he caught up with Mason, the group had nearly reached the auditorium. They were joined by additional police officers.

Danny approached Mason and said, "Chief, what's up?"

"This is the guy who's supposed to help out with the DHS connections. He's also going to tell us about his personal experience." Mason's preoccupation with the visitors seemed to allow him to drop his guard with Danny.

"You think he can help?"

"We'll see, I guess."

Danny followed Mason into the conference room and took a spot next to him, standing and leaning against the back wall. Other members of the force sat in chairs and began to exchange conversation with the older man.

The older man took several minutes to explain his philosophy and insights into criminal behavior. He then took questions from some of the detectives. He came off as professorial, elitist. The younger men he'd come in with appeared dispassionate, disconnected. Danny wondered who the guys were: the man's bodyguards or handlers?

"What's this guy's story? he whispered to Mason. "Did headquarters outline how they think he can help?"

"Well, that's a real good question. He's Matthew Bishop. Well, Colonel Matthew Bishop. He was a POW in Vietnam. Some expert on guerrilla tactics while he was over there. But no one really seems to know for sure."

What? They don't really know his background? What the hell is he doing here? Danny wondered.

Mason went on. "From what I've learned, the guy has built himself up as this big enigma who knows a lot from all this heavy experience. I haven't been able to find much more info that that. And he seems to need to travel around with this . . . what would you call it, entourage?"

His dismissive tone was clear. Danny was sure Mason doubted Bishop really had anything to offer the precinct. "You're not buying it, I guess," Danny said. He thought he might get to know Mason better if he met him in that cynical place. After all, he felt the same way.

"Not really. Something's not quite right about him. I don't doubt he's been in the military and seen some shit. But here he is, supposed to share all this great insight with us, and he comes off like a diva. I don't like it. He's not like any real warriors I've known, and I've been in the military about as deep as anyone could be."

Mason seemed more real to Danny than he had previously thought. And he was more serious and intuitive than Danny had expected. It was also the first time Danny had heard Mason speak of his time in the military. Others had mentioned he'd been Special Forces, but Mason never talked about it.

"I get what you're saying. Seems like a whole lot of style, if you wanna call it that. Let's hope there's some substance there."

"Agreed," said Mason.

Danny turned his attention on what Colonel Bishop was saying.

"You have to understand that any terrorist you encounter harbors a deeply held belief of the need to maim and destroy." Bishop was pacing at the front of the auditorium as he spoke, limping slightly. "You need to understand the necessity of having a much different mindset—a feeling of being invincible. I've come to call it an 'Invictus' mindset."

"What do you mean by that, sir?" one of the detectives asked.

"The word is Latin. Meaning 'unconquered.' I've had the privilege to know at least two men who used this mindset to persevere through all types of hell. Let me share with you how remarkable the men were who embraced this belief, for it made them incredibly powerful. Highly effective.

"I met one of them in a battle tour and the other while I was in captivity. Both had endured terrible, almost unfathomable trauma—trauma that had scarred them internally as much as externally. But it had also forged them, and it allowed certain qualities to come forward, including a level of resilience that neither of them had previously dreamed possible. In both cases, strange and powerful abilities emerged that had been latent until they were triggered, over time, by their ordeals."

Bishop was proving to be a master storyteller. Any superficial pretense Danny had about the man fell away, and his genuine belief in what he was saying was coming through. He kept the officers and detectives rapt with attention.

"These men were pushed to their physical and emotional limits. But once they reached them, something amazing happened. One developed the ability to steal glimpses into the thoughts and motivations in someone's mind. The other became nearly invulnerable to any injury resulting from physical attack."

A crack appeared in Bishop's storytelling. The group gathered was visibly taken aback. Several of them shook their heads in disbelief.

Bishop paused and took a deep breath, then exhaled quickly. "Quite a lot to believe, I'm sure you're thinking. Creatures of this nature are truly rare among us, and I've had the uncanny privilege to be in the presence of two of them. The lesson here is that Invictus is as much about what's inside of you and what you let emerge as it is about who the enemy is and why they do what they do. Nonetheless, all of this relates to a need to go deep into your purpose, your calling, and follow your instincts. Therein lies the opposite of the fear, injury, and destruction terrorists seek to sow."

Danny's mind was racing. *Craig can do both of those things. Or he used to.* And suddenly, a connection dawned on him: trauma. Craig had endured a series of severe traumas: learning that his father had been killed, analyzing crime scenes, feeling alone and isolated, and even seeing how his father had been killed through a re-creation he had involuntarily conjured. Could these events have triggered the fantastic powers in Craig that Bishop was describing.

Danny rubbed his sweaty palms. He needed to learn more about Bishop. But he was also aware of the need to fall back on his training and keep his curiosity in check for now. He felt energized, as he always did when the clues to solving a case began to show themselves. What Bishop described certainly seemed to match Craig's experience, but Danny also wondered whether he might be stretching his imagination too far in linking what he'd just heard to Craig.

Another half hour passed before the colonel began to

wrap up. He announced that he needed to leave, but that his colleague Deborah Wood would be happy to arrange for him to stop by again soon.

Bishop and his entourage were briskly making their way toward the back of the auditorium and the door near where Danny and Mason stood. Seizing on this brief opening, Danny stepped into the aisle in front of him.

"Mr. Bishop! May I ask you something?" Two members of the colonel's entourage stepped between him and Danny.

"Boys, it's fine," Bishop said, calling them off. "This man is clearly a detective."

Danny lowered his voice so it wouldn't carry to others that might still be in the auditorium. "The two men you spoke of earlier. You talked how strong and resilient they were. Was that more about them having some kind of mindset of steel, or do you really believe they were able to do the things you said, read minds and be invulnerable to physical attack?"

Danny was deferential as he spoke, not wanting to raise any concern with what appeared to be Bishop's bodyguards.

"The two men I knew were unlike any other humans I have met. They had gained a special form of resilience that kept them from being hurt, either inside or out. What they shared in common was that they saw themselves and their work as something important that needed to continue. Others would describe the powers I witnessed in them as supernatural, or perhaps a hoax." Bishop's eyes flared wide. "But I witnessed them. I saw firsthand the power each man possessed. Truly unconquerable—Invictus."

"But does that mean—" Danny started.

"My apologies, I'm pressed for time and need to go. My talk has concluded," Bishop replied abruptly. Though he had been engaged with his audience during his presentation, seeming open and approachable, he now suddenly reverted to the aloof, arrogant tone he displayed when he arrived.

"No, wait!" Danny called out as Bishop and his entourage swept through the auditorium doors. Danny snatched up his cane to follow them, but Mason intervened.

"Walsh! Wait up. What're you doing? Let him go." He looked Danny up and down. "What's with this sudden fascination with the diva?"

Danny tried to downplay the fact that he'd ignored his own advice to proceed carefully. "No, nothing like that. I just wanted to pin him down on some of his nonsense."

He was saved from further scrutiny when they were joined by one of the desk sergeants, who was looking for Danny.

"Hey, Walsh. Remember that informant you were interviewing last week?"

"Yeah, what's up?"

"Patrol found his body just outside a warehouse down in Brighton Park."

"What?"

"Yup. Looks like he was killed last night."

Danny frowned and pursed his lips. He slowly shook his head. Mason lingered nearby and appeared to take note of the news and of Danny's reaction.

"Is Forensic Services still on the scene?" Danny asked.

"I think so," the sergeant answered.

"Radio out to them. Tell them not to touch anything else."

Danny reached into his sports coat pocket and pulled out his phone. He dialed Craig and waited for him to answer. Focused on the call, he dimly registered Mason trying to draw his attention. Danny held the phone to his ear with one hand and held up his index finger to Mason.

Several rings passed. "Come on," Danny muttered under his breath.

Finally, Craig answered.

"Listen, Craig," Danny said. "I'm gonna need you to—"

Mason had moved into his line of sight. He did not look pleased. "Hang up the phone, Walsh," he ordered.

"Just hold on a sec," Danny responded as he pulled the phone away from his ear.

Mason's eyes widened at the challenge to his authority. His jaw muscles flexing, he repeated, "Hang up the damn phone."

Danny hung up. He and Mason stared at one another.

"What the hell was that about?" Danny asked.

"I should ask you the same thing."

"Come again?"

"Let me just put it this way, Walsh. A precinct can be a real circus sometimes, but that doesn't mean I'm going to let a detective bring in just anybody they think can help, especially somebody outside the force. I don't care if they can do some carnival tricks in the field."

Well, this was an interesting development. "Just exactly what are you saying, Mason?" Danny asked.

The boss seemed calmer now, back in charge of himself and of the situation. "I had several conversations with Hammond before I took command here. Pressed him on what went down with that serial killer business a while back. Let's just say that Hammond is real protective of you. And of your cousin, it would seem."

"Well, what if he is? What does that have to do with me trying to find out went down with this informant?"

"I don't want my men or this precinct taking risks with things I don't understand or won't be told about. That ig into re-creating a crime scene was a missed opportunity. Maybe a very important one for their understanding of the puzzles they'd been chewing over for the past two years. That damned branding had to figure in here somehow. "So, Walsh," the desk sergeant said. "You going to do anything about this informant? What's your next move?"

Danny glanced at him and then eyed the door.

"I'll tell you what my next move is: I'm gonna have a talk with Eric Hammond."

7

VULNERABILITY

Craig wore a light windbreaker as he made his way from the L toward the aikido studio to work out. For the third day in a row, he was hoping to catch the mysterious woman he had seen the week before. He wasn't sure why, but her assault on what appeared to be a random person on the street—and what happened in its aftermath—had stoked an intense curiosity. Craig had felt compelled to follow his instinct then, and he felt that urge again. Who was she? And what was it about her that he felt the need to understand?

Lauren was still in Minneapolis, and aside from a few brief conversations, they hadn't spoken at length since their strained parting.

It was midmorning and chilly. As Craig neared the studio, he remembered that Lauren agreed to meet him and Danny for dinner Friday night, so he needed to let Danny know about the arrangement and ask if he could come early. Craig was very interested in catching up with his cousin on recent events.

Craig's supernatural abilities had been dormant for more than a year, but now they seemed to be returning. Danny would surely be interested in hearing about Craig's broken arm repairing itself within moments of being injured. But most relevant was his dream about Emma. It was similar to dreams he'd had of his father just as he was beginning to understand his supernatural abilities, specifically re-creating violent scenes and sensing others' thoughts. He had learned he could also project a destructive force from his hands and heal himself spontaneously after the dreams he'd had of his father. And now he was dreaming about Emma. Was there a connection?

Craig was within eyesight of the martial arts studio as he drew out his phone and called Danny, who picked up instantly.

"What's up, Craig? I was actually planning to call you. Need to run some new developments by you."

"Well, I guess my timing is good, then. I only have a few minutes. I wanted to see if you're open for dinner with Lauren and me on Friday."

"Great idea. But no offense, I've got sensitive things to talk about. Things Lauren might not know about."

"Really?" Craig responded, surprised that he and Danny seemed to be headed in the same direction in their thinking.

"Yeah. I don't want to talk about it over the phone though."

"It's interesting you want to talk about 'sensitive things' because something new happened in my last aikido session. I'll tell you about it when we meet up."

"Ah, come on, Craig. You can't leave me hanging with that."

"Let's just say that I'm pretty sure my arm was broken, but a few minutes later, it was fine."

"What? That's great, man!" Danny exclaimed.

"Great that I got my arm broke?"

"You know what I mean. But, for real, no more talking about this now. Where we gonna meet?"

"Santori's," Craig suggested. "Tomorrow at six. Lauren won't be there until about seven." Craig greatly cared for

Lauren and trusted her intimately. But the full extent of his inexplicable powers was something he still wasn't ready to share with her.

"All right, see you then," Danny said.

Craig hung up as he entered the building that housed the studio. After a few quick turns up the staircase, he pushed his way through the doors and surveyed the open grappling session that had just started. He looked around the room, hoping to see the young woman again. His diligence in coming three days in a row was rewarded when he saw her on the other side of a large mat where other students were practicing.

She was adjusting her *karategi,* the traditional uniform for practice and competition, and appeared to have recently arrived. Craig quickly slipped off his shoes and removed the sweatpants and jacket that were covering his own *karategi* and crossed the mat.

As was the custom with open practices, Craig motioned to Jason with a nod in the woman's direction, indicating that he wanted the instructor to come over and sanction their practicing against one another.

As Jason approached, Craig stood in front of the woman to catch her attention.

She looked at him. "What's this?"

"Hi, I'm Craig. I don't have a partner this morning."

"Well, I guess you're in luck, Craig. You sure you're ready for this?"

She was confident, clearly at ease with her skills. Tall, slim, and fit, she had long, straight black hair. She swept it up into a ponytail and then into a bun atop her head as they talked.

"All right, you two, over here." Jason directed them to an empty portion of the mat.

"Yeah, I'm ready," Craig said. "I didn't catch your name."

"That's because I didn't throw it."

Put off by the line, Craig frowned.

"It's Samantha. You can call me Sam." Softening some, but not much.

Craig rolled onto his back on the mat in the guard position, rather than starting from a standing position where a larger opponent might have an initial advantage.

"What are you doing?" she asked, offended by this deference. "No, no! None of that bullshit. On your feet. We start up here."

"You sure?" Craig asked as he looked at Jason. Jason nodded as if to attest to her skill.

"Begin," Jason said, and walked toward another pair to supervise their progress.

Craig stood up. "Okay then. Let's go."

They circled each other in a crouched position, their arms held out in front of them. Craig thought about how he could take her to the mat without hurting her.

"I saw you outside the studio about a week ago. Seemed like you were working an older guy over. What was up with that?"

She stopped circling for a moment, a wave of understanding dawning in her face. "Oh, I thought I recognized you. You were the guy who bolted into the street—and into the path of a car, I should add. Why did you do that?"

"Seemed like the older guy needed help."

Her expression hardened. "Hardly."

"Why not?"

"Let's just say he deserved what I was giving him."

"For what? What did he do?"

"You mean what he was *gonna* do."

"Huh?" Craig said. "You were working him over based on what you thought he *might* do?"

"What do you care, anyway? Come on, we're wasting time."

With that, she lunged and jumped, landing on Craig with her arms and wrists wrapped around his neck and shoulders. Even though she was smaller in size and weight, the full bulk of her body entangled his until it started to pull him over. She twisted her body to one side before torquing him and slamming him into the mat.

The impact nearly knocked the wind out of him, and Craig realized he had underestimated both her skill and her aggressiveness.

Her tone condescending, she asked, "You okay there, Craig?"

"I'm fine," he gasped, catching his breath.

They grappled on the ground. The woman's technique and speed were superior to Craig's, offsetting what she lacked in size and strength. For every move Craig made to gain an advantage, she found a way to parry it or offset it.

As they continued their practice, Craig felt the presence of Samantha's thoughts hovering just out of reach. He remembered seeing Emma's thoughts when he first met her, which was right after he'd accidentally sipped from her wineglass. Now he wondered if he was sensing Samantha's thoughts for a similar reason: physical contact.

His curiosity intensifying, he refocused his energy to visualize his mind reaching out to tap into hers. Not surprisingly, as his focus shifted, his countermoves became less and less effective.

"Hey! What's going on?" Samantha said, irritated despite dominating the match.

Craig closed his eyes as they writhed on the mat. He

could feel the movement of his thoughts, his consciousness, beginning to seep into her head.

Suddenly, Samantha stopped sparring and pushed him away with a violent shove. Craig's focus boomeranged back to his own thoughts, and he opened his eyes just as an open-handed blow came down across his forehead. He fell back onto the mat as Samantha sprang to her feet.

"Get outta my damn head!" she shouted.

Craig was momentarily dazed, but then noticed a burning sensation spreading across the bridge of his nose. He touched it and noticed he was bleeding; a fingernail must have grazed him during the blow.

The other combatants had stopped grappling and turned toward the source of the commotion. Jason loudly called, "Hey, what's going on over there?"

"You tell me, Sam," Craig said. "What the hell was that about?"

"You *know* what it was about." She glared at him.

She must have somehow sensed his trying to infiltrate her thoughts, Craig guessed. *But how?* Thinking this might be his last chance to satisfy his curiosity, he said, "Seriously, Sam. Tell me why the guy you worked over deserved it. What did he do?"

"You want to change the subject? Okay. What did he do? Like I said, it was what he was going to do. If I can put some fear in him that'll keep him from messing with little kids, damn right I'm gonna shake him up."

Suddenly, the anger in her face shifted to a look of disgust. She pointed at his face. "Maybe you should tell me what the hell *your* deal is."

Craig brought his hand to his face again. The bleeding had stopped. Had she seen the cut heal over?

Jason had made his way over to them. But before he could learn what had happened, Samantha had darted off the mat. Grabbing her shoes, she ran out of the gym without saying anything.

Craig sat up, his head spinning.

———◆—◆—◆——◆———

Danny walked briskly down Dearborn Street, aided by his new cane. "All right, see you then," Danny said as he shoved his phone in his coat pocket and waited on the corner of Dearborn. When the light turned, he crossed the street toward the Richard Daley Center.

In the middle of Chicago's Theater District, the Richard Daley Center housed the administrative headquarters of the Chicago Police Department. It was also where Lieutenant Eric Hammond worked. Hammond had been a sergeant and Danny's commanding officer during the period when Danny had significant success as a CPD homicide detective. Part of that success had come from Danny enlisting Craig's help in the Tourist serial killer case, in which he re-created crime scenes to help Danny track down the killer.

But Hammond was more than Danny's former superior officer; he was also his friend. He'd covered for Danny, concealing some of the more sensational aspects of their battle with the Tourist. Though neither Craig nor Danny had revealed many details to Hammond about what Craig contributed to that investigation, they both suspected Hammond had figured out a few things.

Hammond had abruptly moved into an administrative role just as Danny was set to rejoin the force following his convalescence, and Danny found that puzzling. Now feeling marginalized and constrained by his new supervisor, Danny thought it would be good to pick Hammond's brain about Mason and see if his old boss could clue him in to anything that could lead to a better working relationship with the new lieutenant. He was also overdue in thanking Hammond for the cane. He entered the Center and made his way to Hammond's department.

"Detective Walsh to see Eric Hammond," he told the administrative officer at the desk.

"He's not here," the officer said.

"What do you mean, he's not here? I called this morning to make sure he was on the job today."

"I know, Detective. And he was. But some things came up about a half hour ago, and he is taking the rest of the day PTO."

Danny let out a sigh and closed his eyes. "You have got to be kidding me."

"No, sir. Sorry. I'll let him know you were here. You said Walsh, right?"

Danny nodded, his eyes still closed.

"Oh, wait. Walsh. Are you Daniel Walsh? The guy who brought down the Tourist?"

"Yes," Danny said reluctantly. The attention associated with the case always made him uncomfortable.

"Man, that had to be some rough stuff you went through. How are things going for you? I heard you're still working to get back on some regular duty."

Danny had no desire to hang around and grow increasingly offended by reminders of his injuries and the long road back to recovery.

"Something like that. Listen, if he's out for the day, I've got a few others to connect with while I'm down here. Take care, pal."

The man looked like he had more to say, but Danny walked away before he had the chance.

Back out on the street, he stewed over a string of missed opportunities. *Damn it!* The tattooed informant had been killed before Danny could learn more from him. The failure to get back to meaningful work because Mason was limiting his involvement. And now Hammond was a no-show when Danny really wanted to catch up and seek his advice. He needed to walk off his frustration before he made his way back to the Seventh Precinct, so he continued along Washington Street as he took inventory of the myriad of things crowding his mind.

The sidewalk was teeming with pedestrians, and instead of calming down, he was becoming further annoyed by the difficulty of navigating with the cane. He decided to cut through a wide alleyway between Washington and Madison streets in hopes of finding a little more solitude while he planned his next move.

He was mentally juggling so many things. *Meeting Craig tomorrow will help,* he thought. Especially sharing with him what Colonel Bishop had said. But he also really needed to be fully engaged and back at work.

The alley was shadowed by two tall buildings, but it was well lit and clean, with a complex metal web of ladders and fire escapes above. As he made his way through the alley, Danny passed a panhandler. Despite the fact that the temperature was in the upper fifties, the scraggly-looking man wore a heavy winter coat. Odd maybe, but no more odd than anything else he'd seen in Chicago's homeless scene. He glanced at the man and kept walking, returning to his thoughts.

He didn't see or hear the panhandler drawing close until he felt a tug on his coat.

"What the hell!" he exclaimed as he spun around to face the vagrant.

"You're gonna part with a few dollars, you crippled bastard," he said. He pushed Danny back against the brick wall, grabbing at his pockets.

Then Danny realized the panhandler hadn't recognized him as a cop and was trying to mug him.

Danny strained to get his balance and gathered his strength. He shoved the assailant back several feet, and before the man could lunge again, he swung his cane and hit him squarely just below the jawline. It stunned the mugger but wasn't enough to stop him, and the force of the cane's blow knocked Danny off balance. He stumbled and came to rest with his back against the alley wall.

The assailant looked ready to attack Danny again. "Listen, you little bitch. Give me money!"

For the first time since his rookie days a decade ago, Danny panicked. He was pinned in a vulnerable position, and worse, he felt afraid of someone who would have caused him no alarm before being injured. Now he was struggling to balance himself with his prosthetic arm while he used his other hand to reach inside his coat and draw his pistol out of its holster.

The attacker spotted the holster, and Danny watched as the realization spread across the man's grimy face. "Oh shit!" he yelled, as he ran toward Washington Street.

Danny remained there, his heart racing and his breath coming in great gulps. He watched as the mugger turned onto Washington's crowded sidewalk. "Yeah, you better get the hell outta here!" he yelled between gasps.

The mugger was gone. Danny was now alone in the alley, frustrated and embarrassed that a guy like that could get the drop on him in broad daylight. Did he really look like such an easy target? *Is this what it's going to be like? Is this what I have to live with now?*

He shuddered with anger as he bellowed, "What the fuck!"

He struggled to his feet and did his best to brush the dust and debris off his coat. Streaks of dirt remained. Then he made his way down the alley and onto Madison Street.

Once on the street, he knew he must look disheveled, maybe even rattled. As he walked, leaning heavily on his cane past a construction worker, the guy asked him if he was okay. He waved him off and kept going, now desperate to get out of sight and take some time to collect himself. He felt as if all eyes were on him.

He was approaching a large Catholic church that was nestled between two modern buildings about half a block away. He wasn't sure, but he thought he remembered it as St. John's. It would probably be empty in the middle of the day, certainly compared to the sidewalks he was so keen to escape right now. He quickened his pace.

A large stone carving of Jesus's crucifixion stood at the front of the church between two sets of double bronze doors. He reached for a door on the right and made his way into the narthex.

The moment he was inside, the weight of the street's unwelcome attention lifted, and a sense of comfort and ease took its place. He was reminded of the times when he had gone to church with his mother. It was odd to feel this way again after so many years.

A half dozen stairs led to a glass wall and a set of glass doors through which he could see into the sanctuary. Feeling the need to retreat even further, he made his way toward the doors.

He pushed through the glass and took in a truly impressive sight. The size and grandeur of the church were greater than anything Danny had ever seen. Its entire interior was constructed of earth-toned smooth stone and marble. The floor was paved in marble squares. All the pews were of honey-colored wood; there were fifty or more rows.

At the front on either side of the altar stood two religious scenes carved in stone. Another large carving of the crucifixion stood between them. The lighting accentuated key areas of the sanctuary while shrouding others in darkness, creating dramatic contrasts.

It was very quiet. A few dozen people were scattered throughout the church, but it was large enough that no one was very near to anyone else. Everyone seemed to be in quiet reflection. Danny was alone now and free from the stares on the street. He felt himself growing calmer, a welcome contrast to his frustration in the Daley Center and his panic while fighting off the mugger.

Yet he still felt conspicuous just standing there. He walked to the font, a bathtub-sized pool near the entrance. Dipping two fingers in the holy water, he made the sign of the cross and turned to go deeper into the sanctuary.

As he started down one of the aisles, the soft thud of the end of his cane marked his progress. He looked left and right, ceiling to floor, admiring the space. With each step, he felt drawn deeper into the church while becoming more at ease; it was almost as if the place was inviting him in. He suddenly realized how he must look, like a tourist who had stumbled in, gawking at it instead of treating it with the reverence it deserved.

He made his way to a pew and sat down. He glanced around to see who might be observing him, but no one seemed to be paying him any attention. Several other visitors had flipped open the kneeling benches on the backs of the pews in front of them. Danny did the same, gingerly bending his injured leg. But rather than sit with clasped hands as the others were doing, he made a fist that covered the end of the cane and used his prosthetic hand to cover it. For several minutes, he simply gazed at the marble reliefs of religious scenes that lined the high side walls. A priest emerged from a door along one of the walls. Danny closed his eyes and let his mind drift peacefully.

The cane slipped out of his hand and clattered onto the marble floor. Startled, he let out a groan.

The sound had caught the attention of the priest, who was now walking toward him.

"Hello. Everything all right, my son?"

"Yeah, sorry about that," Danny whispered.

"Please, might you be more comfortable in our adjacent space?" The priest motioned toward an antechamber near the front of the sanctuary. Danny interpreted this suggestion to mean that he was causing a disturbance for others.

Slightly irritated, Danny bent down and picked up his cane. He thought momentarily of leaving, but he liked this church and decided to acquiesce to the priest's request.

The antechamber was small, secluded, and quiet, out of earshot from the nave where he had been sitting. Wide eyed, his expression now quizzical, the priest motioned Danny to sit. Though still somewhat agitated, Danny complied, hoping to regain the sense of calm he had been enjoying a moment ago, longing to return to that sense of solitude. The priest, however, was unprepared to leave him alone.

"You have a cane. Just like my uncle Fred. He had a cane. Yes, for sure. And you're quite big, like Fred was. Are you from Milwaukee too?" The priest was looking at Danny as he spoke but also seemed to be staring past him, or through him, with a foggy look in his eyes. Danny estimated the priest was in his early seventies, with tousled white hair and flushed red hands. His clean-shaven face had a kind of innocence, but mentally, he seemed a tad off.

"Listen, um, Father. Maybe I should be going . . ." Danny started, thinking it best that he leave. He figured the respite he had received by ducking into the church had served its purpose.

Just then, a younger priest entered the antechamber. "Ah, there you are, Father Timothy." He turned to Danny. "I'm sorry, sir. He wasn't bothering you, was he?" Danny wondered about the relationship between the two men as he stood and adjusted his coat.

"Um, no. Everything's fine here. Sorry if I caused a disturbance."

"Not at all," said the young priest. "Father Timothy is quite harmless. He just likes talking with others. He's getting along in years, and his mind succumbs occasionally to periods of dementia. Let me move him along so that you can have your time in solitude."

Father Timothy was smiling. He looked at Danny, then his gaze wandered from object to object in the small space.

Understanding the situation now, Danny came to the old priest's defense. "No, please. It's completely fine. I'm just taking a few minutes here before lunch. I'm enjoying the discussion. Getting to know Father Timothy here."

Appreciative of Danny's effort, the young priest smiled. "All right. Just so long as you are sure, Detective."

Danny was momentarily surprised that the young priest had recognized him as a cop, but then looked down and saw that his shield on his sports jacket was visible through a gap in his coat.

"Yes. Totally sure," Danny said. "I appreciate you stopping over, though. I've got him."

Satisfied, the young priest nodded, turned, and left the two men to continue their conversation.

Danny felt sorry for the old man, and what the hell, he figured he had enough time for a little small talk.

"So, it's Father Timothy, then. I'm Detective Walsh."

Without acknowledging his comment, Timothy resumed his questioning. "Do you know Fred or are you just from Milwaukee too?"

"No, I don't know your uncle—"

"Oh, look at your arm. Oh my. How did you make it that way?"

"I didn't actually 'make it that way,'" Danny began. "Just got injured, is all."

"Oh, look at it. May I touch it?" the priest asked, pointing at the prosthetic end of Danny's forearm.

Not wanting to offend, Danny indulged the priest's request. "Uh, sure. Here." He pulled up his coat sleeve.

But Father Timothy didn't touch the prosthesis; instead, he reached for the exposed skin just above it.

The sense of the space, the very air between the two men, seemed to change at once. Father Timothy's appearance and countenance shifted as he touched Danny's flesh with his fingers. *This is getting weird*, Danny thought. *I think I'd better go.*

Now Father Timothy was looking directly into Danny's eyes, his own eyes clear, bright, aware. As if sensing Danny's thoughts, he said, "No, Daniel, please stay." He gently placed his hand on Danny's shoulder in a gesture signaling him to remain seated.

"Hey, wait a minute. How do you know my name? No, I think I need to be going."

"Please," said the priest. "You should stay. We need to talk."

"Why?" asked Danny.

"Because, Daniel, I've waited precisely thirty-two years and two hundred forty-six days for you to enter this building so we could speak."

Danny's mind raced. *Thirty-two years and what?* Then he connected those numbers to his own age—exactly.

Alarm rose in Danny's chest, and he defensively closed his hand into a fist.

8

32 YEARS AND 246 DAYS

Danny's training had kicked in; he perceived a threat and clenched a fist tightly. Father Timothy was no longer the quirky priest asking random, eccentric questions. He was up to something, and whatever it was, it felt threatening.

But before he could draw his fist back to unleash a blow, his arm froze in place. He tried again but couldn't move his arm back any further. It was as if his arm was being clasped in place by an invisible force, with his elbow rooted to his side.

"Hey, what's this?" Danny said in a raspy whisper. He motioned with his chin at his paralyzed arm. "Are you doing this?"

"Yes, I have stayed your hand," the priest responded softly. "There is no need for you to defend yourself from what is to be merely a discussion."

Feeling trapped and with no idea what to do—or what he even *could* do—Danny played for time. "All right. Then talk. What's your story, old man? What the hell is going on?"

"As I told you, I have waited more than thirty-two years to have this conversation with you. I won't abandon this opportunity just because you've become alarmed."

"I'm not alarmed." Danny managed to sound defiant. "But where the hell did 'Father Timothy' go?" he said, indicating that something fundamentally had changed about the priest.

"Ah, so you are aware that he is no longer present, that I am not he."

"Sure as hell seems that way," Danny responded.

The "priest's" confidence was clear. Danny suspected he possessed advantages that went well beyond being able to immobilize someone without even touching him. He glanced around; the few people visible outside the antechamber were quiet, heads bowed, oblivious to this interaction.

"Father Timothy is a real man, and he hasn't gone far. I have chosen to speak through him and have simply pushed him gently aside while you and I talk. Now, please. Calm down, Daniel Christopher Walsh. You have nothing to fear."

Danny seethed with impatience. "Okay, so you know my full name as well as my age. Fine. I don't give a shit. Come on, spill your story. Let's get this over with."

The priest nodded and then obliged. "I know what you faced in that church. I know you and your cousin encountered a physical representation of humanity's dark enemy."

Danny's eyes grew wide. *How could he know anything about our battle with the Tourist in Iowa?*

"I am here to enlighten you, to resolve some of the mysteries you have been struggling to understand." He paused to survey Danny's reaction. "Can I trust you to relax now so we can talk?"

Danny's alarm had given way to deep curiosity; the man had his full attention. He nodded, and the invisible restraint that had pinned his arm ebbed away. He relaxed his hand out and looked at it. He moved his fingers, now assured that he had full range of motion.

"All right. What do you want to talk about? And how do you know the things you know? I don't have time for games. I've had a rough day, and it's not even noon yet."

"Ah, yes, that. It could not have felt good to be assaulted in the alley as you were. Or to feel infirm, so obviously vulnerable, and to be exploited as a result."

"So you know about the mugging too. Go on." While it was alarming that the priest knew so much about him, Danny was also eager to learn more.

"Your physical presence was near the church—that's how I was able to sense that you were harmed. You shouldn't anguish over your infirmities, Daniel. You have healed faster than anyone else could have, given the extent of your injuries. Why do you think that is?"

While he remained intrigued by the priest's uncanny knowledge, Danny was becoming aware that the glare of attention he had sought to escape when he entered the church had been replaced by a different type of scrutiny. This, too, made him uncomfortable, and he wanted to leave as soon as possible.

"I don't know the answer to that. I didn't even know I was healing faster than somebody else would. But why don't you get to the point?"

"You are not what happened to you, Daniel. More importantly, you must understand that what's inside of you remains perfect and unharmed in His eyes."

"*His* eyes?" Danny asked. "Him who?"

The priest's expression softened. "He knows and understands what you have been through, Daniel. And with you, He is well pleased."

Danny narrowed his eyes. *Where is this guy going now?* He felt his impatience dwindling, replaced by a fascination with each new sentence the mysterious stranger uttered. The old man had drawn him in.

The priest seemed to recognize the shift in Danny and

continued. "An ancient war from another place has never been resolved. It continues to be waged, here and now. You and your cousin are part of a very fundamental—and extraordinarily important—calling."

"Craig *is* part of something bigger. The things he can do— that he's done for me in my work—and the other things . . . there's a reason for them. I knew it."

Realizing he'd been thoroughly sucked into the old man's orbit and had let down his guard, Danny recovered. "Look, I need you to tell me how you know what you know and exactly who the hell you are. Was the priest-with-dementia act some kind of game to get me here so we could talk?"

"My real name is Michael. To understand who I am and what I represent will require you to open your mind more than you have."

"You're gonna have to break that last part down a little more, pal," Danny clapped back. He had calmed down and felt less alarmed.

"You and your beloved cousin faced a force together that you struggle to understand. I know you are both still trying to piece together its meaning and his abilities. I'm here to make you see that they are gifts he should embrace in this continuing battle."

"And why do you think *you* understand these things?" asked Danny.

"Because although angels and humans are different orders of beings, the two forms can occasionally intersect for a period of time. As I am doing through Father Timothy now."

"Angels," Danny said in a low voice. "Now we're talking about angels?" Completely baffled, he glanced around at the few people sitting closest to them, wondering if any of them could overhear this fantastical conversation.

Observing Danny's concern, the priest appeared to assuage it. "No one can hear anything we are saying, nor would they understand it even if they could. Our conversation is entirely private."

Danny returned his gaze to Michael's eyes.

"Do you believe in the devil, Daniel?"

"You mean, like, as a concept?"

Michael ignored this response. "The beast you and Craig faced was physical in nature, solid flesh. Yet it had the ability to navigate and manipulate time and space as well, did it not?"

"Uh huh," Danny managed to get out. The description of their battle with the Tourist rolled so smoothly off the stranger's tongue that it didn't register with Danny as to how this Michael could be so all-knowing.

"What do you think it was, the thing you faced?"

Danny crossed his arms. "We don't know. That's what we've been trying to figure out. All we really know is that he had to be stopped—*we* had to stop him when we had the opportunity. He was murdering people."

"He and others like him have carved a wide swath of carnage for a long time."

"Others!" Danny's eyes lit up. "So that's it! Craig brought that guy down, and now he's supposed to find the others like him?"

"You have but a fragment of understanding of the adversary and the roles you are to play. This is why it is important that you understand more completely—if indeed you choose to do so."

"Choose? Of course, I choose to! We need answers!" Danny's patience was wearing thin again. "We've been trying to understand Craig's ability to do crime scene re-creations for years now. And since we've learned he can do so much more—could do, that is—it's only gotten more confusing."

This conversation is having such an odd effect on me, Danny thought. It felt like his responses were being coaxed or drawn out of him, much like he could coax admissions from a suspect in one of his cases.

"You need to realize, Daniel, that your cousin has been a steward of power he hasn't been afforded the opportunity to understand. Your pursuit of their origin and purpose is natural."

Danny wasn't sure how to respond to that, so he remained quiet and listened.

"You have both been sorely tested in the extreme. This has been going on for some time with Craig. First, with the death of his father. Then, his isolation and loneliness. His helping you in your drive to bring killers to justice was also debilitating—another testing ground. He questioned why he had survived as a child and in what direction he should go as he got older.

"As for you, Daniel, your test has been more recent. You suffered the loss of a woman you cared for. You were taunted and goaded by the actions of a killer, and then maimed to the point where you now question your ability to move forward every day. You despair that you will be able to fulfill your purpose with the same vigor without your former physical abilities. Yes, you and Craig have suffered significant trauma: mental, physical, and emotional."

Trauma, thought Danny. *There it is.* It was the word Colonel Bishop had used. To hear Bishop tell it, trauma had been the catalyst for the rare powers he had witnessed in certain individuals.

"You're right," he said. "We've been tested. Been through some shit. But we made it out the other side, ready to tackle whatever lies ahead. Whatever that *thing* was, if there are more of them in this world, they need to be stopped. And Craig can do it—I saw it with my own eyes."

Danny felt emboldened by these new insights but wanted more.

"So, are you here to tell us where the others are?" Danny asked. "Then we can take them out as well? Is that what this is all about? You're saying that Craig was given those powers for a reason. And he and I have already agreed that we're gonna take on all the sons of bitches we can find."

Michael sighed and shook his head. "Daniel, why do you think you were drawn to law enforcement? Other than the fact that it was your father's vocation."

Danny's narrowed eyes flashed annoyance. The string of facts, these details the stranger knew about him—was starting to feel off-putting, like a carnival trick.

"For the same reason we're all called into it. To protect—"

"And serve?" Michael finished. "Precisely. But protecting and serving are not the same as getting revenge."

"I don't follow."

"It's true that you both play an important role. But the way to defeat enemies like the one you faced in the church is by shielding and defending others, not by seeking confrontation."

"You expect me to believe that good-versus-evil bullshit? Coming from someone I've never met, speaking through a priest who couldn't remember my name after I gave it to him?" Danny's voice was rising as he expressed his exasperation.

"You disbelieve, despite the fact that you know my words reflect the truth. All right. Let me show you then. Place your uninjured hand in mine."

Danny eyed Michael with suspicion.

"Really, Daniel? If I were truly a threat, don't you think I would have harmed you by now?"

Danny chuckled. "Fair enough."

He placed his hand flat atop the priest's open palm. Instantly, a surreal sequence of events began to unfold. The room seemed to darken around them. It reminded Danny of a concussion he had suffered while playing football years ago. A tunnel of darkness closed in around his field of vision until only the priest's face was visible. That face now commanded a power and presence that Danny had not sensed before. Then, for a frightening moment, Danny's vision went completely dark, and he was frozen in place.

He was completely unprepared for what happened next. Images flashed through his head: random people, places, snippets of interactions. He was at ground level, with people and buildings whisking by him. He could hear words and phrases as they passed. Nothing seemed related to anything else until Danny noticed a pattern: they were all taking place in earlier time periods. The flurry of modern buildings and cars gave way to early scenes of horses and buggies, with people dressed to match the era. It was as if time itself was rewinding.

The images then sped up, revealing scenes from colonial America, with settlers boarding ships. Then crowded streets in old European cities gave way to vineyards in what looked like the Italian countryside. Next, the terrain shifted to the Mediterranean as the succession of images slowed and Danny pictured a new scene: a clearing at the base of a gently sloping hillside. A young man wearing a long robe reminiscent of Biblical times stood with his back to Danny. It was nighttime, and a full moon brightly lit the young man and a clearing just beyond him. The young man had parted the branches of two adjacent trees and was peering through the gap. The image drew ever closer until Danny felt himself merging with the young man and seeing through his eyes.

And what he saw was unreal.

A large man clad in a long black cloak flung another man to the ground. The man lay crumpled as his attacker shouted angrily into the clear night sky, his face partially hidden in shadow by a hood that fell down past his forehead. But Danny could clearly see the outline of a strong, clenched jaw. The color of his face was almost gray; his face was clean shaven and looked as if it could've been chiseled from stone.

The man on the ground rose to his feet and dusted himself off as he spoke. "No. We are finished here. The pebble that began its journey down the hill will roll forward to its ultimate resting place. You must go, Abaddon, for my Father needs my path to continue."

The larger man spun around, his rage evident. "You would give yourself up for this lot? This worthless rabble? You may choose your Father's path this night. But if that is your choice, for those who believe in what you represent, I will make sure that theirs is a path of constant pain and punishment!"

Danny watched in shock as the menacing figure raised a powerful left forearm and held four fingers up in the air. Then, with one quick chopping motion of his right hand, he severed those fingers, and they fell to the ground.

Impossibly, each severed digit writhed and came to life. In a matter of moments, each had grown to the size of an adolescent child and taken the form of a simian-like creature. All were naked and hairless, with gray skin. They turned their attention to the man who had just risen to his feet.

"My children will stalk yours everywhere!" the attacker bellowed. "Never will they be far from my reach. Those who carry on in your name will be cut down until there are none left who truly believe in you. Nothing will be gained from the sacrifices you embrace, not after tonight."

The four naked creatures approached the smaller man and formed a half circle around him. Then they lunged at him, lashing out with their limbs and striking him several times. He was thrown to the ground again, with cuts on his arms, his cheek split open from one of their blows. He lay there panting, stunned. The creatures looked eager to resume their attack, but the massive, dark figure held up his hand, holding them in place.

"Do you see now? This is what your followers will face."

The man on the ground revived, furrowed his brow, and rose resolutely. "Those who trust in my Father will have . . . strength."

The creatures lurched forward. But this time, their victim attacked with unnatural speed. He thrust out his hands, and from his palms shot out ripples of vibration of such intensity that they bent the very air through which they passed. The waves crashed into the creatures, not only arresting their advance, but sending them sprawling. He shot forth another volley of pulses that pounded into the creatures' bodies. The force from the blasts knocked them across the clearing and sent two of them hurtling up and over a grove of trees. The remaining creatures turned and quickly ran out of sight.

The man returned his hands to his sides and exhaled deeply, but before he could fully regain his breath, the menacing man grabbed him by the neck with his massive right hand, lifted him off the ground, and held his wriggling body aloft.

"You may have driven them away tonight, but they're not gone from this world. They exist still, and they will continue to live long after you are gone."

"So . . . be it," the man choked in response.

Danny was terrified. This dark attacker had an aura of malevolence about him, and he appeared vastly more powerful than his victim despite the smaller man having vanquished his attackers in such a startling way just moments before.

"I offer you one last chance, young prince," the giant roared. "Follow my guidance, and you will become the king on Earth you were meant to be."

"Know this now," the smaller man rasped. "I reject you and all that you stand for. There is nothing you can say tonight that will keep me from fulfilling what my Father asks of me."

"As you wish." The large man lowered his captive to the ground and released his grasp. "But the die is cast for those who believe in you. This much I have shown you tonight."

With those words, the frightening figure grabbed the edge of his cloak and snapped it toward the ground, his shape and form momentarily replaced by thick, dark wisps of oily smoke that soon wafted away.

Then the young man, through whose eyes Danny had been watching the scene, ran over to the fallen man, who was collapsed on the ground in exhaustion.

"Rabbi! Please tell me that you're all right! Who was that strange being? Why was he attacking you," the young boy stammered.

"John," the rabbi interrupted, holding up his palm as if to quiet him, "waste no further thought on the man you saw tonight. Neither he nor the four he created have the power to make any lasting mark upon me."

From his strange perch behind the eyes of another, Danny noticed that the many cuts on the Rabbi's arms and the gash on his cheek were gone. He wondered if the man had really suffered those lacerations or if Danny had only imagined them.

"My lord, you were bleeding, and now there is no blood!"

"John, please," the man replied. "I need you to pay attention to what I'm about to tell you." He grasped his servant's hands, guiding him to sit next to him on the ground. He looked down at their intertwined hands, then up into the young man's—and Danny's—eyes.

"John, I put to you a most difficult task. You saw the four that appeared tonight and vanished away from this grove?"

"Yes," John replied.

"This is their import. It is now up to you to lead a resistance. Those four will try to destroy those who believe and all those who seek to do good works. You must repel them as I did tonight and instruct others to do the same."

"But, teacher," John argued gently, "I have not the power nor the understanding to challenge those things as you did tonight."

"You will have the ability, my loyal friend, and you will teach others how to do the same." He looked down at their hands. "Do you feel that, John? The sensations in your hands. Take note. I am empowering you with the same ability. In the name of my Father, you must not shrink from the challenge those four pose to you and to others with whom you choose to share the gift I bestow upon you now. Do you understand?"

As the question hung in the air, Danny felt himself falling backward, as if out of the scene before him and away. But he didn't want to leave. *Wait! No! I don't understand—not yet*, he thought.

Abruptly, the visions vanished, and Danny found himself once again sitting next to the old priest—no, Michael—in the pew. The priest had released his hand, and Danny looked around the antechamber, then cast his eyes out into the church, wondering what others might have seen or experienced. But nothing had changed, and no one seemed aware of the astonishing journey he had just undertaken in his mind.

"What . . . was that? What did you do?"

"You told me you want to understand what your cousin is a part of and why he can do the things he can do. I showed you."

Questions hurried from Danny's lips as he struggled to process his experience. "Was that . . . what I think it was? Were me and Craig facing one of those creatures in the battle at the church, when Craig did that thing with his hands? And the man who fought them off, the one who passed along his abilities to the guy whose eyes I could see through. He was called Rabbi. He gave the same power to John? Was the encounter you showed me what I think it was? Christ with one of his disciples?"

The priest nodded. "It is very important for you to focus on understanding what you've just seen."

Danny looked down at the floor and heaved a sigh. "I'm kind of a . . . scriptural novice."

"Come now, Daniel," Michael challenged. "You're exceedingly bright, possessing more than the simplistic perspective you choose to show others. This is how the dots you have been examining connect. It may not be what you expected, but it is the truth you wanted to understand."

"This is heavy. I didn't see all this coming. I . . . I'm not sure we're ready for it. Not Craig . . ." He looked down at his prosthetic hand. "Or me."

"Daniel, you were built for so much more than you have accomplished so far, and you know it."

"I mean, sure. I want to play the part I'm supposed to.

But look at me," Danny objected. He stood and faced Michael, spreading his arms wide.

"You need to heal in your mind first, Daniel. Then the body will follow." Michael motioned for Danny to sit back down. As Danny complied, Michael reached out and touched the flesh adjacent to Danny's prosthetic. "You continue to cling to a notion of yourself as something less than you once were. Release it."

There was truth in that, Danny knew. He shook off the thought and refocused. "Why did you show me that particular scene?"

"You and Craig have made little progress in your understanding thus far. You must now move more quickly. After the events in Iowa, things will be coming to a head. Everyone has a path they need to follow. Perhaps yours is to help guide Craig into understanding and embracing that which he truly is."

"But what *is* he?"

Michael left the question unanswered. "The way to defeat the dark descendants you saw—"

"That's what they're called? The thing we faced in the church is a 'dark descendant'?"

"The way to counter them is to serve and protect those who are their targets. That, and to ensure that the abilities Craig has acquired are eventually passed on to another."

Michael fell into silence as Danny struggled to absorb it all. It had been a minute or more. Danny's eyes darted about, as if trying to process everything he'd heard and seen.

"Daniel, think about the speed of your healing. That was made possible because of the power in your cousin's palms. Remember that he held you together with his hands until medical care could repair you. Now it is time to heal your mind, and Craig must do the same. This is the journey you are on. It will challenge you both, but if you see it through, the reward is beyond measure. Release the old to embrace the new. Think about what that means in terms of what you and Craig need to let go of."

"I think I'm following," Danny said, as he tried to grasp the meaning in his words.

"I want you to take this," Michael said at last. "This is something Father Timothy would want you to have as much as I do." He reached into a pocket on the back of the pew in front of them and withdrew a Bible. He handed it to Danny.

"Read a few passages from it, especially those by John. As well as Revelations; John wrote that as well. We'll talk again another time."

"Wait," Danny said, "I need to understand better. There's so much that I just don't get yet."

Michael shook his head. "Perhaps next time, when you return. We will soon be unable to discuss this further today."

Just as Danny opened his mouth to ask why, the other priest reentered the antechamber and headed toward them.

Danny looked at Michael. He had drawn his hands into his lap and sat peacefully. As Danny watched, Michael's eyes became cloudy and unfocused, and his expression shifted to the simple smile with which Father Timothy had greeted him. *Michael has left Father Timothy's body*, Danny realized.

"So, Detective, did you and the Father have a nice chat?

"Yeah, we had a really nice talk," Danny responded. He patted Father Timothy on the shoulder. "You have a great day today, Father. I'll see you the next time I'm in."

The old priest looked at him. "And then we'll talk about Fred?"

"Sure, we can talk about anything you want."

Danny rose, tucked the Bible under his arm, picked up his cane, and walked past the other priest toward the sanctuary entrance. "You have a good day too," he said.

Once outside, Danny felt surprisingly calm. He looked over the Bible in his hand, then gazed into the distance, seeing things from a new perspective and with a million thoughts racing through his head.

9

FOR WHAT PURPOSE?

Craig's arm was awkwardly pinned under his chin and against his throat. Try as he might, he couldn't think of a maneuver to escape.

"You seem to have hit a wall, haven't you?"

Master Jason clutched Craig from behind on the mat. He had wrapped his arms around his student's torso and was holding him fast as Craig struggled to counter.

Breathing heavily, Craig responded, "Something like that. Been a long week."

It had been. Craig couldn't remember how many days in a row he had been in the studio practicing. With Lauren gone for most of the week, he was intent on using the time to hone his skills. But he was also hoping to attend a session that Samantha might be in. During their first match, she'd seemed to be aware of Craig's attempts to reach into her thoughts. He had *almost* succeeded in making use of this telepathic ability, one he hadn't been able to access since the night he drank from Emma's wineglass nearly two years ago.

Exhausted, Craig tapped his palm sharply several times on the mat, submitting to his instructor. Jason released his grasp and untangled his limbs from Craig's. They rolled up to a seated position. Craig took a few moments to gather himself and catch his breath. Jason rose, walked past a few other pairs who were sparring on the mat, grabbed a towel off a bench and tossed it to Craig.

"Thanks." Craig snatched it out of the air and wiped the sweat from his face and neck as Jason approached. He knelt down to get Craig's attention.

"What?" Craig asked.

"Perhaps you should try to smooth over whatever happened the last time you two met."

"What are you talking—"

Just then, a tall, striking woman entered the room. Sure enough, it was Samantha.

Jason strode away to watch another sparring pair.

Samantha was standing near a bench along the wall next to the door. She didn't seem to be there to work out—she was wearing jeans and a hooded sweatshirt. Maybe she had come here to talk to him. Or maybe to confront him. He wasn't sure, but he felt like he'd been in the wrong when they sparred, even if Samantha might not understand why. It seemed impossible for her to know he had tried to read her thoughts, but whether she did or not, Craig knew it was wrong of him to have tried.

He walked over to her slowly. Seeing his approach, she sat down on the bench, upright and alert, waiting.

He sat beside her but a cautious few feet away. Neither looked at the other. Instead, they gazed at the mat and the wrestling students.

Craig spoke first. "It's Samantha, right? Sam, you told me."

"Uh huh."

"So, what are the odds that I'd run into you again so soon?"

The question seemed to annoy her. Not yet sensing where

their conversation might be headed, Craig tried levity. "I hope I didn't scare you off or anything." He glanced at her and smiled, but her face remained fixed, serious.

"I don't really scare easily."

That rang true for Craig. She looked strong, determined, even intimidating.

"No, no, I guess you probably don't. Especially considering how you kicked my ass the other day." Another attempt to lighten things up.

She said nothing, so he went on. "Listen, I didn't mean to offend you by asking questions about the confrontation you had with that guy." He was guessing here. Maybe his witnessing that scene had been the cause of her angry reaction. Maybe it wasn't his attempt to read her thoughts after all.

"Do you think that's why I got pissed off and left?"

"Well, I figured—"

"No, that's not it. I could feel something, or someone, in my head. Maybe they were looking around or talking—I don't know. Not sure I can explain what I felt. All I know is that it seemed like it was you. And when I smacked you and cut your face, well, that was an interesting trick too."

She had seen his wound heal itself. *Damn.* Craig suddenly felt vulnerable, and he thought she might start to get angry again. He moved to calm her. "Now hold on—"

"Don't worry about it," she interrupted. She didn't seem upset. "I don't need to know about any of that shit. That's your deal. I started coming to this gym a while back. I like it. Let's just say I'm not interested in being banned from the place just because I went off on you."

"Wait, no, it's cool, Sam."

Finally turning to face him directly, she pivoted the

discussion. "I came in today hoping you'd be here. Just to make sure there's no harm, no foul. But also to see why you gave a shit about what I was doing with that guy outside."

Here was the opening Craig had been hoping for when he'd sought her out in the first place. "Well, who was he then? Someone you knew and had an issue with?"

"Hardly."

It wasn't the response Craig expected. She seemed like a pretty normal person, if a little one-dimensional. She reminded him of Danny that way—intense, focused. But why did she have this mysterious pull on him?

"I'm not gonna stand by and watch something like that happen to little kids," Samantha said.

Craig squinted. "He was going to do something to a kid? Multiple kids?"

"Let's just say I've had these feelings before. I'm always right about them. I used to not want to get involved, but then I always wished I'd done something to prevent it. I vowed I wasn't gonna look the other way anymore."

"I'm confused. So this guy did something, or he was going to do something? And if whatever it was hadn't happened yet, how did you know he was some kind of threat?" Craig asked.

Craig was walking a fine line. He wanted to divert attention away from his attempt to see her thoughts. But he also wanted to tease out how she could sense things about others.

"I don't expect you to understand. I could just *feel* what he was about. And just so you know, when I confronted him and told him that I knew what he was going to do, all the color left his face. That was when I knew I was right about him. Like I said, I'm always right."

Craig's perception of her was changing. She was describing some type of sense she had about people who intended to do something bad and felt compelled to try to stop them before they could do it, to protect those she saw as innocent or defenseless. Her desire to do that would certainly pair with her obvious strengths: her physical power and martial arts skills.

Things went quiet for a moment, then Samantha said, "Anyway, since you asked me when we were sparring, I just wanted you to know that there was actually a motive behind the message I was trying to send that guy. Ask Jason about me—he understands that I wouldn't use my skills to kick some random person's ass."

"I wasn't thinking that."

Breezing past that comment, she said, "But it *is* my responsibility to protect those who can't protect themselves. Especially from a predator like I knew that guy was. I'm not going to turn my back on it."

"But unless you're sure, unless you have proof, don't you think what you did was a little too aggressive?" Craig asked.

"Too aggressive? If you can help someone and can make a difference, and you have the skill to do it, I think you have to. What's the purpose of having that skill if you don't even try?"

Crag nodded. He didn't want to push her further. He was beginning to appreciate why he might have been subconsciously drawn to her in the first place. He wanted to know more but sensed that would need to wait for another time.

"Well, thank you for sharing that with me and for coming in to talk things out," Craig said.

She moved the conversation to smaller talk. "It seems like you know Jason pretty well. Do you come in here a lot? Do you work second shift too? Is that why you're in here during the day?"

"Not exactly," Craig answered. "I left my job, and I'm

getting ready to go back to school. It hasn't started yet, so I've got a fair amount of time to work a little harder here."

"Did you quit your job to go back and get your degree?"

"I already have a bachelor's degree in business. I'm going back for grad school because I'm trying to find out what I'd really like to do."

"Oh, I see. It must be nice to have that kind of financial freedom."

Craig felt like he should explain his good fortune. "I guess I got lucky. I recently learned my dad had set aside a fund to help me with school."

"Recently learned? Why did he wait so long to tell you?"

"Well, he didn't actually tell me. He died when I was younger."

"Oh, sorry about that." She paused for a beat. "You're just coming into the money now. That's great, but, damn, someone took their sweet time with that news, didn't they?"

"Yeah. Strange how things worked out."

"What are you going to do with a degree?"

"I don't really know," Craig admitted with a sigh.

"But it seems like you would have to have some idea of what you are going to do if you're investing a lot of your time and someone's money in it."

Craig shot her a curious look.

"I work a regular forty-hour job in a warehouse," she continued, "so I don't have a ton of extra time. That's why I like to make sure I've got other priorities. Like with that guy: when I see someone's a piece of shit, I step up and do something about it. I make sure I have time for that."

Not to be outdone in giving advice, Craig offered, "Well, you want to watch getting caught up in too much of the negative and the cynical. I've found that it leads down a path of being angry and resentful. I've been there, and it's not a fun place to be. It's taken a lot for me to heed Lauren's advice and work on it."

"Lauren?"

"Oh, my girlfriend."

"I see. Then I guess I shouldn't read too much into you charging across the street in traffic to meet me that day." It was the first time Samantha had attempted a joke.

"No, it wasn't anything like that . . ." Craig stammered.

"Relax. I'm just messing with you," she said, and he chuckled. "Seems like you're looking for what you're supposed to do, and I know exactly what I'm supposed to do."

Samantha was keen and assured in the things she said, not unlike Lauren, Craig thought. Maybe because she had a confidence like Lauren it made it easier for Craig to relate to her. In any case, Craig was glad to get to know her better after the tense interaction they had last time.

Danny hadn't accomplished anything all morning. Content to stare out the windows of the Seventh Precinct, his mind hopped from one thing to the next. It wasn't an understatement to admit to himself that his time in the church had been one of the most pivotal days of his life.

He kept trying to dissect the time he'd spent the priest in some rational, logical way. But the circumstances of the meeting, and the enormous implications it revealed, stretched his mind's ability to process what had happened.

This much was undeniable: Michael had transported Danny in his mind to a long-ago confrontation to convince him that he knew both the origin and the purpose of Craig's uncanny powers. He had implied that the abilities Craig's father had passed down to him had originated in an event that occurred thousands of years ago.

Danny shook his head for what must have been the fiftieth time that morning. It was hard to believe that the things Craig could do might actually link back that far, and to such a significant time for the world.

And then there was grappling with Michael's true identify. He didn't come across as having ill intent, but rather as someone showing Danny what he and Craig had long needed to know. Michael couldn't have the information he claimed if he was a regular person. Danny wondered if Michael was some kind of spirit or divine being. In the end, as incredible as it was, the explanation for the origins of Craig's powers finally seemed to make sense. The purpose for Craig's abilities was still hazy in Danny's mind, but Michael had challenged him to see it as something greater than mere vengeance.

With every question Michael seemed to have answered, more were raised in Danny's mind. It drowned out everything else that Danny was preoccupied with recently.

His first instinct after his encounter with Michael had been to reach out to Craig. But given the gravity of it all, he needed time to think about what he'd learned. Besides, he was set to see Craig soon at the dinner they had planned.

Mason walked through the buzzing activity of the main floor of the precinct and approached Danny, who was sitting at his desk.

"Looks like you've got a bunch on your mind today, Walsh."

Momentarily startled, Danny wrenched his mind out of the stew of thoughts. "Oh, right. Yeah, no worries. I was daydreaming, I guess."

"I know you've got a lot going on, a lot you're working through. Just let me know if you need anything, all right?"

The gesture gave Danny an opening to push his point, and he quickly took it.

"Honestly, Lieutenant, the thing I need the most is for you to loosen the reins on me a little."

Mason nodded. "I get that, Walsh."

The things Danny had been pondering had put his career concerns in perspective. They loomed so much larger than his duty assignments, and that somehow made it easier to speak freely about his irritation.

"Honestly, I was kinda pissed that you wouldn't let me in on the case when that informant I interviewed was killed. Hell, you were the one who asked me to interview him in the first place."

"True. But like I said, it wasn't your case at that point."

"But you said it was a way I could get back in."

Mason's demeanor remained calm and dispassionate, despite the frustration of his subordinate. "I didn't say you could phone your cousin about getting involved," Mason said.

"Why not, if it can help get the job done?"

"Because a lot went down with you and him a couple years ago."

"Tell me about it," Danny said, his jaw set and his expression grave. The critical connections between those events were fresh in his mind; he'd spent the entire morning mulling them over, drawing on the fresh insights he had received from Michael.

Thinking he needed to give something more to get any further with Mason, Danny offered an explanation. "Craig's got a unique insight, a different way of looking at things. He's helped this precinct get a hell of a lot of bad guys off the street. Did shit go off the rails with the serial killer? Yeah. But how completely out of the norm is that? Plus, it's over now. And he and I paid a damn heavy price for dedicating ourselves to seeing that one through."

Danny felt zero intimidation as he made the point, despite his lower rank, and the determined look in his eyes conveyed it.

"I get it, Walsh. I do. The way you treat things on the job—you're an owner, not a tenant."

"Look, Mason. I know I can't force you to trust me or give me more rope. Even if I could skirt around my orders, I'm too respectful of the colors and the rank to do that. But I'd sure as hell like a little bit of the consideration I feel I've earned, that I've bled for, for this city and the department."

They lapsed into silence. Danny tuned in to the low-level rumble of activity on the floor while he pondered his next move. It was Mason who finally spoke.

"I can see this isn't a game to you, Walsh. At the same time, there's still a lot I'm getting used to with you. How about this? Let's you and I continue to work through questions we both have, continue to ease into things. You need to know that I get what you're saying. For guys who put on the uniform, whether it's the one I did in the military or the one you and I wear now, I know that the people who will literally bleed for it are few and far between. For that, you've got my respect and that of the force."

"And I'd do it again today, without hesitation."

"No question. I hear the sense of purpose you feel in this job. And you've earned some trust by being straight with me today. I appreciate it. I can imagine that both you and your cousin have been through hardship. Maybe even call it trauma, like the Bishop guy said."

Trauma. There was that word again. Michael had used it too. It echoed in Danny's brain.

"That Bishop guy had some interesting things to say about trauma and its effects, didn't he?" Danny said.

"You think?" Mason replied. "Maybe. Call me still a skeptic about that guy. He's actually down in one of the conference rooms today talking to some of our guys from counterterrorism."

Danny perked up. "Really?"

"Yeah, I thought you knew that he was scheduled back in today."

"Oh, I had something come up." The truth was that he had blown off the meeting to give himself time to digest the mind-blowing download he'd received in the church.

"Well, he's been down there for a good amount of time already."

As if on cue, Bishop appeared on the floor, flanked again by two younger men. They made their way across the room and headed toward the doors.

"Please excuse me, Lieutenant, but I'm going to try to catch him real quick," Danny said. He hastily stood, grabbed his cane, and strode past his boss.

"Sure, knock yourself out," Mason said to Danny's back.

Danny met the group just as they were about to exit.

"Excuse me. Mr. Bishop?"

"Ah, yes. Detective . . . ?" Bishop raised his eyebrows and slowly nodded his head.

"Walsh."

"Right, of course."

The two young men accompanying Bishop stood by his side, alert but expressionless.

"Sir, may I ask you a quick question?" Danny started hesitantly. "The last time you were here, you said a couple of things that clicked with me. The comments you made about how trauma can affect people."

"Oh, of course." Bishop's face showed concern as he took in Danny's prosthetic and cane.

"No, this isn't about me. It's about my cousin. He's been through a lot, and he's become a pretty exceptional person because of it, I think. I'm just trying to understand him."

"You seem like you've been through some things as well."

"Yeah, but he's part of the reason of why I'm even here. I owe him."

"Interesting." Bishop's brow furrowed and the wrinkles on his head deepened. "We have somewhere we need to be currently, but if you give me your card, I can see about making some time to reach out to you."

Danny fumbled inside his jacket pocket and retrieved a business card. "I appreciate any time you could spare." He held out his business card to Bishop, but one of the younger men quickly snatched it from his fingers.

"That'll be enough," Bishop said, his eyes flashing. The interception had clearly annoyed him, and the younger man gingerly handed the card over.

"Detective Daniel Walsh, then. I'll endeavor to reach out to you soon," Bishop repeated.

"I appreciate it."

"Certainly, Detective. By the looks of it, considering your sacrifice, it is the least I can do."

Without further comment, Bishop exited through the doors, handing his visitor badge to security as he left.

Just then, one of the desk officers approached Mason with an armful of folders. Without taking his eyes off Danny, Mason hailed him. "Can you help me get a lunch scheduled with Eric Hammond? He works down in administration at the Daley Center."

"Sure, Chief. How soon are you looking?"

"As soon as you can make it happen."

10

SANTORI'S

Danny drummed his fingers on the table at Santori's restaurant as he waited for Craig to arrive. He had reserved a secluded room at the back of the restaurant, which was his and Craig's preferred spot. Doing so was easy, given the history Danny had of coming here and knowing the owner— Arturo Santori or 'Artie'—for so long.

He glanced down at his watch. It was 6:05 p.m. Craig was only a few minutes late, but Danny was antsy. He had an array of developments to discuss, most importantly his conversation with Michael in the church.

His anticipation was also grounded in the knowledge that Lauren was supposed to join them around seven, which didn't leave much time. Danny had to make the most of it before Lauren showed up.

Santori walked back to check on Danny.

"He has not yet arrived," said Artie.

"Okay, but when he does—"

"I know, Daniel. Bring him here straightaway. I will be sure to do that." Though he was at least in his early seventies, Artie embodied the sprightly energy of someone half his age.

"Thanks, Artie."

For years, Danny had been a frequent customer in his restaurant. Artie had witnessed his rise to prominence in the detective ranks. He had also watched him struggle after suffering serious injuries in the line of duty. Of everyone who had known Danny before and after the nightmare with the serial killer, Artie had remained most constant, his respect for and deference to Danny unchanged.

"It will be good to see you and Craig together at the table again. Always good when the two of you can share a meal together." He beamed, then turned and headed toward the front of the restaurant.

Before Danny's anxiety could resurface, Artie reappeared with Craig in tow.

"And look, Daniel. As soon as I return to the front, *Eccolo!* Craig has arrived."

Artie nodded politely to Danny as Craig slipped past him and into the small room.

"Thanks, Artie. Good seeing you again, young man," Craig said. Artie smiled, waved his hand dismissively at Craig's joke, and then left them to settle in.

Danny rose with a wide grin to greet Craig. The two men embraced, clapping each other on the back.

"Man, it's been too long. You're getting strong!" Danny said.

"It's been, like, two weeks. You're talking like we haven't met up in a year," Craig said.

"I know. But it seems like there's been a lot going on. So tell me. What's up?"

They settled into their seats. A server came by to pour water. They exchanged pleasantries.

When they were alone again, Craig asked, "Are you sure you wanna talk here?"

"Yeah. No one will get seated in the back while we're here. I asked Artie to make sure."

"Okay then," Craig said. "Things have been moving along.

You know, I've been making progress. It's been going well with getting ready for classes to start, working the martial arts—"

"I'm not asking about that stuff," Danny interrupted. "I mean, yeah. That's great." He lowered his voice. "But I mean the other things. I'm a detective, and I know it's hard to work on a mystery without clues. It seems like you've got a few clues that you haven't shared with me yet."

Craig took a sip of his water. "You've got a good sense for things. Right after we talked on the phone last week, a couple of things happened on the way to aikido and during one of my sessions."

"And?" Danny perked up.

"Let's just say I had an injury that spontaneously healed."

"Right. You said you thought your instructor broke your arm. That ability you have to heal quickly—hell, instantly—is back," Danny concluded.

The conversation paused as Danny surveyed his cousin. He could sense that Craig was still withholding something.

Craig smiled, confirming as much.

"Give it up," Danny said. "Dude, we've been wondering why your powers hadn't returned for like two years now. If there's more than just your arm healing then spill it."

"Well, there's been a few other things. Remember those dreams I used to have about my dad? I had another dream that was kind of similar. I tried to talk to Lauren about it, but then we got into an argument, and I haven't really explored it since."

Danny's eyes widened. "Go on," he said. "So anyway . . . this dream was about Emma," Craig said.

"Emma? Really."

"Are you okay with hearing about it?"

"For sure," Danny said. Remembering his slain girlfriend

always hurt, but nothing was going to change that, and he wanted to see where Craig was going with this dream.

"Okay, then, if you say so. It was weird. The dream lasted just a few moments. But she was crying, or at least I think it was her. She appeared to be in my room in my old apartment. Remember that box of memorabilia I had?"

As soon as the words left his mouth, Craig thought back to when he first withdrew a letter from the box. It was typewritten and yellowed, dated 1917, and was a letter of condolence written to his great-grandfather. It had come from some group or organization, written very respectfully and solemnly. But it had referenced death as a relentless enemy that pursued them. It closed with a signature, written with quill, and embossed at the bottom with the letters C–O–I.

"You mean the one that had the creepy letter in it that was addressed to your granddad?"

Craig nodded. "Well, a box was sitting next to Emma in the dream, and it looked like that box. When I got closer to her, it didn't look like she had been crying after all. But she was mad."

"Mad at who? You?"

"Sure seemed like it," Craig said. "She kept saying stuff like, 'Are you really going to walk away?' She told me I was supposed to protect someone. She accused me of turning my back on something or someone, but I'm not really sure. Then she got up and walked through the wall. Just like that."

"She walked through a wall," Danny repeated.

"Yeah. And then she was gone."

Danny squinted and shook his head. "Well, that's pretty bizarre."

"I know, right?"

Danny held his tongue for a moment, trying to process the dream's meaning.

"But, hey," Craig said. "You said some things were new with you. How's work? Have you been able to get back in the groove?"

"Uh, yeah, some," Danny said. But his mind was preoccupied with the mysteries they had been chasing for so long. "Things are getting there. I got to question this twitchy informant at the precinct. And there was something odd about him, or at least there was a strange coincidence. He had a tattoo on his arm. It was more of a brand, really."

"A brand?"

"Like where you take a hot iron and burn a symbol or something into the skin. It's a gang thing."

Craig's face contorted in disgust.

"Anyway, how about this for a coincidence? The brand on his arm was three letters: *C, O, I*."

Craig's eyes widened. "The same letters that were written on the letter to my grandfather!"

"Yeah. So naturally, I wanted to look into that. But then someone let him out of the interrogation room when my back was turned. I was really pissed. I was going to find him and ask about the letters, but he turned up dead a few days later. And I think what I was able to get out of him might have been what got him killed. That made me even more determined to investigate, and I tried to pull you into the crime scene to see if you could do another re-creation."

"But you never told me you wanted my help," Craig interjected.

"Because my new lieutenant wouldn't let me reach out to you. In fact, he ordered me to hang up the phone when I tried to call you. Anyway, I think he has some ideas about the things we used to do together at crime scenes, though I don't know where he got 'em."

"Wow, that's tough. But I thought things were getting better for you on the job."

"Oh, they are. But I've still got some ground to make up there. That part is on me." Danny shook his head as if to clear it. Their discussion had taken a detour. He redirected. "Back to those abilities returning—the spontaneous healing, the dreams. I mean, it's not *totally* new. It's happened before. But does anything feel different about it this time?"

"Hmmm, not that I can think of." Craig seemed uncomfortable. "You told me you wanted to know when it started happening again. And you seemed to somehow know it was. So now I'm telling you. But why the preoccupation with how it made me feel?"

"I don't know. I'm just thinking about why your abilities are coming back now, and I wonder if maybe it's happening by design in some way. Are you up for something like that being true?" Danny lifted his chin as he spoke.

"What are you getting at?" Craig asked suspiciously.

"What I'm getting at is whatever that thing was in the church was real. Same with the others like it. And if we go down this path again, I guess I want to make sure we're ready for where it might lead—and what it might mean."

"I know," Craig said. "You're always talking about understanding these supernatural things as unfinished business for us. And that was really a pull for me, helped me think about how everything might fit together. But now I've got other things that are primary in my life: I'm getting more fit, and things have been pretty good with Lauren. Heck, I even get to go back to school without worrying about how to pay for it."

"That was quite a stroke of luck," Danny agreed. "You and

I never did talk about how that came about, the trust fund your dad had left for you. Kinda weird that it took so long to find its way to you."

"I know, but why do we have to try to explain it? Can't you just let me enjoy it? Can't I be happy that I've learned something positive about my dad, something he thought of and planned ahead for, something I can remember about him other than his death?"

Danny furrowed his brow but let Craig keep talking.

"Maybe I don't want to raise my hand and volunteer anymore, not for anything like the ass-beating we got from the Tourist in Iowa at least."

"Maybe you don't have a choice, Craig," Danny said quietly.

"What's that supposed to mean? Sounds like you know, or think you know, more about this than you've let on, Detective. So that's why you were so eager to see me tonight."

Craig smiled. Danny did not. His jaw was set and his gaze steady.

"Tell me again about everything you can do with your hands," Danny said.

Craig crossed his arms. "Hold up. Now I feel like I'm being interrogated."

"It's called 'tactile transference,' isn't that right?"

"Yes, that's the name for it. And believe it or not, I talked to Dr. Burris about it, and she actually seemed helpful for once. Why are you pushing me about my hands?"

"There just seems to be something pretty important about your abilities. I don't think you can stop it this time, Craig. I don't think you can turn it off just because you've got some good things going on. And I wouldn't want to let you stop it even if you could. Don't you think it must mean something that you can do this thing that nobody else can do?"

"I understand what you're saying, but . . ." Craig's voice trailed off.

Danny pressed his point. "People were *killed* by the Tourist, Craig. Good people. All in an effort to draw you out in the open and put an end to you and the powers you have. I gotta believe that there's more you're supposed to do with them. The people who died played a part in this path we're on. Now we need to be ready to play our part."

"We. You said it again. How come it's *we*?"

"No one succeeds alone in tackling something big. Not you, not me. And definitely not with something as big as this."

Their server approached the table. Danny waved him off brusquely.

Craig rubbed his face and the stubble that dotted it. The intensity of this conversation seemed to be wearing on him. "Look, Danny, where's this coming from? You've been acting weird."

Danny ignored him. "Has anything else happened other than the dreams and the healing thing?"

"No, already. I told you I had some updates for you and now you know." Craig opened his palms as if that's all he had to offer. "So how about it's your turn? How about catching me up on what you've been so coy about."

Danny scanned the room. "When's Lauren getting here? What I've got is gonna take a minute."

Craig flashed a surprised look. "Now you've got my attention." His eyes widened. "So?"

Danny took a deep breath and exhaled. "Okay . . . what I'm about to tell you remains between you and me, you got that?"

"Of course," Craig said.

"I stumbled upon a guy and got to talking to him in a church."

"In a church," Craig repeated.

Danny nodded. "Do you remember when we were in that hospital in Iowa, and we talked about where your path might lead and if you were prepared for that. You said you were. Is that still the case, after your powers had gone cold for so long? Because if you are, I have some new info."

"You're sounding like Lauren with the finding-a-purpose-in-life stuff. Can we just slow down for a minute?"

"I sound that like her, huh? How much does she know anyway?"

"Not all of it yet," Craig said, his voice low, his eyes cast downward. He fiddled with his fork.

"Why not? Don't you trust her?"

"Not completely."

Danny was puzzled at Craig's response but didn't want the conversation to stall. "I'm going to guess that you probably haven't told Lauren about shooting the surges of force out of your hands. What's kept you from opening up about that?"

Craig remained silent, not having an answer.

"Look, I get it that it's not easy to get inside a lady's head, to anticipate how she might feel about something that sounds so crazy."

"Inside her head," Craig repeated. "There's something else that happened in the sparring session I told you about."

"Oh?" Danny's eyebrows shot up. "What's that?"

Danny was nearly ready to share his experience in the church with Michael. But the chance to learn more of what might be reemerging with Craig was too compelling to ignore.

"It was the woman I was sparring with. There was

something about her that I felt drawn to, I guess. I'm not exactly sure why, but I started to sense her thoughts, to look inside her head. It was kind of like I did when we had dinner with Emma when we were . . . here, actually. You remember?"

"Oh, yeah, sure, I remember. What was it about this woman, and what did you learn from her thoughts?"

As Craig opened his mouth to respond, his eyes drifted over Danny's shoulder. Artie was escorting Lauren to their table.

She tilted her head to one side. "Please don't let me interrupt your train of thought, Craig," she said.

"Leave it to me to have perfectly set him up," Danny said as he smiled and rose from the booth to greet her.

"Hi, Danny," she said.

Artie waved and slipped away. Craig then rose, and leaned in to greet her as well.

Craig helped her peel off a light windbreaker and draped it over the back of her chair, and they all settled down at the table.

"Why haven't the three of us gotten together more over this past year?" Danny asked.

"Oh, I don't know. You boys have been pretty busy getting back into the swing of things."

Danny thought for a moment. Craig certainly did seem to keep him and Lauren separate for the most part, following the period of a few weeks in Iowa after the episode with the serial killer.

"There's certainly been a lot going on, that's for sure," Craig admitted.

A smirk played on Lauren's lips. "Well, it sounds like Craig was telling you about when he raced across the street to see a girl, and that he almost got run over by a car." She looked at Craig. "You wanted to stop her from roughing someone up, right?"

"Um . . ." Craig stalled.

Danny looked at Craig in surprise. He failed to mention that it was the same woman from his class.

"Or maybe you hadn't gotten to that point of the story yet?" she added.

Danny couldn't tell if Lauren was really annoyed with Craig or was just being playful. To avoid any tension, Danny turned the spotlight on Lauren. "So how are things going with you?" he asked. "I heard you were traveling."

"They're good," she said. "I've been on the road a little. I came straight here from my flight back from Minneapolis."

Now that their party was complete, the server came over to review the specials and take their drink orders. Danny and Craig would share a bottle of red wine, as was their custom at Santori's. Lauren opted for seltzer water.

Once their drinks arrived and they had dug into a shared meatball appetizer, their conversation flowed more smoothly, bouncing from current events to other topics. They talked about the unusually early spring weather, the latest alarms and terrorist warnings, Lauren's job, and Craig prepping for school.

Lauren turned her attention to Danny and his job. "It's pretty impressive how far you've come in a relatively short time."

"Uh huh," Danny mumbled as he took a swig from his wineglass. He let the statement lie there. He wasn't interested in revisiting the limitations he was still dealing with, or the vulnerability that went along with them.

"From what I've seen, and from what Craig tells me, you've gone about your recovery pretty much on your own. That takes a lot of inner strength."

"Sure, I guess." Danny wondered what she meant by "on your own." Was she calling out his lack of dating? He hadn't dated anyone since his injuries. Or was she simply noting that he had chosen to keep to himself more than he had in the past?

"Taking some time alone to process is good. That's the advice I give Craig when he wants to think through the open issues about his dad, or what happened in Iowa."

"I'm not sure that I've really brought those things up that much," Craig said.

"You talked about them the other morning," Lauren chimed in a light tone. Turning back to Danny, she said, "I guess I don't see it much differently from the way you've approached it. I like to think that most questions people ask can probably be found within themselves."

"You mean Craig is just supposed to sit and wait for some kind of epiphany?" Danny said, frankly.

"No, I just think he was fortunate to learn so much from the vision he saw in the church, finally learning circumstances of what happened to his dad. And maybe that's enough. It certainly seemed to have provided Craig closure about how his dad had died, and that he was the source of Craig having his abilities."

She glanced over at Craig for confirmation. Craig shrugged his shoulders in agreement as he took another bite.

"And you think that's it? That's all he needs to know?" Danny's words were tinged with frustration. "You don't think there's anything else he's supposed to discover about the things he can do? Like, what the hell he's supposed to *do* with those abilities?"

Recognizing that she'd hit a nerve, Lauren tried to bring the temperature down. "Oh, sure," she said calmly, "he could find out more. I just think that search should start by looking inside, rather than looking for something new to happen or some kind of trigger that magically explains it."

"I kind of get that," Craig interjected. "That's why it's been important for me to have the freedom to explore on my own, doing aikido, and going back to school."

Danny shook his head. Neither of them understood what Craig needed to do.

"I just think it's time for him to release the old and embrace the new," Lauren said. "Letting go creates space for whatever else life has in store. The way to do that is to look inside, try new things, and leave the past behind so you can move forward. Craig's got a great perspective on things that he finally *does* understand. He can share that with others, if he's looking to help."

At the mention of volunteering, Craig broke off a piece of bread and used it to draw circles in a small pool of olive oil on his plate.

"Leave the past behind," Danny said. "Right. You make it sound easy. But some of us find that a little tough to do."

"Danny, I'm sorry. I didn't mean to make light of—"

"It's fine, it's fine. I get it," Danny said, waving off her apology. "I just think this whole situation is . . . big. There's still much to learn, and more things might come up that could help Craig better understand what he's dealing with."

Lauren shifted her gaze from Danny to Craig and back again, eying both men with suspicion. "Well, maybe I'm not privy to everything there is to know about these strange events. But what I do know is that Craig was in a kind of emotional bondage for a long time" She stared at Craig. "And now you're free. What are you going to do with that freedom? Are you going to be a point, staying in one little spot? Or are you going to be a line?"

"I get what Danny is saying, though," Craig countered gently. "And I want to respect what I've learned I can do, and honor what my dad went through and why he felt it was so important to pass these powers along to me. I want to make sure I measure up."

"I've found that it's a person's power, not their perceived shortcomings, that scares them the most," Lauren responded.

"Who said anything about being scared?" Craig asked. "You know I can do some pretty powerful things. I find them strange, but not scary."

"Yes, I know you have some very unusual . . . tools to work with. The question is, what do you want to create with them?"

"Well, it seems like they were pretty important in Iowa. I helped bring a serial killer down."

"Do you really think that's all you can do with them? Fighting criminals? That would seem a bit limited, a little hollow, don't you think?"

"I think that's the point Danny's trying to make," Craig said. "Shouldn't I further explore exactly what these powers are? I mean, I know they have names now—telekinesis, clairvoyance. Dr. Burris gave me some other terms."

"Telekinesis." Lauren mulled over the word. "That means being able to move things with your mind. But that isn't something you can do."

Craig and Danny fell silent. She looked from one to the other again. "Or maybe it is," she said cautiously. "I guess

I don't know. But I do know that once you put a name to something, you begin to place limits on it."

She blew out a breath and sat back in her chair. "Honestly, it's hard for me to know how to give helpful advice when I don't know the full story. I think it's best to keep moving forward and not dwell on the past. If you feel the need to explore further, look inside and meditate."

Danny jumped in. "I'm not trying to downplay the value of . . . introspection. But I think the gravity of what we've been through demands a more complete answer about what the hell it all means. We both survived an attack by what I believe was some kind of supernatural being. And there was something special about the way Craig held my guts in to keep me alive that night—"

Lauren interrupted. "I know that. You both told me when we were still in Iowa how you had to fight for your lives when you faced down that serial killer. But that was then. You're here now, alive and well, and in a good position to move forward."

"Are you serious?" Danny said, his agitation showing. "Blood has been spilled, Lauren, innocent people's blood. I think we have an obligation to understand if there are others out there like the Tourist and learn what our role is in fighting them."

"Look, Danny, I'm not trying to argue. I think we both want what's best for Craig. And I know you both have dealt with some pretty extraordinary experiences these last few years. Things I obviously can't understand. Now, if you'll excuse me, I need to find the ladies' room."

She rose from the table quickly, and Craig and Danny hustled to stand as she left. When she was gone, the tension that had enveloped the small room lifted. Craig sighed audibly.

"Do you think I pissed her off?" Danny asked.

"I don't know. I seem to be doing that a lot lately. Every decision I've taken, every angle, is met with her disapproval."

"Who's to say her perspective is the right one? You and I know a whole lot more about this stuff than she does."

"I know," Craig said. "It's been difficult for me to understand what's going on inside her head lately. Really, it's kinda been that way since we first got together."

"Well . . ." Danny said slowly, "you could, maybe, try to take a look. See if you can still do that."

"What. You mean probe her thoughts?"

Danny arched his eyebrows, sensing that Craig was also curious about the idea. Then Craig shook his head, as if he struggled with Danny's suggestion, tempted but worried that it would violate her privacy.

"You really think I could do that?," Craig said. "I mean, I could use her water glass and see if I can get her thoughts off it, like I did with Emma."

"That's what I mean. But you better make it quick."

Craig reached over and grabbed Lauren's glass. Keeping his gaze on Danny, he took a sip from it. Then he closed his eyes and held the glass near his forehead.

For a moment, there was silence. Then Craig broke it. "Nothing," he said, "I don't feel anything, or see any thoughts or images. It's just . . . a blank expanse."

"Craig, " Danny whispered urgently.

Craig opened his eyes. Lauren was standing several feet in front of the table, gaping at him. Her arms were crossed. Craig froze under her piercing gaze.

"Really, Craig?" Lauren snapped. "Are you kidding me with this right now?"

11

MICHAEL

"Wait up, will you?" Craig called out.

Lauren marched briskly ahead of him down the street, pointedly ignoring him. She'd gotten a head start out of Santori's while Craig was saying goodbye to Artie, and it was taking a while for him to catch up to her. When he finally did, he tugged at her jacket. "Would you just give me a second? It wasn't what you think."

She yanked her jacket out of his grasp. "Really? Then what was it?" She was still walking quickly and looking straight ahead. "Why have I suddenly become something else you think you need to investigate?"

"You're not, Lauren. C'mon!"

Craig matched her stride and tried to catch her eye as they made their way toward the train stop.

"Danny is always trying to push me to uncover clues to what's been going on with me. It seemed harmless enough."

"So it was his idea to try that little stunt? What clues do you think I hold? The two of you have never been entirely forthcoming with me about this whole situation!"

"Okay, you're right. It was a dumb move."

"It was insulting."

"Right, I get that," Craig said, searching for a way to placate her. "He's just . . . he wants to make sure we understand all we can about my abilities so we'll be better prepared to stop anything else that should come up."

"He does? Or is it you? And why are you even in this picture, Craig? It's Danny's job to stop the bad guys. Or at least, it used to be."

"That's a bit mean," said Craig.

Lauren cringed. "I'm not trying to be mean, really," she said as she marched ahead. "But I can see how limited he is now, and I think it would serve you better to look inside, not outside, for answers, and to stop playing these games." Lauren veered away abruptly onto a side street, opting for a shortcut to the train station they rarely used. "At some point, you have to have a little faith in how things are supposed to work out, Craig. Not everything needs to be a threat or some mystery you have to solve."

"Lauren, come on. If there's one thing I have learned in my time spent helping Danny, it's that there are some real bad people in this world who like nothing more than to do terrible things."

"I know that. But do you really think that's the norm? The negativity you're talking about is the exception in the real world, not the rule. Ultimately, the good prevails."

Craig rolled his eyes. "You can't be this damn naïve. I've seen enough of the real world with Danny to know that's not the case."

They slowed their pace, and she turned to face him. As she did so, an elderly vagrant sidled up beside them. He looked old and frail, harmless. He stretched an arm out toward them, palm up, seeking a handout.

"Spare a little change please?"

"Listen, pal, not right now," Craig said, waving him off.

Lauren kept her eyes locked on Craig's. "Why are you so intent on looking to everyone and everything for answers instead of yourself?"

To Craig's great irritation, the old man walked along behind them as they argued, continuing to beg. "Spare change? A dollar? Fifty cents?"

Craig waved him off again, trying to maintain his focus. "Look, Lauren, clearly I have some unusual powers. Don't you think I'm supposed to do something with them? Don't you think I should find out what that thing was who killed my father?"

Just then, the vagrant pushed his hand toward Lauren's face. There was something in it, and without a second thought, Craig pounced.

"Craig, what are you doing?" Lauren shouted.

Ignoring her, Craig grabbed the man's hand, yanked it downward, and, as the beggar struggled to pull it back up, torqued his wrist up to his head, forcing it awkwardly toward his back. The beggar flipped off his feet and onto his back. He drew his arms up to his chest and cowered as Craig stood over him.

"Craig," shouted Lauren. "Why did you do that?"

"He was shoving something at you!"

"Yeah, he shoved something at me—it was this!"

Craig spun around and looked at her, puzzled. She reached down and picked an object up off the street—a single red rose. Apparently, the old man had tried to offer it to her in exchange for money.

She angrily tossed it at Craig's feet.

"But . . . but . . ." Craig stammered as his overreaction began to sink in.

Lauren drew out a twenty-dollar bill from her pocket-book, then handed it to the man. "I'm so sorry if he startled you. Thank you for the rose. Please buy yourself some food."

"Thank you, ma'am," the old man said as he cradled the bill.

She smiled at the man, then glared at Craig. "Seeing someone suffering or in need of help should move you to want to do something."

Emotion drained from her face, and she turned and walked away, continuing toward the L stop that would take her back to their apartment.

Craig stood and watched her for a moment, then looked down at the man. What he saw was a pitiful-looking guy, malnourished and grubby. He clutched the money Lauren had given him as if it were gold. His lips quivered, his eyes expressing terror as he tried to read in Craig's face what he was going to do next.

Flooded with embarrassment and shame, Craig held up his hands and looked at them, hands that had just thrown a broken old man to the ground.

Danny glanced around the church, feeling on edge. He had been here for some time and hadn't seen Father Timothy.

Dressed in a dark windbreaker over a T-shirt and jeans, he sat near the antechamber at the front of the sanctuary where he had talked with Father Timothy—that is, Michael.

While he waited, he gazed at the colorful biblical scenes that occupied the high marble walls of the huge sanctuary. He hadn't noticed them before. He found their scenes of struggle and triumph in ancient times intriguing.

He watched the activity in the church, growing impatient.

There were more people quietly seated than he had seen on a weekday. In a far corner, a choir prepared for rehearsal. A few people striding through the space appeared to be administrative personnel.

Danny was reluctant to miss a chance to talk with Michael again, but he felt like he was spinning his wheels. He decided to leave. Just then, Father Timothy appeared, framed in a doorway along the opposite wall. Another priest was speaking to him and gesturing, apparently encouraging him to make the rounds through the cathedral. Probably to keep the forgetful old man occupied, Danny thought.

Danny's gaze locked on Father Timothy as the priest made his way cautiously through the sanctuary, wide-eyed, his expression innocent. Finally, the priest felt the weight of Danny's stare and looked his way. He immediately beamed and walked toward him.

"Oh, hello! Aren't you the man who knows my uncle Fred?"

"Father Timothy. Yes, that's me, Danny. Won't you stay and talk with me for a while?"

"Oh, I don't know," the priest hesitated. He peered into Danny's eyes. "Do I know you?"

This must be the dementia, Danny thought. *The old guy clearly recognized me just seconds ago.* "Come on, Father, take a seat. I'd love some company right now," Danny urged.

At first, Father Timothy was unconvinced. Then he appeared to make a decision. He sat down on the pew next to Danny but retreated beyond arm's length.

Danny suddenly remembered the priest's fascination with his prosthetic. Maybe it could serve as a touch point again, and then Michael could be channeled through him with their conversation.

"Oh, my arm aches," Danny feigned. He pushed up his

jacket sleeve to where his wounded arm attached to the prosthetic.

Instantly, Father Timothy perked up. "Oh my! Is that real? Does it work?"

"Sure, would you like to see?" Danny offered his arm.

Father Timothy slid closer to Danny and gently touched the plastic surface. Then he moved his hand higher and made contact with Danny's bare skin.

In the blink of an eye, the nature of the priest's face underwent a dramatic transformation. The vacant wonder in his eyes drained away, replaced by a steady gaze of focus and intensity.

"Hello again, Daniel."

Michael had returned.

"Michael?" Danny asked tentatively.

"Yes, Daniel, the very same. I'm glad you chose to return."

"So am I. I want to know more," he said with purpose.

"As you should. Learning more will make you stronger."

"Stronger," Danny repeated, suddenly distracted. For the first time, he noticed that the section of the sanctuary where they were seated had emptied. They were now secluded, and the buzz that had filled the church was reduced to a dim whisper. *How did he manage that?* Danny wondered.

"Not many people in this world would forgo the chance to have a discussion with an archangel in order to seek the truth and be imbued with understanding."

Danny was transfixed, hanging on to Michael's every word.

"Let us continue then. Have you come to grips about what you learned the last time we spoke?"

"Come to grips—I wouldn't go that far." Danny leaned back, underscoring his unease. "There is still a lot I don't understand about Craig and his powers. But I'm willing to hear you out. That's why I'm here."

"Your cousin is eminently more important than those who have come before him. But the difference is not in what resides within him. It is in *how* he was gifted. He had no knowledge that it happened, or any knowledge of the true meaning behind it. Do you recall the scene I revealed to you?"

Danny nodded. "Of course. Who could forget a thing like that?"

"Craig lacks that understanding. And if he does not make an effort to accept the powers he has been given, and to pass them on—always to be used for their intended purpose—he will leave many more innocents vulnerable to these dark descendants."

"What you just called them—descendants. Who are they? *What* are they?"

"What do you think they are?"

"Why won't you just tell me?" Danny asked.

"Because part of truly understanding is to gain awareness through your own efforts."

"Okay, then help me with that. Help me learn how to do that."

But Michael pivoted from the request and changed the subject. "Have you told Craig what is now contained within him?"

"No. I thought about it, but I held back because I'm not quite sure what the hell to think about it myself. You say he's important, that *we're* important." Danny tilted his head as he struggled to understand. "And from what I've learned so far, it certainly seems like there's a meaning or a purpose to . . . what is contained in Craig, as you say. But I'm a detective by nature, and I can't put it together yet. I don't want to share what I know with Craig until I can do that."

"I understand your need to stay rooted to a process. But the way to get to an understanding of anything new is to let go of that which no longer serves you well."

"You're not the first person who has said something like that lately," Danny said, remembering Lauren's insistence on the same point.

"At certain points along the course of our lives, we will be tested—deliberately tested—in order to prepare us. And through this testing we are made stronger for the roles we are destined to play."

"Craig certainly appears to have gotten stronger, both mentally and physically, since what went down in Iowa."

"Power has been given to Craig. If he understands what he has received, he will also understand that he is responsible for how he wields it."

Danny paused. "Are you saying it's up to me to make sure he's using this stuff the right way?"

"Whether you realize it or not, you have done exactly that with Craig to this point, through the service you've provided to others, the selflessness of your vocation. You have provided him with an example of the enlightened use of power."

Danny wasn't interested in discussing his career on the force. He now knew that he and Craig had a nemesis out there—make that *nemeses*, and supernatural ones at that. He had to know what they were up against. "Tell me in plain English what we encountered in Iowa."

"You already know, Daniel. You just want it confirmed. You know that what you battled in the church was far deadlier than anything you could have imagined."

Danny's stomach clenched as he remembered the Tourist

beating him with superhuman ferocity. He had thought time and healing had erased the fear he'd felt back then, but it stirred again as Michael reminded him of it.

Michael studied Danny's face with some concern. Then he sighed, apparently resigning himself to explanation. "You want confirmation, Daniel? Then let us do that. The Tourist, as you call him, was one of four beings I showed you in that flashback. Their charge? First, to endure. Second, to terrify, torment, and ultimately eliminate those within whom a positive light shines and good deeds flow. To annihilate those people who are willing to stand up, to inspire, to heal—those who choose love."

Daniel gulped. "Was it the devil's hand the descendants were cut from?"

"You need to understand how the Dark One intends to use his descendants. Over time, he has chosen the most benevolent among us to inflict the greatest harm. He reserves his deepest animosity and revilement for two groups: those he sees as the great guides of humanity, and ordinary people who feel the call to stand up for good. In short, the more charitable and noble someone is, the more the descendants seek to destroy them—and along with them, the benefit they bring to others."

"You showed me there were originally four of them," Danny jumped in. "But there's one less now that Craig and I dealt with it."

"That is true. Actually, only two of the original four remain. But do not take any measure of comfort from that. Each of the four has operated differently, which makes it harder to recognize them. And over the years, they have learned that the most effective way to bring pain and suffering to the hearts of good people is to seduce others to follow them. Their actions of cruelty and hatred can be a powerful draw for those who are adrift."

"But if two have already been destroyed, it *can* be done."

"Yes, this is true. Their physical presence on Earth enables them to deliver suffering. But it also makes them vulnerable because they can only carry out their plan if they assume some form of flesh."

Clarity and resolve converged in Danny's mind. "So these remaining two—they've got to be stopped, somehow. We're supposed to destroy these things. And Craig has the power to do it. *That's* the responsibility he carries, the duty that comes along with the crazy things he can do. Just like his dad."

Michael shook his head. "Your cousin's real gifts are inner sight and the ability to reveal truth. The defensive power you witnessed him wielding in the church— "

"Shooting force out of his hands," Danny interjected.

"Yes, that power. That defense will only emerge when he faces these adversaries or their agents. His true responsibility is much greater than acting in such moments."

"But it's not only the way Craig fought in the church." Danny paused, wondering how much he should reveal. Finally, he reasoned that Michael probably already knew. "I've seen him heal himself. He can't be harmed."

"Yes, Daniel. Craig is invulnerable to human aggression."

Danny's mouth fell agape. He leaned back against the pew and looked steadily at Michael.

"I said invulnerable from *human* aggression, Daniel, not immortal. Either of the remaining descendants can kill Craig, as well as anyone who stands between them and their prey."

Michael fell silent for several moments, giving Danny time to take that in. When he resumed, he said, "Daniel, I cannot stress enough that Craig's intended path is to protect and preserve those who are vulnerable, not to seek conflict with the two dark progeny that remain."

Danny's head was spinning. "If Craig is as powerful and important as you say, why shouldn't he—*we*—go after the remaining two descendants? They're the threat in the first place!"

Michael sighed. "Why are you so obsessed with trying to roll back the darkness? What do you think you can do, capture it, contain it? It's like trying to catch wisps of smoke. You and your cousin should look to enhance the light in others. Think about it, Daniel. What has been your focus? To protect and serve. Not to hunt and kill."

Danny felt pangs of anxiety as he struggled to accept the idea.

Michael repeated his earlier advice. "Protect those who are vulnerable, and pass Craig's abilities along to others."

"But there are only the two of us. We can save only a handful of the good ones from these things. How could doing that have a bigger impact than wiping out those two things altogether?" Danny argued.

Michael smiled as he looked across the sanctuary. "Ah, harmony," he said.

Danny caught the sound of the choir warming up on the far side of the cathedral.

"There is such beauty in the way singular voices come together and produce an even sweeter collective sound."

"What the hell does that have to do with what we're talking about?" Danny asked, irritated by Michael's shift of focus.

"Daniel, people want to share their goodness, their kindness, with one another through their words and deeds. But you should know better than most that to do so they must be willing to be vulnerable. They have to *choose* to be unsteady, uncomfortable, even to endure pain in order to do the right thing. You and your cousin must commit to protecting others who are willing to step out in that way, as you have done before in your line of work, even if you did so unknowingly."

"I'm still not sure I follow," Danny admitted.

"It takes a catalyst, someone willing to lead by example, to show people a better way, a different way. Those who serve in this manner must not perish at the hands of these dark descendants. People need to feel safe and supported if they are to move toward the light. But once they do, they shine like so many stars in the night sky, making a collective, positive impact that astounds. Don't you want to play a part in setting that into motion? Doesn't Craig? Before you answer, you should know that it can be a lonely path. It means being satisfied with that path, being able to thrive in anonymity."

"If all we're supposed to do is work behind the scenes protecting others, why did Craig get all these awesome powers?" Danny countered. "What you say we're supposed to do doesn't seem to make the most of his gifts."

"Your cousin's abilities flow through him because he is a tool, an instrument. But for what purpose, he will wonder. Just as you are doing now. He is powerful, yes, but still ignorant of his purpose." Michael looked intently at Danny. "Let me ask you, Daniel. Is he ready to listen? Is he teachable?"

Danny thought the question ironic, given Craig's studious nature and how much Danny often learned from him.

"Everything in his life has led to these moments, these very decisions," Michael said.

At last, it clicked for Danny. "New challenges are coming at him. It's going to get harder, isn't it?"

The priest nodded.

Danny wanted to help Craig on his journey and felt

mentally up to the task, but he worried that he might not be up to it physically anymore. Without realizing it, feelings of inadequacy spilled out of him.

"I failed Emma. I'm of little use to Craig now. Hell, at work, I'm more and more useless each day."

"The greatest way you can help Craig is to bring him into awareness. Who people become is rooted in their memories and experiences. Craig doesn't have any memory of what his father sparked in his palms so long ago. But you now know. You have seen its origins. You can guide him."

"I can try," Danny said hesitantly. "This is a lot to process."

"Craig needs to claim his power while also understanding why he has it and how to be responsible in the way he uses it. Without you to help him, he risks going down his own dark path."

Danny pressed his lips together. "Craig on a dark path? I don't see that. That's not Craig."

"Darkness doesn't fall each day because of the setting sun. It's the rotation of the earth—and the humans who choose to rotate away from the light—that creates the darkness."

"Again with the riddles!" Danny said, exasperated. "Come on, Michael, Craig is as good as they come. Hell, I would've died in that church if he hadn't kept me alive."

"Did he?"

"What do you mean? Of course he did."

Michael smiled. "This time I won't give you a riddle, but are you familiar with the biblical saying: 'I will exalt you, my Lord, for you have lifted me up and have not let my enemies triumph over me. I cried out to you, and you restored me to health. You brought me up from the dead, restored my life, as I was going to the grave.' Does that sound similar to what happened to you in Iowa?"

"Are you saying Craig wasn't the one who kept me from bleeding out?"

"I'm saying he is a vessel through which power can flow. Its outcome can be positive or negative. Your cousin's situation is unique—it has not been encountered before in the entirety of the long line of defenders of this faith. He didn't *agree* to accept it, and therefore he could be seduced to use his powers in ways that were never intended."

"Craig's been through a lot. He's the type of guy who'll wanna make a positive impact," Danny said.

"As I said, the way Craig received these powers is unique. But equally rare was what he did when you both battled the Tourist. Faced with his own death, he offered himself as sacrifice so that you might live. In doing so, he was cleansed, made pure."

"But pure is good, right?" Danny asked.

"Like anything that is pure, it is currently absent of any influence, a blank slate on which can be written good or ill intentions. It can take on the traits of that which it embraces, whether the influences it succumbs to are charitable or malevolent."

"You mean he's vulnerable right now. Like, in his heart. That these descendants could take him down a bad path."

"Once more, Craig is unlike any other who has received this gift. The way it came to him and the sacrifice he made for you has made him powerful. But he himself needs to be enlightened. If he isn't, what he's been gifted will be squandered at best. At worst . . . " Michael didn't finish his sentence.

"C'mon! You can't leave me hanging with that."

"I know that both of you have been impatient to grasp the meaning of these powers during these last two years.

Know that the time is now upon you. The need to help him understand has become urgent."

Danny opened his mouth to press on, but Michael raised a hand. He let the other hand drift to his forehead.

"Our time today is ending." Michael closed his eyes and quietly coughed. It was the first time in their conversation that he looked vulnerable, human, not the powerful force that spoke behind Father Timothy's eyes.

"What is it? Are you all right?" Danny asked.

"Father Timothy is sick and slowly getting worse. I have long accompanied the good Father so your path and mine could cross in this time and place through his soul. But the human frailty from which he suffers is something I cannot mend."

"But I still have so many questions. Are there others like Craig in the world? Can't we keep talking?"

"Yes, there are others—a precious few—though their numbers dwindle. But yes, they do exist. As for our discussion, we cannot continue today. Father Timothy is waning under the physical toll of my speaking through him. We can certainly meet again, however. And it would be best if Craig can accompany you when we do."

"Why have you told me all of this instead of him?" Danny asked.

"He has been in his own head for too long. He needs someone he trusts to bring him into this awareness before he sees me. He needs you." Michael grew quiet for a moment before resuming ominously. "Dark times lie ahead, Daniel. Craig must surrender to a greater plan. He needs to push ahead—and survive—so he can pass along what he has within him. You must first make him understand that."

Michael stared at Danny with steely eyes. "Know this. The

next battle Craig faces will be one of temptation."

12

COALESCENCE

Master Jason was in a rare position. He grimaced through the pain. Craig had cocked Jason's arm behind his back and pinned him face down on the mat with his legs atop his body. He was bracing Jason's arm with his knees and was awkwardly twisting his instructor's wrist toward the ceiling with both hands.

Then, slowly, as if reluctant to relent, Jason reached out his free hand and tapped sharply twice on the mat, the sign that he had submitted. Craig released him from his grip, and both men relaxed on the mat.

Jason shook his head, clearly impressed. "That was good, Craig. Your skill and precision have definitely ticked up lately. There's real power and authority in the way you're fighting."

Craig sat up on the mat, a satisfied smile curled on his face. "Yeah. I feel different, for sure. Good, I think, but different too."

Craig's hair was tousled and damp with sweat, his *karategi* disheveled from the match. But he didn't feel tired; rather, he felt empowered.

"That did seem to go pretty well," a woman's voice said from across the room.

Jason and Craig both turned to locate the speaker. The gym was nearly empty except for the two of them and one other pair sparring on the far side of the mat. Samantha was seated on a bench and had evidently been watching their encounter unfold.

"Oh, you again?" Craig said, his tone light and mocking. He felt confident, emboldened by the success of his sparring session. He stood and walked toward her. She tossed him a towel as he approached.

As he caught it, she said, "I know it's Craig. But Craig who?"

"Henriksen. Craig Henriksen." He sat down beside her.

"Fancy college guy's got a fancy name."

"And yours is Samantha . . . ?"

"Wall. And it's Sam. Sam Wall."

"Good name for a stubborn girl who likes to put up—"

"Walls," Sam interrupted. "Cute. I get it."

She seemed genuinely interested in getting acquainted and willing to play along. Craig noticed how easy their banter was today, not as tense as conversations had recently been with Lauren, especially after their evening at Santori's. His interaction with Sam was refreshing.

With no trace of shyness or hesitation, Craig went on. "Going to get in some groundwork today?" he asked, referring to the term that described the sparring done while wrestling on the mat.

Sam pointed to her jeans, T-shirt, and jacket. "Nah. Got a few things to take care of before my shift in a few hours. Thought I'd catch up with you."

"Oh? Think maybe I'm not done peeling back your layers?"

"Ha! Let's just say I might have learned you've got a few layers yourself." She cocked one eyebrow, as if to remind him of the strange things she'd noticed in their last encounter.

"Let's not get carried away," Craig said modestly.

Sam maintained the slightly furrowed brow and direct

stare she had leveled at him before, but it appeared to soften. "I just—it's just not easy to find people who give a shit about things. Someone who will take an interest. You seemed interested in the fact that I can sense it when people want to do harm to others."

"I think you'll find that I give a shit about a lot of things," Craig said as he smiled.

They spent the next several minutes in lighthearted conversation, sometimes pausing as they watched the other students come and go. They discussed their schedules, how long they'd been practicing martial arts, and current events. Craig had several commitments to keep during the day, but their free-flowing conversation had pushed them to the back burner.

Then Craig's phone rang in his gym bag. "Sorry," he said as he retrieved it. It was Danny. "I need to take this," he told Sam, then answered the phone. "Danny, what's up?" Craig said.

"What's up?" Danny repeated. "What's up is that I've been trying to get ahold of you."

Sam turned her attention to the matches taking place on the mats.

"I know," said Craig. "I haven't been avoiding you. Just trying to smooth things over."

At that, Sam cast a puzzled look in Craig's direction.

"Right," Danny acknowledged. "But listen, I *really* need to bring you up to speed on that guy I've been talking to."

"What guy?"

"At the church."

"Oh, right. We didn't get around to it before Lauren showed up at dinner—"

Danny kept talking, but Craig stopped short as he looked past Sam toward the door.

Lauren had entered the gym, her eyes fixed on Craig and Sam. Sam returned the stare. Anxiety flooded through him, but he wasn't sure why; he wasn't doing anything wrong. But Lauren had never shown up at one of his sessions before. Something must be up.

"Uh, Danny, I've got to go," he said.

"Why? Dude, we have to talk, and soon."

"I hear you, but I've got a little situation here."

"Lauren again? By the way, how did the other night turn out?"

"Going now," Craig said, singsong. As he hung up the phone, he could hear Danny say, "Call me back."

Lauren walked confidently toward them. Craig glanced from Sam to Lauren as he hastily introduced the two. Sam seemed completely at peace in the situation. For her part, Lauren didn't seem jealous exactly—not angry—but she definitely looked curious.

"What brings you here?" Craig asked his girlfriend.

"I was just in the area and thought I'd swing by before you head off to meet with Madison."

Craig knew that reason didn't add up, but he wasn't about to question her, not with this tenuous interaction underway.

"Right, Madison," Craig said. Now he remembered that he promised Lauren he would make good on his commitment to meet her friend.

"And also to remind you that we have dinner tonight with my folks—"

"At seven. I remember," he said. Had Lauren slipped that in for Sam's benefit?

"I should leave you two to your planning," Sam said.

Without taking her eyes off Craig, Lauren responded, "No, you're fine right here. No worries."

"Actually, we probably should get going," Craig said to Lauren.

"You should get going, Craig. You do have a busy afternoon planned. We'll be fine here without you," Lauren demurred.

"Um . . ." Craig started. Then the light bulb went on: Lauren wanted to talk to Sam alone. He quickly resigned himself to the inevitability of a conversation between the two of them.

"Okay. Well, I'll catch you next time, Sam?"

"Yeah, sounds good."

Trying one last time, Craig said, "Lauren? You sure?"

"You go on ahead, Craig. I'll be fine."

Craig snatched his gym bag and headed for the door. This was a strange feeling; he'd never been the focus of two women's attention before.

Turning back as he pushed the door, he said, "Okay, I'll see you at the apartment later."

"Yup, before we head to dinner," Lauren confirmed.

Craig started down the stairwell, apprehensive about how their conversation might go down.

Lauren turned to survey Sam, who stood silently under her gaze, unfazed.

"Actually, I need to leave soon too," Lauren said. She eyed Sam up and down and cocked her head to the side. "I just wanted to meet the mystery woman that Craig spoke of. You don't look like you came here to work out."

"Nah. Just wanted to catch up with Craig again," she said unabashedly. "We had a misunderstanding in one of our sessions, and I wanted to make sure things were good."

"And were they?" Lauren asked, offering nothing further, instead watching for Sam's reaction.

"Yeah, they were," Sam responded, still looking at ease. "So, you just popped in today to see who the heck I was?"

"Something like that," Lauren responded coldly.

As if to reassure her, Sam said, "Craig's a good guy. I'm starting to find that out about him. But I'm sure you already know that."

"He is an extremely good guy," Lauren agreed.

An awkward silence extended between the two women. Sam appeared like she was about to advance the conversation when Lauren broke it off.

"I'm sure we'll cross paths again. But until then, I'll ask that you be careful."

Sam flashed a puzzled look. But before she could speak, Lauren spun on her heel and pushed her way through the door and out of the gym.

13

RECONNECTION

Danny exhaled sharply and glared across the squad room from his desk, oblivious to the bustle of the precinct office. Craig had just hung up on him. He needed to sit his cousin down and finally come clean about his conversations with Michael and his new depth of understanding about Craig's abilities. And the situation it put them both in.

"Sounds like you're a man on a mission to tell someone something." Lieutenant Mason had walked up behind him. Danny twisted around to look up at him. He wasn't in a mood to ingratiate himself with his boss and his greeting reflected that.

"What's up?" he said tersely.

Mason walked around to the front of Danny's desk. "Just wanted to let you know I've been trying to see things a little more from your perspective."

"Oh?" Now the lieutenant had Danny's full attention.

"Yeah. I don't think I've given you enough credit for what you've gone through and how difficult it's been to get back to this point."

"Really? That's what you've been thinking? Huh. Well, this shit hasn't been easy, that's for sure. What made you come around to seeing things from my perspective?"

"Funny you should ask that," Mason said. He pulled a chair from a neighboring desk, spun it around backward, and sat down to join Danny. "When I first read your file, I thought it curious that our paths hadn't crossed since I joined the force."

Danny knew Mason had only been with Chicago PD for a few years after leaving the military, so it didn't seem altogether implausible that they hadn't met.

"I got to know Eric Hammond pretty well when I joined. We were both in the same branch of service, so we got connected through an informal buddy network the force makes available to vets."

Hammond is a veteran? "I didn't know he served," Danny said. "So you got to know Hammond."

"Yeah, and he was a real help to me early on. When I took over here, I thought it would be a good idea for him and me to catch up because he was your CO when things went down a couple of years ago."

"You've talked with him recently?" Danny kept it to himself, but he was annoyed by this, given how difficult it had been for him to connect with Hammond lately.

"Sure. Had lunch with him last week. He's been in and out a lot lately, with his mother recently passing and all. But we finally connected."

"Hammond's mother died?" Danny was stunned. He hadn't known.

Mason nodded, compassion plain on his face. "Yes, and his mom was a huge influence on him. Raised him by herself—you know that? Ever since she took ill a couple of years ago, it's been hard on him."

Danny shook his head, then gazed out the window. He regretted not having known something so important about a man he considered a friend.

"I . . . I didn't know," Danny admitted, turning back to look at Mason.

"Ah, it's okay. Eric was pretty private about it. Anyway, he gave me a pretty good perspective on you. And your cousin."

The last statement caught Danny by surprise and made him suspicious.

"It must have been a lot for you to shoulder at the time, a lot for both of you. I appreciate that more now that Eric has walked me through it."

"How so?"

As if ticking off a laundry list, Mason said, "Well, you were becoming the shit with your investigative work when that serial killer landed on the scene."

Danny couldn't keep a slight smile from crossing his face as he reflected on it. What Mason said was true.

"But then things got difficult—at least, that's what Eric shared."

"What exactly did he tell you?"

"It would've been a tall order for anybody," Mason repeated. "Not only was the Tourist taunting you with notes, but he kept getting closer and closer to you, hitting home, first with your informants and ultimately, well . . ." He hesitated.

"Go on," Danny said.

"Finally reaching your girl. That had to be hard to bear."

Danny took a deep breath but said nothing. His first thought was about Maggie, an older lady he had gotten to know on his beat who was killed by the Tourist. Then his mind went to Emma, whom Mason was referencing. She had added much to his life in a short period, and her death had left an emotional hole larger than he sometimes realized.

"I'm not one to bitch about it," Danny finally said, "but unless they have most of the picture, like Hammond does, it's hard to get people to understand."

"About your cousin," Mason went on. "Craig."

Danny perked up.

"I know I gave you grief about wanting to pull him into crime scenes," Mason said.

"You gave me grief, all right."

"Well, Hammond had high praise, not just for you. He told me to ask you how Craig was doing. He knew Craig was reluctant to get pulled into cases, but that he didn't shy away from them when push came to shove. He said you wouldn't even be here today if not for Craig."

"That's absolutely true," Danny said.

"And he told me your cousin had scars left over from when he was growing up."

"Hammond shared all that with you?" Danny was surprised by the extent of it.

"Yeah, he did. I think Eric felt like he had left you both hanging when he opted for the administrative role downtown. When I went to meet with him—and I'll admit now that I was skeptical about you both—he set me straight."

"Eric's been about as stand-up a guy as I've met since I've been on the force. What's it been . . . ten years?" Danny reflected.

"That's a good call, stand-up guy." Mason paused. "Eric also told me you and he have been playing tag recently, haven't had a chance to meet up. But he did tell me he's been keeping an eye out for you from a distance."

Mason eyed Danny's weaponized cane, which was leaning against his desk. Sensing where his gaze had drifted, Danny absently reached out and grabbed the handle. A knowing smile spread across Mason's face. *So Mason knows about this too*, Danny thought.

"Anyway, what he's told me about you two carries a ton of weight. I want to make sure you know that. I'm coming to understand your situation—and Craig's—a little better."

"Thanks, Lieutenant. I appreciate you making the effort to do that."

Mason placed his forearms on the back of the chair and leaned forward. "So how can I help, Walsh?"

Taken aback by the unexpected offer, Danny had to think for a minute. Finally, he said, "Let me do my thing. Trust me when I tell you I can get things done like I used to. I can be 'the shit' again if you give me the chance." The two men locked eyes and Mason nodded while he thought it over.

An officer from the dispatch desk approached Mason to brief him on some recent disturbances in the industrial area known as the Stockyards, where an increasing amount of criminal activity had been occurring. It was the same area Danny had questioned his twitchy informant about. His mind wandered to that encounter as Mason and the desk officer talked.

When the officer left, Mason turned to Danny and said, "Let me check this out first, but if you're gonna be available, I might want you to dig into it further. With so many of our resources getting siphoned off to terrorism, I feel like we've been going too light on the usual characters."

"Sure, makes sense," Danny agreed. He hoped this was the opening he'd been waiting for.

"Good. I got a feeling that things are building up with the gangs there, and the mob of course, while we're off chasing the feds around. If we can learn more about what's going on down there, it might help us to head off further trouble." He paused briefly, his thoughts returning to Danny's request from a few moments before. "I had read up on you, Walsh, before Hammond gave me this latest intel, and one thing I remember is that you were a damn good detective."

"I don't believe that's changed, Lieutenant. So yeah, I'm game. Let me grab a couple of uniforms and get on over there."

"Agreed," Mason said.

The desk officer returned and asked Mason to take care of some issues that had cropped up in the intake area to triage.

Before he left, Mason said, "Walsh, I want you to know that I'm okay with it if you look into what's going down there and see the need to involve that friend of yours." Though Mason had coded the message in the officer's presence, Danny heard it loud and clear: thanks to Hammond, Mason had come to terms with the fact that Danny and Craig had been a team, an effective one—and that Danny might need to use him again.

The question that remained was how much Mason knew about what Craig had actually done on their team. Did he know about Craig's supernatural powers? Was he deliberately trying to create an opening for Craig? He needed to meet with Hammond sometime soon to find out exactly how much he had spilled to Mason. But until then, he intended to take full advantage of his newfound investigative freedom.

He stood and looked across the squad room, then walked over and looked out the window. It had been a surprising turn of events, and he felt invigorated. The cell phone on his desk buzzed and started dancing toward the edge. Danny snatched it up, hoping to hear Craig's voice. But the display number was blocked.

Danny answered, his suspicions aroused.

"Is this Detective Daniel Walsh?"

"Who is this?"

"Of course. My apologies, Detective. This is Colonel Matthew Bishop. We met at the precinct. You gave me your card."

It took a second to remember because there had been so much on his mind lately that he'd put it out of his thoughts. "Right, yeah, I remember."

"Is now an acceptable time for us to talk?"

"Sure."

"You mentioned something when we spoke that I haven't been able to let go of. Specifically, you spoke of someone you knew who had undergone a series of traumatic events."

"That's right. Someone I know really well."

"You said you were drawn to the discussion I had with you and your colleagues about men I've known who were transformed by trauma in ways that are truly remarkable. Does that sound like what may have happened to the person you described to me when we met?"

"Yes, it could be. He's been through a lot. And since you and I talked, he's learned quite a bit more about his . . . remarkable abilities." This was a tough call, and Danny was struggling with it. He didn't want to share too much information, but he didn't want to lose the opportunity to explore Craig's abilities with someone who might have some expertise to offer. "He and I have been trying to figure out what they are and what they're all about. You seemed to be describing people who may have become similarly . . . empowered."

Feeling tense, Danny stewed in his thoughts but resisted the urge to break the silence.

"Empowered," Bishop said at last. "That's a good word for the unique people I've encountered in my travels."

"Okay, good. Because I think Craig needs to know there might be someone else out there who's been down this road before and can help him."

"Craig is his name. I see."

Danny grimaced. He hadn't meant to reveal personal details so soon.

"Well, you and I weren't able to talk at length when we met," Bishop continued, "and I would be remiss if I didn't offer to help a man who may be experiencing a phenomenon with which I am familiar."

"That would be great, Mr. Bishop."

"Please, just call me Bishop. It's a form of brevity I still prefer from my time in the military."

"Sure, Bishop. I appreciate your offer. He's been trying to unravel this mystery for some time now."

"Even more important that I meet your friend. I have time this coming Friday. Would that work?"

"Sure, where are you thinking?"

"Chinatown," Bishop said.

"Chinatown? Why there?" It seemed a curious location to suggest.

"I'm sorry if that sounds strange, Detective. There is a World War II center nearby that I like to frequent. Also, I like the obscurity I can find there."

"Huh," Danny said. He found the colonel's desire for anonymity odd, but he didn't want to press him further on the point right now.

But Bishop seemed to sense the question. "Let me explain," he said. "You see, aside from specific engagements, such as addressing your police department or other speaking obligations, I try to avoid the glare of publicity. I'm sure you understand."

"Sure, I guess so." In truth, though, Danny didn't understand at all. He filed this unusual tidbit in the back of his mind to consider at a later time.

Bishop gave Danny the address and suggested a time in the late afternoon. Danny agreed without knowing whether it could work for Craig. The need to schedule the meeting would strengthen his resolve to catch up with his cousin about the myriad of things they so urgently needed to discuss.

"I'll see you then," Danny said.

"Very good," Bishop replied. "One of my men will be available at the door to escort you in. Good day, Detective."

Danny hung up the phone. Michael had told him there were only a few others who had been gifted and tasked as Craig had been. Danny was eager to find out whether Bishop had known any of them and if he might be able to help convince Craig of the importance of pursuing his destined path.

The desk officer who had come to fetch Mason returned. "Walsh, the Lieutenant has you green-lighted to take two uniforms out for the rest of the day to check out the Stockyards. You know who you want?"

Danny provided a few names, men he was comfortable with and who were quick on their feet, and the officer went off to queue them up.

Danny collapsed into his chair. Suddenly, he felt overwhelmed. He was still desperate to talk with Craig about Michael and get everything he knew off his chest. He needed to catch up with Hammond. And while he longed to take advantage of the unexpected opportunity to return to field work, the job he'd been so good at was now competing with so many other things.

Too bad, Walsh, he thought. *You'll have to deal with every-thing else later. Right now, you'd better get your ass down to the Stockyards.*

14

HELL'S FAITHFUL

The near west side of Chicago had long been an area of mob and gang-related activity. Whether it was the Back of the Yards, New City, or Canaryville, the proximity of these neighborhoods to the intersection of various freight train lines and extensive warehousing space fostered a hotbed of nefarious activity. It was a perfect spot for crime rings to steal from the shipments that passed through in relative isolation, and then fence what they stole in the more heavily populated areas to the south and west of the city.

In a large administrative area of a dilapidated warehouse, an animated discussion was taking place between members of one of the area's long-active gangs. The three men who carried on this debate offered their varying perspectives.

"Those assholes got the drop on another one of the electronics shipments, I'm telling ya. It had to be them, Clint!" one of the men said as he paced along a wall. He was short, bald, and cleanly shaven. Several tattoos crawled out from under his shirt and leather jacket and wound their way up the side of his neck. His jacket flapped open as he walked, and his diminutive stature cut an almost cartoonish figure every time he turned.

"You're probably right, Roddy. But raging about it here ain't gonna do a damn bit of good, Clint said.

Undeterred, Roddy went on. "Those damn Russians know

this is our area, but they roll in here a couple of months ago and are already siphoning off our flow?"

Clint was one of two of Roddy's associates in the warehouse. He sat at a large metal table, spartan and bare, devoid of any paperwork that would be associated with an honest business. Clad in a black T-shirt and dark jeans, Clint wore sunglasses perched on his nose well below the eyes. His thick black hair dangled along one side of his face.

Looking over the glasses, he said to Roddy, "What will make a difference is if we teach them a real, painful lesson."

"We've said that before, man. The last couple times," Roddy went on, still agitated and fidgety. "We've hit one of their boys before to send that lesson, but it clearly ain't getting through."

The third gang member stood with his back to them, taller and more imposing than the others. Long hair trailed out in a braided ponytail from under a bandana that covered his head. He was looking out a grimy window. He wore a leather jacket, biker style, with dense embroidery on the back: a skull with wild, manic-looking eyes and the words "Hell's Faithful," one word above the skull and one below it.

The dingy light coming through the window waned. The biker turned to the other men. A lit cigarette danced on his lips as he spoke.

"Those Russian bastards are gonna learn to move on to other work," he said. "We're gonna hit them *hard*. Let's start with that scrawny piece-of-shit capo of theirs, Anatoli, or whatever the fuck his name is."

Instantly, the dynamics in the room became clear. The other two men were energized now that their leader Vince had spoken up.

Roddy stopped in midstride and nodded his head vigorously in agreement. "Hell yeah! Vince is goddamn right."

Clint concurred. "You got the right idea, as usual."

Suddenly, a new voice entered the conversation, coming from a doorway on the far side of the room.

"The menacing figures you gentlemen cut would no doubt strike fear into anyone."

Clint leapt out of his chair and drew a handgun. He leveled it in the direction of the stranger's voice. A thin, older man wearing a dark driving cap entered the room.

"And who the fuck are you?" Vince demanded. The other two remained on alert but let the old man approach. He stopped about thirty feet from them, keeping a little extra distance between himself and their leader.

"Who? Me?" the older man said mockingly, pointing to his chest.

Vince gestured to Clint to lower his weapon, apparently seeing no threat from an old man who had stumbled into their meeting. Clint complied, slowly, but kept the firearm ready at his side.

"Who the hell does this guy thinks he is?" Roddy said. "C'mon! We're letting this old boy walk right in here?" He shot a look at Vince, challenging his boss to exact some kind of penalty for trespassing.

Taking the cue, Vince said, "Looks like you wandered into the wrong fuckin' warehouse, padre. You looking for something?"

The stranger's dark eyes stared at the men from under his cap. "Of course I am!" he answered with contrived cheerfulness. "Friendship! We four have similar intentions. That should make us natural allies."

"I don't know what the hell you're rambling about," Vince responded, "but if you think you can walk in here where you don't belong and then walk right back out, well, that just ain't gonna happen."

Apparently unintimidated, the old man walked farther into the room. It was as if he was talking to himself rather than the three gang members in the warehouse.

"I need to show him what we are capable of," the old man said, "so he will choose to embrace his power for his own self-protection. That would be splendid," he added, half to himself. "Oh, and as for me? I have no intention of leaving just yet." The false cheer fell away and the old man's voice took on a deadly seriousness. "I'm afraid none of you will ever leave this building."

Confused, the men looked at each other, contemplating their next move.

In a flash, the old man launched himself into the air and hurtled toward Clint. He tried to raise his gun, but the old man immobilized his arm, and the thug squeezed off a round that went into the floor. Then the old man grabbed Clint by the neck and slashed out his windpipe with his bare hand. The gun dropped as blood sprayed from the gangster's neck. He died as he fell to the floor.

The other two, stunned by the speed and ferocity of the stranger's attack, fumbled in their jackets for their own weapons.

But they weren't quick enough.

The old man snatched up one of the heavy metal chairs that surrounded the table and fixed his eyes on Vince. With a strength that belied his slight frame, he raised it above his head and threw it at Vince. It hurtled through the air at unnatural velocity, as if some unseen force was powering it faster than any man could possibly toss it. It slammed into Vince, sending him crashing against a wall and crumpling to the floor.

The old man was now focused on Roddy, who had finally moved to draw his own gun. The attacker was on the gangster in an instant, clutching his wrist in a talon-like grip and driving wrist and gun together forcefully against the wall. Roddy's wrist shattered and the gun dropped to the floor. Roddy bellowed in pain. Then the old man wrapped one hand around the thug's neck, squeezing his windpipe, and fashioned the fingertips of his other hand into a knife-like point.

He paused for a moment and smiled into the face of his victim, who stared into his cold, dark eyes with an expression of helplessness and terror.

"What the hell do you want? What's this all about?" Roddy croaked, pleading.

The old man drew back his arm and drove his pointed fingers into the gangster's chest, piercing him just below the collarbone.

Roddy let out a high-pitched scream as he absorbed the blow. He gasped for air and slumped toward the floor as the old man held him up by one arm, then withdrew his hand from the thug's chest.

"Normally, I have no quarrel with your kind at all," he said, neither his words nor his voice betraying any acknowledgment of the melee he had just caused. "You're helpful, actually, in some instances. With the work I usually do, of course. But now I need you to serve a different purpose, a very important one. You see, I must flush him out. We have come close before, but now we need him to show himself and confirm his identity for us."

"What the hell are you talking about?" gasped Roddy,

growing woozy and disoriented from shock and the loss of blood. He gathered himself up as best he could to beg for his life. "I got no idea what you're talking about, man! Please, just let me go. Please!"

Ignoring the thug's begging, the old man said, "I hear your friend stirring across the room. Oh, let's check on him. This will be fun! A treat for both of you."

The old man dragged Roddy across the room to where Vince was sprawled out, barely seeming to exert any effort in accomplishing this task. As they approached Vince, he rose to his hands and knees and attempted to crawl away, but he soon realized there wouldn't be time.

"Wait! Hold it, hold it! Just wait a minute, man!" Vince rolled onto his back and held up his hands in a gesture of surrender as the old man stopped just in front of him. "You ain't gotta do this. Just leave, and I ain't gonna say anything about this."

"Of course you aren't." The old man narrowed his eyes in annoyance. Then the cheery voice was back. "And now, the treat I promised!"

He pulled Roddy to his feet and propped him up next to Vince. He had both men's full attention.

"Now look! Look, my friend, at your partner in crime. Watch the truly spontaneous nature of his reaction. One who witnesses death!"

All Roddy had time for was to feel a rush of apprehension. Then he saw his own blood spray across the face of Vince. For an instant, he registered shock and horror on that face. Then his vision went black forever.

Tossing Roddy's lifeless body aside, the old man crouched to engage Vince. He flipped off his driving cap, revealing a ruddy, wrinkled face and cold, dark eyes that flashed with excitement as he spoke.

"A treat it was, don't you think?" he sneered as he leaned over Vince.

"Please! Please, man. I'm begging you!"

"Of course, you are." He smiled into the gangster's blood-speckled face. "But now it is your time."

The old man ripped off Vince's bandana and grabbed him by the hair, pulling him up off the floor and toward him with one hand as he plunged his other hand, fingers pointed, deep into the man's chest near his heart.

Craig had been in the Wicker Park apartment for some time waiting for Lauren to return from work so they could go to dinner with her parents. He still felt uneasy about having left Lauren with Sam at the martial arts studio. He didn't know why Lauren would want to talk to Sam. He also felt a tinge of guilt despite knowing he had done nothing wrong.

He was in the bedroom changing for dinner. He slipped on a T-shirt, then stood in front of the full-length mirror. Something in his reflection caught his eye. He looked stronger than he'd realized. The precise definition of his chest and arm muscles reminded him of the image of his father he had seen when he re-created the battle his father had waged with the Tourist.

Just then, his phone rang on the nightstand where he'd left it. It was Danny.

"I'm glad I caught you, man," Danny said.

"Danny. What's up? Anything wrong?"

"No, not wrong. I've just been processing a lot lately. I'm gonna need your help with it."

"I can't really talk now. Lauren's going to be here in a second, and we're heading to her parents' place for dinner in the city."

Danny huffed. "I need us to talk."

"Then talk, man. What's holding you back?"

"Not over the phone."

"Never over the phone, I know." Craig had grown tired of this standard response. "Listen, I've been pissing Lauren off in a bunch of different ways lately. I can't afford to do it again tonight."

Craig heard the rattling of keys in the front door.

"Shit. She's here. I have to go, Danny."

"Craig. For real?"

"Tell me this, Danny. Are you hurt? Or in some kind of distress? Anything like that?" Craig had learned some time ago how to ferret out whether Danny needed him for a personal issue or wanted to use him for some professional reason.

"No, it's not like that. But—"

"Then we can talk later. All right? You've been way better lately about being considerate of my time. Let's keep that trend going."

"Craig, you gotta promise me—"

"Later. We'll talk later. Take care. With that, Craig ended the call. He threw on an Oxford buttoned-down shirt and quickly made his way out of the bedroom.

"Hey," he said to Lauren. "How was the rest of your day?"

Lauren let her work bag slip off her shoulder and onto the couch, surprised by his attentiveness but with an inkling of why he might be behaving that way. "It was . . . interesting," she said.

Craig cut to the chase. "Did you and Sam talk for long? I mean, she's been a good sparring partner, just a little tough to figure out, so I've been drawing her out. But that's really all it's been."

"Craig, relax. I can see that. And remember what I've told you before about our relationship. You don't have to feel the need to explain things to me. You're your own person. I trust you."

She smiled, but Craig thought he sensed a certain reluctance in her expression.

"Well, sure. I know that. Just didn't want you to get the wrong idea."

Lauren thumbed through a few pieces of mail on the table. "She's nice, I can see that. And harmless, I think." She gave him a coy smile.

"Oh, really?" Craig flashed a smile back at her, relieved.

Lauren turned away from Craig and said under her breath, "At least, to you."

"What was that?" Craig asked.

"Nothing. We should get going soon, if you're ready."

"Yeah. I just want to make sure you and I are good." Craig said cautiously. This was the first time he worried that Lauren might be genuinely jealous, something he didn't want to result from his desire to learn more about Sam. His interest in Sam was real and still unexplained, but he wanted to make sure Lauren knew that it wasn't romantic.

"You and I are fine, Craig." Lauren patted Craig's shoulder as she moved past him.

After Lauren freshened up, they made their way to the elevated train platform a few blocks from the apartment. A light mist fell as they waited for the train to arrive from the north. There were few other people waiting on the platform to board.

"Little light for a Thursday," Craig mused.

When the train pulled in and they entered a car, they were surprised to find that they had it all to themselves.

"Look at you, arranging private transportation to dinner." Lauren smiled.

"Well, I thought you'd probably had a rough day," Craig grinned back.

They sat down and snuggled together.

"You do know how precious you are, don't you?" she asked.

Lauren had a way of making him feel cared for, a feeling he had been denied when he was young after his father passed. He let her question settle onto him like a warm blanket as the train left the platform and proceeded toward downtown Chicago.

After a few minutes, Lauren said, "Oh, I forgot to ask. How was your meeting with Madison?"

"Um, well . . ."

Lauren's curious expression melted into one of disappointment. "You're telling me you didn't visit with her like you said you were going to?"

The truth was that Craig had been so flustered after leaving Lauren and Sam together that he had completely forgotten. Instead, he'd spent some time clearing his head and then went to the university bookstore to buy the books he'd need for his classes.

Rather than feeling guilty to the look she'd shot him, he decided to press in a different direction. "You're not going to make a 'thing' out of this, are you?"

Lauren's brow dipped as she eyed him critically.

Just then, the train came to an unexpected stop. They glanced out the windows, looking for landmarks. They were somewhere between the Damen and Division platform stations.

"I guess you *are* gonna make it a thing—that was a dramatic way to make your point," Craig joked. Then he looked around again and frowned. "Think we should be worried about this?"

"I don't think so," she said. "This happened during my commute about three times in the last couple of weeks."

A voice on the intercom announced there had been a minor mechanical issue that should be resolved in just a few minutes.

Lauren took up their earlier conversation where Craig had left it.

"No, I'm not trying to make a thing out of it."

"What gives, then?"

"Let's just say I think the universe supports the highest and best use of what we each have to offer."

"The universe," Craig repeated skeptically. It wasn't the first time Lauren had talked about a higher way of thinking, an idea that was a bit too metaphysical for Craig.

"Sure, the universe." she said, "Hear me out."

Craig recognized the signs: she was intent on landing a point with him. It frequently worked, and he always found it cute. He liked to indulge her.

"Clearly you've been gifted with some special powers. Don't you think their purpose might be to benefit others? To help people who don't have them?"

"Are you saying I should stop trying to understand the things I can do and instead see how they might be used for—what? Complete strangers?"

"Doesn't that make sense?"

"No, it doesn't. Does it make sense to you, Lauren?" Craig challenged.

She looked hurt for a moment. A crack had emerged in the foundation of understanding she had hoped had been building between them.

Without waiting for her answer, Craig tried to seize the upper hand in a debate with her. "I've come a long way so far, building a box around all this." He placed his fingertips together for emphasis, his hands forming a cage. "Trying to piece everything together, to hold on to everything I've learned and understand what it means."

"I get what you're saying, Craig. But we become who we are either by embracing power or giving it away. I just think it's important for you to resist fitting this neatly in a box, or you'll soon get defined by it."

Craig squinted and shook his head in frustration. "I know, you've said that before."

"And it's still true. You need to realize that you still have the ability to shape who you become and what you do."

"And that's what I'm doing, aren't I? I'm trying to learn more about these bizarre things, like the crime scene stuff. And I've also been focused on my future. You said you've seen me sharpen my focus—going back to school, working on martial arts. Isn't that enough?"

She let out a sigh of impatience, as though he still wasn't getting it.

Craig pushed ahead. "You said when we got together that I was depressed, cynical. Well, I've gotten better because I'm focusing on myself. Trying to figure things out *about myself*. And I'm happier now."

"So that's it?"

"What's it?"

"The guy was happy."

"Huh?"

"That's what you want on your tombstone?"

It was an overly dramatic statement, even for Lauren. Craig frowned and fell silent.

"Seems to me you'd want more than just 'the guy was happy.' In a meaningful life, there's usually some positive struggle for real growth. I just want you to be able to feel like you've persevered through the challenges of your life to achieve something meaningful."

"Yeah, great. So, I don't deserve a little happiness by now," Craig said, his defensiveness plain.

Lauren stared at him as they sat in the quiet of the stopped train car.

Craig sensed a question in her silence and felt the need to respond. "Do you think I haven't struggled? Haven't you known me at all these past couple of years? You think all the shit that I've been through since I was little is no big deal?"

"Honey, you know that's not what I'm saying. I know you've had a lot of pain in your life." She continued to challenge him, but more gently now. "But do you think those struggles are unique to you? No doubt others have had similar ones. But do you know what you and those others have in common?"

"What?"

"Time," she said. "Ask yourself: time for what? To have what impact and to what end? None of us is guaranteed a tomorrow. How do you want to use your time?"

Craig clenched his jaw. "I have some awesome abilities, and I need to understand them."

"Fine, but you also need to do something with them," she countered. "Point them at something and move forward."

"I've got no problem moving forward. But in terms of the

present and the future, shouldn't I focus more on happiness? With you, for example?"

She softened, happy to be mentioned as a focus of his search for happiness. "There is a ton of literature that says the reason souls come to Earth is to experience adversity. To see the difference between bad and good, or dark and light. You still struggle with your past. I just don't want you to get stuck there. Life is about moving forward."

Craig opened his mouth but found he was at a loss to counter her argument—again.

"I worry that you're searching for conflict," Lauren said, "either within yourself or elsewhere. Maybe start thinking of ways the world can benefit from what you can do."

"I've gotten a lot of bloody lips from 'the world' over the years. It's tough to shake."

She remained silent, giving him time to realize he was playing the victim role. They had been here before.

Finally, he realized it too. "I'm doing it again, aren't I?"

Lauren's expression had become distant. She glanced around the train, as if wondering when it would start again. Without looking at him, she said, "Ultimately, you need to walk your own path, Craig."

Craig was caught off guard. It was the first time that he felt Lauren was deliberately trying to put distance between them.

"Life is about those nuggets of truth and insight that only get delivered to you one at a time," Lauren continued. "You'll slowly start to see how everything fits together. It can, and should, be a long slog. Sometimes disappointing, sometimes painful. But ultimately, it gets you where it's supposed to take you and to the role you're supposed to play. Whether or not that's clear to you yet or makes sense, I just think you have to be open to it."

Her words pushed a button inside of him that he had struggled to resist: the pull he felt to become reanimated by his uncanny powers. The ability to spontaneously heal that had recently returned. His inexplicable curiosity about Sam. It was ironic that now, when he was otherwise free of burdens and was receiving Lauren's love and attention, her words stoked within him a sense that some purpose remained unfulfilled.

He opened his mouth, not knowing what would come out of it. But he was sure of one thing: a schism had developed between the two of them that he hadn't known before.

Just then, the train started with a jerk. They were in motion again, heading toward the city.

15

SILHOUETTES OF THE SHADE

Craig and Lauren were having dinner in the downtown apartment of Lauren's parents, Jeff and Lynn Harris. The last time they'd been there was under markedly different circumstances. The Tourist had killed Emma, throwing Danny into a rage to find him. The police were watching over Craig and Lauren lest the Tourist take aim at others who were close to Danny. But they snuck away from their police escort to hide out briefly here, an apartment Lauren's father barely used. It was after this brief stay that Craig found the resolve to follow his gut and drive to Iowa to find his cousin and ultimately fight the Tourist with him.

Jeff and Lynn Harris greeted them at the door and invited them in. Craig remembered the tenth-floor apartment as modern but spartan in its furnishings. It now looked brighter and well-appointed. Large windows allowed for a nice view of the constellation of city lights and buildings all around. Craig had understood that Lauren's parents were spending much more time there than in their suburban home these days. As Jeff's retirement approached, they wanted to see if living downtown full time appealed to them.

They sat around a dining room table. Lauren's mother had prepared a meal of pasta and salad and had served wine. Craig hadn't spoken much to Lauren since their train ride into the city. Their argument there seemed to have ended flat, and neither of them wanted to advance that debate, least of all at her parents' apartment.

"So, Craig, how have things gone since you left GPH?" Jeff asked, referring to his accounting firm, Grey, Parker, and Harris.

"It's good," Craig said, between bites. He looked sideways at Lauren, trying to gauge her reaction. She had none; she was focused on eating her meal.

Noticing the silence around the table, Craig tried to expand on the answer. "I mean, I've been fortunate to have some extra time before classes start. I've been getting everything squared away with school—schedules and books and such—and working on some personal improvement, things like that."

"Well, we're glad someone is able to spend time with Lauren," Lynn said. Lauren flashed her a puzzled look. "Honey, I just mean that you spend a lot of time by yourself. And your relationship with Craig has been good for you in that way."

Craig could tell Lauren was put off by her mother's remark. But when he thought about it, he realized Lauren didn't have a big circle of friends. She worked in HR for her dad's firm, so he figured she would have a lot of interaction with others. This, coupled with her warm and congenial nature, didn't match the person her mother described.

"Mom, Dad, please." Lauren countered. "You're making me sound like a recluse or something."

"I didn't mean anything negative by it, dear." Lynn tried to mollify her daughter. "More like what your aunt Ginny used to say about you when you were growing up: 'That little girl of yours is such a saint!'"

"Oh, you were a *saint*, were you?" Craig said, grinning.

Lauren rolled her eyes in irritation.

Craig expected that any tension this evening would be between Lauren's parents; she had told him their marriage had been troubled in the past. But they exchanged warm glances throughout dinner. It was Craig and Lauren whose interaction was awkward, a hold-over from their discussion on the train.

"You mentioned personal improvement, Craig. A lot of introspection going on for you?" Jeff asked.

"Well, sure. It's a big life change, going from the workplace back to school, so I feel like I need to step back and think it through," Craig said. He hoped he didn't come off as too lackadaisical or self-interested. He was intent on being gracious this evening and hoped to wipe away any skepticism Jeff and Lynn might have about his being a worthy partner for Lauren. He worried that his departure from GPH had made him look selfish.

"How has your cousin been?" Jeff asked, changing the subject.

Craig raised his eyebrows, caught off-guard by the question. Lauren paused, waiting to see where her father was going.

Lynn appeared uncomfortable with her husband's question. "Jeff, I'm sure he's doing much better now. He's had well over a year to recuperate from his injuries, hasn't he?"

"Mom's right," Lauren cut in. "Danny's doing just fine. He's been working to get mainstreamed back onto the police force. The progress he's made is pretty impressive."

Craig flashed Lauren a smile. He appreciated her standing up for Danny.

Jeff furrowed his brow as he looked at his plate, picking

indiscriminately at his dinner. Then he looked at Craig and said, "I'm sure his recovery has been fine. But we've been thinking about what you two went through, and what his job still exposes him to every day. And the fact that it all comes so close to Lauren. And frankly, it makes us uncomfortable."

Craig set out to ease Jeff's concerns. "But he hasn't been out in the field that much so far. And, honestly, he and I don't really talk about his cases a lot—"

"But he *could* get back into the types of cases he used to, right?" Jeff interrupted. "And given how close you two are, you'll know about those cases. That could place our daughter awfully close to real danger. Again."

"Dad, really?" Lauren interjected.

"But it's really not—" Craig started.

Jeff was determined to make his point. "We just want to know our daughter is going to be safe, and that you're going to be every bit as solid for her as she says you are."

"Oh, Dad. Stop. You know I can take care of myself."

Lynn cut in, an edge in her voice. "Lauren, Craig and his cousin had a serial killer tracking them barely two years ago, didn't they?"

Lauren had raised her finger, preparing to argue, when Craig saw his cue to try to defuse the situation.

Turning to Lauren, he said, "Your dad's right."

Lauren now raised her eyebrows.

Drawing in a breath, Craig went on. "I get what he's saying. What happened to Danny and me in the church was a wake-up call. It's certainly changed him in all the ways you can imagine. You should know that it changed me too. I understand the danger in that line of work, the gravity of it.

And I wouldn't throw myself or anyone else who is important to me into that mix again."

Lauren's demeanor toward Craig instantly thawed. She smiled lovingly at him and placed her hand on his.

Craig faced Lauren's parents to underscore his point. "I'd never let anything happen to Lauren. I wouldn't hesitate to jump in front of a truck for her."

There was silence at the table as Jeff and Lynn considered what Craig had said.

Then Jeff said, "That's good to hear, Craig. Adopting Lauren was one of the greatest joys of our lives, the answer to a prayer for a couple who couldn't have children of our own. Her well-being means the world to us. We're glad to know you feel the same."

It took a moment for his words to sink in. Then Craig turned to Lauren and said, "Adopted?"

———◆•◆•◆———

"Why won't you just let it go?" Lauren called back over her shoulder as she continued walking. Craig stopped momentarily with his hands on his hips before quickening his pace to catch up to her. This chasing after her, talking to her back, was starting to become a pattern he wasn't eager to continue.

"After all the time we've spent together, I find out that you were adopted. Don't you think it would have been good for me to know that sooner?"

Lauren seemed offended. "Why? I've always known them as my true parents. Besides, I'm pretty sure I don't know the full extent of everything about you. In fact, I think you've got some nerve faulting me for not having brought this up before."

Walking beside her now, he shivered in the chill air of the late-spring night. They were nearly at the entrance to their apartment building when Craig jumped in front of her and stopped.

"Just let it go," Lauren huffed. "It's not a big deal. Why would it matter to you anyway?"

"It matters because you've helped me peel back a lot of layers of my own past. And thank you for that, by the way. But you didn't think to share this important layer of yours with me."

"Craig, I don't know. It slipped my mind."

"You *forgot* you were adopted? Come on, Lauren. What you mean is you didn't trust me enough to let me in on your secret."

Then a new voice entered the conversation. "Listen, I don't want to separate you two, but if I did, it would be the first domestic dispute I've worked since my rookie days." Danny was sitting on the low wall that stood several feet from the apartment.

"Dude! How long have you been there?" Craig asked.

"Not long. You didn't answer upstairs, so I've just been hanging out for a bit, thinking I might run into you."

"Just *thought* you might run into us?" Lauren asked, skeptically. "You know we live here."

"Hi, Lauren," Danny replied.

"Okay, Danny, what gives?" Craig asked.

"So, here's the deal. I need you for something. I need you to tag along with me and check out a scene one of our patrols came across near Fuller Park."

Lauren took a couple of steps toward Danny. "Tell me you're not taking him with you to do cases again."

"I'm sure it's not that big of a deal, Lauren," Craig seemed to downplay, perhaps excited that Danny was being called in to crime scenes again. He liked the feeling of being invited. But he also hated that he liked it.

"Seriously, Craig?" Lauren snapped. "And right after what you just told my dad at dinner not even an hour ago?"

"You know you and I are on the same side, right?" Danny said.

"Really?" Lauren snapped back. "I'm trying to help him move forward. You keep dragging him back into the past and these mysteries."

Craig's head moved back and forth as he watched them banter. It made him feel important and energized.

Danny seemed to catch excitement on Craig's face and pressed ahead. "Craig, we have to get going."

"You two do what you need to do," Lauren said. "I won't wait up." She then turned and stormed into the building.

Danny turned away and headed toward his car. "C'mon, Craig. Let's go."

———————

Craig looked around the dimly lit interior of a warehouse in the Back of the Yards area of Chicago's South Side. Danny stood near a back door and poked his head out to verify that the patrol officers who had initially arrived on the scene to secure it had followed his instructions and left. He nodded his head once, satisfied that he and Craig would have undisturbed access, then shut and locked the door and crossed the room to where Craig was standing. He had also ordered a delay in bringing in the Forensics unit, pending his initial assessment of the scene. This would buy them some time, he said.

"You sure those officers are gonna be okay with just leaving us in here alone?" Craig asked as he ventured further into the building.

"Craig, it's damn near eleven. None of those guys wants to keep hanging out until Forensics gets here. Plus, they'll help hold off the news crews once this hits the scanner. And I've got a little pull around here again."

Craig noticed Danny had regained some of his confidence and even some swagger, qualities that had been elusive since his recovery and return to the force.

"I've already looked things over," Danny said, "and there's some interesting stuff going on here besides the obvious. If you can, you know, do your thing again . . . it might help us piece together some info that's been missing since the Tourist."

Craig scanned the scene, the gruesome aftermath of three murders. Danny had shared with Craig on the ride over that the three victims were gang members. One had fallen near where Craig stood and suffered a lethal injury to his neck. The other two were further into the building. One of them appeared to have his throat slashed. He was lying in front of a third man who appeared to have been stabbed.

"Grisly stuff," Craig remarked. He wasn't sure if it was because of the time he'd spent away from this type of work, or because of the hardening he'd experienced after he and Danny fought the Tourist, but he was fully engrossed in the scene. He no longer felt dread or anxiety at the prospect of re-creating what had happened to these men, or with seeing who had done it.

"So, what's so interesting that you felt I needed to be here?"

"You'll see how it fits in," Danny replied coyly. "But first, tell me: are you ready to give it a shot again?"

Craig shrugged. "I might as well find out if this power is coming back along with the rest of them."

Craig scanned around the victim nearest where he and Danny stood, looking for a spatter of blood or some other bodily material that had been cast off but was still near the body. He spotted a small, angular streak of blood on a near wall close to the floor.

"There," he said.

Danny bent down and squinted at it. "That enough, you think?" he asked.

Craig raised an eyebrow. He felt strangely confident. "Hasn't it always been?"

He walked around the dead body, giving it a wide berth, then squatted near the stain. "Well, here goes nothing," he announced.

Standing several paces away, Danny drew in a breath and held it.

Craig held out his hand, paused briefly just short of the blood spatter, and then touched it.

The room grew lighter, and a surreal red mist gathered in the space, obscuring everything that had been previously visible. The chairs, the table, and the dead bodies all faded away as they were consumed by the haze. Only Craig and Danny remained visible, rooted in place but floating as the slow-moving reddish fog moved almost imperceptibly about the room. It unfolded as it had in previous times.

Then three dark silhouettes—the three victims—appeared. Craig felt a rush of adrenaline fill his chest as he watched the re-creation animate itself.

For his part, Danny stood up straighter as he leaned against his cane. An excited expression spread across his face. Craig was using one of his most extraordinary gifts again: tactile transference, the ability to replay a crime scene by touching the victim's blood.

"Look, Danny, it's starting to happen!" Craig exclaimed.

As they watched, the action began. A baldheaded man, short in stature, paced nearby and between them, clearly agitated. Another shape sat still at a table in the middle of the room. The third victim, a tall man striking an authoritative pose, stood across the room.

"These three guys look like they're some kind of trouble," Craig observed.

"Shh," Danny whispered.

Craig thought it odd at first that the scene was silent. But Danny's frowning intensity offered an explanation: he needed quiet in order to concentrate.

Suddenly, the three victims turned to face a doorway to a room located near a darkened corner. The shadowy outline of a person emerged. The seated figure sprang from his chair and leveled a handgun in the direction of the new arrival.

This figure stepped out of the shadows. He was an older man, small in stature and slightly bent over. He seemed at ease, unfazed by the gun pointing in his direction.

Craig observed the old man for a moment. Then a great sense of trepidation rushed through his body, and he winced. *Was this how the re-creations used to feel?* He didn't remember it feeling this way.

The old man walked toward the two silhouettes closest to Craig and Danny.

"Oh, here we go," Danny said.

The man who had risen from the table lowered his gun. This was followed by a few moments of conversation. Then the scene dramatically changed.

The old man vaulted halfway across the room, landed, and gripped the man holding the gun by the throat. With one quick movement, the attacker ripped out a chunk of his victim's neck, tossing away the flesh. Dark spatters of blood sprayed toward where Craig was standing, a streak of it landing against the backdrop of the misted veil where Craig held his hand.

Craig and Danny recoiled at what they had seen. What they were witnessing seemed incomprehensible, even taking into account the supernatural re-creation of the scene. This attacker had moved with preternatural speed, and with a strength and ferocity that didn't align with either his stature or his even-keeled attitude when he had first entered the room. Dawning awareness of what this attacker was washed over Craig—he had seen only one other killer move in such a way before.

But before Craig could verbalize what he saw, the attacker let his first victim fall to the ground and grabbed an object— *Maybe a chair,* thought Craig—and briefly held it up before tossing it toward the far side of the room. It crashed into one of the men, sending him sprawling.

"What the hell did he just throw at that guy?" Danny blurted out.

The attacker quickly faced the bald man. The victim's shadow appeared to struggle briefly, as if trying to draw a weapon. He wasn't fast enough. In an instant, the attacker was holding the bald victim and drew back one of his arms. Then he struck his victim, using a motion Craig and Danny had witnessed before, one that sent chills down their backs. The attacker fashioned his forearm and fingers into a point that resembled a dagger and plunged it into the victim's chest.

The victim appeared to survive the blow but slumped to the floor while the attacker held his torso upright.

"Look how quickly he killed the two of them!" Danny exclaimed. "His speed and the way he's attacking them, it's just like the way the Tourist came at us!"

Craig kept his hand pressed tightly against the wall, in contact with the bloodstain, but he was becoming increasingly lightheaded as he watched the savagery unfold.

The attacker rapidly—even effortlessly—dragged the bald man behind him as he pursued the remaining victim across the room.

The third victim was on his stomach, trying to crawl to safety. As the attacker nearly reached him, the victim rolled onto his back, drew in his arms, and cowered in mortal fear.

The attacker crouched down in front of the third victim, his silhouette appearing to talk for a moment. He then lifted up the cowering man's head and held it in front of the second victim.

In a flash, the attacker slashed the bald man's throat. Blood sprayed across the face of the third man. Then the attacker crouched over the third victim and plunged his forearm deep into the man's chest.

"How . . . how is this happening? How is he able to do all of this?" Craig shouted.

Danny was more composed. "You know exactly how he can do it."

"Can I shut this down now?" Craig asked Danny. It was becoming too much, and he wanted to get out of here.

"Wait!"

Danny had noticed something. While the third victim lay quivering on his back, near death, the attacker ripped a sleeve from the man's arm to expose it. Craig squinted, trying to make out what the attacker was doing to the man's arm. It seemed like he had scratched the victim's arm.

"What is it? What do you think is going on?" Craig asked.

"I dunno yet," Danny said. He was trying to keep his eyes fixed on the scene.

Then the attacker did something Craig and Danny had seen once before. He stopped and looked purposefully around the space of the warehouse room. Then he fixed his gaze directly on the exact location where Craig was crouched down and holding his hand to the bloodstain.

"Are you shitting me?" Danny said.

Craig saw it too. Heat and humidity enveloped his face, and dizziness overtook him. He watched as the attacker took two initial steps before launching into a sprint in Craig's direction.

"What the hell?" Craig cried out. He immediately withdrew his hand from the bloodstain and stood. Instantly, the mist dissipated, as did the lunging silhouette of the killer.

A near miss. If Craig had pulled away just a fraction of a second later, the shadow of the evil thing would have reached him.

Craig stared at the palm of his hand in shock, as if he regretted that it had made him see the grizzly scene. He then eyed his body up and down and patted himself all over, checking to make sure he was still in one piece.

"Danny! Did you see that? The killer noticed me—right here, and just now. Just like the Tourist did when Maggie got killed!" Danny didn't need the reminder. When Maggie had been killed by the Tourist and Craig conjured the re-creation of her death, it was the first time that they saw how the killer's shadow became aware of their presence. The shadowy figure of this killer that now vanished into the ether of the warehouse displayed the same awareness.

Danny strode over to the third victim. The dead man's arm was bare, and the sleeve of his black leather jacket was ripped away.

Craig was frozen with alarm as he watched Danny lift and survey the victim's arm.

"It looks like we're back in business."

Craig cocked his head to one side, confused. "What do you mean?"

"There are letters carved into his arm. They spell C–O–I."

16

ESPRIT DE CORPS

It was past midnight when Craig and Danny made it to the all-night greasy spoon near the warehousing district. After their harrowing experience, the first re-creation Craig had channeled in nearly two years, they needed to debrief.

Kenny's Hamburger Haven lived up to its name. It was a refuge for the area's laborers working odd shifts, as well as cops on their breaks in need of a bite. It was just a short drive up Pershing Avenue from where Craig and Danny had left the arriving Chicago Police Forensics team. They would be processing the crime scene under the direction of another detective.

The diner looked to have been built in the late 1950s, with glass windows surrounding a familiar arrangement of tables and booths, as well as a counter where patrons could sit near the service line. Tonight, two customers sat at the counter, while two others occupied the last booths at each end of the building.

Craig and Danny settled into a booth near the middle. They ordered decaf coffee and waited with bated breath for their server to collect their menus and move out of earshot.

"Well, that was a lot," Craig started.

Danny didn't waste time. "Tell me. Did you see the arm? Those initials? That's the third time with those letters. First, on that letter you found, the one you keep in that box. Then there was the informant from the precinct interview I told you about—the damn letters were branded into the skin on his arm. And the killer carved the letters into a dead guy's arm."

Craig rubbed his temples. "I saw it. You know who that guy was, don't you?"

"Yeah, I know," Danny said. "He was another one of those 'things.'"

"He saw me, Danny. Through the re-creation. Just like the other one did. I felt that same nausea too." Craig looked wide-eyed. "Hell, he came right for me, just like the Tourist did!"

"I know." Danny kept his voice low in an effort to keep Craig calm. "Seems like they were both able to sense you." He looked off into the distance. "I'm so damn glad Mason finally relented and let me get involved again. This is what we've been waiting for."

"What are you talking about?" Craig said.

"Remember what you said in the hospital after the Tourist almost killed us both? You said that, even though you might not understand why you got these powers, you'd be ready to use them again if they were needed. Do you remember that?"

Craig did, and he was surprised at the detail Danny remembered from that conversation. "Yeah, but I expected that we would do our own investigating. Maybe get the element of surprise over the remaining two. Now it looks like at least one has already locked onto us."

"But everything you and I went through back then—all the injuries, all that trauma. You ever think about what those events might have ignited?"

It was an odd pivot, Craig thought. "What do you mean?"

"Maybe some of what your dad transferred to you was activated by that trauma. You sure as hell couldn't send surges of force out of your hands before we confronted the Tourist that night. I'm thinking it was the emotional trauma of you seeing your dad getting killed that did it."

"Maybe." It was a concept that Craig hadn't considered.

The waitress returned with their coffee and asked if they were sure they weren't ordering food. Danny shook his head, and she left them to their private conversation.

Danny pushed his cup aside and leaned forward.

"I'm trying to share with you what I think might be the 'how' part of what you're able to do. There's this guy the force has hired as a consultant to work with us on the 9/11 and terrorist shit. He's been interesting to listen to. A bit mysterious, but he describes people he's met in life with unusual abilities . . . people like you."

"People like me? You've been talking to this consultant guy about the things we've encountered? Things we haven't told anybody? Jeez, Danny." Craig pushed back his chair and glared at his cousin.

"Don't worry. I spoke about it in a very general way. But it's not like we haven't been trying to figure things out for a long time. Maybe we can use some help. Isn't that why you talk with that shrink every now and then?"

"Yeah, but—".

"His name is Matthew Bishop. He's a former military guy. He seems to know other men like you and has talked about the miraculous things they can do. What he said really struck a chord with me because it seemed like he already knew some of the things you've been through in your life. It appears that trauma is a common thread among people who can do what you do. Various kinds of pain, distress, shock. And I'm thinking maybe that's what activates the powers you got from your dad."

Craig was intrigued by his cousin's belief that this Bishop guy might be able to help.

"It's definitely a new way of thinking about it," Craig admitted. "You're saying I've always had all these abilities inside of me, but they don't get activated unless I'm tested, like when we were in the church?"

"Exactly."

"Huh." Craig looked down at his coffee cup and fiddled with it. For a moment, he felt his nagging feeling of lack of purpose lessen. His thoughts drifted back to the warehouse. "And if we're going to face more of those things like we did tonight, it's critical we know as much as we can about everything I can do."

Danny let out a satisfied exhale. "I'm glad we're on the same page, Craig. What I just told you gets at the *how* of what you can do, how it gets activated. Now you and I need to talk more about the *why*."

"Go on," Craig said.

"Even with everything we've seen so far—how crazy it all is—what I'm about to say may still be a stretch to wrap your mind around." Danny glanced around the nearly vacant diner, his normal prelude before sharing sensitive matters with Craig in open spaces. Then he said, "It came from this chance encounter I had with a priest in a church."

"In a church. You did mention something about a church." Craig laughed. "How the heck did you find your way into one of those?"

"It's not actually funny, Craig. And you're gonna think I'm fucking crazy. But this priest I met—I've talked to him twice now—he knows things about you and me that we don't even know."

Confused, and still feeling on edge, Craig threw his hands in the air. "What the hell are you talking about?"

"Well, let me back up. He isn't really a priest. He's someone who speaks through a priest."

"That makes zero sense. Danny, are you all right?"

Danny kneaded his forehead. "Yeah, I'm fine. Just listen to me. You gotta hang in there with me for a minute. Hell, more than a minute. I've spent days turning this info over in my mind, and I still can't quite get used to it."

"Well, just spill it," Craig said, getting annoyed.

Danny leveled his gaze at him. "What I learned from the priest—I mean, through the priest—gets to the reason why you can do all the amazing things that nobody else can do. And as crazy as it sounds, it originates in history. Biblical history."

Craig's expression was pained. "Wow, Danny. You've never been, how do I say it, religiously inclined. But I know things have been tough for you since you got wounded, and if that's what you need now—"

"It's not about me, Craig."

But before he could continue, a voice carried across the diner.

"Craig?"

Craig turned to look over his shoulder as Danny instinctively reached inside his coat toward his shoulder holster. He gestured with his chin. "Craig, do you know this person?"

Craig flashed a smile of delight.

"Sam! What the heck are you doing here?"

Sam smiled back, stopping a few feet away, fists on her hips. "I was about to ask you the same thing. This isn't exactly Stanton Park down here," she said, referring to the nice area of the city near their gym. She wore a black sweatshirt, dark jeans and boots and looked perfectly placed in the diner.

"I'm just here catching up with my cousin." Craig half stood and motioned to introduce him. "This is Danny Walsh, He's a—"

"Cop," Sam finished. She took a step forward, reaching out, and firmly gripped Danny's hand and shook it. Danny remained seated. "No offense," she continued. "I just know 'em when I see 'em."

Danny relaxed and shook back, asking with curiosity, "How do you know Craig?" Sam held her space with an air of confidence, despite being in the presence of someone in authority.

"We roll together, occasionally," Sam said, casually.

Danny raised his eyebrows.

Sam said, "Martial arts, I mean. Mat work. We go to the same gym."

"So how is it that you're in this area? And at this time of night?" Craig asked.

"I work second shift, remember? There's a logistics ops company a few miles south of here. How about you, what's your excuse? You usually catch up with your cousin in a place like this, and in the middle of the night?"

"He helps me work through some of my cases," Danny jumped. "He's a good listener. I was just getting his thoughts on some leads I've been chasing down. Helps me if I can process things with someone I trust."

"Oh, I see," Sam said, smiling. It was clear she knew a bullshit answer when she heard it, and that she'd caught Danny's interruption and read it to mean he wanted to be left alone with his cousin.

Danny looked her over, unsure whether to decide if he was impressed or annoyed.

"No worries, gents. Didn't mean to interrupt. Just pleasantly surprised to see a friendly face in here for once." She smiled at Craig again.

"It's fine, it's fine," Craig said. "We can talk any time. Have a seat."

But Sam had picked up the impatience on Danny's face. "No, you two carry on. Any chance you'll be at the gym later this week? We can talk then."

"Yeah, for sure. I'll be there. And Sam . . ." Craig turned away from Danny and spoke softly. "Everything go okay with you and Lauren?"

"Dude, really? Relax. Your girlfriend's super nice. We talked for a few minutes, and it was all good. She's just looking out for you, I think."

Strangely, Craig didn't think the statement had anything to do with jealousy but was more about looking out for his overall well-being.

"I told her I wasn't quite sure what she saw in you," Sam laughed, and Craig chuckled nervously. "I gotta get going. I'll see you two. And Officer Walsh, you keep things safe around here." She mockingly wagged her finger at him.

"It's detective," Danny said as she walked toward the door. When she was gone, he said, "So that's the girl from the gym, the one who bum-rushed a guy on the street?"

"Right, that's her. Not sure what it is about her that feels like such a mystery to me."

"Craig, who gives a shit!" Danny said bluntly. "Can we get back to what I was trying to tell you?"

Craig caught a glimpse of his watch and flinched as he saw

the time. "Crap. It's close to two. I've gotta get home, Danny. One of my classes starts in the morning."

Craig was still worried about smoothing things over with Lauren, but he also felt the urge to try to catch Sam outside.

Danny put up both hands. "No—wait, wait, wait. You can't do this to me again. There's an arc to what I'm telling you. You need to hear all of it."

"And I get that. And as far as this Bishop guy goes, I'm totally down with meeting him. Maybe learn more. Count me in for that."

Danny became visibly flustered as Craig slid out of the booth.

"Goddammit, Craig," he said, his voice rising. "This is like the third time I've tried to walk you through what I know— things you *need* to know too."

"I get it," Craig replied, "But it's late, man. Plus, what went down in the warehouse is freaking me out, and we'll need to talk more on that. Let me know tomorrow what the Forensics team learns? Then we'll get together again, promise."

"Craig, it's wrong that we keep kicking this can down the road."

"Sorry, Danny, gotta go. We'll talk tomorrow." He tossed a five-dollar bill on the table and hastened toward the door.

As Craig opened the door, he glanced back at his cousin, who was angrily muttering under his breath and clenching his fist.

Craig stepped outside and walked briskly in the direction he'd seen Sam go, but then stopped. There was no sign of her as far as he could see down the darkened street.

◆◆◆

Danny felt heavy fatigue descend upon him. He had arrived at work nearly on time this morning, despite having stayed out so late with Craig the night before.

He combed through his thoughts about their discussion. He had gotten Craig to bite on agreeing to meet with Bishop; that was a win. But he hadn't yet been able to reveal the astonishing things he'd learned during his pivotal discussions with Michael. His investigative experience told him it was best to pay attention to pacing when you had to share dramatic, disorienting, and even shocking new information; you had to lead the subject there in such a way that he could best absorb it. Danny concluded that he had completely failed last night. *Damn that young woman showing up when she did!* he thought. *If I'd been able to make a good start down that road, I bet Craig would have stuck around until dawn if it meant getting the whole story.*

Danny barely had time to settle into his office chair with a fresh mug of coffee before a desk officer stopped by to tell him that the chief wanted him in the conference room.

Shit. Mason had gone out on a limb when he let him bring Craig into the crime scene on the assumption that it might accelerate cracking the case. But what would Danny share with him now? Once they learned through the re-creation that these killings had been done by another dark descendant, Danny had abandoned trying to solve the murder case in favor of working with Craig on how this knowledge might further help connect dots in their own long-running investigation.

He made his way down the hall, leaving his coffee and the noisy common area behind.

He stopped at the conference room door. Mason was sitting at the head of the long table inside.

"Come on in, Walsh."

Danny instead held his ground at the doorway.

"Suit yourself then," Mason said. "I wanted to see how things went with that trio you and your friend caught in the Yards last night. Wasn't easy for me to get you the air cover for that. Was your friend able to help?"

His tone was direct with a critical edge. Danny wondered if Mason thought he should have sought him out right away to debrief him on the crime scene. Or was he reading too much into it? Danny's fatigue and preoccupation kept him from filtering his response.

"Lieutenant, I appreciate you letting me get back into action. But are you just coming at me right out of the gate this morning, looking to bust my chops? Well, I'm pretty wiped out this morning—it was a long night."

"I can see that. Listen, I'm trying to help you out, Walsh. Just come in here and close the door behind you."

Danny grudgingly complied. When he stepped inside, he was surprised to see his former supervisor, Eric Hammond, tucked into a corner out of view of the doorway, leaning against the wall.

"Hammond? What the hell are you doing here, man?"

"Walsh! How've you been?"

Hammond stepped forward to shake Danny's hand and slap him on the back as they embraced.

Danny made a mental note to leave behind his recent irritation. His old colleague and boss—his mentor in some ways—was a welcome sight.

"You've been a pretty elusive character for a while now. You know that?" Danny said.

"I know, I know. So how are things?"

"I'm good. I mean, I'm getting there."

Danny looked from Hammond to Mason, growing

suspicious. "Okay, now wait," he said. "This isn't some kind of disciplinary action going on here, is it?"

Hammond let out a laugh. Mason's expression remained stoic.

"Walsh," Mason said, "you need to know that you're among friends here. We've had your back all along. Always have. Eric and I have been tight ever since I got out of the army and joined the force. I've told you that. You need to know you can trust me as well."

Danny let out an audible sigh. "Okay, maybe it's an intervention then," he joked, relieved. "God knows, I probably need it!"

"So, what about last night?" Mason asked again.

"Wait. First, with all due respect, can I take a minute?"

"Sure," Mason replied.

Danny grabbed the nearest chair and sat. Hammond remained standing. "Eric, what the hell's been up? For real," he began. Now he was intent on confronting Hammond. "You've been pretty damned hard for me to corner since you left the precinct."

Mason opened his mouth to object to the change of topic, but Hammond waved him off.

"It's a fair question," he said to Danny.

"Let me be more specific, then. You know I've been working my ass off to get rehabbed. But not too long after that, you just disappeared." The memory of that hurt, and Danny's voice betrayed the pain.

Hammond sat at the conference table, appearing resigned to hearing whatever else might be coming at him.

"I start to get my physical act together, and you just transfer off to headquarters. Why? It left me feeling like I was on my own out there."

"Yeah, I get that," Hammond conceded.

"Then there's this parade of new lieutenants coming through here who don't make it any easier for me." He looked at Mason and said, "No offense."

"None taken."

Hammond interlaced his fingers. "I'm sorry, Danny. Truly. I hate that you felt that way."

Danny was caught off guard by the direct, heartfelt apology, and the fact that Hammond had referred to him by his first name. But it wasn't enough. "You're sorry? Well, I guess that makes everything all better."

"Danny, you and me? We're good. Always have been, always will be," Hammond said. "But around the time when all that shit was going down between the Tourist and you and your cousin, my mom got real sick. It went on for a long time, and then she passed when you were between surgeries."

Danny grimaced, remembering what Mason had told him about Hammond's loss.

"And you weren't supposed to know that at the time—it was just about the last thing you needed, I figured. So I kept that pretty much to myself. You sure as hell had your own load to carry."

He paused and looked down at his hands before continuing.

"My mother—Sophia, I wish you had met her—was fighting a wicked battle with cancer. And I had to make sure I was there for her. But I also followed what was going on with your recovery, and I made sure I knew at least the broad strokes of what happened to you and Craig when you went up against that . . . thing. I knew it was a bigger deal than the way we spun it."

He paused again, as if it was a struggle to revisit that time.

"Still, I couldn't risk pushing to find out more. Or

stretching myself too thin by being more involved with you two. That was the main reason for taking myself out of the mix, getting transferred down to HQ. Trying to help my mom recover was the most important thing to me at the time, and I didn't want to do anything that might jeopardize being there for her."

"I'm so sorry about your mom. Eric. I understand. You don't need to—"

Hammond ignored the interruption. "I think it would've been different if it hadn't been for my concern for my mama. I think I would have jumped right into helping you and your cousin untangle what I knew was still a mystery for y'all. But my mother was big in my life. She trumped everything else."

A silence filled the space among them for a few moments.

Then Hammond sighed. "Anyway, I learned something important from that business with the Tourist, namely that there's something pretty special about your cousin. And while you were working to get back, I learned the same about you. After everything you've gone through, you came out on the other side more determined than ever to get back on the job.

"I also got the sense that you and Craig felt like you had opened some kind of door. But I wasn't strong enough, or even available, to acknowledge it or help you with it. But knowing that you were doing your damnedest to get back into the action—well, that's why I had that cane made for you.

"I've been careful not to mess with your mojo these past few months while you've been trying to get back on the job. But believe me, I've been your biggest cheerleader behind the scenes."

"That he has," Mason chimed in.

"See, Danny, I know you better than you think I do. I knew that for you to get back to what you expect of yourself, *you* would need to be the one who makes it happen." He glanced at Mason. "And *he* would be the one who would need to see it firsthand, regardless of how much I sang your praises."

Danny's irritation had melted away. He stood and moved to a seat directly across the table from his old boss.

"Thanks. It's good to know you've been in my corner."

"I hope now you understand why it had to be that way. But I recently caught up with Jack and heard that you and he might be seeing eye to eye a little better. I guess I thought it might be time to stop making myself so scarce."

Danny nodded. "You've seen, from afar, that it's been a hell of a road. But I finally feel like I'm back. And I appreciate all you've done—the things I've known about, and the things I haven't."

Mason nodded approvingly.

"Good," Hammond agreed. "Let's leave it at that for now. So, how is Craig?"

"He's really good. You think I'm getting my shit together? Hell, you may not even recognize him next time you see him."

"What do you mean?"

"Our guy is getting ripped, and he's gained a ton of confidence," Danny said. "Learning some things about his past has been pretty liberating for him."

"And how's Lauren?"

"I'm not sure," Danny mused, "there's just something a little different about her now."

"Different how? You mean like a bad vibe?"

"I wouldn't say bad. Just different. I've been trying to piece it together," Danny said.

Mason chimed in, "The *esprit de corps* going on here is something that has been a while in the making. Walsh, I knew you wouldn't take me at my word when I said I was getting more comfortable with your work. You needed to hear this kind of testimony from Eric. That we both understand where you've been, what you've gone through, and where you're looking to go."

Danny finally felt what had been missing. Satisfaction. Belonging. Legitimacy. Things he'd worried might be lost forever after what he'd suffered at the hands of the Tourist. Not only were they still there, but the way the two men were talking vindicated his dogged march forward in the face of his own injuries and the continued mystery of his and Craig's roles in this saga.

Mason seemed to sense Danny's epiphany and decided it was time to move on. "Now, about the killings last night. Were you and your cousin able to extract any clues? Beyond the obvious blood and gore, I mean."

Danny was pretty sure that Mason—and presumably Hammond too—saw Craig's involvement as simply a unique set of eyes at the crime scenes, and that they were still in the dark about the extent of supernatural abilities he had employed. The time to clue them in on that might come, but not before he and Craig learned a lot more about the forces at work.

"The killer made cuts into one of the victim's arms. They were letters. They matched a tattoo on an informant I interviewed a couple weeks ago." Danny looked directly at Mason. "It was the informant you had me catch the morning after one of our weekly briefings in the auditorium."

"Really? That's interesting. Forensics did pass the word up this morning that they might've gotten a little more off the bodies that could be of interest. I've got Dixon running point administratively on this and with the press. But you have access to go down there and see what they've got if you want. You still in?"

"Of course," Danny said confidently. The morning's fatigue had vanished.

"Good."

"As for me," Hammond said, "I probably need to scurry back to that hole we all affectionately call 'headquarters.'"

They all smiled knowingly as they got up from the table.

"Well, I'm going to get on this," Danny said. "But before I do, I want you to know it's been a big deal for me to hear what you've had to say this morning, Eric. What both of you did, really," he concluded, turning toward Mason.

Mason nodded. "It's my pleasure, Detective."

Hammond responded, "It's been overdue."

As Danny turned and started for the door, Hammond said to Mason, "Jack, remind me to send you and your admin the schedule for next week's counterterrorism experts. They'll be coming back in. Bishop been working out okay for your people?"

Upon hearing Bishop's name, Danny momentarily froze. Mason took notice.

"Walsh, you good?" he asked.

"Yeah," Danny called back over his shoulder. "Yeah, all good here."

He was through the door and halfway down the hallway before he remembered it was Friday, and he and Craig would soon meet separately with Colonel Bishop.

17

BISHOP

As Craig dreamt, a flood of images slowly began to crystallize. He felt anger building up inside. Emma was pacing back and forth, and they were in one of the crime scenes Craig had re-created, though he couldn't discern which one. It didn't matter; his focus was on Emma.

She was challenging him. Again.

"You really refuse to listen to anyone else, don't you?" Emma said.

"That's bullshit. All I've ever done is try to help Danny—with *this*!" Craig motioned to the dead body in the center of the murder scene. "Why are you being this way? You didn't used to be like this."

"Because no one else will tell you the truth," Emma replied.

She stopped pacing and leveled a stare at him. "And why do you think that is? Do you think it's because you can't handle the truth? You're too scared to face it?"

"Scared?" Craig shot back. "You know what I've already faced? That thing *killed you*. And I defeated it. Me! So don't act like I'm scared of anything."

Even in his dream, Craig felt the pull of reality.

Emma locked eyes with him. "You really don't know anything, do you, Craig?"

Craig jerked awake, his heart pounding and his hair damp with sweat. For a moment, he worried he might have also woken Lauren. He looked over to find that her side of the bed had been slept in, but she was gone.

He vaguely remembered sneaking into bed the night before, careful not to disturb her as he collapsed into sleep. His time with Danny, first during the re-creation of the crime scene, then later as they discussed things at the diner, had worn him out.

He swung his legs over the edge of the bed and placed his feet on the floor. He cradled his head in his hands. "Why do I keep dreaming about Danny's dead girlfriend?" he said. He looked at the clock on the nightstand and groaned.

"Damn it!" he exclaimed. It was just after ten. He had slept through his first class at grad school. He kneaded his forehead with one hand, as if trying to work through a hangover. Then, in an attempt to get himself going, he snatched his phone from the nightstand. He hoped he had missed some phone calls, either from Danny or Lauren. Nothing.

He could understand Lauren not calling. They had been at odds about his going back out with Danny to a crime scene and coming home so late. But if she knew he'd overslept and missed his first class, she would be truly disappointed in him.

Not hearing anything from Danny didn't make sense. The night before had been a watershed: the first re-creation he'd conjured in such a long time. As that sank in, Craig realized he had fully come back into his powers.

He glanced out the window at the late morning sun spilling though intermittent clouds. The busy doings at the Wicker Park intersection were already on full display.

Craig was awash in apprehension, unsure of which direction to go. Last night's re-creation had confirmed that another nemesis like the Tourist was somewhere in the city—and even more worrisome was he was aware of Craig.

Craig was also concerned about Danny. As he'd prodded Craig back into action, Danny had seemed almost manic about it. It was as though there was something more intense and personal about these latest turns. There were at least two people Danny wanted Craig to meet, and the Bishop guy was supposed to have some inside information about Craig's abilities. Danny's ramblings about the priest he had met in church were worrisome. What did it say about Danny's mental state? Considering the lasting effects of his injuries, and things heating up at work again, Craig wondered if it was all starting to take a toll.

Then there was Lauren. He closed his eyes and shook his head. As much as he cared for her, it felt like he was ruining their relationship.

He entered the kitchen for something to eat. A sheet of notebook paper was situated on the counter beside a jug of apple juice. He saw how well Lauren knew his morning routine.

His chest felt tense as he picked up the note and read it.

"I'm not angry. Let me start with that, since I'm sure that's where your focus is as you start to read this. But I am concerned. I've enjoyed seeing how you've developed. But you're all over the place now. There are pieces of yourself that you are leaving or have already left—you're getting increasingly fragmented in your thoughts and direction. You're unfocused. I don't know why, and I've tried to help, but I'm not sure you want that or if it would even work. I just want you to remember what makes up your core."

He paused, steeling himself for what he would read next.

"All I can do is remind you that you are already whole. Sometimes I think people forget that, when everything they've been through in their life still dominates their thoughts. There's so much for you to give to the world—it just frustrates me that you haven't seen that yet. I know how much symbolism has meant to you in your life, and especially how you're anchored to your father's cross. Let me try and see if I can help you focus on something else. If you're open to it, I've left you a new charm that might help you. I'll be honest with you, Craig, I'm trying. And what I'm leaving for you might symbolically lay out a path so you can move forward."

She had underlined the last sentence.

"Take a look at it. I'd be happy to explain its meaning to you if you want. I'm on an overnight recruiting trip in Indy. But I'll see you when I get back, and then can we talk? Please? For both of our sakes. Good luck with your classes."

Craig was relieved. She hadn't given up on him, and she was obviously trying to reach out.

He reread the sentence about his dad's cross and pulled it out of his shirt to touch it. He then carefully opened a small brown paper packet that sat beside the note. Inside was a small coin-shaped medallion with a loop for attaching a chain.

Craig had never seen anything like it before. It was smooth and a pale gold color. One side looked to be a cross along with various letters and symbols, and on the reverse was the outline of a bearded man. Maybe a holy man, wearing a hat and holding some type of staff.

He appreciated the effort Lauren was making. He took a deep breath and removed his father's cross from the chain around his neck. He placed it into the empty paper packet. Then he attached the new medallion to the chain and clicked the latch back in place.

Whether it was the symbolism of wearing Lauren's gift or relief that she hadn't yet given up on him, Craig felt a deep apprehension drain from his body.

It was early afternoon before Craig made his way to the only place that helped ground him and allowed him to work through his thoughts over the last couple of years.

Sitting on a bench along the wall at his martial arts studio, he collected his thoughts in preparation for joining others on the mat to spar.

"What are you waiting for this morning, Craig?" Jason asked.

"Just thinking. Meditating, like you always say I should do."

Jason flashed a quick grin and then looked away to supervise the others.

In truth, Craig was hoping Sam would show up. After her unexpected entry at the diner last night, nothing seemed too far-fetched anymore. He had nearly given up on the thought when she pushed through the door, rubbing sleep from her eyes. Not yet seeing Craig, she headed toward the other end of the studio's main floor.

Craig had risen to join her when he recognized someone else enter the room. It was Danny.

"Danny! What the heck are you doing here?" he said.

"No one was at your apartment, so I thought I might catch you here."

Craig held up his hands. "I know, I know," he said, thinking Danny was there to rehash the events at the crime scene. "We said we'd go over last night again when we're fresher and try to figure out what it all means. And we will."

"No, it's not that. Remember that guy I told you about? The military guy from work. How I was lining us up to talk with him. Well, that's today."

"Today?" Craig said, surprised. "Damn, Danny. There's just a lot going on."

Craig's mind was spinning. The re-creation still echoed in his thoughts, his tenuous circumstance with Lauren was weighing on him, and he wanted to talk with Sam, who had now taken notice of Craig from across the gym.

Danny nodded. "I know, Craig. I'm not sure, but this guy might be someone who can tell us if there are others like you."

"Yeah?" Craig had to admit he was intrigued. "Well, okay. But as soon as we meet with this guy, my ass has to get back home and get ready to mend fences with Lauren." The words from her note rang in his ears: *move forward*.

Sam sauntered up and stood next to Danny. "Guys, we have to stop running into each other like this." She smiled.

"We're a little busy with something," Danny responded, his eyes still fixed on Craig.

"No, it's fine, Sam. How's it going?" Craig said, glossing over Danny's rudeness.

"You're back here with Craig so soon, Detective? Are you here so you can 'exercise' some of those demons you talked about last night?"

Danny wrinkled his nose and gave her a sidelong glance, clearly taking offense.

Craig laughed at the joke but then tried to blunt her approach. "Sam, maybe don't push him so much," he said, letting any humor fall away.

How do I always get in the middle of tense situations? Why is it always up to me to defuse the situation? Craig thought.

Unfazed, Danny said, "You're cute. Not as threatening as you'd like to think. But cute."

Sam's expression soured as she registered the disrespect.

Craig had been looking forward to talking with Sam, but

he felt the pull of the meeting with Bishop too. And a quick exit from this uncomfortable situation had an even greater appeal.

"Listen, Sam. I've been meaning to get your take on some things. I think you might be able to . . . sense them better than I can. I've gotta go with Danny now, but can I give you a call?"

She eyed him with amused suspicion, then softened. "Sure, fine. But you don't have my number."

To hasten their departure, Danny handed her one of his business cards and a pen. She flipped it over to the blank side, scribbled a number on it, and handed it to Craig.

"Let's go, Craig," Danny said, and they moved toward the door.

As they exited, Craig glanced back at Sam.

"What the hell was that all about?" Danny asked, noticing Craig's apparent fascination with Sam.

Craig turned around. Sam was staring at them with her arms folded. He sighed. "I don't know," he said, and they left the building.

------◆·◆·◆------

They stepped out of the car at the edge of Chinatown as a light, misty rain fell. The neighborhood looked a little rough to Craig, with a variety of shoddy and dilapidated storefronts.

"Where exactly are we supposed to meet this guy?" Craig asked, squinting against the rain.

"Should just be a few buildings away from here," Danny replied. "There's supposed to be a World War II Asian-American center or something."

"So, this guy's Asian?"

"No, he's not. I'm not sure why he said this would be a

good place to meet. Maybe it has to do with him having served overseas. I dunno."

They walked quickly, eager to get out of the rain. Their surroundings perked up as they approached a modest brick professional building. The sign above the doorway read "Asian American Military Center."

Craig ducked under an awning a building shy of their destination and grabbed Danny's arm to stop him. "Tell me again what I'm supposed to talk to this guy about."

"I think it's mostly about listening to what he has to say."

"But what if it gets into knowing people who can, you know, do things like I can do. What should I share with him? Jeez, I don't even know anything about this guy. And it sounds like you don't know much either."

"Just trust me on this, okay? Bishop seems to know something about what we've been trying to figure out for so long. And he's talked several times about getting into the mind of a criminal."

"How's that supposed to help us?" Craig looked skeptically at Danny.

Danny eyed the door of the Center and tried to quickly get Craig on the same page so they could make their way in. "Well, he's gone off on a tangent a couple times about people he's seen who have special abilities."

"Like what kind?"

"I don't know exactly; he didn't get into specifics. But he said these abilities were extraordinary, and they were all activated by some type of trauma they had gone through. Sound familiar?"

"I've had my share," Craig snapped.

"If he asks for a lot of specifics, just keep it vague. You've helped me with crime scenes. You're able to see visions of past scenes, how they might've unfolded. And that you can sense how people think or feel."

"Really? That much?"

"C'mon, Craig. There's a shitload of people who go on and on about how they have some type of sixth sense for things, right?"

Craig conceded. "I'll go along with it. You're the one who's already been around the guy."

Bishop might know something that I'm still missing, thought Craig. His dream with Emma, and Lauren's note telling him to move forward, were both fresh in his mind. Then there was the re-creation he had channeled the night before. If there was ever going to be a time to learn the full extent of his powers and why he had them, it was now.

"Let's go," Danny said as he led the way out of the dry pocket where they had sheltered.

They entered the building and shook off the raindrops from their coats. The small, modest reception area housed several exhibits containing war artifacts and maps related to World War II. A few shelves full of books were located behind the welcome desk. Craig's impression of the Center was one of understatement: a small but authentic collection of memorabilia.

It was nearing their meeting time, but there appeared to be no one else in the center. Danny glanced down at his watch. He looked up again in time to see a short, older Asian man emerge from a back room.

"Good afternoon, gentlemen. Welcome."

"Afternoon," Danny replied affably. "We're a few minutes early, but we're supposed to meet an older gentleman here, a former military man . . ." Danny seemed to struggle with a fuller description.

"You're describing Bishop," the man said.

Danny nodded.

"He likes to hold his meetings in our storage area," the man said. "Please follow me."

Craig and Danny were led into the back of the building and down a short staircase into a basement that had the feel of a rathskeller. At the back was the storage room, where the man called Bishop sat at a large wooden table. There was a small tumbler filled with brown liquid in front of him. The man who had ushered them in bowed to Bishop, who acknowledged the gesture with a nod of his head. Then the man retreated up the stairs.

Craig had no idea what Bishop would look like; Danny hadn't described him much. The man had mostly gray hair and weathered, wrinkled skin; Craig guessed that he might be approaching seventy. He wore a tan wool sports coat and a plain white dress shirt. Craig noticed the way he held himself: he appeared calm, confident, with an air of authority. He seemed to exude a youthful energy that belied his age.

Two young men flanked Bishop, one at each end of the table. Both wore dark pants with matching windbreakers and seemed uninterested in the meeting. They avoided eye contact, instead gazing off into the distance, as if providing Bishop some measure of privacy or respect.

Craig didn't understand the presence of the two men, and Danny hadn't shared ahead of the meeting that Bishop wouldn't be alone Were they his handlers or bodyguards? Craig wondered.

"Detective! It's great to see you again," Bishop greeted him warmly but not bothering to stand.

"Colonel Bishop," Danny returned.

"And you are Craig, of course." Bishop rose from his seat and motioned for Craig to sit in a chair across the table from him.

"Hi," Craig said and didn't offer a handshake. He was still feeling out the stranger and his two assistants.

As Craig lowered himself into the designated chair, the medallion Lauren had given him briefly bobbed outside of his shirt before falling back into place. It was only a split second, Craig thought he noticed Bishop's pleasant demeanor seemed to vanish.

Bishop smiled. "I've been looking forward to meeting you, Craig, based on what your cousin has shared with me. But first, if you'll indulge me with a bit of housekeeping, may I ask that Thomas and James"—he motioned to the two men flanking him—"hold on to your phones until our meeting has ended?"

Craig looked at Danny.

"Huh? What for?" Danny said.

"Forgive me, but I like privacy in these types of discussions. To ensure nothing inappropriate is inadvertently disclosed. I'm sure you understand."

The request struck Craig as strange. But he reasoned this might be an aspect of Danny's work when it involved sensitive topics that weren't to be shared. He shrugged off the request and withdrew the phone from his jacket, then laid it on the table as Danny relented and did the same.

Each assistant retrieved a phone. The man who collected Craig's turned it on and reviewed the display.

"Hey, pal!" Danny warned.

Bishop turned to his assistant. "That will be quite enough, Thomas." He turned back to Danny. "My apologies, Detective. Please, won't you have a seat as well?"

"I'm okay to stand," Danny demurred. "My knee tends to lock up."

"Oh, of course. I'm sure it does."

Craig looked over at his cousin, who obviously had his guard up. They were in an unfamiliar part of the city, in the basement of an obscure location, flanked by two men whose presence and purpose still wasn't clear to him. And now they were without their phones.

Craig brought his attention back to Bishop and watched him intently. Bishop had a sense of gravitas about him, as if he was in command of the situation: of his assistants, the setting, even himself and Danny. And he made it look effortless. Now Craig was even more intrigued about what this stranger might be able to offer them.

"Tell me a little of your story, Craig," Bishop said. "Your cousin, no doubt, has shared with you at least some of what he and I have discussed."

"Yeah, so, about that . . ." Craig looked at Danny as if seeking his blessing.

"Go ahead, Craig. Tell him about how you've been able to see things. The images in your head. After your dad passed things on to you. And how you're able to sometimes understand what goes on in other people's heads, and that it all seems to be rooted in the challenges you've dealt with throughout your life."

Craig took his cues from Danny. He didn't share how he had conjured in the Iowa church the re-creation of the night his dad was killed. It was then, when Craig was only ten years old, that his father first hid Craig from view and then seemed to pass energy from his hands to Craig's. Right after that, Craig's father was attacked and killed by the Tourist.

He did, however, talk about the emotional trauma he had endured after his father abruptly died. Craig spoke of the physical ordeal of being bullied as a child, and that he was now addressing it with martial arts training. He delved into some of his powers, including the work he had done in the past few years helping Danny interpret grisly crime scenes by making physical contact with their surroundings with his hands. He avoided the detail that he could accurately summon those scenes visually for Danny to see as well.

Bishop's eyes grew wide in amazement as Craig recounted this brief history.

Craig paused to consider whether to describe his most dramatic powers, his spontaneous healing, and his ability to project force from his hands in self-defense. But he fell silent.

Bishop clearly registered the pause.

"Fascinating," he said, his eyes alight. "Clearly, trauma has sparked these abilities. But you've also been able to reach inside yourself and bring them to life."

"'Reach inside yourself,'" Craig repeated. He glanced up at Danny. "That sounds a lot like a Lauren Harris saying, doesn't it?" Craig hoped Danny might now see that Lauren's metaphysical ideas could have some validity.

"Ms. Harris is . . . ?" Bishop questioned.

"My girlfriend."

"The struggles and difficulties you have revealed certainly seem in line with some of the extraordinary people I've told the detective about," Bishop said. "I've had the good fortune to spend time with some truly special people who could do seemingly miraculous things. I feel privileged to be in the company of yet another who has shown such budding promise."

Craig realized he was holding his breath. Suddenly, it seemed as if all the questions about his strange powers were about to be answered. "Tell me more," he said.

As he watched Craig's reaction, Danny shifted uncomfortably.

"You must know," Bishop said, "that each of these individuals bore a heavy burden, one they gladly shouldered. Eventually, they all displayed even more abilities—attacking powers that they used against those who sought to employ the heavy hand of villainy."

"Villainy," Danny repeated, puzzled. "But fighting villains is law enforcement's job."

"Forgive me, Detective, but these unusual individuals possess quite another set of tools. They can see things that have occurred, sense the intentions of others. They have the power required to deal with certain threats that law enforcement oftentimes cannot."

"Exactly!" Craig exclaimed. *Finally I'm listening to someone who understands.*

Bishop nodded. "What appears to be emerging with you, Craig, is something I've witnessed in others. They are part of a larger community of similarly gifted people who are critical to delivering balance to the dark nature of others."

The room fell silent, and then Bishop leaned across the table, speaking slowly and intently. "Against those who spread, you might say, evil. People like you have the power to stop it, and a noble calling it is. It's a brotherhood of sorts. One that has proven to be quite resilient. In fact, they call themselves 'unconquerable.' They have adopted the Latin term for this: *Invictus*. They refer to themselves as a community or a council, and they often mark their work and their presence by means of but three letters—"

"*C, O, I?*" Craig interrupted, wide-eyed.

"Precisely," Bishop answered, smiling pleasantly.

"Wait, what?" Danny stepped closer to the table. The closest assistant locked his attention on Danny, as if letting him know that Bishop would be protected.

Neither Danny nor Craig could suppress their reaction to the meaning of the letters that had posed such a mystery to them.

"You're telling us that Craig is supposed to be part of this group?" Danny asked.

Bishop ignored Danny's question, keeping his gaze leveled on Craig. "The Council of the Invictus, as they call themselves, has shown a great willingness to stand in the struggle against dark forces."

"So I haven't been alone in this for my whole life," Craig whispered.

"Oh no. Anything but, actually," Bishop replied.

Craig let out a sigh of relief. "That's good to know. I'm not gonna lie, but there have been times when I've wished I could just be normal."

"Normal? Why would you want that, son? You have extraordinary talents." Bishop narrowed his eyes. "You have been cloaked with amazing abilities. You just need to focus them and loosen yourself from any angst or confusion that's restricting you. Let your abilities flow and impress upon the world what you feel is proper and right."

"I guess that is what my dad wanted for me," Craig acknowledged, his eyes drifting to the floor. A sudden rush of confidence filled him.

Danny seemed to have sensed it. He mumbled, "That's not the way Michael talked about it."

"Huh?" Craig said, trying to understand what his cousin just said.

Bishop continued to press his case. "To be part of this cause, one must truly embrace the power that simmers just beneath the surface. The individuals I've known had real power. Maybe in time, you could be similarly empowered to do the Council's work. But for that to come to pass, you would need to be able to do things like this."

Bishop lifted one hand off the table and extended his palm toward the small glass of brown liquid. He grimaced slightly. For a moment, nothing happened. Then faint ripples emanated from Bishop's palm toward the glass, appearing to push against it and nudging it several inches toward the middle of the table. It kept moving until it stopped in front of Craig about a foot from the edge of the table.

Craig and Danny were stunned speechless.

"What the hell . . . ?" Danny gasped at last.

Craig's eyes darted between the glass and Bishop's hand, which was still outstretched across the table. *He can do what I can do!* he thought.

Without acknowledging their reaction, Bishop went on. "Craig, you said your father passed on these gifts to you. A curious origin. How did he counsel you about your path ahead? How did he explain it?"

Craig struggled to refocus after what he had just witnessed. "Well, that's just it. He didn't. That's why we've been so puzzled for so long. In one of those visions I told you about, I saw my dad give me the things I can do. He passed it to me as I slept. He passed it into my hands. I was a child, about ten years old. He didn't have the chance to tell me about it before he died."

"A child? You have known nothing of this cause and your journey?" Bishop looked surprised at first, then crestfallen. "Oh, this is unexpected."

"Why? What's wrong with that?" Craig asked.

"Unless you have been trained and mentored, it's impossible for you to truly embrace the calling and become what you're intended to be."

"But I've been working to understand," Craig pushed. "And there's really a lot I can do already—"

"Craig, stop," Danny said firmly.

Craig looked up at Danny, irritated by the interruption. "I think the colonel can help us understand."

Bishop's keen eyes moved between them. "Is there something more here that you'd like to discuss?"

"No," Danny snapped. "There have been other things we've discussed, but I don't think now is the time."

Craig glared at his cousin, frowning in anger. *Why are you blocking this?* he thought. *We've finally found someone who can enlighten us, and you want to hold back now?*

Craig looked at Bishop and said, "You're like me, at least in some way. I need to understand everything—why I can do these things, what I'm supposed to do with them. Please, help me. I have to know more. I really want to embrace this power you've told us about, this 'Invictus.'"

"I'm sure you do, son." Bishop took a deep breath and gently clasped his hands. "I am sorry. But through no fault of your own, the unique gifts within you are incomplete. You have not yet become worthy of wielding the power."

"Not *worthy*?" Danny piped in.

"No offense is intended, Detective. What Craig has shared is truly unique, remarkable. But the Council is very intentional in selecting those in whom they will cultivate such abilities. Craig will need more time to develop his."

"But I can do things like what you just did. I know it."

"Perhaps."

A voice calling down the stairs interrupted them, speaking in a tongue that sounded like a Chinese dialect. Bishop responded in the same tongue, then turned back to Craig and Danny.

"Gentlemen, your story is truly something to behold, but not what I expected. I think you have seen that I am a good judge of these things. I'm not sure how and when your abilities were given to you, Craig. Please understand, I do not doubt you. However, those who are special enough to be part of the Council need to understand and embrace their gifts more than you have had the chance to do. It is a league of truly extraordinary people, and not of children."

"I'm not a child," Craig shot back.

"Oh, I know you are not now. But you received your gifts as a child, and this means your understanding is likely clouded, muddled."

"Then show me. Teach me," Craig pleaded.

"I mean no offense, young man. This is heavy and powerful work, and it is only for those who are ready to unleash themselves to do what needs to be done."

"What do you mean 'what needs to be done'?" Danny jumped in.

Bishop's expression soured, as if he was offended by the inquiry, but he kept his attention on Craig. "Best of luck to you, young man," he said. "I have other commitments that I must see to now." He raised his gaze to Danny. "I wish I could be of more help, Detective. I'm sure you understand."

With that, Bishop stood. His two assistants rose and tossed their cell phones back to them. The three men quickly ascended the staircase and then they were gone.

18

SCATTERED PIECES

By the time Craig and Danny exited the Military Center, a steady rain had resumed. Craig's mood matched it.

"You bring me to see this guy. He can actually do the same things that I can! Tells us there's this secret society I'm supposed to be a part of. Then he bolts before I can learn more!" Craig vented, barking over his shoulder as he walked briskly ahead of Danny and toward the car, trying to shield his head from the rain with his hand.

Danny struggled to keep pace while cinching his trench coat against the rain and pivoting off his cane. "I don't know why that happened, Craig. Wasn't expecting that."

"Damn it, Danny! Why didn't you let me go into more detail with him?" Craig shouted.

"Because it didn't seem right. The way he was describing the situation—it seemed off."

"But this was the guy *you* thought was so important for me to meet. Now I'm not supposed to talk to him? Besides, how would you know if the way he's describing things is right or not? You know less about this than me. I've got the power; you don't."

The last sentence landed on Danny as they reached the car. He whipped open the door. "Get in the damn car!" Danny ordered as they clambered in.

They sat inside, shaking off the rain.

"So close. So damn close," Craig muttered. "We've got to get in front of that guy again. Can you arrange it? Like you did today?"

"Just hold on for a second," Danny cautioned.

But Craig wouldn't let up. "Why wouldn't you let me share anything more? I deserve an answer."

"You were the one who was tentative at the beginning, remember? As the conversation went on, I thought it best that you didn't lay all your cards on the table."

"But this was your guy, Danny."

"Yeah, and he turned out to be an asshole," Danny spat. "And you're not. At least you're not supposed to be. Look, I didn't get that attitude from him at all in our other interactions."

Craig blew air out of his nose. "This guy has abilities like mine. Maybe knows others too. And he crosses our paths when we learn there's another one of those . . . things here in Chicago. We have to learn as much as we can so we can be ready. We found someone who might explain it all, and now he's tossed us aside because he thinks I'm unworthy."

"Which is bullshit," Danny replied. "And you're right that there's something to Bishop. But I've uncovered other leads too, and hell, I've been begging you to listen. This guy is just one of the pieces that's coming into place."

Craig rubbed his forehead and closed his eyes as he calmed down. "It's just a lot right now, Danny. The powers are back. Lauren's mad at me. There are these new people. I'm just trying to figure shit out, you know?"

"Of course, I know, damn it!" Danny braced himself against the steering wheel as he gazed at Craig. "We're in this thing together, aren't we?"

"Of course!"

"Today may not have turned out exactly as we wanted, but the guy panned out," Danny said. "And the other guy will too. In spades."

"And you're sure about this? This other guy? I feel like we missed our chance right here."

"Just leave that for now, will ya? Let me connect this one other major dot." He paused to make sure Craig was with him.

Although he was still feeling irritated, Craig appreciated that Danny's search for answers was rooted in more than his own self-interest. "Okay, shoot," he said.

"There's so much more to this than we've known before, Craig. Things are about to get deep for you, even deeper than what you learned from that asshole in there."

"Yeah? How?" Craig asked, looking for something, anything, to latch on to.

"There's someone who can clue you in better than I ever could. Tomorrow would be a good day to drop in and catch Michael . . . I mean, Father Timothy, at St. John's on Madison Street. He can bring you up to speed."

"This is the priest you've been talking to?" Craig shook his head, skeptically. "I don't know, man. First Bishop, and now some priest? I feel like we're chasing after phantoms or something. Maybe Lauren has been right all along, that the answers are supposed to be found inside, in the gut. Meanwhile, here I am struggling to see where all these other people might fit in. Think I'm just too desperate?"

Danny let out a slow, decompressing sigh. "No, you're not. You'll see. She *is* right. There'll be a time for looking inside. But you need to know everything I know first."

Craig drew in a long breath and blew it out. "Okay. Let's see this through then. I trust you."

Craig was still uncomfortably wet as he entered his apartment. He locked the door behind him and leaned against it, still brimming with anxiety as he shook his head and mulled over what he still believed was a missed opportunity with Bishop. Especially now that he knew there was another supernatural adversary that was aware of him and Danny. His sense of urgency seemed completely out of step with the pace of their efforts.

He heard a voice coming from the kitchen and stopped cold. Focusing intently, he thought he heard running water.

"Lauren?"

She stood in the doorframe of their small kitchen dressed in jeans and a T-shirt.

"Hi, Craig," she said. She didn't seem particularly enthusiastic to see him.

"I wasn't expecting you to be here," he said.

"My trip got cut short."

"You want to talk?"

She nodded, appearing resigned as she headed back into the kitchen. Craig followed her, noting that her attitude was at odds with the desire to reconcile that she had expressed in her letter. She tended to a pot on the stove, keeping her back to him.

Craig pursed his lips as he lowered himself into a chair at the kitchen table. "Where do I even start?"

"There's a lot competing for your thoughts up there, isn't there?" She turned and nodded her head, then returned to the stove. "It feels like we're growing apart. The distance, the secrecy. Seems like we're starting all over again. Looks like you've blown off school, you don't work, and you don't take any of my advice on volunteering. And now you're getting pulled back into riddles and mysteries with Danny."

Craig no longer felt the need to disagree. Everything she said was true. "I genuinely feel bad for not sharing with you the full extent of those riddles, all the twists and turns. There are so many pieces."

"What kinds of pieces?" Lauren switched the flame off under the pot and leaned against the stove, facing him now and inviting him to continue.

"You keep telling me to look inside and dig deep. But there's still so much I don't know about my powers, and there are other people who know more than I do. Seems like there should be a way that these pieces come together. It's like a big jigsaw puzzle I'm supposed to solve, except I don't even know what the hell the picture looks like."

"Maybe you're not supposed to know what the picture is yet. Maybe that's what you're supposed to visualize inside . . . how it makes you feel." Lauren's tone was argumentative.

"I get what you're hinting at," he said. "Because I do feel different. Stronger. It might sound stupid, but even though I've blown off everything, I also feel like I might be on the right path. I don't feel so vulnerable to what life throws at me." Craig's hand was outstretched as he spoke, as if trying to grasp an unknown concept in his palm.

"Okay," Lauren snipped. Her demeanor was deteriorating by the minute. She had apparently grown tired of Craig ignoring her advice.

"But these clues," Craig continued despite sensing her impatience, "these people I'm coming into contact with . . . it's like I *have* to explore them. Like they're supposed to unlock something for me. I know what you always say: move forward, look inside. But it's a hell of a pull, Lauren—a pull from the past and from what's unknown in the present. I just can't deny it. You know as well as I do that it's only a matter of time before Danny and I face another one of those things." *If only she knew how soon*, he thought.

He knew he was floundering in trying to explain himself. Lauren simply stared at him, refusing to rescue him.

He forged ahead. "Like today, Danny introduced me to this guy who could be someone who knows more. And he's got someone else lined up for tomorrow who might be able to help me."

Lauren shook her head. "Danny always seems to have that potential silver bullet, doesn't he?"

Craig closed his eyes and shook his head. "I know what you think about Danny, but—"

Lauren cut him off. "Listen to me, Craig. Life is about bringing the things you have to offer to their highest and best use. That highest and best use is what I'm always challenging you to find out about yourself. We become who we are either by embracing our power or giving it away. It's great that you're feeling more empowered, but I worry that you're also seeking a conflict."

"Of course, all of this likely leads to conflict," Craig said. "You were there in Iowa seeing it firsthand—" He caught himself before ending the sentence, thinking he might have been too harsh. But Lauren didn't seem fazed.

"Don't you think there's a more important use for your powers? The negativity you surround yourself with is incompatible with a better, more positive outcome." She always explored the psychology of his situation, and right now Craig was tired of it.

"Maybe—" he started.

"Once you understand that, you'll have what you need to

discover your purpose. To stand on your own. Because at some point, it won't be about Danny, or any of these new people, or even about me—it's just going to come down to *you*."

"Right, but . . ."

Lauren crossed her arms. "Remember what I said to you on the train?"

Craig tried to recall that conversation, but recent events jumbled in his mind.

Lauren narrowed her eyes. "The nuggets of truth that life reveals—remember?"

It finally came back to him. "I do."

Her face relaxed. "Maybe there is something to what you're finding, the clues you and Danny are pursuing. The new people who might help enlighten you." Lauren moved closer to the table and her expression grew serious. "But when things get dangerous again, like they did before, you'll need an anchor inside of yourself. If things are dicey, it won't matter what anyone else can do for you. And that includes me."

"You?" Craig responded, puzzled. He was suddenly struck by the weight of recent developments, and it was all just too heavy. He decided to lighten the mood. "Well, that's not really true, is it now? You left me that note and some kind of good luck charm."

Lauren stood in silence, looking Craig up and down. She seemed to be debating whether it would do any good to press ahead. Finally, a smile creased her lovely face.

"I suppose you're right," she said softly.

"You going to tell me all about it?" Craig tugged on the chain around his neck until the silver medallion popped out and fell against his shirt. "What's this all about?"

Lauren smiled again. "It's a Saint Benedict medal It's

used by a lot of different denominations, and it's one of the oldest and most honored medals there is, believed to have great power against evil."

"Yeah?" Craig's interest was piqued.

"It's known as the 'devil-chasing medal,' and it's used to ward off dangers related to evil, poison, and temptation."

"Let's hope it can do more than just ward things off," Craig said, "because you know as well as I do what's waiting out there."

"Remember my note. It's more than a good luck charm, Craig. I want you to see it as a symbol that reminds you to steer clear of danger and to chart your own course. Like everything I've been pestering you about." The last line was delivered with a sarcastic expression that made them both chuckle.

"I guess I'm loaded for bear with this, then."

"Let's hope so. It's intended to protect the person who is worthy enough to wear it."

"Funny, I heard recently that I might not measure up."

"Measure up to what?"

"Being worthy."

"Oh, Craig. If there's anything you've learned from your life's journey, it's that you're definitely worthy."

They smiled affectionately at one another. She pulled out a chair and lowered herself onto it. She gently rested a hand on his.

"I need to leave in the morning. I'll be gone until the first of the week."

"Where? Why? It's the weekend." Craig didn't bother to hide his irritation.

Lauren let his reaction wash by. "My mom's best friend

passed away suddenly. I want to accompany her to Wisconsin while she checks in on the family."

"Oh. Sorry," Craig said. "Did you know her? Were they close?"

"I knew her a bit. And, yes, they were close."

"I'm sure that's tough on your mom. But do you really need to go? I mean, right now?" Craig was acutely aware of his own anxiety. The fear of a new nemesis. The apprehension of meeting Bishop and whomever he would meet tomorrow. He needed her.

Lauren withdrew her hand, her mood cooling. "Of course right now, Craig. My mom needs my help."

"So you won't be around at all this weekend?"

"That's right. And I would think that is perfectly understandable."

Craig opened his mouth but then closed it, then tried again. "It's just . . . there's just a lot going on right now. And more still is likely to unfold."

Lauren raised one eyebrow. "There are other things you're keeping from me?"

Craig lowered his head. He dared not share the scope and gravity of what he'd recently experienced.

Lauren sighed. "Craig, I've done my best to be with you through everything. Even when there are pieces of your jigsaw that I'm not allowed to see. Anyway, I need to pack a few things. I've got an early start tomorrow."

She rose from the table and Craig stood too. Before she could turn toward the bedroom, Craig tugged at her arm gently.

"Listen, I'm sorry if that came across poorly. I appreciate your putting up with me. With everything."

He leaned in for a hug. Lauren returned it, but in a way that felt hollow, too formal somehow. She patted his back before they separated but kept hold of his shoulders.

"You've got this, Craig. You'll see. I'm always with you, even if it's only in there." She placed a finger on his chest. For a moment, his anxiety seemed to fade. Then she gently but firmly pushed him away and made her way toward the bedroom.

She must have sensed that Craig was puzzled by that push. She stopped and turned. "You know how much I care about you, Craig. But whatever steps you take next, you'll need to decide them on your own."

He watched as she disappeared through the door, wondering where that left things between them.

— ◆—◆—◆ —

Danny leaned his head on his palm, his elbow resting on his desk, and stared out at the late afternoon sunlight. The rain had cleared, and his eyes were heavy. The quiet pause was a welcome respite following that business with Bishop. The view out of the third-floor window of Seventh Precinct headquarters gave way to darkness as his eyes closed. He was tired, drawn out from recent events and the jumble of thoughts turning over in his mind.

"Long day, Walsh?"

Briefly startled, his eyes flew open to find Lieutenant Mason standing in front of his desk.

"Oh, Lieutenant. What's up?" He knew he no longer needed to put on any pretenses with his boss after their conversation with Hammond.

"You've been busy as of late, haven't you?"

Danny straightened. "It's exactly what I've wanted."

"Right. Any new leads on the warehouse killings?"

"Huh? Oh, that. No, unfortunately not." With everything he'd learned from Michael and now the mystery with Bishop deepening, that event seemed so long ago. It was ironic that it seemed so distant given that it had revealed the threat of another nemesis, whose reappearance could be imminent.

Mason squinted and looked skeptically at Danny. "You seem a little off, Walsh. Despite getting back into the action. Anything I can help with?"

Danny drew in a breath, his first instinct to dismiss Mason's concern. Then he remembered their recent meeting of the minds and slowly exhaled. He felt like he could trust Mason. Finally.

"Things are a little complicated, I guess. With my cousin. With how he's helped me and how I've tried to help him over the years."

Mason appeared open and ready to listen. "There's no question Craig has come a long way since we were kids," Danny continued. "He's, well—how do I say it—a lot more advanced. He's gone beyond where I thought he'd get. He's become powerful, I guess I'd say."

Mason looked at him quizzically.

"I mean, his confidence and inner strength are just at a different place. And me, well, we've talked with Hammond about what I've been through and how it's . . . diminished me by comparison."

Mason took on an authoritative tone. "Walsh, you need to feel confident that you're a hell of a cop. That didn't just disappear after Iowa. Maybe you got a few pieces taken out of you during that ordeal, but I've seen how you carry yourself. Don't let that shit bug you."

"Thanks. I know. I'm just not sure I carry the same credibility with Craig that I used to."

"What you've had to lean on more than anything these days is your mind."

"How do you mean?"

Mason snatched up a neighboring chair, as was his habit, and plopped down in front of Danny's desk. "Let me tell you something about when I was in special forces."

Danny leaned forward, eager to hear more.

Mason waved his hand dismissively. "I don't talk much about it, so don't you get hung up on it either. Just hear me out." He scooted the chair closer to the desk and lowered his voice. "On our team, I took on the role of a linchpin."

"Linchpin?"

"Yeah, a linchpin is a thing that holds it all together. I had a knack for knowing what kind of work everyone's skills were best suited to, and how to use them to build a team that holds together."

"I'm not really that familiar with a team working like that," Danny said. "I've typically worked solo since I joined the force. What did that look like in the military?"

"Let me give you an example. There was this one guy on our team—he had skills, no doubt. He was probably the strongest and most physically deadly guy I've ever met. But he was raw. Unfocused. We were on this mission, and he was out of control, ready to confront or kill whatever came up next. Regardless of whether it was within our orders or even something that was morally right."

"What did you do?" Danny was genuinely intrigued.

"I finally had to grab him and throttle him to the ground. Talk directly in his face. Don't get me wrong, he could've snapped me in half. But in that moment, he needed the guidance, and after I got his attention, he was finally ready to listen to reason. When you have a more advanced perspective and knowledge about something than someone else, you've got to jump in there when the time is right. Set them straight."

"Sometimes I wondered if I've actually got the best angle on things."

"Walsh, I'm guessing you've seen a ton. And that you understand a hell of a lot more than your cousin does."

Danny returned Mason's gaze silently, not yet ready to reveal any of his secrets.

"Anyone can come into a situation thinking they've got a handle on their abilities," Mason continued, "that they know exactly what they're capable of. But at some point, they're gonna need help. Guidance. Perspective. And you need to focus them and aim their skills where they're most effective. You'll know the situation when you see it." He paused. "I'm guessing you already know a person like that, and you know what he needs to hear."

Danny sat quietly as he ruminated over Mason's words.

"You know what I mean, Walsh?"

"I think I do," he finally said. "I've struggled to understand how I can play my part, not only on the force but for my cousin too. This gives me a different way of thinking about how I might go about it."

Mason stood. "Just something you might want to keep in mind. I'm sure I don't know the half of what you're trying to process in that head of yours. But at some point, you'll have to make the decision to take control. Make your voice heard and bring him along."

"You're right," Danny said. "I've doubted plenty about myself over the last couple of years. But I think I have a better perspective now."

"Good. If the shit jumps off, you'll be ready."

"Thanks, Lieutenant. I appreciate it."

"Just trying to help out. I think you know that's what I want to do."

Danny nodded to his boss's back as he walked away. Then he turned back to the window to let his new perspective sink in.

19

HIGHER PURPOSE

Though it was early May, the crispness of the midmorning air helped further awaken Craig. He marched along Wells Street, trying, unsuccessfully, to keep his mind off Lauren. She had left with her mother before he rose this morning, not bothering to wake him to say goodbye. That alone told him everything he needed to know about the state of things between them.

As he approached the old four-story factory building that housed the martial arts studio, he was unable to get the emotions swirling inside him to abate: dread. Knowing there was another supernatural nemesis in the city that awaited Danny and him caused him dread. He felt confused about the myriad clues and people who had recently appeared just as his powers reemerged. He felt depressed over where things stood with Lauren. He was frustrated with Danny and his inability to seize on the opportunities to finally understand everything. And curiosity—in general, and about Sam in particular. He had made plans earlier in the week to meet her at the dojo this morning. It was the only part of his emotional state that felt positive, assured.

He paused in front of the door to the building, staring off into space.

"Are you going in or not, pal?" someone said behind him.

"Oh, sorry," Craig said over his shoulder as he reached for the handle.

Good question, he thought. *Where the hell am I going, anyway?*

✦

"I'm graduating both of you from groundwork to the heavy bag for a while," Jason said.

Sam and Craig stood side by side on the edge of the mat dressed in their *karategi* uniforms. They glanced at each other for a moment, unimpressed by this news, and then turned back to Jason.

"This isn't the first time you've had us or anyone else in class focus on stand-up fighting," Sam said.

"Ah, that's true," Jason replied as he led them to a corner of the gym and away from the others on the mat. "It's also true that aikido is generally a form of defensive techniques, joint locks, and countering another's offense." He stopped in front of a large, heavy black bag that was hanging by an intermesh of chains from a thick wooden beam overhead.

"But the Americanized version of aikido also blends in strikes and blows. You'll need to perfect the ability to project force and use your skills to be more offensive." He smiled. "And who better to transition to this phase than my two best students?"

His comment was intended as flattery, but it was also true. Craig had advanced to the point where he could best his instructor in groundwork about half the time. And Sam had always had a technical proficiency that rivaled and often eclipsed Craig's.

"Here's a set of bag gloves." Jason tossed them underhand to Craig. "Let's have you start first. I'll call out the combination

I want to see as you work around the bag. Get it jumping."

Both students understood what their instructor meant. The bag was about the size of a person's head and torso. And heavy. The only way to get it moving, bouncing up and down on the chain, was to hit it hard.

"I don't need any bag gloves," Craig announced as he tossed them to Sam and stepped forward to face the bag.

"Oh, ho, that bag had better watch out!" Sam quipped.

Craig smirked.

"Have it your way, Craig," Jason said. "Let's see if you can use the techniques you've learned over the years and turn them into real power."

Craig knew it wouldn't be easy. The bag was big and immobile, its mass difficult to overcome. It was also unforgiving to the knuckles without the thin, padded bag gloves that Jason had offered. But Craig didn't care to lessen whatever pain he might undergo. In fact, he welcomed it.

"All right, let's go!" Jason commanded.

With that, Craig began while Sam watched. Letting loose an occasional punch, he bobbed and weaved around the bag as if he were fighting a real attacker. It took only a minute or so for him to work up a healthy sweat. His fists thundered against the heavy bag as he tried to match the combinations and strikes Jason called out.

He was winded, and his knuckles ached with each successive blow he landed. After a few minutes, Jason offered him a respite.

"If you're wearing down, take five and Samantha can step in."

Craig dismissed the offer. "No way."

Instead, Craig stepped up his intensity. The ferocity of his attacks increased with each punch, backfist, or elbow stroke, and the bag bounced on the chain—until a loose end of chain fell down against the bag just as Craig landed a glancing blow against it.

The pain of knuckles against steel was instant. Craig stopped and drew back his hand. He cradled it against his chest.

Sam cringed. Jason moved quickly toward Craig. "Craig! Your hand, is it all right?"

The pain subsided almost as quickly as it had come on. As the sweat dripped off his brow, Craig looked at his hand. The flesh across three knuckles had been gashed open by the chain, but the wounds closed in a matter of seconds, sealing the cuts as though they had never been created.

A smile curled across Craig's face as he drew both fists back up in front of his face and turned to look at Sam and his instructor.

"Are you kidding? I'm fine." A wild look momentarily came to his eyes and then, shaking off any fatigue, he resumed pummeling the bag.

"Wow," Jason remarked as he watched Craig pound the bag, seemingly uninjured.

"Hell yeah!" Sam exclaimed, impressed by the speed and power Craig was unleashing.

After another minute or two of this impressive work, Jason finally called Craig off.

"That'll do. Take a break. I need to see what Samantha can throw at this."

Sam snatched up a towel from a neighboring shelf and tossed it to Craig as he walked away from the bag, panting.

"Damn, Craig! You were throwing all kinds of hell at that. Where'd that come from?"

"I don't know. Maybe it just felt good to burn off some frustration. There's been a lot of bullshit going on lately."

Sam looked at him with curiosity as she slipped the bag gloves on her hands, readying herself. "What kind of bullshit?" she asked.

A phone rang loudly, echoing across the gym. Jason held up a hand and retreated to answer it. "Just hold for a moment, Samantha. Let me get this first."

Still winded, Craig collapsed on one of the wooden benches that lined the side of the gym and began toweling off his face. Sam plopped down beside him.

"Impressive bag work, Henriksen. But seriously, what kind of bullshit are you dealing with?"

Craig thought better of telling her. "Oh, I shouldn't have been venting. It's just . . . there's a bunch of different directions I'm supposed to go in," he stammered. "Or maybe only one. And each time I take one, I get more confused, or disappointed, or alarmed. Oh, you don't want to hear all this crap."

"Hey. You and I are starting to get to know one another a little, right?"

Craig nodded. "I'm just feeling a little overwhelmed, I guess."

"Then trust that I've got the time and interest to listen."

Time, thought Craig. He glanced up at the wall clock. It was almost one o'clock.

"Shit, Danny will be here soon."

"Not to pry," Sam began, "but what is it with you and your cousin? I mean, you seem tight. But you also tend to get worked up when you're around him."

"It's not that. It's just . . . we've been through a lot."

They both went quiet, and Craig worried about what she might be sensing.

"I know you've got a 'thing'—that you can sense about people. Threats. Whatever. Trust me, that's not Danny, even if you're getting that vibe," he said.

Sam's demeanor softened. She drew in a long, deep breath and studied Craig's face.

"What?" asked Craig.

"One of those waves is coming over me."

"Oh, stop it." Craig laughed.

"No, I'm serious. I've told you about this, these feelings of hate I can sense about a person. Knowing something negative about them and their intentions. But I haven't felt one like this before."

"Like how?"

"It's a wave of . . . it's not negative. I guess it's just an uneasy feeling." She frowned and shook her head.

Just then, the door to the gym swung open and Danny marched through it. He wore a black long-sleeved T-shirt, jeans, and boots. His eyes found Craig, and he pivoted off his cane briskly as he made his way over.

"Hey, Danny."

"It's time," Danny responded. "Let's get moving if you've wrapped up here."

"Is the church only open until a certain time or something?" Craig said.

Danny tilted his head to the side, irritated.

"Craig and I were just getting into things," Sam pushed back.

"Listen, Sam. It is Sam, right?" Danny remembered her name perfectly well but couldn't resist needling her. "We've got an appointment, and I'm just trying to get us there on time."

"All right, all right." Craig intervened. "Let me switch into some street clothes. I'll be back in a minute."

———◆—◆—◆———

As Craig disappeared out of sight, Sam rose to face Danny.

"Seems to me Craig's got a lot on his mind. There's a lot that's concerning him."

"Oh, he does, does he? Listen, I know you two have a friendship or whatever this is." Danny waved his cane around the gym. "But I can take care of him. No need for you to worry."

"Worry? I thought *he* was the one who helped *you* out. You pull him into police matters. What kind of things are you using him for?"

Danny slid his eyes away. "'Using him'? Sure, I pull him into some cases. But it helps him too."

"You said you 'take care of him.' What is it about Craig that you think needs taken care of?" Sam's face scrunched quizzically.

Danny grew tired of their banter and locked eyes with her again. "Let's just say I need to look out for him and leave it at that."

"Well, if you'd seen what he was doing to that heavy bag before you arrived, you might realize you don't have to."

Danny sized her up. How much did she really know about Craig, and what were her intentions for their friendship? She didn't seem at all intimidated by his stare.

Sam broke the tension. "At a loss for words, Danny?"

"It's Detective Walsh."

"Oh, then for me, it's Sam. Craig's friend. Regardless of your history and relationship with him."

Danny thought about engaging with her, and he was relieved when Craig emerged from the locker room, one hand pulling a Henley shirt over his head and down, unbuttoned to the middle of his chest, the other holding his gym bag.

"This work for the church? Should I have dressed nicer?" he asked.

"You're going to church?" Sam asked.

Intercepting her comment before Craig could, Danny said, "I've got this. And him. Remember?" He planted his cane and turned toward the door, trying to hasten Craig along.

"I'll catch you to start the week. You'll be around for the Monday night session?"

"Sure. But wait, Craig."

Danny barked at Craig as they both moved toward the door. "You said one o'clock. Now let's get moving."

Sam watched them as they pushed through the doors.

◆—◆—◆

Craig and Danny stood in front of St. John's Church on Madison Street in downtown Chicago.

"And you sure meeting this guy is the right next step for me? I mean, you thought meeting with Bishop was the right move too."

Danny countered, "I'm not sure Bishop's take was what we've been searching for. But this guy? I think this is it."

As Craig dropped his gaze to the glass doors, he took in their reflections. They were both wearing jeans and casual shirts. Danny was thinner than he'd been in the past. And as he leaned on his cane, he seemed shorter—he'd always been much taller than Craig. Craig noticed that his own image looked stronger, that he held himself with more confidence than he had before the horror in Iowa. The contrast was striking, and he found himself liking it.

Craig followed Danny inside. In less than a dozen steps they had passed through a glassed-in lobby and pushed through a set of wooden doors that revealed an expansive sanctuary.

Craig's eyes widened as he took in its grandeur. He hadn't thought about what it would look like inside but found himself impressed, and a little intimidated.

"Good, not that many people here," Danny said as he surveyed the others scattered about in the pews. Most were sitting in quiet reflection or in prayer.

"Is this how it always is on a Saturday afternoon?" asked Craig.

"It's the way I was hoping it would be."

Craig watched as Danny glanced around the church impatiently. "What's up, Danny?"

"I'm looking for our guy," Danny said. "Follow me."

They made their way up a long aisle, each side lined with dozens of rows of pews. Craig was still wide-eyed as he scanned the room. The floor was overlaid with a speckling of pieces of tan and gray glass that formed a mosaic. The pews had a look of deep mahogany and were covered with red cushioned seats. He looked up while they walked and noticed the cool tones of the sandstone walls decorated with an occasional religious scene carved in relief.

When they were near the front, Danny led him to the smaller antechamber.

"We're supposed to meet him here?" Craig asked.

"I've got to find him first."

Danny stayed on the hunt for Father Timothy. Finally,

a young priest approached them slowly from the front, his attention focused on a bulletin he was reading.

"Excuse me, I'm sorry. It's Detective Walsh." Danny brought his hand up to his chest. "I've had the pleasure of visiting Father Timothy a few times recently."

"Ah, yes. How are you, Detective?"

Danny ignored the question. "Is Father Timothy here today?"

"He is, but he hasn't been feeling his best lately, Detective."

"I'm sorry to hear that." Danny paused for a moment. "I know this may sound a little rude, but my cousin is visiting from out of town. I've told him how much Father Timothy reminds me of his own uncle. May I ask if we might visit with the Father, if only briefly?"

The priest glanced at Craig, who indicated his interest by raising his eyebrows and smiling.

"Sure, gentlemen. Let me get him."

As the young priest left them, Craig sat down on a pew, staring up at Danny. "Tell me what's so special about this priest."

Danny ignored the question. Instead, he looked around so as to make sure they were out of earshot of others. "The Father's mind is failing him. That priest you just met looks out for him."

"You're telling me that a man whose mind is failing him is the one who can help us unlock the secrets of my powers?"

"It's not like that, exactly. Yes, he's got dementia. But the person I want you to talk to is actually able to speak *through* him."

"Huh? You okay, Danny?"

"You'll see. I didn't expect it either. Just hang in there with me on this."

The young priest reemerged with an older priest Craig assumed was Father Timothy.

"Here's the good Father. How about I check back with you three in a bit?"

"Perfect, thanks," answered Danny. "We'll be fine. I promise we won't keep him long. We had an uncle with the same . . . issues I know Father Timothy has been dealing with."

After the young priest left, Father Timothy looked nervous and uneasy. "Do I know you?" he asked cautiously, looking at each of them in turn.

"Of course, you do. I'm Danny, the guy you thought might know your uncle Fred. Remember?"

"I'm not so sure. No, I'm not sure I know you. I'm sorry, but I should go back."

Danny stepped tentatively toward the priest. "No. Please, Father. Just sit with us for a few moments."

The situation was getting awkward for Craig. He stepped closer, trying to sort out what Danny was doing that made the priest so uncomfortable.

"Danny, maybe you should just let . . ."

"Oh, what's this?" Father Timothy's attention was drawn to the silver medallion that was only partially hidden by Craig's half-buttoned shirt.

Danny tried to distract the priest. "Don't worry about that, Father. Remember this injury I have on my arm?"

Father Timothy reached for the silver medallion and clasped it.

"Um, Danny," Craig said, "I think we need to just let the Father go back and rest."

"Oh, my son. Look, you were once injured." The priest's hand drifted to a scar just beneath Craig's collarbone. It was where he had been wounded by the Tourist when the serial killer plunged his pointed fingers into Craig's chest. Both he and Danny barely survived that confrontation in the church in Iowa nearly three years ago.

As the priest touched the scar, Craig was unnerved. He glanced at his cousin. "Danny—"

Father Timothy's voice seemed to change. "I see you have brought him to me at last."

"Yeah, it took a little while to put it all together," said Danny.

Craig's head swiveled back and forth between the two men. "What exactly is going on?"

With calmness in his movements and authority in his voice, the priest said, "Craig, please sit." He released the medallion, placed his hand on Craig's shoulder, and ushered him onto a pew. "I am Michael."

Craig obeyed, though he wasn't sure why. It felt like the priest's eyes could see right through him.

"It has been a long journey we have traveled to arrive here together, Craig. I appreciate the point you've reached in that journey and your willingness to embrace your role."

"I—I'm really not sure what this is all about."

"The truth is being revealed to you, I trust," Michael said. "I can now help complete the rest of it."

"Um, no, not really. Okay, what exactly do you know about Danny and me?"

Michael turned to Danny. "You've told him, I'm sure."

Craig jumped in before Danny could respond. "Father, I'm taking this in . . . whatever this is . . . for the first time." He looked at Danny, annoyed to feel so clueless.

"He doesn't know? He hasn't yet been made to understand— any of it?" Michael leveled a look of disappointment at Danny.

"Don't worry about that," Danny tried to redirect. "I haven't had the opportunity to tell him. Can you please tell him what this is all about, and why he can do what he can do."

Michael turned to Craig. "You may not desire these things. You may want to shrink from what they require of you. But these gifts . . . these powers? They reside in you now, regardless of how they came to you."

Craig swallowed a lump in his throat. "Danny and I have encountered things I don't think you can understand. Sometimes I'm not sure I was meant to get this far. But I'll bite. Why is this happening to me?"

"What do you think is the purpose of these powers? If no one has explained that to you, at least let me ask: How does it feel to you inside?"

Craig was getting impatient. "What is that supposed to mean? Am I getting more 'look inside yourself' spiels?" He turned to Danny. "I don't have time for this. You say the dots are getting ready to connect? It's never that simple. Each encounter leaves us hanging. And in the meantime, I'm pissing Lauren off at every turn and spinning my wheels with everything else."

"Just be patient and listen," Danny countered. "You'll find out why we've been having such a hard time figuring it out."

"No, *you* need to figure out if you truly want to help me," Craig challenged. "Or if you just want to indulge some crackpot priest who may have helped you with your own issues."

"My own issues?" Danny seethed in anger.

"Daniel!" Michael broke in on the commotion. "It is difficult for me to conceal when the two of you are carrying on." His whispered command was harsh and authoritative.

Danny brushed off Michael's concern. He was focused on his cousin. "Craig, it's okay. You can trust him."

"I think we could've trusted Bishop," Craig snapped.

"Who is Bishop?" asked Michael.

"Listen," Craig said, "I'm not sure what the two of you have discussed, but I can see how my path is unfolding."

"Your path is that of a humble servant," said Michael.

The meeting with the priest had taken an abrupt, bizarre turn. Craig didn't understand the nature of the priest and Danny's relationship, and he didn't care. His patience had run thin. Those he trusted with his secrets had failed to help him get the clarity he needed. At this point, he felt he might as well go it alone.

"My path is letting whatever I'm coming into flow through me. I can be ready for whatever he and I come up against," Craig challenged.

Michael turned to Danny. "Did you not act on anything we discussed?"

Danny brushed it off. "Craig, you need to listen to what Michael has to share with you."

"Are you gonna help or not?" Craig challenged the priest.

Michael looked hard at Danny. "He is not prepared for this."

Craig grasped his head in his hands as Danny shot Michael an incredulous look. "So first it was Timothy. Now it's Michael. Whatever. I *knew* this would be a bust. We missed out on our chance with Bishop. His perspective made the most sense. We're wasting time here." Craig felt the anger and frustration that had been building over many weeks bubbling to the surface.

His voice rose. "You bring me in here to see this guy. Then after some personality swap or whatever, I'm supposed to take whatever advice he's got? Come on!"

"Craig, lower your voice," Danny admonished.

"Listen, Father. I know what I can do. I know the power of it, and I'm ready to point it in the direction where it's needed. Is that something you're willing to help me identify?"

Michael crossed his arms. "What help do you think you need, son?"

"Okay, enough with the twenty questions. I'll discover the purpose for all this. But I'm leaving."

"It is a purpose higher than you yet understand," Michael said as Craig rose and began making his way toward the front of the church.

"I'll be outside," Craig said to his cousin as he turned to leave.

———◆—◆—◆———

Danny kneaded his forehead in frustration and scoffed. "I've got to catch him."

"Wait, Daniel."

"What? *Now* you want to be helpful?"

"You were supposed to prepare him before bringing him to me."

"I couldn't. He and I have been trying to deal with a lot of stuff. Besides, you're the best one to tell him—you're my source for the origin story."

"You should have begun awakening him to his purpose. Creating a bridge that would permit him to take in what I can share. It was overwhelming to you when you saw the scene in your mind's eye. Imagine how it would be for him, the one anointed with these gifts! He needs a guide to bring him further down the path. Only when he is closer to the truth can I show him the rest."

"Well, you could've made that a little more damn clear."

With Craig gone, the intensity of the conversation between

them was growing, and others in the church were taking notice.

"I did!" Michael looked angered. "He didn't agree to the gifts, and he doesn't yet understand. And now he sits at a most perilous point. It was your job to initiate his understanding."

"*My* job!"

"Just as this burden was thrust upon Craig without his consent, so too has it been thrust upon you to serve as his guide. Until you can no longer. He can't understand and accept his calling unless he is prepared."

Danny snatched up his cane that was leaning against a pew. "I know that. But there's been a hell of a lot vying for his attention right now, and I haven't been able to break through."

"You must do your part, Daniel. You agreed to it. With me, and within your heart."

Danny was frustrated, as much with himself as with the situation he was in.

Then the aging priest started coughing.

"Hey, you okay?" Danny asked as he leaned closer to the man. As the coughing continued, he noticed the young priest hustling over toward them, no doubt spurred by the recent commotion and now the coughing.

Michael looked at Danny through the priest's eyes. "Without you to guide him, Craig risks embracing a dark path."

"What do you mean by that?"

"Make him understand," Michael said. Then the priest's eyes went vacant, and the presence of Father Timothy was back within them. His coughing resumed.

"Is everything all right, Detective?" the young priest asked upon reaching them.

"It is. I'm sorry, but my cousin became a little emotional—the Father reminds him so much of his uncle."

"Oh, I see." The priest placed his hand on Father Timothy's shoulder. "Best we get you a bit of water, Timothy?" he asked.

Father Timothy nodded. Danny voiced his appreciation for their time and quickly set his cane to the floor, hurrying back up the aisle toward the main entrance.

Once through the outer glass doors, he squinted and looked up and down the length of Madison Street, but Craig was nowhere in sight.

20
A GATHERING FOG

Craig stood in a dark, decrepit place, staring at two necklaces with charms attached. In his left hand was the old Scandinavian cross his father had given him so long ago, the one he had lost and then found in the church where he and Danny had faced the Tourist. In his right palm was the Saint Benedict medallion Lauren had recently given to him, as she had hoped it would help steer him on a more constructive, forward path.

He felt his heart being pulled between the two.

"What's the problem?" a voice asked. Craig looked up to see Emma, Danny's deceased girlfriend, come into view. Her eyes were critical.

"I think I can only have one," Craig said. "I just don't know which one."

"They're the same, Craig. Why is it taking you so long to figure it out?"

"What do you mean?" Craig implored. "No, they're not the same. One is from my dad, the other from Lauren."

"They're both the *same*. Isn't it time you realized that and did something about it?"

"Why do you always challenge me like this?" Craig asked. "I did nothing but offer you kindness when you were with Danny. You weren't like this then."

Emma's face softened and began to fade. "You feel the power, but you don't know what to do with it," she said, now nearly translucent. Her final words rang out clearly: "Figure this out—it isn't about you. Please."

Craig awoke, drawing in a quick breath. The room was dark, and he glanced at the digital clock. Its red numbers told him it was half past five in the morning.

He turned toward the side of the bed where Lauren slept. A feeling of longing washed over him as he remembered why she wasn't there—the trip to Wisconsin with her mother.

He wished so much she was there for him when he awoke from yet another disturbing dream. For all of his progress and the flashes of enlightenment he'd experienced over the past few years, he felt alone yet again. Was he destined to solve all these mysteries by himself? Increasingly, he was feeling that this might be the case. He wanted Lauren to be here, nonetheless.

He rolled onto his back and looked up at the dark emptiness of the ceiling. It was very early on Monday morning. Sunday had been a lost day. After his confrontation with Danny at the church, and after what Craig felt was another dead end—their frustrating conversation with the priest Danny had hyped— Craig felt adrift. Again.

He had ignored several calls from Danny on Saturday night, instead stewing over what he felt had been another fruitless lead in unraveling the mystery.

Craig spent most of Sunday wandering through the city, trying to clear his head and anchor to something that might provide him with direction. When he got home, there was yet another missed call from Danny that had rolled to voicemail. Irritated, Craig flung his phone toward the nightstand before collapsing into bed. Now he was awake in the pre-dawn hours having dreamt of yet another cryptic interaction with Emma.

He shook his head as he reviewed all the key connections

that had existed and those that recently emerged: Danny, Lauren, Bishop, and Sam. And most critical of all, another supernatural enemy lurking somewhere in the city had revealed himself to Craig and Danny.

Craig looked over to Lauren's side of the bed and imagined her sleeping there. He was alone. His mind raced for an hour, and then another, until many hours had passed.

Craig's eyelids separated as bright sunshine streamed through the bedroom window. A glance toward the clock on the nightstand told him it was early afternoon. He heard a strange rattling sound somewhere near the side of the bed. He dropped his head over the edge and saw that his phone had come to rest underneath the nightstand. It hummed and beeped periodically, announcing the missed calls and voicemails from the previous day or so.

He closed his eyes and sighed. He didn't want to face any more expectations or disappointments. The only thing on his mind was how much he was looking forward to training with Sam at the gym later that evening. After that, he could look forward to Lauren's return. He hoped she was still due home soon, as expected—he hadn't heard from her since the start of the weekend.

Finally summoning the energy, he stretched down to pick up his phone. In addition to the notifications of missed calls and voicemails, it was flashing with a low battery warning. He saw there were several missed calls from Danny. Remembering Lauren's advice that he was in control of what he became involved with, he said, "I get to choose."

As he scrolled through the missed calls, he noticed an unknown number had called two hours ago. *Strange*, he thought. He tossed the phone onto the bed and headed for the shower.

Once he emerged from cleaning up, he plopped onto the bed just as his phone began to ring. Snatching it up, he noticed the caller was listed as "unknown."

Craig answered it. "Hello," he said tentatively.

"Mr. Henriksen? It is Henriksen, correct Craig?"

"Uh, yeah. Who's this?"

"Colonel Matthew Bishop. Am I interrupting you, son?"

"What? No, not at all." His hesitation vanished. Craig was excited to have another chance with Bishop. "I'm just surprised to hear from you."

"I understand. I regret the way I left our conversation, and I wanted to offer the opportunity to meet again to discuss your . . ." He paused. ". . . situation."

"I'm so glad you reached out. The talk we had was helpful, and I really wanted to explore it more." Craig felt as if he needed to avoid being too specific.

"I was too dismissive of the origin of your gifts. And the ways in which I and the rest of the Council might be of help to you in activating them and focusing them."

"That would be great. I'd be all in for learning more."

There was a brief pause before Bishop continued. "Then let's plan to meet. Later tonight, if your schedule can allow it."

"Right, yeah." In his excitement, Craig's mind went blank as to his schedule. "I can definitely make the time."

"Splendid," replied Bishop.

Craig thought for a moment. "I'll just need to check to make sure my cousin, I mean Detective Walsh, is available too."

"Oh," Bishop said. "Detective Walsh. Of course. Will he need to accompany you?"

"I guess so," Craig wondered aloud. "He and I have kinda been in this together."

"Been together in what, son?"

Craig didn't want to try to explain. "It's nothing. He's just usually been a part of figuring all this out."

"I understand. I actually do," Bishop said, his voice reassuring. "And I know how challenging the journey toward understanding has been."

There was another pause, then Bishop went on. "By all means, have him join us if you like. It's entirely up to you. But you should understand that you do not need the detective with you in order to come into your own with these gifts. You must realize how singularly powerful you are becoming. These abilities were bestowed upon *you*. Both I and the rest of the Council are prepared to guide you."

"Yeah," Craig said, nodding, energy and confidence now flowing through him. "That makes sense."

"There is a window during which you can gain understanding. I do not want it to close for you. I am prepared to help you if you are ready."

"I'm ready," Craig said.

"Then let us continue this conversation in private. If you're available, there is an industrial park where the Council meets. I can give you the address, and we can plan to meet there early this evening, if that is agreeable."

"That sounds great." Craig fumbled in the drawer of the nightstand for a pen and a paper. "Fire away." Craig jotted down the information.

"I will see you soon," Bishop said, and hung up.

Craig felt both relieved and excited. For the rest of the afternoon, a feeling of anticipation coursed through his veins. It felt like everything was coming together at last, an opportunity to finally get to the bottom of the mystery and the role he was supposed to play. And it was on his terms. Not Danny, or Lauren, or Emma and her cryptic words in his dreams. He was illuminating his own light on something that had eluded him for so long. He had seen with his own eyes that Bishop not only understood Craig's powers but also possessed powers of his own.

It was nearing five o'clock when he left the house. The air was chilly for a late May evening as he made his way toward the Damen platform to ride the L to the south side of the city and the address Bishop had provided. The sun shone through intermittent clouds as he climbed the metal stairs to the elevated platform. As he walked out to the boarding area, he watched a train depart toward the city. He would be alone with his thoughts for another seven to ten minutes while he waited on the next one.

He stood apart from the few other people who trickled out onto the platform to wait. His mind began to drift, anticipating the meeting with Bishop and what he would learn. His thoughts then gave way to pangs of guilt. He was excluding Danny from a process they had been following together for so long. The irritation he had been feeling with his cousin over the past few days began to give way.

He withdrew his phone from his pocket. He stared at it resting in his palm. Within his chest, his excitement and apprehension gave way to calmness and surety. As his eyes fixed on the phone, he had the impulse to call his cousin. But then the phone blinked red, indicating a low battery.

"Shit," Craig said. As distracted as he had been all day, he hadn't bothered to plug it in to recharge.

Then, almost as if his other hand were guided by something

else, he pressed a key on his cell phone that served as a shortcut to dial Danny's number.

◆━◆━◆

Danny stepped from the stairs and onto the second-floor squad room of Chicago's Seventh Precinct. He was tired, disillusioned. He'd given up trying to reach his cousin after their meeting with Father Timothy two days ago.

It was the end of a long day in which Danny had helped investigate some routine robberies and other small crimes in the area. He walked over to his desk, ready to toss aside—literally—the files and paperwork he would need to complete from the day's activities, looking to leave them for tomorrow.

The breast pocket of his blazer buzzed and, feeling resigned, he withdrew his phone. His demeanor changed instantly as he saw who was calling him. He quickly answered the phone.

"Craig! Thank God."

"Hey, Danny. You got a minute?"

"A minute? Of course. I've been trying to reach you. Listen, I think I know why the meeting didn't go as planned at the church. It was my fault. There are some things—"

"No time for that right now. There's a meeting going down tonight that I thought you would be interested in."

"Oh? What's that?"

"That Bishop guy. He called me this afternoon. Said he changed his mind and is willing to meet again."

"Really?" said Danny. "That's good, I guess. But he called *you*? I haven't heard anything from him today."

"I was surprised by his call too. This guy probably holds the key to a lot of this for us. I don't want to let this window close again."

"Right, I get your motivation about that." Danny was

shifting gears in his head, away from prepping Craig for another encounter with Michael and toward absorbing this latest twist. "He called you directly today, did he?"

There was a brief pause. "Yeah," Craig said. "It sounded like he wanted to meet with me one-on-one."

"With you. Like, *just* with you?"

Craig huffed. "I'm the one with these powers. I can see why he'd want to come straight to the source."

Danny remained silent, waiting to see what else his cousin would say.

"Anyway, I thought I should involve you. After all, you're the one who came across this guy. I mean, we are in this together."

"We are."

"And you found him. I want to hear what he's got to say. I want to jump at the chance he offered tonight, if you can move on it with me now."

"Makes sense. Where are you right now?" Danny was cautious, still trying to understand the situation and gauge Craig's attitude toward it.

"I'm at the Damen platform getting ready to come down into the city."

"Okay," Danny said. "I think we need to meet for a few minutes before we go to him. Talk through where he might be coming from."

"Fine, but I don't have a ton of time. He said to meet at seven. It's pushing six now."

Danny checked the watch he wore on his prosthetic wrist. "Then let's meet up once you get down here. Where are you taking the L?"

"The address he gave me looks like it would be closest to the Forty-Seventh Street station."

"Really? What's the address?" As Craig gave it to him, Danny felt a presence approaching from across the squad room. But he didn't turn toward it—he wanted to keep all his attention on Craig.

He closed his eyes to do some time management. "Okay, so it will probably take twenty to twenty-five minutes to get there from where you're at. I'll meet you there with a car. Okay?"

"Sure," Craig agreed.

"If you get there before I do, just wait. I'll be along soon. Gotta run," Danny said.

Then something dawned on Danny. "Wait a minute. How did Bishop get his number?"

"How did Bishop get whose number?" Mason asked.

Danny turned to engage. "I'm just thinking out loud."

"I never did understand what interest you had with that guy a few weeks ago when he was here doing the terrorist profile briefings."

"I don't think I had an interest in him so much. I was just . . ."

"C'mon, Walsh. What gives? We're all in this together. Remember the understanding that you and I and Hammond reached? It still holds."

"I know, I know." Danny wasn't up for playing games, and he genuinely felt like he didn't have to anymore with Mason. "Craig's been through some shit in his life, and I thought Bishop might be someone who could help him."

"I see. Well, I hope he's doing okay. Although I'm not sold on how legit Bishop's help will be. Your cousin deserves the advice of someone who isn't as egocentric as Bishop comes off."

"Agreed. And I appreciate your asking about Craig. But I

need to get a move on right now if I'm to catch up with him before he meets Bishop."

Mason flashed Danny a puzzled look. "You are meeting Bishop somewhere? Like, tonight?"

"Yeah. I just got a call from Craig about it. It's a little spur-of-the-moment, but that's probably on brand for this guy."

"Where are you supposed to meet him?"

"South Loop warehouses, near Halsted Street. Shooting for seven p.m."

"Kind of an odd spot. It'll start to get dark close to eight."

"True," Danny replied. He scrunched up his nose and closed his eyes, suddenly remembering something.

"I'm off shift, so second shift has it."

"Huh?" Mason wasn't following.

"I don't have a car now. Richards, the detective on second shift, would've already taken it out."

"Just take my car then. It's on the second deck of the garage. Here's the keys."

Danny shifted his cane into his prosthetic hand so he could catch the set of keys that Mason tossed.

"Dark gray Impala, space twelve. Just tell the booth when you exit that you have the go-ahead from me."

Danny breathed a sigh of relief. "Perfect. That'll help a ton." He was already feeling tired and anxious to meet up with Craig, and he didn't need any additional complications with getting there as soon as he could.

One of the desk officers hurried over to them.

Mason raised his hand to his chest. "You need me?"

"No," the officer said. He looked at Danny. "Detective Walsh, I'm supposed to give you a heads-up on a call. This woman called your desk phone not even an hour ago. She was pretty irritated that she got your voicemail and transferred out to the desk. I told her I couldn't take her info and sent her back to your voicemail. She made me promise to give you the heads-up at the end of your shift. But not before she let me know she was none too happy."

Danny looked down at his desk phone, and there was indeed a flashing light indicating that a message was waiting.

"Thank you," Danny said.

The desk officer left them. Mason stood close as Danny held the receiver to his ear and listened to the message.

"Danny, it's Lauren. Listen, I'm not sure what you and Craig have been up to. But I don't appreciate being manipulated into meeting. If you want to have an intervention with Craig to try to get him pointed forward, I'm all for it. But not like this. I don't like what you're proposing in your message, and I'm not comfortable with it. But you should know by now that you and I both want what's best for Craig. If this is something I have to do to show you, then I guess I will."

Mason raised his brows. "What is it, Walsh? What's up?"

Danny lowered the phone onto its cradle and stared absentmindedly into the distance. "That's genuinely strange," he mumbled.

"What's strange?" asked Mason.

"That was Craig's girlfriend, Lauren. The one Hammond mentioned when the three of us talked."

"Yeah, I remember the reference."

"And she was pissed."

"Pissed about what?"

"Something about me leaving her a message about roping her into a meeting to confront Craig. Or something. Not sure." Danny's eyes darted around. There was already so much swirling in his head, and now this. "But the thing is, I didn't leave her any messages. So what the hell was that about?"

"Call your cousin."

Danny quickly called Craig on his cell phone and waited as the phone rang, then the call connected and instantly rolled to voicemail."

"Dammit. His phone must be off or outta charge or something."

"Who knows, Walsh? Maybe Lauren thought it was you who left the message, or maybe—"

"Fuck!" Danny looked up at the wall clock. "I don't have time to try to figure this out. It's already after six!"

"Then get outta here, Walsh. Get the car and roll. I'll help you with this later if you need it."

Without another word, Danny spun on his heel and made his way toward the stairs.

———————— • ••• • ————————

He casually glanced around the squad room to assess whose eyes, if any, might be on him. It had only been a few minutes since Danny disappeared down the stairwell.

Feeling appropriately inconspicuous, Mason walked a few paces to the window closest to Danny's desk. He withdrew his cell phone from his pocket, scrolled down to a saved number, and dialed.

"Detective Adams? It's Mason. Remember that thing we talked about? I think something could go down tonight. If you're ready, I'll need your support on it."

Mason paused and listened to the response.

"I knew you'd be in for this if it was needed," Mason said.

"I need you to meet me in the garage as soon as you can get here. See you then."

He ended the call and then searched for another saved number on his phone. He dialed it and glanced around the squad room impatiently as he waited for someone to pick up.

"Hey, Jimmy, how you doing? It's Jack," Mason said. "I'm going to need your help tonight with that thing we talked about. Adams can meet us in the garage in about twenty minutes. I need you to haul ass over here and we'll go in your car."

He ended the call and shoved his phone into his pocket. He took a deep breath and stared at Danny's desk.

"All right, let's see where this goes."

21

THE INVICTUS

Craig looked nervously at his watch, his impatience growing.

"Come on," he mumbled as he stood on the lower platform of the Forty-Seventh Street station, scanning the street for Danny's police sedan.

Letting out a sigh, he pulled his phone from his pocket, forgetting it was dead. "Shit!" he exclaimed. He shoved the phone back into his pocket and glanced at his wristwatch again to check the time. It was quarter to seven. "Where are you, Danny?"

A couple of short bursts of a car horn drew Craig's attention to a sedan that had just rolled up to the curb and parked near the station exit. *It must be Danny*, Craig thought. He didn't recognize the car, but he saw his cousin sitting behind the wheel. He made his way to the car, pulled the door open, and slid in.

"What's this?"

"Long story. It's Mason's car," Danny shot back. "What gives with you? I've been calling you."

"Phone's dead. Forgot to charge it last night."

Irritated, Danny said, "Speaking of last night, where have you been? I keep trying to get ahold of you, in case you hadn't noticed."

"Oh, I noticed. I needed to clear my head."

Craig fidgeted in his seat as they sat near the curb, the

sedan's flashers on. "Can we get a move on? I thought you'd be here sooner."

"I know. I tried. Listen . . . this meeting seems weird to me."

Craig scoffed. "No, what seemed weird was when Bishop blew us off last week. He's come around, and we should be grateful for it."

"I get it why you'd think that way," Danny said. "Give me the address."

Craig recited it as Danny drove away from the curb.

"We should be fine," said Danny. "It's near a couple of the other spots where we've been recently—the warehouse area where you did the re-creation, and the military center where we met Bishop."

"It probably makes sense that he'd want to meet around there if he hangs out at the military place," Craig rationalized.

"I know you want to get off and rolling with this but hear me out. About what went down at the church with Father Timothy . . ."

Craig rolled his eyes. "Just stop, all right? I respect whatever reason you have for going to church."

Danny shook his head as he turned onto a side street. "That's not what this is about, Craig."

"Whatever. I'm just not sure that—whoever that was—can help. But Bishop? He can help us pull the pieces together."

"There's something there, sure. But this is bigger than you know, and you need to understand all of it."

"I agree that it's big!" Craig blurted, exasperated. "It's not lost on me that my abilities start returning right when there's another one of those things in the city. And he's aware of us! That's why we can't turn down a chance to learn more from Bishop."

"Craig," Danny said and then stopped.

"*What?*" Craig gritted his teeth.

"I screwed up by not painting a better picture for you before you met Father Timothy."

"That's all right. You've been taking the lead and serving up the pieces and the clues. I appreciate that. But Bishop is the play, not Father Timothy or Michael, or whoever he was."

Danny shook his head. "It just doesn't feel right to me."

"Well, I'm all in for it," Craig said with intensity. "No offense, but I don't want to listen to you or Lauren or anybody else right now. There's only one person we've met who has hit the mark, and that's Bishop."

At the mention of Lauren, Danny perked up. "Lauren . . . so what's up with her? She left a message for me about you."

"Oh? What did she say?"

"She said she's uncomfortable with what you and I have been up to. Wondered whether the three of us should have an intervention. It sounded something like that anyway."

"She said that to *you*?"

"Yeah. She didn't sound happy, but I couldn't figure out why."

Craig looked down, feeling embarrassed that he always left Lauren out of the loop, so much so that now she felt the need to reach out to Danny.

"We're here," Danny announced. They were in an industrial park. He pulled into a driveway that led to a large brick warehouse. The parking lot was practically empty as Danny glided the car into a parking spot near the entrance.

"So, what's the deal with Lauren? Why would she leave a message like that?" Danny asked.

Craig deflected. "Don't worry about her. She and I are trying to work some things out."

Danny twisted in his seat toward Craig. "You *still* haven't told her everything?"

"C'mon, it's almost seven. Let's not keep this guy waiting." Craig opened the car door.

They stood in front of the car and stared at the building. It was four stories high, with a dark red brick exterior. On each side of the entrance, there was a grid of leaded paned windows, starting at about seven or eight feet off the ground. Several of them were cracked or missing glass.

As they assessed their destination, Craig's mind dwelled on Lauren. His hand fiddled with the medallion she had given him, which hung from a chain just inside his shirt collar.

As the low sunlight bathed the front of the factory building, Craig pulled out of his thoughts and turned to Danny. "So?"

Danny lifted his eyes to look over Craig's shoulder. He raised his eyebrows to indicate they weren't alone.

A man emerged from a door near a corner of the building, raising his hand to hail them. He had an athletic build and was wearing a navy windbreaker and dark jeans. His brown hair was cut short and framed a clean-cut face.

Craig glanced over his shoulder. "Okay, good. Let's go."

"Craig, wait."

"Come on, Danny. This is what we've been waiting for." Exasperated, Craig shook his head and stomped off toward the man and the door, ignoring Danny's caution.

Danny opened his mouth to speak but instead hurried to catch up. They followed the man through the entrance. Danny was the last through. He left the door open behind him.

Once they were all inside, Craig asked, "Is this where we're supposed to meet the colonel?" Instead of responding, the man, who Craig could only assume was a bodyguard, wordlessly nodded in the affirmative and pointed to an area above them.

Danny and Craig stopped about a dozen paces into the building. The bodyguard moved to their left and took up a position about twenty paces into the room. He turned to face them, his arms drawn behind his back in the parade rest posture, an informal stance that a soldier might take.

The interior of the building was tiered. Craig, Danny, and the bodyguard stood on the entrance level before a three- to four-foot ledge that resembled a stage riser. The "stage" was much larger than the entry level. It appeared to have once been the main shop area, but the space was sparsely occupied now, with only a few pieces of equipment scattered about. Scanning the setup, Craig noted a short staircase near the wall to their right that led up the riser and onto the shop floor.

The auburn rays of the falling sun streamed through the grid work of windows behind Craig and Danny, illuminating the interior of the shop floor. The glow had already started drifting up toward the ceiling, revealing yet another level of the building and what looked like a foreman's office. A split flight of stairs led down from the office, with the first set of steps reaching a wide landing and the second set arriving on the main shop floor.

"Do you know this place?" Craig asked Danny.

"Seen it but haven't been inside. Looks like a machine shop or a tool factory. Odd, though. Looks like it's been out of business for a while."

"What's it used for now?"

"I like to call it a home away from home, for myself and for others like me," a voice called from above.

Craig and Danny looked up as Bishop emerged from the elevated office. He made his way down the first set of stairs and stopped on the landing. He wore a plain gray suit and a white dress shirt with no tie.

Craig greeted him. "Colonel Bishop, good to see you."

"I'm so glad you could make it on such short notice; my apologies about that."

"It worked out fine," Craig said.

"And I see you've brought the good detective with you," Bishop added, acknowledging Danny.

Before Danny could address him, another bodyguard entered and closed the door behind him. He walked past them and took up a pose similar to his colleague's on the opposite side of the room.

Bishop recaptured their attention. His presence was authoritative, and he spoke almost as if he were holding court. "Mr. Walsh must certainly have much else on his investigative plate that should be commanding his time. Nonetheless, I welcome him to our discussion."

"Danny's been an important part of my journey," Craig acknowledged.

"That's something I could clearly sense during our last meeting, Craig. In truth, I've worried about your situation since that conversation. I've conferred with other members of the Council, and we thought it wise that I engage you concerning your gifts, despite how you came to inherit them."

"Really. Why is that?" Craig prompted. He was keen to take in Bishop's every word.

An odd configuration of people was assembled within the space: two members of Bishop's entourage were stationed at either end of the floor, and Bishop towered over them on the stairway landing. Craig seemed oblivious to the full picture, gazing up at Bishop as if he held all the answers. The whole scene seemed surreal—and entirely out of place.

"I've been concerned about the threat you could pose to others, Craig. I need a better understanding of your abilities to ensure that you do not harm anyone."

"Me, a threat?" Craig asked.

"How is he a threat?" seconded Danny.

Bishop glanced at Danny before turning back to Craig.

"We can answer your questions, Craig. And we can guide you. But first I'd like to know that you will comply with what we ask of you."

Danny prodded Bishop. "There are others like you—is that what you're saying? I mean, like Craig?"

"Of course there are," Bishop answered.

"And the others, are they are like you? I mean, like me too? How many of us are there?" The thrill of being on the verge of real answers drew the questions out of Craig in rapid fire.

"I was hoping you might be able to tell me," Bishop replied.

Danny countered Bishop's odd comment. "How would Craig know? Why wouldn't you and your . . . council know?" Danny was growing more disconcerted, but not Craig. He was entranced, as if on the edge of a great discovery.

Bishop ignored Danny and kept his eyes fixed on Craig. "It is trauma that brings forth the gifts. There is no way we can know exactly how many people both have accepted the gifts and transformed them into powers through trauma."

"Colonel, wait a second. So what you're saying—" Danny started before Bishop plowed ahead.

"You are finally beginning to understand the power behind the letters that have long vexed you," Bishop asserted.

Craig nodded. "The Council of the—"

"Invictus!" Bishop finished with enthusiasm. "Your connection to this group is within reach. We welcome you, and others like you, because we understand how powerful you are."

Craig's eyes were wide, his chest thrust out and his hands drawn into loose fists. He felt almost hypnotized.

"The Council must draw together all of those who share these abilities. Don't you see, my boy? This hasn't been merely a strange coincidence, some obscure geometry of chance."

Craig dropped his gaze. He looked down at his hands as he unfolded his fingers from his palms.

"You have borne a heavy burden, haven't you?" Bishop said.

"Yes," Craig answered. "But I know it will have been worth it when I finally understand."

"You need to unburden yourself. To let loose. But you will need guidance on where to focus your power."

"My father—he was a part of this. And I'm to be part of it too."

"Yes. We leave clues for those who pay attention, hoping they will understand and find their way to us."

Danny appeared confused about what was going on between Craig and Bishop. He glanced at the two members of Bishop's entourage, who remained at their posts. Then he said, "The clues I understand. The letters have appeared to us in different ways over the years. But some of the clues surfaced through my police work. And it was I who crossed paths with you on the force, Colonel. Not Craig."

Bishop flickered a glance in Danny's direction before locking eyes with Craig. "Your father accepted his calling—willingly—and was part of this Council. He took his direction from us and helped further our important work."

"What kind of work?" Craig asked.

"Those who have caused you trauma also bring it to others

every day. Giving false hope. Beguiling them with the idea that their gifts are for others, when in truth they have been reserved to obstruct those who must be stopped."

"But how will I know who those people are, the ones who have to be stopped? And *why* do they need to be stopped?" Craig asked.

"We will guide you. We will lead you to those who have earned the kind of judgment that you can levy upon them with your powers."

Craig was only a few feet from his cousin, but it seemed like a gulf had grown between them that widened with every word that rolled off Bishop's tongue.

Danny took a step closer to Craig and tried to jump in again. "Craig, how can you be sure he's right? How do you know what you're supposed to do with your powers is what *they* say it is?"

Bishop answered instead. "Because he, like myself, as well as a few others, have been entrusted with this responsibility, Detective. You cannot begin to understand. And you certainly cannot be brought into the effort yourself. Your injuries have made you infirm."

Danny bristled at the characterization. He leveled a stare at Craig so piercing that it couldn't be ignored.

Craig met his eyes. He shrugged his shoulders in apology, acknowledging that, despite their traveling on this path together over the years, Danny's role might have come to an end.

Bishop's voice boomed, "Craig, *you* are the one who has been gifted. And you have advanced beyond the detective's ability to guide you. Your path forward is one that he cannot follow."

Craig seemed to be slipping further away from his cousin as Bishop's words drew him in.

"Craig, listen to what I'm saying," Danny appealed. "I don't believe for a second that you are supposed to use your powers as some kind of an enforcer. You're not like that. Your dad wasn't like that."

"You have felt this path coursing through you, haven't you, Craig?" Bishop said, teasing back his attention.

"Craig, don't look at him. Keep looking at me. Does this feel right to you?" Danny spoke urgently now, as if he was running out of time to distract Craig from the spell that was being cast on him. "What he calls you, what he's asking of you, doesn't change the core of who you are." Craig stared at him blankly.

"Craig, think for a second. Don't be defined by what he's describing. You really think you're just supposed to be a weapon to get pointed at the people that *they* decide deserve it? Your purpose has to be more than what he's saying." Danny flipped his finger in Bishop's direction.

Something in Danny's intensity got through to Craig. "Wait . . . wait a minute, Danny. What did you just say?" he asked. He blinked rapidly as if emerging from a fog or a dream.

"What I'm saying is that it doesn't matter what picture he's trying to paint for you. You're still *you*. Don't let him limit you. You're the one—the *only* one—who gets to define yourself and your role in this world. Believe me. I can feel it. You don't need this guy or his council."

Danny's words echoed Lauren's voice inside Craig's head. *What was it that she said?* Craig thought. *Once you put a name to something, you begin to put limits on it.*

Danny must have sensed the opening. "I know this has been hard. But, damn, you must see that I'm giving everything I've got to help you. It'll come together; I know it will. I just don't think it's *this*. And I think I know what it should be instead."

"Mr. Henriksen," Bishop called out in a sing-song tone, trying to lure Craig's attention once more.

Danny's words were starting to break the spell.

Craig took a step toward his cousin. As he did, he felt some of the energy, the raw power, that had been building within him recede. Replacing it was calm, a sense of surety in aligning with Danny. Craig noticed the grave concern on Danny's face, and a flood of memories washed through his mind: all the times when Danny had guided him and protected him, well into adulthood. The time he was prepared to give his life to save Craig from the Tourist's destruction.

Danny kept pushing. "Whatever your gifts mean, you'll figure it out. And I'll have your back the whole way. Like I always said I would."

Craig sighed heavily. "You're right, Danny," he agreed.

Bishop broke in. "But is he, Craig? You are a young man with extraordinary powers. Are you really going to choose to cast your lot with someone who is uninvited to such powers? So disappointing." There was a sharp edge in Bishop's voice now.

Danny dropped any pretext of respect. "Who the hell are you?" he demanded.

Bishop ignored him. "You can be everything you've wanted, Craig . . . everything you have found lacking in your life. You can exact justice on those you know deserve it. Come with us, and we will teach you how to deliver it."

"Colonel Bishop, this is the second time I've met you, and the second time you've wanted me to put aside my history with Danny. Why? It doesn't make sense." Craig was beginning to see Bishop with fresh eyes.

"My boy, do you think he can aid you anywhere near as powerfully as I can?"

"Just *you* now? What happened to the Council?" Craig threw back.

"Oh, it exists. And I think you will need its help as well."

Craig could feel every fiber of muscle in his chest and arms tightening. "Yeah, well, I think I'll be just fine."

"We shall see, won't we?"

There was movement up on the shop floor. To their left, a man emerged from the shadows, dressed similarly to Bishop's other men and conveying the same dispassionate air. A noise came from the right side of the shop floor, and Craig and Danny noticed another bodyguard taking up his position. An eerie silenced gripped the factory.

It was Bishop who broke it. "It has come to this. How truly unfortunate."

"What are you talking about?" Craig asked, confused.

Danny's eyes darted around the building at the suddenly elevated threat. They were outnumbered.

Bishop's mood seemed to shift, now less intense but more self-assured. "You have been a bit of a puzzle for us to tease out, Craig. But I'm sure I don't have to explain that to you."

All of the bodyguards had shifted their focus squarely on them, as their hands drifted toward the interiors of their windbreaker jackets.

"Now, wait, wait. Let's just hold on a moment," Danny growled.

"Danny, what the hell is going on?" Craig yelled out.

"Ah, Mr. Henriksen. I was certain that you had a muse to guide you. I just believed it was someone other than the detective. Right, my dear?"

Bishop looked up toward the foreman's office and beckoned

with his hand. A man emerged from the office, and he was pushing a woman in front of him.

Craig gasped. "Lauren!" he called out.

She looked distressed as the man behind her grabbed her shoulders.

"What the hell are you doing with her?" Craig demanded.

As the entire situation spiraled out of control, Danny drew his handgun from his shoulder holster and leveled it at Bishop, who stood his ground on the landing. "I don't know what game you're playing, but you need to let her the fuck go," he barked.

The four bodyguards flanking them reacted as if commanded by some silent cue, each drawing out a handgun, two aiming at Craig and two at Danny.

Bishop was calm. He nodded to the man above him, who then led Lauren down the stairs toward the landing. Before they reached it, he gave her a rough shove and she stumbled. Bishop stopped her fall by clutching her shoulders.

"What am I doing with her, you ask? I am just facilitating your reunion. My dear, haven't you long sought to understand the exploits of these two?" Bishop's words seemed both carefree and foreboding.

Lauren looked at Bishop in silent terror, her body frozen in place as he held her.

"Lauren, are you okay?" Craig said. *Why isn't she answering me?*

"I had planned for her presence to be your reward for our reaching an understanding between us," Bishop said, "for your choosing to take guidance from me."

"Lauren, don't worry. Everything will be fine," Craig said in what he hoped was a reassuring tone. But he recognized the words were hollow as they left his lips.

Bishop spoke with comfort and ease. "Imagine how silly I feel now. This lovely lady was not the one who served as your muse, the one who counseled you as you struggled to understand your place." He glared at Danny. "Rather, it was this pathetic cripple. And I suppose he was attempting to be both your muse *and* your protector."

Craig and Danny looked at each other, bewildered.

Bishop's carefree attitude suddenly vanished. An evil grin creased his lips, and dark malevolence wrinkled around his eyes. "But can he protect you? Of course not. In fact, nothing can now."

As Craig eyed Bishop's grip on Lauren, panic overwhelmed him. He looked wildly around the room at the bodyguards who had their weapons drawn.

"Craig, Craig! Look at me!" Danny called.

Craig spun around and found Danny's eyes, which were wide with fear. Beads of perspiration instantly speckled the entirety of Danny's cheeks and brow. The only other time this spontaneously happened was when they encountered the Tourist in Iowa.

"Oh no!" Craig said as he brought his hands to his own face. It, too, was slick with perspiration. A thick humidity had descended upon them. "He's one of them!" he shouted "They're back!"

"We never left, you fool," Bishop snarled.

"Lauren, honey. Hold tight. It's gonna be fine. Please, trust me," Craig pleaded. But she remained unresponsive, her eyes fixed on Bishop's.

"Do you honestly think you are in a position to ensure the safety of this lovely woman?" Bishop taunted.

"Let her go. Right now! Or I'll hurt you." Craig clenched his fists, ready for combat, but he and Danny were outmatched. Bishop's men meant business.

Silence hung thick in the air.

Then came the sound of shattering glass as two, possibly three, windows on the wall behind Craig and Danny burst into pieces. A moment later, several steel canisters clattered to the floor and slid and spun across the room.

In the brief instant while everyone tried to regain their bearings, Danny drew his gun close to his chest and clutched his cane tightly as he braced for impact.

The flash grenades detonated in rapid-fire sequence. Blinding light and deafening sound blasts echoed through the building, and smoke billowed throughout the space.

The canisters had accomplished their intended purpose: Bishop's bodyguards had been thrown into disarray. Stunned by the explosions, they had dropped their weapons. Craig cowered and grimaced, not yet understanding what was happening.

"No! It's a diversion!" Bishop shouted from the stairwell. "Take them!" he ordered.

The four bodyguards gathered themselves, two of them scanning the floor to locate their weapons while the other two made their way toward the cousins, prepared to launch a physical attack. Just then, a new booming noise echoed through the building, this time coming from the main door behind them.

With smoke clouding the scene, confusion reigned, and Bishop's entourage halted as Danny and Craig spun around to face the door.

A final deafening blow ripped the door off its hinges and hurtled it into the room, followed by a metal battering ram that clanged to the floor.

Three men burst through the door.

"Mason!" Danny shouted as if to announce the first of the three to make it inside.

Undaunted by the three new entrants to the scene, the bodyguards bore down on the cousins.

"No!" shouted Bishop, enraged to find that the imbalance of power he had orchestrated for the meeting was unraveling.

Jack Mason, along with two others, fanned out. "Adams!" Mason shouted as he pointed at the two bodyguards who were closing in on Craig. He turned and shouted similarly "Sullivan!" who then ran in the opposite direction, blocking the two men who were pushing headlong toward Danny. Mason jogged his way into the middle, his eyes flashing around the scene as smoke curled, voices shouted, and the first gunshots rang out.

Bishop still held Lauren. Mason ran straight to the ledge, as if preparing to leap up and engage Bishop. A fifth bodyguard came into view above the ledge with gun drawn. Mason quickly ducked below the ledge, barely avoiding the gunfire from the new attacker.

His voice booming, Bishop yelled, "Henriksen! Get him! Quickly!"

Craig had been grabbed by two of Bishop's men, but not before Adams shot one of them and clipped his shoulder. Closing the distance, Adams tackled the wounded man to the ground.

The other two men were closing in on Danny. As the first one reached him, Danny swung his cane and smashed it against the man's head, sending him crashing to the floor. Sullivan pushed past Danny and leveled his firearm at the second attacker—but not fast enough; the attacker retrieved his gun and shot Sullivan in the thigh. Sullivan crumpled to the ground.

Mason stayed crouched near the ledge. "Shit!" he yelled. Danny's confrontation continued to unfold. He swung his cane again and knocked the second man's handgun away. Though unarmed, the bodyguard still laid into Danny, taking him to the ground. Mason drew his gun and aimed it at Danny and his attacker. Meanwhile, Sullivan lay wounded nearby, and the first man who had attacked Danny seemed to be gathering himself, ready to rejoin the fight.

Mason holstered his weapon and ran toward Danny.

Across the floor, Craig grappled with one of his two attackers while Adams tackled the wounded man. For a fleeting moment, Craig realized that the three men who had burst into the building were law enforcement. He recognized the name 'Mason' that Danny yelled to be Danny's new Lieutenant. He was grateful they came to his and Danny's aid, since the situation had devolved into a life-threatening confrontation. The injured man was still in fighting shape, and Adams was locked in a fierce wrestling match with him on the floor.

Craig's attacker had the advantage now—Craig was on his back in the guard position with his legs pinned. The man had drawn a gun and was struggling to bring it up and point it at Craig's head.

Craig's martial arts training took over. Using the force of the attacker's downward push against him, Craig reversed his resistance. Pulling the force toward him instead, he smashed the man's gun hand into the concrete floor. The bodyguard bellowed in pain as the gun dislodged from his hand and scooted across the floor. Grasping the man's injured hand with one of his own, Craig placed his free hand on the man's shoulder and twisted, pinning the man's arm against his own neck and chest. Then, with an upward thrust of his hips, Craig deftly flipped the man off him. But he kept the arm securely pinned.

Bishop continued to shout orders from the landing, guarded by the only bodyguard who had not yet attacked, as the fighting dragged on: Craig and Adams with their attackers and Danny, Sullivan, and Mason battling the other two. Danny was trading blows with fist and cane against one man. Mason seemed to jump in front of the second one a mere instant before Danny would have had to deal with them both. This attacker was larger and more skilled than the others, and quickly threw Mason off him and got to his feet. But Mason looked unintimidated. He dodged or parried away every blow, returning thunderous punches to the face or kicks to the ribs.

The man then drew out a knife. Mason blocked his stabbing motion, locked his arm, and drove him onto the concrete floor, where he lay stunned and gasping.

Meanwhile, Danny had been thrown onto his back. His attacker stood over him and was fishing inside his jacket to draw out another handgun. But too late. Danny drew up his cane, balanced it on his bent knee, pointed the tip at the attacker, and pulled the trigger that was secreted under the handle. The shotgun blast caught the man squarely in the face and he fell into a heap.

Craig heard the shot but kept his focus. He was desperate to reach Lauren and needed to neutralize his attacker. He slithered beneath the man he had pinned, thrusting his forearm under his chin and against his throat, and wrenched it tight, cutting off his oxygen supply. The man fell unconscious. Craig rolled out from underneath him and onto his feet.

Bishop looked down on them, scowling. His eyes locked with Craig's, and Craig saw pure malice in Bishop's dark, beady eyes. Bishop still gripped Lauren tightly with one hand. Craig winced at the look of horror on her face.

Bishop narrowed his eyes and moved his hand to Lauren's neck.

"No!" Craig screamed. He took off in a run toward the ledge.

Then, unbidden, Craig heard words echoing in his head. It was Bishop's voice: *Your soul will forever dwell in darkness.*

Bishop was now lifting Lauren's body off the ground by the neck, effortlessly—impossible for a man of his small stature.

"Craig!" Danny yelled, as he looked to be keeping his own attacker subdued. "Oh, God, no," he said breathlessly.

Lauren struggled and squirmed, her legs flailing helplessly in the air and her hands straining to tear Bishop's grip from her throat. But Bishop was crushing her windpipe, suffocating her.

"Lauren, hold on!" Craig yelled. He bolted toward the ledge, poised to vault up and battle Bishop. But just as he reached it, he was tackled from behind. One of the bodyguards had somehow wrested free and was forcing him to the ground just feet from the ledge.

Craig unleashed his fury on the man. He let loose a hail of punches and blows that the man tried to counter, but he was no match for Craig's skill, driven by rage. He knocked the man out with one final blow to the head. Craig quickly got back up. He saw Danny out of the corner of his eye, careening toward the ledge, determined to rescue Lauren.

Adrenaline surging, Craig vaulted onto the ledge and ran toward the staircase. Pure terror flooded through his body as he felt Lauren's life slipping away. She was in mortal distress, and her gaze began to soften as she looked off vacantly into the distance.

As he ran toward her, Craig extended his hand, feeling once again the funnel of power building in his palm. He would wield it against Bishop to dislodge his choke hold on Lauren. But before he could unleash it, he felt the searing pain of the gunshot at the exact instant he saw the flash of a gun barrel.

The blast caught Craig squarely in his ribs. He was thrown to the ground, clutching his chest with both hands. He had forgotten about the fifth bodyguard, who was now at the base of the stairs. Through the pain he watched Lauren cease to struggle. Her hands fell limp to her sides.

Bishop released her lifeless body and let it fall onto the staircase landing as Craig's vision went black.

22

TEXTURE OF JUSTICE

Mason was holding the assailant who had tried to stab him to the floor when he heard a gunshot ring out. He glanced up at the upper tier of the shop floor as Craig fell forward and collapsed onto it. Turning back to his opponent, Mason delivered a final thunderous blow to the assailant's head. He paused for an instant to see the man was unconscious, then clawed inside his vest for his police radio.

"Squad Seven, this is Mason. I've got a ten-one. Repeat: a ten-one. We have multiple men down! Machine shop building on South Wolcott, just south of Forty-Fifth Street. Copy—now!"

A barely comprehensible radio message responded in the affirmative.

Out of the corner of his eye, he spotted Danny, who remained frozen after seeing Craig fall. Mason instinctively ducked as he heard several more shots popping off from the stairs. Both he and Danny were now crouched beneath the shelter of the ledge. The bodyguard who had just shot Craig had fired several shots at them from his elevated vantage point at the foot of the stairwell.

As Mason peered over the ledge, he got a good look at Bishop's face. The man was glaring down at Craig where he had fallen, a look of disgust twisting his features. Mason was perplexed by the snarl that curled Bishop's face. Wouldn't he be happy to see Craig, the target of his rage, so grievously injured, effectively neutralized?

The bodyguard drew out another handgun and squeezed off several more rounds of covering fire. Danny, Mason, the other detectives, and their assailants on the lower floor huddled on the ground. After a moment, Mason heard the sound of running feet. He raised his head just enough to see Craig still lying on his back. Bishop and his bodyguard raced up the stairwell toward the office and their escape. Bishop hesitated for a moment as he looked back down at Lauren's body and shook his head dismissively. Then Bishop looked at Craig's body a last time, bolted through the office door, and was gone. The bodyguard who had kept them at bay followed immediately behind.

With the threat of further gunfire gone, Mason jumped to his feet and trained his attention on Craig. His finger jabbed in the direction of the stairs and Lauren. "Walsh, get up there and see to her! I've got your cousin."

Mason leapt up onto the ledge and raced across the floor toward Craig. He rolled Craig over onto his back. Craig's eyes were closed, and his body was rigid. Mason feared the worst.

Craig's hands were clutched to his chest. When Mason pried them off, he saw blood staining the front of Craig's shirt. "Shit!" Mason shouted as he ripped open the top of the shirt. Mason dug inside his vest where he kept a handkerchief. He was preparing to press it against the wound he expected to find. Then he froze, and his mouth fell open. He peered at the flesh underneath the bloodstain but found no visible wound at all. Mason shook his head in confusion as Craig took in a sharp breath and his eyes flew open.

"What the . . . ?" Mason exclaimed.

Craig looked to be coming back into consciousness as

Mason squatted over him. Mason watched Craig's eyes grow wide as if coming back into awareness. Craig's head jerked around and toward the stairwell. "Get off me, damn it!" he shouted.

"Henriksen, wait! Where are you hit?" Mason asked.

But the words had barely left his mouth when Craig clutched the hand that held his shirt and used his other hand to shove Mason's shoulder hard enough to send him rolling off to the side.

Craig jumped up and ran, calling Lauren's name as he made his way to the stairwell. Danny had just reached her and was kneeling to provide aid. Mason heard shouts and a commotion behind him as he got to his feet. Adams was busy securing one of Bishop's men, zip-tying his hands at his back and then around a steel support column that rose to the rafters.

As Craig ran toward the stairwell, Mason pulled himself upright and shook his head in disbelief. *That dude just took one square in the chest. What the hell?*

Mason looked back to where Craig had fallen. A glint of metal on the floor caught his eye.

"Well, what's this?" he said under his breath. He reached down and picked up a small, flattened slug. He rolled it about in his fingers—it was still warm. And it had a tackiness to it, as if it had been in contact with flesh.

"I'll be damned."

"Jack!" shouted Adams. "What gives?" He nodded in the direction where Craig had run.

"Dunno."

Mason turned his attention to Sullivan. "Sully, how bad are you hit?"

Sullivan was seated with his legs straight out in front of

him, only a few feet away from the man whose face had been blown off by the blast from Danny's shotgun cane.

"Not that bad. I should be good. Think it's only a surface wound. I'll be up there in a sec."

Sullivan was already busy fashioning a tourniquet out of his belt and wrapping it around his leg to stem the bleeding.

Adams finished securing the bodyguard Craig had choked out—who was now conscious—and walked up the side stairs to meet Mason. Mason was still perplexed, but he shoved the spent bullet into his pocket.

"What the hell was up with him?" Adams said, referencing Craig.

"I thought he'd been hit. I guess he wasn't," Mason answered.

"Did you call it in?" asked Adams.

"Yeah. We probably have a couple more minutes before one of us needs to get outside to flag them in." He turned to see Danny crouched over Lauren with Craig behind him. "I need to figure out just what the hell is up with Walsh. Until then, I need you to get square with Sully—make sure you two keep this on the down-low until I can tease it out."

"Jack, this is fucked up."

"I know. What's more fucked up is that the same guy who's been consulting the force on terrorist shit is the one who orchestrated this. He lays a trap to take down Walsh and Walsh's cousin. And the cousin's girl? And us too, if they could've pulled it off."

"I hear what you're saying. I'll close the loop with Sully. For now, Jack."

His tone seemed to indicate that he expected to get an explanation for these bizarre events from Mason later. But

Mason was still baffled by the situation. He knew that any answers would lie with Walsh.

———◆—◆—◆———

The precious few minutes that passed had seemed like an eternity.

"Danny, how is she?" Craig's voice, tinged with desperation, rang out from the platform on the stairs. "Come on, Danny! Is she . . . I mean, how is she?"

Squatting over Lauren, his back to Craig, Danny held two fingers against Lauren's neck. He held still, hoping—praying—for a pulse. His eyes were tightly closed. His teeth were grinding. Then he shook his head slowly, almost imperceptible. But Craig, peering down with utmost intensity, wide-eyed, seemed to understand what that meant.

"No, Danny. No! Say something, damn it!"

Danny's chin dropped to his chest. He opened his eyes and gathered a type of courage that he had never thought he would need to summon.

Turning toward Craig, he declared it. "She's gone, Craig. I'm so sorry."

As Danny rose, Craig pushed him out of the way and dropped to his knees. Caught off balance, Danny stumbled but grabbed for his cane to steady himself. Once fully upright, he stepped out of the way to give Craig a moment with Lauren.

Craig knelt down and gently lifted her head off the platform floor, his other arm supporting her limp body. Her eyes were slightly open, but vacant. Expressionless. It was Lauren's face, but she was no longer there.

Danny felt his insides plummeting. He could only imagine how Craig felt.

"No," Craig whispered. And with great care, he drew her body against his own. His hand disappeared into her wavy auburn hair.

Danny had no words. He knew Craig needed time alone with her. He climbed down the stairs and walked toward the ledge where Mason had come up to meet him.

"Is she . . . ?" Mason started.

Danny nodded.

"Oh, shit," Mason said, his hand drifting up to his forehead. "This is terrible."

Danny wanted to present a proper front to his superior given the complexity of what had transpired that afternoon. "I don't get it. With Bishop. Why? How? And why pull Lauren into this? It makes no damn sense."

As Danny spoke, a wave of guilt descended on his heart. Bishop had now been fully revealed for what he truly was: one of the dark descendants that Michael had shown him in the ancient vision in his mind. The same as in the re-creation Craig had conjured of the three gang members' murders. Bishop had laid this trap tonight, using Lauren as bait—or leverage—against Craig. And while the fortunate arrival of Mason and the other detectives had disrupted his plan, Lauren had still paid the ultimate price.

"There'll be time to figure that out, Walsh. But the situation is kind of a shit show right now." Mason seemed to grow impatient, knowing the limited time they had before others would arrive. "I'm sorry, but you need to focus with me."

———— ◆◆◆ ————

Mason paused and scanned the scene. A thin veil of smoke

still hung in the air. The factory looked like the aftermath of an ambush he'd seen in his military days. The eerie quiet that enveloped them was broken only by the sound of Craig sobbing.

Suddenly, there was a commotion on the lower floor.

Mason, Adams, and Danny turned their attention to it.

Two bodyguards had come to and were now up and blazing a path toward the open front entrance where Mason and the two other detectives had blasted through.

Adams reached beneath his arm for his shoulder holster, but Mason cut him off.

"Let them go!" he shouted. "We've still got that guy." He nodded toward the one who Adams had zip-tied.

"Jack? What the hell?" Sullivan shouted, struggling to stand up on his wounded leg. He could only watch as the two escaped.

"That guy!" Mason reiterated. "If we got that guy, he'll be able to lead us to the others."

"Right," Sullivan said with a hint of resignation. "That guy," he repeated, looking appraisingly at the only remaining assailant who was tied to the column. Then Sullivan cocked his head to one side as he watched the man's behavior. "Hey, what the hell's he doing?"

Mason and Adams peered down from the top floor to see what the lone remaining bodyguard was up to. Although his hands were tied tightly behind him and around the column, it looked as if he was trying to gnaw at the collar of his windbreaker.

"Jack, what's up with him?" mumbled Adams.

Then Mason's face looked as if a realization had hit him. "No way!" he yelled as he sprinted across the floor and leapt from the ledge onto the main level. Adams followed quickly after him. Danny stayed back, as if wanting to keep an eye on Craig from a distance.

In only the handful of seconds it took for Mason and Adams to reach the man, the cyanide capsule he'd bitten off the top button of his jacket was taking effect.

Mason grabbed him by the hair as Adams stood back.

"Spit it out! Goddamn it, spit it out!"

The man began convulsing uncontrollably. Foam formed around the corners of his mouth.

"Did he just do what I think he did?" Adams asked over Mason's shoulder.

The man's eyes rolled back in his head and his body became still. Mason dropped the man's head to the floor.

Appearing to shudder with anger, Mason shouted, "What the hell is going on here?"

———◆—◆—◆———

It had been barely an hour since the ambush and was late in the evening. The area around the factory that had been dormant was transformed. Rather than darkness and quiet hanging over this rundown area of Chicago's Bank of the Yard warehouse district, the street outside the machine shop was lit up. Flashing lights from police vehicles outside pulsed through the windows.

Craig, Danny, and the three detectives who had come to their aid were all still there, but they were now by no means alone. The only attacker Mason and the other detectives had in custody was dead, having taken his own life rather than face questioning.

The entire building was teeming with numerous elements of law enforcement: medical examiners were analyzing the bodies of Bishop's bodyguard and Lauren; a forensics team was talking to Danny, Craig, and the other detectives to piece together what had happened; and a special weapons unit was sweeping the complex, assessing the calculated nature of the assault.

Most notably of all, James Haggerty, the superintendent of the Chicago Police was onsite, a testament to the brazen nature of the attack on his officers.

While law enforcement busied themselves about the scene, Craig sat apart from the others against a wall, his head in his hands and his eyes fixed, as though in a catatonic state.

Paramedics tended to Sullivan and his leg wound. Adams was giving a statement to another detective on the scene. Danny stood off to one side, observing the Chief engaged in discussion with Mason in the middle of the entryway.

As Danny's gaze scanned all the activity underway, he had a new perspective, different from other crime scenes. The aftermath of such a confrontation wasn't new, but it usually included Danny's use of Craig's abilities to comb for clues and to re-create a shadowy view of what had transpired. But neither he nor Craig needed those shadows now; they themselves had been the victims.

Danny looked over at his cousin's slumped form. He tried to imagine what Craig's perspective must be now. The circumstances—and the finality—of the evening's events were crushingly different this time.

Danny's heart ached for him. There would be no reversing what had happened or its impact; life would be forever changed for Craig. Until tonight, he had been on the periphery of Danny's work and investigations. He would usually choose, or relent, to step in to help Danny. But he had nearly succumbed to an appeal that was both powerful and dreadful, something they both had searched to understand but hadn't felt the full malevolence of—until now. Neither of them could escape wherever this would lead them. Craig had been sucked in, whether or not he was aware that he had come to that unique tipping point. From Danny's loss of Emma, and now the death of Lauren, both cousins bore the deepest of scars in their bodies and now deep within their hearts.

They both felt they were on the cusp of understanding the origin and purpose of Craig's powers. Danny had skated ahead, and he now understood the power and provenance of Craig's abilities. Initially, he thought Bishop was a similar, kindred spirit to Craig, and learning from Bishop could be a "softer landing" before Craig learned what Michael had unveiled to Danny. Danny had worried that Craig wasn't quite ready for this knowledge. The emergence of new clues and the return of Craig's powers had energized them to try to figure out the puzzle. Bishop seemed like a logical piece to it. But now they had to face what Bishop's deception had wrought: one of Danny's fellow detectives was wounded, two of Bishop's mysterious bodyguards were dead, and most painful of all, Lauren had perished during the melee.

As the day's events weighed on him, Danny leaned on his cane and whispered, "What have we gotten ourselves into?"

Danny's quiet remark piqued the Chief's attention. "What did you say, Walsh?"

"Oh, sir," Danny stammered, straightening. "I'm just trying to understand what we've stumbled onto, I guess."

"Come over here, son."

The Chief wasn't so old as to use that label, but he spoke to his officers in this genial way in certain circumstances to put them at ease and to further establish his control.

Danny walked over to the Chief as Mason took a step back from him.

"This is a hell of a mess, Walsh. The second time in two years that you were targeted." He shook his head and furrowed his brow. "You need to know we've all got your back. Mason was telling me that something didn't seem right about the way Bishop asked you down here."

I never told him that, Danny thought. *He must be covering for me. Thankfully.*

The Chief went on. "It's one thing for Bishop to have some kind of sick interest in you. You've certainly had a high profile over the years that'd make you a target. But all of this? Pulling in other officers too?"

Mason drew in closer. "Whatever Bishop had in mind to do here, the scene had clearly gotten too chaotic for him when I arrived with Sullivan and Adams."

The Chief nodded, then faced Danny. "So, Walsh, how were you able to know you needed backup? Is that how Mason and the others were clued in to get down here?"

Danny hesitated. He didn't know how to answer that question.

Mason intervened. "Walsh had a feeling something wasn't right. But out of respect for the old man, he wasn't looking to make a big deal about it. Once he told me that, I thought it best that the three of us come and check things out."

"Uh huh," the Chief said in a suspicious tone. He glanced around, taking in the disarray

"And I'm glad they did. Thank God," Danny jumped in.

"I'm still not understanding this angle, Walsh," the Chief said. "Why was your cousin here? And to have his poor girlfriend dragged into it, as bait or whatever, I just don't get it."

Danny worried he was losing control of the narrative with the Chief. It would only raise more questions.

"That young lady, Walsh, you familiar with her next of kin?" the Chief asked.

Just then, Hammond entered through the front door, flashing credentials to the uniformed officer who was controlling the entrance.

"Chief, you called Hammond down on this?" Mason asked.

Hammond was slowly making his way over to them, scanning the scene in the abandoned factory as he did.

"Eric . . . who the hell at DHS vouched for this guy? This is Bishop's work, or at least that entourage he travels with." The Chief flung out his hands in disgust. "Why the hell does this guy want to infiltrate my force and take down my men?"

"Looks like there's a few less of that entourage now," Hammond said, glancing at the two bodies of Bishop's men. "The dispatch said our men were okay—that true?"

"Couple of scrapes and one wound that cut into flesh." Mason nodded in the direction of Sullivan. "But otherwise, we held up."

"Did I also hear right that there was a female civilian down too?" Hammond asked cautiously.

Mason looked to the floor as Danny reluctantly nodded in the affirmative.

Hammond walked past the Chief and scanned the stairwell and the landing where Lauren's body lay, surrounded by two techs from the medical examiner's office. Silently, he turned back toward the Chief. He patted Danny's shoulder as he walked past him, gently pushing him away at the end. Danny understood this as an attempt to let him disengage from the discussion.

Danny complied and drifted away from them. He began the dreaded walk to rejoin his cousin. He paused a few feet before reaching Craig, who sat with his back against the wall. His jeans and shirt were disheveled, stained with grease and blood from wrestling on the floor.

Danny knew he didn't look much better himself, and he took a moment to smooth his blazer. He passed his hand through his hair to tame it as his prosthetic hand held his cane.

Then he marshaled as gentle a tone as perhaps he'd ever used. "Craig, how are you doing, man?"

Although it was a moment of significance, words came easily to Craig at this point. "Why? Why did this happen? How did Bishop get Lauren here, and why did he take her?"

"You know why, Craig." Danny understood the waves of emotion Craig must be struggling with as he processed it all. As carefully as he could, he sought to drive home the point. "Bishop is what he called himself, but we both now know what he is. The same type of thing as in Iowa. The same shadow that killed that gang. Teased us with those same three letters. Drew you down to this place."

Danny raised his palms and looked around the factory. As he did, Craig pressed his hands tight over his eyes and gritted his teeth, as if he were internally kicking himself for not seeing it sooner.

"You can't be blind to what he represents and what he really came to take."

Craig opened his eyes and looked up at Danny. "What? What did he really come for?"

"You. And he almost had you. I could tell."

"Danny, he *did* get me. She's gone, goddamn it!" Craig said, his voice rising.

"Please, quiet down. We got people for this. There'll be someone you can talk to about this . . . trauma."

"Trauma? That's what supposedly led us to this fucking Bishop guy in the first place! What I can do was supposedly *activated* by it, remember?"

"Craig, I know you're hurting. But you've got to lower your damn voice," Danny answered sternly.

Craig was enraged and didn't care for Danny's admonition.

Their conversation had drawn the attention of the various groups of law enforcement who were scattered about. A few glanced over before returning to their work. They understood the raw emotions of the victims of such scenes.

Danny tried his best to get Craig to focus through his pain. "This is such an agonizing blow. I know, I've been there, remember?" But his reference to Emma's death didn't seem to calm Craig at all.

Danny tried a different angle. "We'll regroup, like we've always done. Together. We've got to lean on each other, Craig."

Craig's body slumped. "Danny, there's nothing left. She's gone. She meant everything to me." His eyes welled up, and his hands shook as he spoke. Then Craig froze. His eyes grew wide as he pushed against the wall to stand up. "My God, her parents. I promised them I could protect her. Danny, I gave them my word!"

"I know it probably doesn't feel like much now, but I'll help you with that."

"I don't need any help. And after this fucking debacle, I don't need you!"

Danny tried not to take Craig's attack personally. "I'm sorry, Craig."

"No, it'll be the rest of those *things* that will be sorry. I'll make them hurt. I'll make them pay for what they've done to me." Craig's jaw clenched as he glanced at the form of Lauren's body lying beneath a police blanket. Danny didn't think he'd ever seen his cousin in such a state of grief before.

Danny touched Craig's shoulder, a gesture meant to calm or comfort. Craig's hand jerked out and swatted it away.

"Get away from me, damn it!"

"Craig—"

"Being involved with you and . . . this stuff has only ever brought me more pain and loss. I'm done with it and with you!"

And with that, Craig spun around and headed toward the front entrance. He brusquely pushed aside the officer who was stationed there as he passed through the door.

The commotion was now evident to everyone on the scene. Danny could feel their eyes on him, but he could only watch as Craig's form stormed away from the building and into the night.

———◆◆◆———

From the shop floor near the foot of the stairwell, the Chief watched Craig and Danny, and he appeared to have heard Craig's words before he left. Danny stood alone.

"Walsh has put it all out there for this force, no doubt about that. But I'll be damned if his methods aren't coming home to roost," the Chief said.

He turned and addressed Hammond and Mason. "We've given Walsh a hell of a lot of latitude, but the shit is officially hitting the fan. I need to know how Walsh's cousin is tied into this, and how and why Bishop got to his girl. That understood?"

Both men nodded.

Hammond took a more informal approach. "Jim, you know

we'll get to the bottom of this. Walsh and I have a long history. And I've gotten to know Craig pretty well."

The Chief went back to the night's events. "But why kill the girl? Why come at the two of them from that angle?"

"Who knows," Mason replied. "Maybe it was for leverage. And when Adams, Sully, and I arrived on the scene, we blew up his plans to the point that he panicked and took her out."

Mason came across like he was making excuses and trying to explain away a situation he clearly didn't understand. It was tragic, surreal, and mind-boggling, especially since he saw Craig take a direct gunshot and emerge unscathed.

"The girl. Henriksen's girl. What did you say her name was?" the Chief asked.

"Harris," Hammond answered. "Lauren Harris. Her father is a partner in a small accounting group downtown. The mother and father live here in the city."

"Well, that doesn't matter right now. They're going to have to wait on any details."

"What?" Mason said.

The Chief lowered his voice. His tone was serious. "Create a story. Get it explained away for now. At least from the outside point of view." He paused for a moment. "Say it was a sleeper cell of radicalized former military. Hell, that's what we're gonna find anyway with those DOAs. That's the way the public needs to see it now until we learn what's really going on. Leverage the spotlight that's on this terrorist bullshit."

"Get a story together?" Mason asked, quizzically.

"Damn right. Until we figure this out. Laying it all out there right now, solving it publicly, that's an old way of thinking. We're dealing with new challenges, especially when it comes to terrorism. We've got to find a way to adapt and keep the details in-house until we learn more."

Mason spoke up, seeming to soften. "When I was in the military, the loved ones of those killed in duty always deserved respect, sir. They were owed a level of decency and transparency. Walsh's cousin, his girl getting killed, we've got to be able to tell the family what happened and how we plan to investigate."

The Chief grunted. "The texture of justice is different here. We need to circle the wagons and keep this in-house, at least until we understand what Bishop's motive was." His gaze fell on the front entrance Craig had passed through moments before. "Ms. Harris's parents will have to wait for more information until we get a better handle on this."

23

HARSH REALITY

Two exhausting days after the terrible events in the warehouse district, Danny Walsh and Eric Hammond pushed their way through the doors of the Daley Center. Their tan overcoats flapped open as the detectives came in from an afternoon that was unusually chilly for late May in the Windy City.

They had just returned from the home of Lauren's parents' where they had delivered the curated official story of her death. Danny fumbled in his pocket and pulled out his phone, hoping for a voicemail from Craig. Nothing. He hadn't spoken to his cousin since Craig had stormed out of the crime scene.

A fresh wave of guilt and anxiety washed through Danny's chest as he and Hammond passed through the metal detectors. Danny slowed as he walked toward a bench in the hallway leading to the bank of elevators, leaning more heavily than usual on his cane. He felt as if he shouldered the weight of the world.

"Eric, just give me a couple minutes, okay?" he said as he slumped down onto a bench.

Hammond let out a long, measured sigh and placed his hands on his hips. "I know, Danny. It's about as bad as it gets right now. But you know how this has to work. Let's just put one foot in front of the other and get up to the Chief's office. He'll be wanting to hear how it went with the Harrises."

How it went? Danny thought. At the Chief's request, he

had stayed in the car while Hammond delivered the news. But how else could it have gone? *Grueling. Awful. Cruel.* It would be bad enough to be parents of a woman taken so early in life and in such a horrific manner. But they were also being lied to and not yet getting the full story. The version of events was staying vague and sanitized for now, and it would fill the Harrises with even more questions. Why had their daughter gone to that godforsaken place to meet Craig and Danny? What did the killer seek to accomplish by killing her in front of them? And where were Craig and Danny when Lauren was killed?

Danny propped his cane against one leg and stared at the floor. He nodded, indicating that he understood Hammond's counsel. He grabbed his cane and helped himself up, and they resumed their walk to the elevators.

By the time the elevator doors parted to let them out on the Chief's administrative floor, Danny had regained some of his energy. But he was nervous about facing the questions the Chief might still have about the entire situation and how it had unfolded.

Mason stepped out in front of them. Clearly, he had been waiting to walk them in. "We'll get to the bottom of this, Walsh." Mason's impatience cut short any further consolation. He looked around and lowered his voice. "But first we all need to be on the same page when we meet with the Chief. There were a lot of things that went down that raise questions about Bishop and other things."

"For sure," agreed Hammond. Danny nodded.

Mason went on. "But I also saw some things the other night that I can't really explain." His eyes darted from Danny and Hammond. It was clear he was referring to Craig being shot and his behavior thereafter. "There's no way any of us want Adams and Sullivan wondering what the hell all that was actually about, let alone the Chief. Am I right?"

Hammond drew in a breath, appearing ready to rebut, but Danny broke in first.

"Yes, but that's for another time. Right now, we need to deal with Bishop." Danny sought to leverage the camaraderie the three of them had recently established. "Jack, you knew something wasn't right about Bishop. That's why you and the other two tailed us there. I'm grateful, please understand that. But right now, we have to keep the Chief's focus on him and only him because Bishop represents a real threat, potentially to others on the force."

"Others on the force?" Mason raised an eyebrow. "Or do you really mean a threat to you and your cousin?"

Danny and Hammond fell silent. They were saved from further inquiry when the door to the Chief's office opened just down the hall. His assistant stepped through the doorway.

"Gentlemen, the Chief has been waiting for you. Are you planning on joining him or not?"

The three quickly broke off their discussion and dutifully made their way into the office. The Chief was clad in his typical dress uniform. Built-in shelves behind him held an assortment of awards, proclamations, and family pictures. He remained seated behind a large wooden desk as they filed in, his large hands clasped in front of him.

"Well, gentlemen, this is a hell of a mess."

"Any word on the identities of the two bodyguards who made it out of there?" asked Hammond. He and Walsh drifted closer to the Chief's desk. Danny hung back near the door.

"So far, not much," the Chief started. "Ex-military. Other than that, nothing really remarkable about either of them in the info we could dig up. Which makes it all the stranger how coordinated it was."

His attention turned to Danny. "Walsh, you gave a statement that Ms. Harris left you a phone message saying you asked her down to the machine shop."

Danny closed his eyes and lowered his head. "Yes, she left a phone message. But I did not ask her to do that."

"Detective, you wrote you took your cousin with you when you went to the Yards after your shift to investigate stray leads."

"Uh huh."

"What the hell for?"

"It's helpful when we go over things together," Danny struggled to explain. "He's . . . he's been good to bounce things off of since I've returned to duty."

"I don't like it," the Chief said. "That's another issue we have to get to."

Danny looked down at his lap, hoping the Chief didn't mean they'd get into it now.

"But right now, let's talk about that voicemail you got from the girlfriend. If you didn't tell her to go down there, who was it? Why would Bishop or one of the others mess with that angle, Walsh? What was she to you? She was your cousin's girl, not yours. Makes no damn sense."

No, it makes perfect sense, Danny thought. The more it became clear that Craig's abilities had reemerged and were gaining strength, the more it made sense that Bishop would want Lauren as leverage.

"You're telling me," Hammond added. "And the discussion I had with her parents was rough."

Despite the horror of it all, Hammond seemed glad to have been the one to break the tragic news. Perhaps he figured it would be too emotionally difficult for Danny. The way Danny was slumped in the hallway when they arrived seemed to validate that.

The Chief didn't seem interested in how the parents were handling it, but he did want details on the conversation. "So? How did it all go down?"

"What story did I give them, you mean? What you told me to say." Hammond replied. "That we don't know how she showed up in the Yards. That no one on the force reached out to her, and that the fact that she was killed during the attack on our detectives is, as of now, an unexplained coincidence."

"How'd they react to that?"

"They're devastated, as you can imagine. And angry at the force, and at the cousin for putting her in danger."

"I get that. How did you describe the attack?"

"I said there's still a lot we don't know, but that it was likely gang violence directed at the police and at people in their orbit."

The Chief didn't seem ready to speculate about Bishop's intentions. He shifted in his chair and stared out the thirtieth-floor window. "The body we dragged out of that shop isn't going to fit the narrative the public is used to hearing about terrorism, about sleeper cells. We need to keep up the story that they're probably part of a domestic gang, but we really don't know. They could be a terrorist sleeper cell that was radicalized here." The Chief appeared to be calculating how to leverage the preoccupation the city maintained about possible terror threats.

"That will be the story for now." He paused. "And, unfortunately, that's the way it's going to have to stay. We won't be letting the Harrises in on anything else."

"What?" Danny barked, his eyes flashing. Mason and Hammond's eyes widened in alarm.

The Chief leveled his gaze at Danny. "What's on your mind, Walsh?"

Danny thoughts churned. He'd had his differences with Lauren. But he had known her well, and he knew how much Craig cared for her. The Chief's cavalier dismissal of her parents' interest offended him, and he didn't care about rank right now.

"They deserve better than that. She was my cousin's girlfriend. How and why she was targeted and dragged into that attack is something we need to learn for ourselves and then share with them. They deserve that." Danny realized his situation was precarious, but he just didn't have the stomach for this.

Mason and Hammond opened their mouths to come to Danny's defense, but the Chief brusquely waved them into silence.

"Walsh, you've got some stones, the way you're addressing me now."

Danny was undeterred. "You know I'm right on this, Chief."

"Better watch yourself, boy. Unless you think you've been around the block the same number of times as I have. We're dealing with gangs, the terrorist bullshit with 9/11, and the recent attacks on you and other detectives. The world is changing, pal. What you're saying is an old way of thinking, how we dealt with the challenges of the past. We have to adapt to what's out there now, and I'm gonna make sure we do it."

Danny gritted his teeth.

The Chief was still irritated. "Plus, this bullshit about getting your cousin involved in crime scenes isn't right, regardless of anything good that might have resulted."

Danny's eyes widened.

"Yeah, I know more than you think when it comes to that."
The Chief turned to Mason and Hammond. "And I'd venture
to guess there are others who have indulged it."

The Chief paused, then took a deep breath, visibly working
to lower the temperature of the discussion. "Look, Walsh, if
you've broken down to the point where you're struggling on
this job without help—from the inside or outside—maybe
you've got some thinking to do."

The words stoked feelings in Danny that he'd suppressed
for too long. The pressure to live up to his father's reputation.
The worries about whether he could be as successful without
Craig's help. The debilitating effects of the assault and his
maiming at the hands of the Tourist. It all flooded through him
now. He'd learned to cover over these recent vulnerabilities.
The tough outward appearance had been a cloak he'd hidden
beneath. But now, finally, Danny felt his inner fire rekindle.

"Listen, it's okay that I might need a little help now in
order to do my job and to put myself out there for this city.
This is the new space for me. There's no going back to how I
was before I was attacked. But I'm willing to try to still do it
all for the force and for the community. The fact is, we all need
a little help from time to time. And damn it, that's okay!"

The Chief shut him down. "I think that will be enough,
Detective. I should have guessed that the experience in the
Yards unnerved you. I'll ask you to wait outside while the
three of us finish up here."

Danny didn't hide his disgust. He glared at the Chief,
glanced briefly at his friend and his immediate superior, then
left, closing the door loudly behind him.

◆———◆———◆

338   The Invictus

Danny was pacing in the hallway. The rage he'd felt in his gut when he'd left the Chief's office was starting to settle.

Michael said the first battle Craig would face would be one of temptation, Danny thought. He surmised that was why Bishop's first plan was to seduce Craig away from his intended purpose. If that didn't work, Bishop would use Lauren and her death to let molten rage push Craig away from his purpose. What he hadn't counted on was the arrival of Mason and the reinforcements.

Danny spun around at the sound of Hammond exiting the Chief's office.

"That was bullshit, Eric. He's a goddamn bureaucrat!" Danny shouted.

"Lower your damn voice," Hammond said in a gruff whisper. He pulled Danny down the hallway some distance from the offices.

Danny had lowered his voice, but he was no less intense. "Eric, it's too damn cold, the way he's treating this. You know it."

"I do know it. And this is the administrative dance. You know that's the way it works. It's just that it's hitting close to home this time, even closer than Emma was for you. Because this time it's not just Lauren dying. Bishop and company tried to cap you and Craig too."

Danny was gathering himself together as Hammond went on.

"Look, this is deep, complicated shit. And I need you to hold it together, if not for yourself then for your cousin."

"Obviously, I need to keep it together for him," Danny shot back, irritated.

"No, here's the thing: I've read Mason's report. And while he doesn't out your cousin, he notes that Craig was fired on squarely yet somehow avoided being hit. Mason's attention to that is way up there."

Danny went silent and looked at the wall. He had never come clean about Craig, although he suspected Hammond knew his cousin was extraordinary in some way.

"Danny," Hammond whispered, "I know that Craig is special. Probably *real* special." He paused until Danny looked up at him.

"You know, I was a little special back in the day myself," Hammond said with a smirk.

"Oh?"

"Before I became this big, strapping man you see in front of you, I was just a Southern boy, thin as a string bean growing up. After getting my ass kicked by a few good ole boys in Mississippi, I took up boxing and weightlifting."

Hammond's face had taken on a gritty edge that Danny hadn't seen.

"And I got damn tough. And mean. I could pretty much whip anyone's ass. Except I was starting to get too big for my britches. When I would get too cocky from time to time, my mom would grab me by the collar and reel me in, setting me straight.

"Now, when I think about this mess and your cousin, I don't care if you know him and you *think* you know what he's going to do. I've been hearing the past couple years how Craig has changed. Probably getting pretty damn strong in his own right. And he's gotta be pretty unhinged right now, Danny. Hell, I would be too. I also know he's . . . different. But in ways I don't understand."

"Eric, it's more than that." Danny sighed deeply. "It's big . . ."

"And I don't need to or even want to know what you mean

by that. Not right now, not while we're in the thick of all this. But I do know you need to rein him in. Get in front of Craig before more people are hurt or killed. I don't care what he's been through. Or what he will or won't do. Sometimes you just need to rein a man's ass in, you know? Before he does harm to himself or someone else."

Hammond's intense gaze was fixed on Danny.

Danny looked away from his former boss, his eyes darting back and forth as he thought through his words.

"You're right. I gotta go find Craig."

And with that, Danny moved toward the elevator with unaccustomed haste.

Once he reached the lobby and was out the door, Danny felt clammy and agitated despite the cool weather outside. It reminded him of the hot, humid ether that surrounded him and Craig when they were in the presence of the supernatural killers.

He also felt a deep pang of regret for not having explained everything better to Craig ahead of their meeting with Michael. *Maybe we could have avoided Lauren's tragedy*, he thought.

A sudden cool breeze found Danny's face, and he stood on the sidewalk for a moment to take it in. "Deep breaths. Just breathe," he said under his breath.

"Are you all right, Detective? It's Detective Walsh, correct?"

He turned to face a small, middle-aged woman, dressed primly and conservatively in a dark gray dress. Her wavy hair was cut short and was speckled with gray. She adjusted her modest wire frame glasses as she looked up at Danny.

"Uh, yeah, who are you?" Danny asked.

"Please let me introduce myself. I'm Dr. Janet Burris."

There was a pause while Danny tried to clear his mind so he could place this woman.

"Wait . . . you're Craig's shrink."

Dr. Burris furrowed her brow.

"Doctor, I mean, psychologist. Whatever you want to call it." Danny shook off the surprise of his discovery. "So, what can I help you with?"

"May I ask how Craig is doing?"

"I'm not sure what you mean."

"Please, Detective. It was not difficult to connect the dots when I learned on the news that Ms. Harris and another civilian were present at the crime scene."

"Why would you think Craig was in any way involved?"

"I am not at liberty to share the details of my sessions with Craig."

Not knowing what Craig had and had not shared with his therapist, Danny was forced to play coy. "I'd like to help you, but just as you can't reveal information from your sessions, I can't really discuss police business with you—that is, unless you have information that is relevant to this specific investigation."

"I need to be careful not to say too much because of doctor-patient confidentiality. But during our sessions, I may have underestimated what he shared with me, what he said he witnessed, and the insights he gained from it."

Danny tilted his head, trying to decipher that cryptic statement.

She looked down, apparently frustrated with how she was articulating her fears. "I guess what I am saying is that I have been wrong to dismiss some of the information he put forward. And that I worry for him."

"Have you heard from him?" Danny asked.

"I have not. But given what I have heard on the news, I'm hoping that you are in frequent contact with him yourself."

Danny remained silent. Patient confidentiality and police business made for this delicate dance.

"Well," Dr. Burris pressed, "do you know how or where I might find him?"

Danny felt a wave of angst. Craig wasn't answering his calls and likely wouldn't. "I'm afraid I can't share that with you."

"Understood, Detective. I respect your situation. But I think Craig may be extremely fragile right now, and perhaps a danger to himself."

Danny's head snapped back. "What do you mean?"

"I'm honestly not looking to play games with you or to be hyperbolic," Dr. Burris said. "Please, when you reconnect with him—and I hope that is soon—let him know I'm prepared to help him work through what he must be feeling."

"Okay, sure. I'll do that."

"Thank you." Dr. Burris nodded sympathetically, turned, and walked away.

Danny was deeply worried for Craig. He was frustrated by his discussion with the Chief. Now he was processing this strange, brief encounter with Craig's therapist. The weight of responsibility grew larger and heavier.

He drew out his cell phone to try to reach Craig. Again.

24

SITUS INVERSUS

Craig was lying on an uncomfortable cot. He opened his eyes and stared at the wall. A shelf slowly came into focus. He was gaining consciousness; he could enjoy oblivion for only a few moments. Then the inside of his chest was swallowed up as he remembered the harsh reality of the events at the warehouse.

It was mid-morning, and he found himself where he had been for the last several days: in the supply room of the martial arts studio. He had gotten up earlier this morning and stumbled out to grab a muffin from a street vendor. Now that he was awake, he heard tumbling and other sounds of a class being held on the mats just beyond the door.

He sat up on the cot and looked across the room at the mirror that hung just above a counter. He barely recognized his own reflection. His face was gaunt. His eyes were ringed with deep, dark circles. More than a week's worth of beard speckled his face. His hair was disheveled, matching his frumpy appearance; he was wearing the same clothes since the attack at the warehouse. The face that stared back at him was devoid of expression, a lifeless husk of a human face.

His attention to this image was broken by the familiar buzzing from his cell phone, which was lying on the concrete floor near the cot.

He strained to reach down to pick it up. As expected, it was Danny again. He had lost count of the number of times his cousin had called—calls he had ignored. At once, Craig no longer felt lifeless, but instead rising anger. If his eyes could bore a hole in the phone, he would have let them. "Goddamn you," he muttered under his breath.

Instead, he channeled his anger, and his power, into the palm that cradled the phone. He gripped it tightly and, with one quick clench, crushed it. He opened his hand to see the screen blink for a moment before the display and case fell in several pieces to the floor.

As he looked down at the pieces, Craig caught a glimpse of his shirt. Just below the top buttons, he noticed a stain, a dark circle of blood. He knew it had come from the gunshot he had absorbed and emerged from unscathed.

His heart felt like it was falling into a bottomless pit again. He noticed a large pair of scissors that rested on the counter. He stretched toward it, wincing at the soreness and stiffness of his body, remnants of the attack and the effects of his inactivity in the past few days.

Scissors in hand, he opened them fully and rubbed his thumb across one blade. It was sharp. He held the single blade with one hand and turned his other palm up, exposing his wrist.

"I wonder . . ." he said.

He pressed the blade against his wrist, pushed down, and dragged it slowly across his flesh. He felt the sharp tear of his skin as it was sliced open. It stung, and the blood started to well up in the blade's wake. But a second after the flesh had opened, the skin melded back together, closing the flesh where the blade had cut. He watched as his skin fully and completely repaired itself.

He shook his head in disappointment and dismissively tossed the scissors onto the counter, and they landed with a clang. Maybe it was a coincidence, or maybe he had been heard, but just then the door opened and his instructor Jason appeared.

"Craig. You doing all right?"

"I dunno. I guess," Craig said in a deep monotone. "I probably shouldn't keep crashing here. I'm not trying to cause you problems."

"It's no problem. What you went through at that warehouse, and with your girl . . . I just can't imagine it. I'm just concerned about you."

Craig ignored the outreach.

"I just don't feel like I can go back to the apartment. I really don't want to, even though that's where all my stuff is."

"That's understandable. You can stay as long as you like—there's no issue with that. It's just becoming . . . awkward each time the detective has come in."

Danny, thought Craig.

"I'm sure he'll come in again today, as he has the past several days."

"I know. I'm just not ready to talk to my cousin right now."

"Are you willing to talk to *someone*, at least?"

Craig looked away, wading into the ether of his mind for someone who might understand what he was going through. Dr. Burris? No, it had been a long time since their last session, and the thought of bringing her up to speed sounded exhausting.

"'Cause if you're willing, I know someone who's ready to listen," said a female voice.

Craig snapped his head back to the doorway.

Samantha stepped forward from behind the instructor. Her face and posture were different than he remembered. The tough, confident body language had softened. She appeared kinder and more cautious.

"I've been threatening Jason, telling him that if he knows where you are, he'd better let me know." She gave Craig a careful smile.

"Hi, Sam." Craig looked up at her from where he sat on the cot. He remembered finding her intriguing, but he wasn't feeling much of anything anymore.

"I'm going to let you two talk," Jason said, "but I'll be out on the mats if you need anything."

"Thanks, Sensei," Sam replied.

Her face drew into an expression of genuine concern. "Craig, how are you holding up? How can I help?"

"You can't. My life's over. It's only a matter of time now," he said.

"Whoa. Whoa, Craig. I . . . can't imagine what you must be going through. But please don't indulge that talk."

She plopped down on the cot beside him.

Craig no longer saw the need to remain closed off from her. "Everything that could possibly go well always gets covered over by this goddamn dark shadow that follows me. Whether it's a new start here in the city. Or grad school that's been paid for, even though I don't attend one damn class. And now the one person, the one woman, who I ever felt understood me. She's gone. Taken from me."

"Craig," she started, "I guess I didn't realize—"

"Everything had been going great, and then what happens? I get sucked back into it."

"What do you mean, sucked back in? And what exactly is 'it'? This wasn't random?" Sam asked. "You're talking like something has its hooks in you."

"Damn right. And now I'm entirely alone with it."

Sam looked down at the broken cell phone on the floor next to the cot. "What happened here?"

"Let's just say I didn't want to talk with my cousin anymore."

"Ah, the detective? Did you ever think maybe he's the one person to talk to right now?"

"Fuck him," Craig shot back. "He's the last person who could help now. He's a big reason why my girlfriend is dead."

Saying the words aloud drove the reality home again. Anxiety tightened its grip on Craig's chest.

"Craig, I'm really sorry that this has happened."

"I know," Craig said, dully. He swept out his arm, gesturing to take in the supply room. "So how did you figure it out that I was here?" he asked.

"I guess I just hadn't seen you around . . ."

Craig tilted his head and squinted, clearly skeptical.

"Okay. I follow the news. The story about a detective and a civilian drawn into some kind of terrorist attack at a warehouse. A young woman dies. Having spent some time with you and your cousin, it didn't take long for me to piece it together. And I'd had that conversation with Lauren . . ." Her voice trailed off.

Craig dropped his head again and stared at the broken pieces of the phone.

"I put that together. Then I pestered the shit out of Jason until he gave up that you were hiding out here. I'm glad he did. I know he's been really worried about you."

"Doesn't matter. It's all over now."

"The hell it is. It sounds like you're damn lucky to be alive based on what I heard went down there."

"What did you hear?" Craig said, then held his hand up before she could answer. "Shit, it doesn't matter. I don't want to even be here anymore."

"Here? What do you mean?"

Craig looked at her with a deep sadness in his eyes but said nothing. Sam appeared to acknowledge how he felt.

"This is a tragedy, there's no question," she said. "But try not to wrap your entire life in this moment. We really endure two types of pain: pain that hurts, and pain that changes us. Sometimes we have to decide which we want it to be."

"You've got no idea, Sam. This has been my whole life." He looked away. "If only you knew the whole story. Then you'd understand that almost every part of my life has been cursed."

"I don't know about being cursed. Seeing it from the outside, this is obviously a terrible shock, but maybe not a surprise." She cringed as she said it.

Offended, Craig glared at her. "What did you say?"

"I haven't known you that long, but I think I've seen how it is. You're angsty. Depressed. And when your cousin is around, I see the tension between you two."

"Well, he's pulled me into his shit. He used me to help solve crimes, no matter the toll it took on me. It's not right."

"Use you . . . how?" Sam pushed. "What would you have to offer a trained detective?"

Craig shook his head. He wasn't ready to go there.

"Oh, come on, Craig. Let go of the mystery. Let me help you," she urged.

He stared into Sam's eyes, and there was kindness and understanding. It felt like a pivotal moment. He wasn't sure he was in a mental place where he could gauge if he could completely trust her, or whether she might run away if she knew the truth. But he didn't care anymore. He was tired of being alone with the weight of all his secrets. Danny knew it all, but Craig's confidence in him had unraveled spectacularly. In those few moments, he reached a decision.

"All right. You want to know it all?"

"Yes, I do."

"Okay, then."

He stood up and walked a few steps away from her. He drew breath into his lungs, bracing for a narrative that he knew would take some time.

With his back to her, Craig set out to explain it all to Sam. He started the story with how his father had met his fate. He told her that he could conjure the shadowy images of past, violent events, and how Danny would use him to decipher crime scenes and crack cases. He told her about the Tourist serial killer, a supernatural creature who had killed Danny's friend Maggie and his girlfriend Emma. About how he drew Danny to Iowa as a way to draw Craig out into the open. He described their confrontation with the Tourist in Iowa, and how they had barely survived that awful night. He explained how he discovered even more talents and powers as he defended himself against the Tourist, including the ability to channel waves of force from his palms. And he shared with her the vision from his past when he was a child and how his father gifted him with the extraordinary abilities that he could now wield.

He explained that only Danny knew the full extent of these secrets. He expressed feeling optimistic about learning the origins and purpose of his powers from Bishop, but how he'd realized too late that Bishop was another supernatural nemesis, like the Tourist who had nearly destroyed them two years ago. Fighting back tears, he told her what had happened at the warehouse nearly a week ago, how Bishop tried to recruit Craig so he could harness his abilities. In vivid detail, he recounted how he and Danny were attacked by Bishop's bodyguards. The arrival of police reinforcements thwarted that effort just in time. Sadly, he finished with how Bishop stared down at him while he squeezed the life out of Lauren.

Sam sat through it all, silent and with rapt attention.

When he finally paused, he tried to gauge her reaction. Surprisingly, she seemed impassive.

"I knew there was something unique about you," she said simply.

"You did?"

"The first time we rolled in a sparring session, I felt that you were rooting around in my head. I knew it was you doing it, but I just didn't know how."

"Yeah, I know you felt that. I could tell you were on to me from the start. But you probably didn't imagine that I'd also become damn-near indestructible."

"How's that?"

Craig pointed at the bullet hole in the front of his shirt, which was ringed with the faint stain of blood. "I caught this from one of Bishop's henchmen. He shot me squarely in the chest. I went down, but it healed in a matter of minutes as if it never happened."

"Crazy," she muttered as she stood and approached him. Her eyes fixated on a small rip near the neck of the shirt, then on a scar that ran down near the collarbone.

"What's this?"

Craig undid a button to show her the length of the scar. "That's where that thing in the church plunged its hand into my chest. Almost caused me to bleed out."

Sam took a step back and looked into Craig's eyes. She

tilted her head. "So . . . obviously you *can* be hurt. It seems you could even be killed. Maybe not easily, but it could be done by a 'nemesis,' to use your word. It looks like you almost bit it that time."

He raised his brow. "So, you don't think I'm nuts? You don't want to get the hell out of the building?"

She shook her head with a quiet confidence. "Hardly. I've dealt with my own crazy situations. Like I told you before, I figured out a long time ago that I could read people and get a sense for them. It may not be this supernatural shit you've got going on, but I can relate some to what you've described. You could say that I have my own set of 'gifts.'"

"Really?" Craig said. He wondered if that was why he had been drawn to her from the moment he laid eyes on her.

"I can sense things—not sure how or why. I try to live in the moment and not carry too much baggage from the past, or worry about what might come in the future. Just live in the here and now. Much to my parents' dismay, probably."

"Why's that?"

"I'm sure they wished I had gone to college or had opted for a more professional career. I like manual labor, a sense of accomplishment, and aikido, of course. It lets me kick some ass where I see that it needs to be done." She flashed a coy smile. "I'm *literally* wired differently. Like, physically."

"How do you mean?" Craig was once again intrigued by her.

"I was born with a condition called *situs inversus*. All of my internal organs are positioned exactly opposite of where they are supposed to be."

"What?" Craig was startled by this news. "Is it serious? Are you okay?"

Sam smiled in response to Craig's genuine concern. It was

selfless of him to put away his own grief for a moment and to be anxious for her.

"Yes, I'm perfectly healthy. Just a rare, fluke condition. But I've always wondered if it has something to do with my being able to sense things about people."

Craig exhaled. "We'll, I'm glad you're doing all right with it."

"I am. I know it's small potatoes compared to the things you've discovered about yourself. I have some understanding now about how much you've been through. But everything you've told me—the arc of it all—if it's true . . ."

Craig's eyes narrowed. Was this conversation going to be like the ones he'd had with his psychologist?

"And I do believe your story is true," Sam added quickly. "Damn, Craig. Don't you feel like you have to get to the bottom of it? You thought this Bishop guy had similar powers and could explain it all to you, right?"

"Until he revealed what he really was, the bastard. He tricked me. He played on my confusion and all of the trauma I've endured. He made me think there was a reason for it, some point to it all. But now I know it was just a way to draw me in." Craig hung his head. "And in the process, he killed Lauren."

"Was that how he tricked you? He implied that your gifts had an overarching purpose he could clue you in to? Well, he obviously thought there was something special about you. Otherwise, why go through all this planning? Why the deception?"

Craig straightened up. "I don't know, Sam. You think you're confused by it all? You think I haven't asked these questions? Try being me and having all this swimming in your head for years. That's exactly what Danny and I have been trying to do since Iowa. And it's led to this."

"How do you mean?"

Craig huffed. "It feels like we've been coaxed along by people we meet and new clues as we try to figure out what's going on with me. Like those damn three letters Bishop referenced: *C, O, I.* He made it sound like I was going to be a part of some sort of 'council.' I felt 'anointed,' to use his term, with these abilities and a part of a larger group."

"What do you think he was trying to do?"

"I guess make me drop my guard so he could take me out. But why? Why me?"

"It seems like he believes you're a serious threat."

"A threat to what, though?" Craig asked.

"That's exactly what you have to find out. Now, I'm not discounting at all how you've tried. And that your cousin the detective has tried too—"

Craig scoffed. It was impossible to hide the frustration he felt with Danny, which had been building over the last few months.

"That's all I've been doing since Danny and I nearly got killed in Iowa. Being this special, this complicated, takes it out of you. I just want it all to end."

"You just said that again: the word *end*."

"I alternate between just wanting everything to end for me and knowing that I have the power to hunt that bastard down." He plopped back down onto the cot and looked up at Sam. "I'm starting to feel more like the latter."

Sam nodded. "I can understand that. I've entertained revenge and retribution for a lot of people who've earned it. Why do you think I'm obsessed with coming here?" She motioned to the gym studio beyond the wall. "But it was always for a purpose, and not for one that did jack shit for me. It was always for others who needed the help. You get that?"

"Yeah, it's what I've heard from Danny. And Lauren . . ." His voice trailed off in emotion.

"I'm not trying to add to your grief. I just want to give you a different way of seeing all this. Maybe ask yourself what you are not seeing right now that you should be seeing. And show a little compassion for yourself. You've been through a massive amount—maybe more than anyone has ever faced—and you're still pushing forward."

"I'll push forward, all right. I'm going to hunt him down. I'll make him pay."

"Let's take our time getting to that point. Like I said, I can be all about revenge and retribution. I think you've seen that in me."

Craig recognized that Sam was reaching out a helping hand, and he felt like he had to grasp it.

"I get your point."

Sam sat down beside him and patted his shoulder. "I'm sorry."

"I appreciate what you're saying, and for checking on me. But a few days ago, I saw my girlfriend get killed by a supernatural villain who wants me dead. So you're gonna need to give me a little time to let any other perspective sink in."

"Totally understandable."

They sat in silence, staring at the wall, which held jump ropes, spare weights, and other exercise equipment.

"You know, I could *hear* him," Craig said.

"Who?"

"Bishop. Right before he killed Lauren."

"What do you mean? He was calling out to you or something?"

"No, I mean in my head somehow. When I was down below and he was up on the stairwell."

"What did you hear?"

"He said, 'Your heart will forever dwell in darkness.' I didn't get it at the time. But now I'm starting to see what he might have meant. Maybe he's right. That's all I'm left with."

"You don't have to be there. I'm a person who takes each day as it comes. Nothing's preordained."

"Preordained. Listen to those fancy words." Craig sounded just the slightest bit playful, the first glimpse of emerging from the grief.

"Have you been able to confide in anyone else who has helped?" Sam asked.

"That's what we thought Bishop could do."

Sam's intensity picked up as she seemed to better understand Craig's plight. "No, you didn't get your powers from him. It was from your dad, right?"

"That's right. I saw it happen through the re-creation in the church. It set into motion everything Danny and I have been trying to understand for the past year and a half. Or at least since Danny got rehabilitated enough to get back into action."

"Rehabilitated?"

"The Tourist really messed him up. Danny was barely hanging on by the time I found him. He tried to warn me to leave him and get to safety, but I didn't listen. Anyway, after we both survived, there were several surgeries, an amputation, and now he walks with a cane. But he's able to do most of the things he used to."

"I'll be damned," Sam said. "Sounds like your cousin went from a selfish, hard-ass cop to a more vulnerable, supportive person for you."

The anger Craig held for Danny waned some as he remembered the intense pain and physical challenges his cousin had suffered.

"You learned as a kid that you could re-create crime scenes?" Sam asked.

"Past scenes of violence, really."

"But in the past several years, you learned you could do much more, like seeing into people's heads and shooting waves of force out of—"

"My hands, yeah."

"Then you got duped by that Bishop character. You thought he might have all the answers, but he was really just another one of those evil things trying to kill you."

Craig nodded. "Bishop was the last real lead I had to try to understand everything, and look how that's turned out."

Sam went quiet for a moment, then said, "There has to be more to it than that. And more places that you can look to for answers. How about your dad?"

Craig drew back from her, thinking it bold to bring up another source of his pain.

"Craig, I'm not trying to twist the knife, but you saw that your dad had similar powers through a re-creation, right?"

"It looked like my dad had the *exact* same powers."

"And what did he do with them? Do you remember him looking for ways he could rain down his fury on others?"

Craig looked away. He didn't feel it happening, but he had slipped back into a selfishness of *what* he could do without contemplating the deeper *why*.

Craig sought to pivot; he didn't want to revisit anything about his dad. "So, you've got your gift of sensing things about people. What's that sense say about me?"

A wry smile subtly curved her faced. "You're more than just the things you've encountered."

"How's that?"

"I'm not getting any evil off you, if that's what you mean, Craig. But I also don't sense much direction."

He cocked his head, puzzled.

She went on. "It's like things are in neutral for you—balancing on an edge that could tip in either direction."

"It does feels like I've fallen into whichever side is the shit."

Sam grew serious. "I feel some massive power bubbling under the surface, and it's been growing. Hell, I've even seen it in our sessions here. That's what concerns me. I wonder what could happen with it?"

"How do you mean?"

"You seem fragile, like you could shatter or explode."

"That's probably a fair description."

"Give yourself a break, Craig. A little grace, as my mom would say. Losing someone they way you have would be hard on anyone. But the other stuff you shared with me? That's even heavier. Dark in ways most people couldn't handle."

Craig slumped on the cot and staring blankly at the wall again. Sam occasionally slid her eyes sideways to check in on him.

"Did you love her?"

Craig swiveled his head toward Sam, surprised by her question.

"I'm sorry. That's probably insensitive to ask," she said.

"It's fine. Honestly, I don't know. I know that sounds bad. And I'm not trying to be that way." He looked up at the ceiling as if summoning an explanation. "She and I were close and connected, but I also felt like she had some level of understanding that I was never able to match. She knew that too, but she accepted and cared about me all the same."

Sam nodded as Craig spoke of Lauren, her lips pursed.

"What did you think of her?" he asked. "Did you get a sense of her?"

She hesitated, then said, "I . . . don't mean for this to sound bad because clearly she was a special person to you. But I didn't sense anything. At all. Like she was just a blank slate."

"Huh." Craig remembered when he tried to peer into Lauren's thoughts at dinner at Santori's. There'd been nothing there for him to sense either. He sighed heavily. He felt so worn down. "Where the hell can I go from here?"

"Only you can lift this darkness from your eyes, Craig."

"Lauren used to say the same type of stuff." He felt his eyes watering. "Life keeps chipping away at me. I'm mad and bitter and wondering if there's anything left."

"There is, Craig. I can see it. You have to start by honoring the wonderful person with whom you once shared a relationship."

"You mean go to the memorial service? I don't know if I can even manage the courage to do that."

"Craig . . ."

"Sam, really, I'm not sure I can face it. Or her parents. My God, I promised them I could protect her! I feel this hole in my chest grow every time I think about it."

"You have the strength to go. It's the right thing for you to do."

"It's my fault she's gone, letting her stay so close to the evil that pursued Danny and me. It was only a matter of time before she got tangled up in it. I'm to blame for it all!"

"No, you're not. You're a victim, just like she was and so many others that these things have gotten to. And you won't be alone. I'll go with you. I'll be there to support you."

"Why? You barely know me."

"I know bad. I know evil. I know that's not you. You've been dealt a terrible hand for a long time. And like I told you before, my purpose is to help protect the vulnerable and those in need."

Just then, there was a light rapping at the door. Jason poked his head in.

"I just wanted to check on you two to see how you are and if you need anything."

"Thanks, Sensei," Craig said softly.

Sam lightly tapped Craig's hands that were clasped in his lap. She turned back to their instructor. "Yeah, we're going to be okay."

25

FLICKERING FLAME

"This is where it's at? I never knew there was a church tucked in here." Craig stared up at the building that he and Sam were approaching.

"That's it," Sam confirmed. "Can't say that I've ever been here either."

Saint James Chapel was off River Loop North in downtown. Its dark stone exterior rose over a half dozen stories as it sat nestled among office buildings. At street level, there were four sets of dark wood double doors, and above them loomed a larger crucifix relief.

Sam was dressed in plain dark slacks, black flat shoes, and a gray collared shirt that rounded out an appearance less edgy than he was used to.

"Does this outfit work for this?" Craig asked of his own appearance.

Sam looked him over. Craig wore khaki pants, his old brown casual shoes, and a blue-striped oxford shirt. The shirt was a little tight, and the pants just a cuff shorter than where they should hang since he had borrowed them from Jason. Still, Craig had finally gotten out of the clothes he had worn for days and cleaned up well after having showered and shaved at the gym.

"You look good, Craig. How are you feeling?"

As Craig's attention was drawn back up toward the large stone relief of the crucifix, his hands fidgeted nervously. "I'm still feeling that hole inside my chest, but now it's wrapped in a ton of anxiety too."

"I can't imagine. But remember, you've got this. I'm with you." She patted him on the back reassuringly, and he dropped his gaze and headed for the entrance with Sam beside him, stride for stride.

The entryway beyond the open wooden doors looked like any other lobby of a downtown building. In just a few strides, Craig and Sam made their way across it. They came to another set of glass doors that opened into a glorious cathedral.

"Whoa," Sam said in a breathy whisper.

A church usher at the door handed them a small *In Memoriam* handout. Neither of them made eye contact with the usher as they soaked up the magnificent setting: the tan grandeur of polished marble and mahogany pews.

As they slowly entered the space, Craig was intimidated by the formality of the setting and the circumstances that brought them there. It felt foreign to him, unlike the Lauren he had known.

Seeming to sense Craig's reluctance, Sam gently nudged him forward. "It'll be okay," she said, her voice low, "I'm here."

They continued on. Organ music played softly. Only about thirty people sat in the pews, silently staring toward the front of the church. Craig guessed that most of those who were coming had already arrived.

As he drew closer to the front where others were seated, a bit of familiarity came into view. There was a poster-sized picture of a smiling Lauren at the altar. It sat on a large rectangular table that was adorned with bouquets of flowers too numerous to count.

Craig saw Jeff Harris, Lauren's father. Their eyes locked, and Jeff's face registered shock when he realized it was Craig. His eyes narrowed, and his lips quivered in rage.

"Oh no," Craig whispered as he stopped in his tracks. Sam halted as well.

Before family or friends could realize or prevent it, Jeff Harris was out of his pew and stormed up the aisle to come face-to-face with Craig, blocking his way.

The smooth, soothing organ provided a stark contrast as the two men eyed one another. Craig was taller than Jeff, but the frumpiness of his outfit and the weight of his guilt made him look small. Jeff, in contrast, wore sport coat and tie and cast a respectful, solemn look.

"You have a lot of nerve showing up here today."

"Mr. Harris, I am so sorry—"

"Cut it! How dare you!" Jeff snarled in an angry whisper. "I warned you not to get mixed up with your cousin's line of work. It's too dangerous! Don't you remember what you promised us?"

"Yes, I do." Craig's chin dropped to his chest.

"She was a gift to us that came into our lives," Jeff hissed. "We told you our concerns. You swore she would be safe. Now the police won't tell us anything. You've been completely AWOL, and *now* you show up here. Why?" His last question sounded almost pleading, desperate to understand. "You let our precious daughter be taken from us!"

Sam looked pained. The encounter was brutal to watch and awkward as others turned to see what was causing the tension.

Just then, Eric Hammond came up behind Craig, wearing his long, dark trench coat. He moved to step in between the two men. "Mr. Harris, I'm Lieutenant Eric Hammond—"

"I know who you are," Jeff snapped.

"If you want a target for your anger, point it at me. The department was unaware that terrorist cells were targeting our officers or their kin. I know that gives you no solace at all right now. You have my and the superintendent's deepest condolences on the loss of your daughter."

Lynn Harris had approached and taken up a position behind her husband while the muted confrontation took place. "Jeff, please. Come and sit. Let's just try to get through this day. The way Lauren would've wanted us to," she said.

His lips still trembling, his face reddened, Jeff acquiesced to her instruction. "You're right, Lynn. For Lauren. No one else matters today except for her."

"Mr. Harris, please know . . ." Craig started.

"Don't even . . ." Jeff warned, before trailing off. Lynn grasped his hand and gently guided him back to their seats.

Craig closed his eyes as a tide of emotions washed through him. He spun on his heel to leave.

"Craig?" Sam caught up with him as he neared the end of the aisle and grabbed his hand. "Sit with me."

"I don't want to."

"You'll regret it forever if you don't. Trust me."

The priest appeared to pick up on the tense encounter. He quickly left his seat behind the altar and hastily made his way to the microphone. "In the name of the Father, and of the Son, and of the Holy Spirit," he said.

Sam and Craig watched as many of the attendants made the sign of the cross and mumbled several words.

The priest began. "It is a mournful and unexpected situation that has brought us all together today. I offer you, the friends, family, and loved ones of Lauren Elizabeth Harris, comfort and consolation. Lauren's family has asked that today not be a traditional Catholic service but instead be a celebration of Lauren's life and her impact on others. In our upmost respect for these wishes, the church of Saint James the Apostle is honored to do so. Please join me in this opening prayer . . ."

As the attendants bowed their heads and listened, Craig looked at Sam, his eyes searching, appearing lost. She reached out and patted his hand.

The priest recounted Lauren's life, her personality and qualities, and Sam and Craig spoke in hushed whispers.

"The Harrises are right. I am to blame for this."

"No, you're not."

"Jeff and Lynn Harris would want you to know," the priest went on, "that Lauren was always the light of their lives and remains so even in this dark hour. Lauren was a gift that came to them when they adopted her . . ."

"Adopted," Craig whispered as he shook his head. "Her big secret from me."

"What? You mean you didn't know?"

"Not until recently," Craig said with an air of resignation. The priest continued, "And I would say to each of you, that even as she passes from this earth, her light will continue . . ."

As Craig stared at the back of the pew in front of him, he wondered why Lauren had never mentioned she had been adopted. Such an important life event seemed like something his girlfriend would have willingly shared with him during the two years they were together.

The priest's words rang true as he went on. "The grief that we feel is all the unexpressed love and emotion that we have for someone. Until we pass ourselves, we will continue to carry a part of this grief. Because we never get enough time with those we care about."

The pit that had opened in Craig's chest since Lauren died felt as though it could never be filled.

"We must appreciate the impact they have on us and honor them through the ways in which we live our lives."

It was true. Lauren had always accepted him and put up with the mystery of his secrets. All of her words of wisdom usually bubbled in Craig's consciousness. There was meaning and purpose. But now, in the stew of pain he felt, it was difficult for Craig to draw any of them from his thoughts.

"A person's legacy is the value of their presence. The challenge when they are gone is to transform that into a living legacy. Grief can be a teacher for those of us left behind. Her parents believe that Lauren was the best of us. Anyone who truly knew her understands this to be true."

He let the words hang in the air. There was silence as everyone in attendance gave space to reflect on this wonderful person.

"A legacy gift can be transformational, something left for you that supplies missing pieces you never knew you needed. After all, what is a legacy? It can be planting the confidence, support, and friendship in others that you may never see blossom. Lauren undoubtedly did this for her parents and for many of you as well. Jeff and Lynn deeply appreciate your honoring Lauren today. But they would also challenge you to ask: What do you want people to say about you when you are gone?"

Sam tilted her head at the curious way the priest's words changed.

"For Lauren, it was her light. The way she reached out to people. Her kindness, her charity. She had a selflessness, and she was always trying to find and recruit those who had gifts but had been marginalized."

Craig looked up as a memory suddenly snapped into focus: Lauren showing kindness to the panhandler Craig had threatened.

"She did it in her work, helping people develop and be productive in their chosen vocation. She was a different level of spirit," the priest said. "Always shining her light on whatever or whomever needed to receive it. She left each of us with an impression. What I ask of you is what are each of *you* willing to do to honor her? What step would you take today if you were brave enough? Are you willing to try?"

It was odd hearing this, Craig thought. The priest's message conveyed, nearly precisely, a sentiment Lauren had often shared with Craig.

"Be brave and remember this challenge, even if you find yourself in the darkest depths of despair that the smallest ray of light cannot pierce. Now, let us think of Lauren in silent reflection."

A pair of ushers made their way up the aisle, one handing out small white candles to be passed down each pew, while the other followed behind with a lit candle used to light them.

Despite the inspiring words, darkness crept into Craig's mind. Nothing could change the fact that Lauren was gone forever, and that a terrible malevolence had grown closer and closer. It had started with Craig's re-creations of the crime scenes. He hadn't known the victims until his re-creation of Maggie's death, for whom he had known only briefly. Then Danny's girlfriend Emma was killed, someone he had gotten to know well. And now with Lauren's death, the encircling darkness couldn't possibly have moved any closer. Even more so, Lauren's death was an event that Craig felt specifically responsible for. He knew he had endangered her by continuing to be involved with Danny in their quest to understand this mystery.

The ushers reached the row near the back where he and Sam sat. As they held their small flames, Sam cast her gaze toward the front and those who meditated there. Craig stared down at his flame instead, tumult roiling within him. His field of vision narrowed; dark black splotches blocked out everything except the flickering light in his hands. The roiling turned to anger. Rage. He felt it welling in his eyes as if it needed to escape. Still his eyes bore down on the flame. The grief and the loss were all consuming. With each spike in emotion, the flame whipped rapidly, as if stirred by a sudden jet of air.

Craig continued to move the flame with his mind. Then, suddenly, he noticed a reflection of the flame in the medallion that dangled against his shirt. It was the St. Benedict medal Lauren had given him. Mercifully, it drew him out of his feelings of rage, but it still left only sadness. He fiddled with it between his index finger and thumb. He closed his eyes and let the feeling of the smooth metal soothe him, if only for a few moments.

The mourners were drawn out of their quiet contemplation by the priest. "Remember that when there is doubt, allow faith. Where there is despair, allow hope."

It sounded almost poetic. Brave. Craig could hear the gentle sobbing of those gathered in the pews.

"Now, I invite each of you to come to the altar to pay your individual respects."

Craig had held on as long as he could. He extinguished the flame of his candle with thumb and forefinger.

"I'm ready, Sam." Without waiting for her, he got up and

headed to the glass doors through which they entered. Sam hastened along to catch up with him.

They were through the lobby and had pushed open the exterior doors when Craig heard someone calling to him.

"Henriksen! Wait up."

Eric Hammond caught up to them on the sidewalk at the end of the block. "How are you holding up, son?" Hammond said, catching his breath.

Craig started to speak, but his throat tightened with emotion. He only gestured back to the cathedral and shook his head.

Sam stepped in. "He's doing the best he can right now."

"And who are you?" Hammond asked.

"A friend," Sam answered, annoyed by his tone.

"It's okay, Sam. Eric is cool. Thanks for checking on me, Lieutenant."

"Miss Harris was a special lady. I could tell that from the time I spent with you all at that hospital in Iowa. I'm truly sorry, Craig."

Craig looked down at the sidewalk. He then brought his attention back to Hammond. "Where's Danny?" he asked.

"Keeping out of sight for now. The Chief thought he was too hot to be out in the open, both with regard to the family and because Bishop might have more plans for him, or for other detectives."

"Whatever," Craig scoffed. He was irritated. He knew that the focus of Bishop's plans would have nothing to do with Danny or the police. Eager to end the conversation, he said, "Anyway, I do appreciate the things you said to the Harrises."

"Least I could do."

"I've got to go."

"Henriksen, wait. I don't think you've had a chance to get back to the apartment you shared with Miss Harris, have you?"

"No. I've heard it's been a zoo around there. You've had patrols hanging out there, right?"

Hammond nodded. "Right, to continue the investigation, see if there was any other angle Bishop might have had with Lauren. I can carve out some time for you when there will be no uniforms there. I could give you a couple of hours tomorrow so you can get over there and remove some of your things if you want to."

"Really?"

"I figured that might be helpful to you." He looked at Sam. "But it may be better if you go alone. It'll draw less attention if just one person is going in and out."

"That makes sense." Craig was relieved for the chance to get into the apartment by himself and gather clothes and other things he needed.

"I appreciate that. Thanks, Eric."

"Tomorrow, say between ten and noon work for you?"

Craig nodded.

"Take care of yourself, Henriksen. I'm available if you need anything. And I know Danny would like to hear from you."

At that, Craig's mood shifted. He held up his hand as if to say he wanted to hear no more. He turned to leave. With a shrug toward Hammond, Sam followed closely behind.

26

CLOAKED IN DARKNESS

It was midmorning, and the air was dry and warm. Craig stood outside the entrance to the martial arts studio clad in a dark T-shirt and jeans. Sam was but a few feet from him wearing her usual black jeans and a black hoodie.

Craig was silent as he stared at the columns of buildings in the distance.

"You need any company with this?" asked Sam.

Craig sighed and broke his gaze. Though it might've given him comfort to have Sam there, he knew Lauren wouldn't have approved.

"I think I'll be okay. Other than clothes and a few personal things, I don't think there's a lot that I need to get. Most of the furnishings were Lauren's anyway. Besides, this is something I should do by myself."

"Where are you going to stay now?"

"Well, I'm pretty sure Jason won't want me to build an addition to the gym." The slightest smile appeared on Craig's face, a small bit of humor amid the recent dark days. "I've got a little money that can get me through until I figure out my next steps."

He looked at Sam as if to assure her. "It'll be fine. I'll see you back here in a few days during a morning session. How about that?"

"I think that would be good. If you need anything in the meantime . . . wait. Your phone is busted. How will you—"

"I've got your number," Craig assured. "I promise to reach out if I need anything."

"You just go and get your stuff. I'll be around to help you figure things out from there."

Craig smiled apologetically. He had no intention of bringing Sam any closer to his affairs and putting her at risk with the monsters that awaited him.

"I appreciate you," Craig said. "For listening to me, for believing me, and for worrying about me right now. We'll talk soon."

With that, Craig turned up the sidewalk and made his way to the train station and on to the apartment in Wicker Park.

◆—◆—◆

Danny knew it had been over a week and a half since Craig was at his apartment. Out of sight around the wall that separated the kitchen from the entryway, Danny leaned on his cane. It was nearly eleven when he heard a key being inserted into the lock. The tumbler turned, and Danny could hear Craig enter and close the door behind him. Still out of sight, Danny peered around the corner to see Craig surveying the setting.

There was a stillness in the apartment, the very essence of quiet, that felt heavy.

"I was hoping you'd show up today," Danny said as he rounded the corner. His appearance startled Craig.

"What the hell?" Craig exclaimed.

Danny leaned slightly on his cane as he stood there. He wore a T-shirt, jeans, and boots, a look altogether uncharacteristic and casual for him.

"How are you, Craig?"

"Why on earth would you care?" Craig's surprise had been replaced by anger.

Without his typical long-sleeved shirt, Danny's prosthetic hand was visible where it attached to his forearm. The look was stark.

"You know that I care. I've been really worried about how you're doing."

"So this was a setup by Hammond. So that I'd be forced to see you here today?"

"No, I just want to talk. I haven't been able to reach you, and this seemed like the best way the two of us could meet up."

"It's not needed," Craig said tersely.

"It is. I can't imagine what you've been going through."

Craig's body stiffened. "You don't need to be concerned. I'm not that frail, little boy you once knew. I've gotten stronger, if you haven't noticed."

Danny started to pace. "Maybe. But I know what you've been up against—how we've been running around trying to find clues. The letters, the informant with the tattoo, Bishop, even the re-creation with the biker gang. And now you're dealing with tragedy on top of that. It would be a lot for any person to handle."

"I'll manage."

"No, you're going to listen. Now." Danny spoke in a tone he'd never used before with his cousin.

"You think *now* is the time for any of this bullshit? Newsflash, Detective! These creatures are back. And one of them just killed my fucking girlfriend!"

Craig's reaction showed zero patience. Danny still had some.

"I know that, and there's nothing that gives me greater

grief than what happened at that warehouse—except maybe the murder of *my own* girlfriend by these damn things. *Remember*?" Danny said, giving it right back to Craig.

"Well, welcome to the fucking club, cousin."

Danny turned away and shook his head. "I've tried to get to the right clues and get us the guidance we need. Clearly, I've failed."

"That much I already know, pal."

"And that's on me. But at the same time, it's time for you to grow the fuck up." Danny stopped pacing and stood to face Craig squarely.

"*What?*"

"The supernatural forces we've been dealing with are ancient, Craig. And as cold as it might sound, the threat they pose, the damage they can do, is bigger than any single victim killed by the Tourist or Bishop. Bigger than Emma. Bigger than Lauren."

"Watch it," Craig cautioned.

Danny ignored the warning. "I learned this about the same time I got introduced to Bishop. I thought Bishop might be the easier bridge to get you there, because what Michael would tell you would blow your mind."

Craig leaned against the wall, scrutinizing Danny. "Explain what you mean."

"Michael took me back through history, literally, and he showed me images of how this all started."

Craig scoffed. "Danny, have you gone mental? Seriously, are you okay?"

"I see things more clearly now than I ever have."

"Oh, I see," Craig said, his voice oozing with sarcasm. "As clearly as you saw through Bishop?"

"There's no denying that I missed that." Danny was beginning to struggle to stay calm in the face of Craig's anger. He knew if they both went that same way, their meeting would be futile.

"No shit. You fucked this up, Danny. Your lead on Bishop nearly got us get killed. Some fucking cop you are. You would've been *nothing* without me! And how do I get repaid for helping you? With a continuation of the torment that started when I was ten years old in that damn church with my dad. I've just been a pawn for you to use to get your job done. What do I get? Losing the only girl I've ever really had a meaningful relationship with!"

Danny held firm against the onslaught of Craig's anger and grief. All the pieces of himself that he'd struggled to manage—the doubt, the fear of what they faced, the gravity of the origin of Craig's powers—all of it had been such a challenge. But Danny had found his voice.

"Listen to me. You've got to talk with Michael. You've got to surrender to the possibility of what your powers mean and what you're supposed to do with them. You've covered yourself so long, Craig. Wrapped yourself in whatever bullshit you felt was heaped on you. Being orphaned. Isolating yourself as you grew up. You've been angry, afraid, pissed. I get it. But it's a cloak you've been hiding under. It's been nothing more than a goddamn disguise. You haven't had the courage to embrace what it all really means."

"Courage? Are you fucking kidding me? I trailed you to that church in Iowa, faced down the Tourist. Saved your ass before you bled out!"

"Are you blind to what these monsters represent, Craig?"

Craig's face scrunched in anger. "I know what they're about, goddammit. What they represent is destroying everything I hold dear. But they picked the wrong person, Danny. I'll show them."

"Honestly, don't you see that it's never been about you? They're deliberately trying to throw you off your path so you can't help others."

"Enough of that bullshit! I'll find him, and I'll destroy him, just like the one we faced in Iowa."

"That wasn't you, and you know it."

Craig lurched off the wall, flashing a disgusted look.

Danny dialed up the confrontation. "You weren't *made* to try and bring them down. You're meant for so much more. To protect others who *can* make a difference. More than anything, the dark descendants want to bring those people down."

"Oh, now you got fancy names for those bastards, huh?"

"Yes. I learned it from Michael. And if you'll listen to him, you'll learn too. You can bring people the protection they need, but in ancient and powerful ways that I could only dream of as a police officer."

"A lot of good that did Lauren."

"She chose to walk her path, Craig. She chose to be with you and accept the ambiguity, the lack of the full picture. And the consequences."

Craig shook angrily at the mention of Lauren and how she accepted remaining in the dark.

Now I've got him, thought Danny. He bowed his head and gritted his teeth. He didn't want to have to do this, but he saw no other way.

"It's your time on the stage, Craig. The discomfort, the scrutiny, the pain—all of it. You're no longer on the fringes, observing. You're in an end game now. It's time to man-up for it."

"You son of a . . ." Craig said as he moved aggressively toward Danny.

But Danny closed the distance first, holding his cane as a weapon, and with a swift thrust, he jabbed Craig in the midsection. Craig doubled over in pain as Danny took a couple of steps back to brace himself for Craig's counter.

In an instant, Craig recovered. He glared at Danny with rage in his eyes. He lunged toward him, but Danny was ready.

Using his good hand to whip the cane up and overhead, Danny swung it down, delivering a glancing blow that caught Craig above the eyebrow. Craig was driven to his knees, and a gash opened across his nose.

For a moment, everything was still. Craig looked up in disbelief at his cousin. "What do you think you're doing, Danny?"

Danny watched the open wound on Craig's face that started at the eyebrow and extended across the bridge of his nose. A trickle of blood ran down Craig's nose and onto his cheek.

Danny held his breath as the blood flow stopped and the gash on Craig's head slowly closed up. The response of Craig's body to the injury was as he had predicted, and Danny gulped a sigh of relief. But it was short-lived, as his assault had driven Craig into further rage.

Launching out of his crouched position, Craig flew across the living room at him. But in his wrath, Craig forgot his structured martial arts moves while Danny's police training held.

Danny sidestepped as Craig hurtled himself forward,

and he swung his cane down on Craig's knee, sapping the momentum and power from the attack. Craig dropped again, and before he could regroup, Danny swung a backfist against Craig's temple in a blow that sent him sprawling across the room.

Craig came to a rest, shouting, "What the hell are you *doing*?"

"Proving a point," Danny said calmly.

The words did nothing more than further enrage Craig, which was what Danny wanted.

Once again, Craig lunged forward, intent on tackling him. Danny dipped one shoulder as Craig reached him, and then thrust himself upward. The result sent Craig somersaulting over the couch and onto the floor.

Danny gulped for air. He wasn't sure how much longer he could keep up the pace of this confrontation.

Have I done enough? Will he do it? he thought.

Craig popped up from behind the sofa as if on cue. With a guttural yell, he shot his arms forward, palms open, intent on blasting Danny with waves of force.

Nothing happened.

Craig drew his hands back, looked at them with a puzzled stare, then flung them out again toward Danny. As he tried to duplicate what he had done to the Tourist in Iowa, Danny walked slowly toward him.

"Do you see? Do you understand now? It doesn't work that way. This power—your ability to shoot those blasts of force like you did before—only works against evil. Against those who come at you with ill intent. And that's not me, Craig."

"What are you talking about?" Craig stammered. "How the hell do you think you know how this works?"

"I learned it from Michael. He told me. You're not supposed to use your power for yourself or for revenge," Danny said.

Craig calmly approached until he was face to face with Danny. Then, with a lightning-fast move, Craig punched Danny in the ribs. As Danny doubled-over, Craig drew up his knee and launched a kick into Danny's torso that sent him crashing to the floor.

"Look, no powers used there," Craig said with spite.

Danny was wheezing, trying to get up on all fours. His prosthetic hand struggled to hold his weight. His cane was now several feet away. He crawled toward his cane, hoping to use it to help him stand up. Just as his outstretched hand had nearly reached it, a quick snap of Craig's foot sent it out of his reach. A devious smile curled across Craig's face.

"Nice, real nice," Danny said. He put his hand on his knee and struggled to stand.

Craig watched Danny's pitiful struggle to get to his feet without the aid of the cane and looked ashamed. But undeterred, Danny pushed to collect himself.

"Oh my God. What am I doing? Danny, I'm sorry. I shouldn't have done that."

Craig took a few steps forward and extended his hand in an offer to help Danny to his feet. Instead, Danny roughly slapped his cousin's hand away.

"Don't touch me, you asshole. That was such a little bitch move."

"I'm not sure what came over me. I know you've got physical challenges. I shouldn't have done that. It's just . . . you just came at me."

Danny wasn't having any of his pity. "It was a test, Craig! Working you over was to show that your injuries can heal. But you can't use your firepower on me. I knew you wouldn't be able to do it because I know the whole story now. I learned it from Michael!"

Danny was now standing. Craig looked humbled and embarrassed, and he turned away. Danny wasn't letting up.

"I'm the only person who's always looked out for your ass. I've always protected you. Even after I lost Emma, I vowed to be by your side to help you figure things out. Hell, I even lost part of my goddamn body."

"I know that, Danny. When my abilities started to return, and I was getting stronger, I thought I'd be the one who got to decide how to use them for once."

"You're pathetic if you think vengeance is what you're made for—that that's why you have this power."

Craig seethed, "You don't understand. You don't have to deal with all of this stewing inside you."

Danny took command of the conversation. Any humiliation he had felt from being laid low moments ago had been burned away. "Just shut up and listen to me. You can kick me down with all your newfound strength, and I'll get back up. I always do. But will you?"

Craig fell silent.

"You feel it, I get that. The injuries and pain, both physical and emotional. Well, I've been there too. Loss? Hell yeah, I know that feeling. I lost Emma. I lost my dignity with the force. So I know a little bit about how you must feel right now. Even if you think you are the *only* person who could understand that kind of pain."

Danny made his way over to an armchair next to the couch and collapsed into it. Craig leaned against the living room wall. A long silence unfolded between them.

Danny gathered a huge breath before letting it out. "It only took me having a busted leg and a cane for you to finally take me down." He managed to chuckle.

Craig joined in. "You've gotten pretty handy with that cane, I've got to say. Where the hell did you get that, anyway? I sure was glad you had it when we were up against Bishop and his men."

"Hammond had the quartermaster at our precinct make it for me."

"Ah, that makes sense."

The brief levity evident on Craig's faced slowly melted into pain. "At the end, Lauren wouldn't say anything at all," he said. "How come? I kept calling out to her, but she wouldn't react. It was almost like she was afraid to, or that she had somehow resigned herself to what was going to happen."

"I'm not sure, Craig."

"Why did he involve her?"

"You know why. It was a way to get to you, to push your buttons."

"But why? Why are they after *us*?" Craig said in a tormented voice. "And this power I've somehow come into—it's so damn extraordinary. But what good did it do? When it came down to it, I couldn't stop him from taking her. I just couldn't stop him!"

Danny took the tremor in Craig's voice as a sign that he was finally ready to listen to reason.

"Bishop and the Tourist, they're the same. They see you as a threat. They want you gone, and they're willing to do anything to either pull you into their thinking and their way of life or kill you. As sick as it was for Bishop to lure Lauren to the warehouse and take her life, his intent was to throw you off your path."

"She was most of the flesh and blood that made me whole."

"And what would she want you to do now?" Danny challenged. "Give up? Track these fuckers down in some hopeless effort to destroy them? Or would she want you to strive for something greater? You know the answer to that."

"I want to destroy him. I *can* destroy him."

"No, you can't."

"The hell I can't. I already did to that one in Iowa. You were there!"

"No, you didn't. It was your dad that killed it for us," Danny said calmly. "You told me as much when I was lying in the hospital after we fought the Tourist. You told me you heard your dad speaking to you. And that was after the Tourist was dragging himself toward us, trying to kill us. Somehow, your dad brought about that violent avalanche of white dust that destroyed him. That certainly wasn't you, so don't go thinking you can kill these damn things on your own."

"Then why can I do the things I *can* do? If not to kill these things and put an end to the death and destruction they unleash?"

"It's about protecting *others* from the death and destruction that they bring. For each person you can protect from that fate, their effort and positive influence will ripple out to a few others. And those others will impact several more, and on and on. Eventually, it becomes a bright light shining out from so many people that those things can't possibly snuff it all out."

Danny rose and walked over to Craig, staring at him

intently. "That's your job, and Michael and I can draw it all together for you."

Craig's hands drifted to his head as he closed his eyes.

"Listen, Craig, these things have taken great, big chunks from both of us. Me with Emma and parts of my body. You with your father and now Lauren. The only thing that makes sense is that you have something they can't allow to remain loose in the world. You're supposed to use your gifts for something more important than going up against that evil directly and battling it endlessly. That's what Michael told me—that's what he *showed* me. If you trust me, Craig, and if you truly think that we're family, then you'll believe me when I tell you that this is the way forward."

Danny brought one hand to his head to rub his brow.

"I failed to prep you for the meeting with Michael at the church. That's a mistake I won't make the next time you see him. But you have to believe me. He's the one who can show you all of it."

Craig started to mumble, then talk coherently. "All those good people who were done in by the Tourist. My father. Maggie. Bishop killing those gang members—it was all right there in the shadows and the mist. If only I could've seen it coming."

"We won't make that mistake again. We've been searching so long for a rationale for all of this tragedy. Forgive me, Craig, for not having found it until now. But I finally have through Michael."

Craig cringed at the mention of Michael.

"You've got to trust me now, Craig. I won't let you down again."

All at once, Craig seemed to go limp, as if the stress and fear and grief was too much. "Danny, I'm just so tired.

Those things are waiting out there for me. To kill me like they have all the others. I'm just so . . . alone now." He began to sob.

"No, you're not," Danny said.

"So much has happened, Danny. So much pain and ruin. How can anything ever be right again?"

It felt like they had come full circle. Danny remembered when they were kids standing at the top of the stairs, when Craig first learned that his father had been killed and Danny sought to comfort him. He'd watched Craig grow up, first frightened and then introverted, wrestling with the strange abilities that bedeviled him. In recent years, he had seen Craig's powers grow to the point that he was able to save them from the Tourist. Now Craig was even more powerful, but he also appeared to be at a breaking point. It was a dangerous situation, and worrisome.

Danny once again felt the weight of responsibility for judging Bishop so wrongly and for Lauren's death.

As Craig sobbed, Danny felt the need to reassure his cousin, and more importantly, to check where Craig might aim the anger and power within him that had grown into a roaring fire.

"I'm resolved to see this through, to see it made right. Are you, Craig? Can you keep moving forward if you know you've got me to shoulder the load with you?"

Craig's sobbing turned to trembling and shivering. Then his legs were unable to hold the weight of his despair, and he fell to his knees on the living room floor.

"I don't know if I can. Danny, you can't imagine what this is doing to me inside!" Craig's breathing quickened. He was beginning to hyperventilate.

Seeing his distress increasing, Danny approached him. "Hey, take it easy."

Danny watched Craig reach under the top of his shirt and fiddle with a coin-looking pendant that dangled from a necklace.

"I can't!" Craig shouted. "I feel like I'm drowning. I just want it all to stop. It has to stop!" he screamed. He then threw his hands over his head as if trying to fend off the weight of a world that was crushing him alive. As he did so, ripples and waves of energy flooded uncontrollably through the room, shaking the furniture, cracking several windowpanes, and finally reaching such an intensity that lamps and other small objects around the apartment were sent flying.

Danny recoiled in alarm. It was as if a small earthquake had shaken the apartment. He looked around at the disarray Craig's uncontrolled power had caused, emanating from the rage and despair that roiled within him.

So much power, Danny thought. *Raw. Uncontrolled*. Craig was in a fragile state. It was like when they were young when Danny tried then to console him. But this time, so much power was welling up in Craig, and so unpredictably, that Danny worried whether he could help Craig keep it together long enough for him to learn the full arc of the powers he possessed.

He turned to Craig, who had buried his head in his hands as he slumped on the floor. Danny slowly knelt down beside him and gently drew Craig's head to his chest. "Please, Craig. Know that I'm here. Things are terrible right now, but we will get you through this. Just try to let it go for right now."

So many questions, and so much worry. Danny felt the weight of his own responsibility to show the way for Craig.

"I'll help you, Craig. You have my word, until the last breath either of us takes."

ABOUT THE AUTHOR

An author, professor, and financial executive, Keith Goad lives in Fort Wayne, Indiana, with his wife. Keith holds a bachelor's degree and an MBA from Ohio State University. In addition to serving as a financial executive, Keith has also taught as an adjunct university professor for over fifteen years.

The *Relentless Enemy* series is based on the real-life history and heritage of Keith's late father, which serves as the inspiration for this epic tale.

The Invictus is the second book in the *Relentless Enemy* series.

·OTHER BOOK·S

in the *Relentless Enemy* series

As a child, Craig Henriksen is sent to Chicago to live with relatives after the shocking death of his father. As an adult, he is reclusive and avoids facing his past, only to discover strange abilities that won't let him escape it. His struggle to find normalcy is challenged by his cousin Danny, a Chicago police detective who uses him to uncover clues at murder scenes.

As Craig becomes involved with Lauren, a woman who offers him the hope of living the life he has always wanted, he is drawn even deeper into Danny's pursuit of the Tourist, a vicious serial killer. But even if he chooses to forgo his chance at happiness to help his cousin, will he understand in time that both he and Danny are being hunted?

Relentless Enemy brings an age-old battle to today's streets, hearts, and lives